CITY OF
DARKNESS

Get the Water Street Crime Starter Library FOR FREE

Sign up for the no-spam newsletter and get *four* full-length ebooks—the thrillers **BLOODY PARADISE**, **FROM ICE TO ASHES**, **TROPICAL ICE**, and **SING FOR THE DEAD**—plus two introductory short stories by the author of **STAINED FORTUNE** and lots more exclusive content, all for *free*.

Details can be found at the end of *CITY OF DARKNESS*, or go here now: mailchi.mp/waterstreetpressbooks.com/ waterstreetcrimemailinglist

CITY OF
DARKNESS

ZACHARY ALAN FOX

Water Street Press
Healdsburg, California

For information, contact Water Street Press,
www.waterstreetpressbooks.com

Published by Water Street Press
Healdsburg, California

Water Street Press paperback edition published 2019

Produced in the USA

Print 978-1-62134-431-5
E-Pub 978-1-62134-432-2
Mobi 978-1-62134-433-9

Cover design by **thecovercollection.com**

Typesetting services by **bookow.com**

For all the grandchildren.

Acknowledgments

I would like to thank Jim Trupin and Elizabeth Trupin-Pulli at Jet Literary Associates for their support and encouragement over the many years we've been together.

"The most dangerous creation of any society is the man who has nothing to lose."

James Baldwin.

Prologue

WHAT was it that they were all living with suddenly? Ann wondered. What walked in the door when Robert left to get her medicine? Fear, she decided.

Fear was something new for their family, something they didn't know how to deal with, but now it was leading their protected lives in this "rich boy's" (her son's angry term) enclave in the middle of the Los Angeles ghetto. Fear was like a snake that slithered in during the night and lay coiled on the living room floor, waiting for someone to take a misstep.

And we did, each of us.

All because of a split-second decision, an act of kindness that destroyed two families. But that's all it takes to ruin your life. "Why can't I have those few seconds back?" Robert asked again and again. "Why can't I reverse time, make a different decision? And not help someone who needs it." No, it simply wasn't possible. Robert had a need to do good. To help. They all did. That's who they were as a family, that was their strength.

And weakness. We worked too hard at being a family. We were going to show the world. Dinner together every night at six. Thursday evenings at the Hollywood Bowl. Ball games, ski trips, weekends in San Francisco or Phoenix or Catalina. We tried so hard...

How naïve they were. Maybe Robert most of all. His *goodness* left him defenseless. He simply couldn't imagine how evil people could be. Especially someone he had risked his life to help.

But the real culprit was ourselves, our family. We loved too much, we were too strong. Closeness squeezed out our individuality, forcibly disassembled us and melded us into the whole. But both families were like that, weren't they? Both close and loving and murderous in their own distinct manner.

1

THE innermost level of hell, the point at which old Lucifer sits back on his asbestos recliner and enjoys the unspeakable torture of the damned, is made up of an endless round of academic parties: Philosophy professors forced to spend eternity talking to linguistic theorists, sociologists arguing with French deconstructionists, historians locked forever in conversation with legal scholars. Or so Ann Binder reflected as she gazed at the several dozen professors, spouses, and college trustees wandering around the grounds of the seaside estate. The political maneuvering masquerading as friendly chitchat, and delicate backbiting raised to an art form, was one of the reasons she'd given up her own tenured position at UCLA eight years earlier. Though only one. *Let me count the ways ...*

"Enjoying yourself?" her husband Robert whispered with malicious glee as he slipped quickly past with a glass of very good chardonnay in his hand.

"Like Joan of Arc as the flames leapt around her body."

But Robert had passed on, probably to collar their host, Edgerton Lee, U.S. Congressman for this part of coastal Los Angeles as well as Chairman of the Board of Trustees of Otis Law School, and Robert's none-too-subtle target all evening. Robert had only a tangential connection to Otis, though a much closer one to Lee, who had been promoting him for several months as an Assistant Secretary in the Department of Health and Human Services. But Lee seemed to have disappeared, so Robert had to settle for Addie, his wife. *Oh well,* Ann thought with her own frisson of marital maliciousness, *second best will have to do for now.*

Glancing around, she found herself wondering how many other African-American women were present. Only one that she had seen so far, though there were eight or ten black men. The same sort of imbalance she had felt at UCLA. But she wasn't going to let it bother her tonight. Or at least wouldn't let it show.

A string of outdoor lights behind her suddenly flickered and died, plunging everyone into darkness before struggling back on again as someone yelled, "It's a sign from God, Edgerton. Repent!" And someone else laughed and said, "Edgerton would never allow God to interrupt his party."

Feeling a chill wind sweep up suddenly from the sea Ann rubbed her arms and began to wander toward the house. Off to either side she could hear bushes trembling in the darkness, ice sloshing in cocktail glasses, and shards of broken conversation from an argument nearby. *Something's wrong, something bad's going to happen tonight. Now where the hell did that come from?* she wondered with annoyance. But she had been uneasy since arriving here. *Anticipating.* As though something was waiting for them out there where the light failed. Something with form. And a face. Forget it, she told herself, and felt another chill creep along her spine to her arms and the very ends of her fingers. *Well, it's my fault. I should have brought a jacket.*

Anyway, she was just over-reacting to a little illness, the twenty-four-hour flu, probably. She would have stayed home if it hadn't been important to Robert that she be here, to offer moral support if nothing else. "You know Edgerton likes you," he'd told her as they dressed—Ann finally getting to wear the mauve Versace cocktail dress she'd bought at an after-Christmas sale—not needing to point out the Congressman's role in their life right now.

"'Future Nobel Laureate Contemplates Trade Imbalance.' Next year's *New York Times* photo caption of a thoughtful Dr. Ann Binder gazing out to sea."

Ann spun around so fast she almost lost her footing. Edgerton Lee, immaculate in his pin-striped Pickett's of London suit, steadied her with his hand. "Sorry," he said, "didn't mean to startle you."

Ann laughed, pleased to see him, pleased to see *anyone* not a professor. At six-foot-three and with a full head of dark hair just beginning to go gray, he was still ruggedly handsome, and looked a decade younger than his sixty-seven years. "Where did you get that 'future Nobel' nonsense, Edgerton? You know better than that."

"Rumors, my dear. The common currency of get-togethers like this. I choose to believe the more knowledgeable amongst my guests since I'm not qualified to judge your work. Robert once gave me an article of yours from *Policy Review*, but I'm afraid I was lost in the first paragraph. Something to do with how people make rational economic decisions."

Ann smiled. After a lifetime in politics, Lee was an expert at putting people at ease with well-chosen, if not always accurate, compliments. In Congress since the late-eighties, he had sufficient seniority to pick the committees he served on, and was thought to have a fair amount of clout in the White House. With the Congressman's backing, Robert hoped to use his appointment to Health and Human Services to go national with RULA—the Rural and Urban Legal Assistance program he ran with Dohr, Haskins, and Poole, his downtown law firm, to provide legal help to the poor by utilizing law students. Still smiling, Ann said, "Not just economic choices, Edgerton. Any form of decision-making where the consequences are weighty."

"Like picking a spouse?"

"I'm afraid that's defied explanation," she said with a laugh. "Though quite a few people have tried. The only conclusion seems to be 'Love is weird.'"

"Well, I congratulate you and Robert for the decision-making that brought you together. Happy marriages seem so rare today, don't they?"

"Especially mixed-race marriages?" she asked with raised eyebrows. She immediately regretted the acerbic tone, but it was a subject she and Robert had both grown weary of.

"Not at all," Lee said easily. "Look around. I'd guess ninety percent of the people here are on their second or third marriages, including myself." A waiter came by with drinks and Lee plucked a white wine from the tray. "By the way, you can assure Robert that he needn't worry about his appointment. His name is going forward next month. It's just a formality after that."

"He'll be relieved to hear it. He's been on edge for months."

"Hell, you know how Washington is. Unless the background check turns up something, it'll be smooth sailing. He doesn't have any skeletons rattling around in his closet, does he? Any little slip-ups we should be worried about? Plagiarized papers, child porn on his phone, nekkid photos sent to city interns?"

"I'm sure not. With Robert... what you see is what you get. You won't have to worry about a last-minute embarrassment."

He took her by the elbow and they began to wander. "The Law School is having its own little embarrassing moment, as you may have heard. They're choosing a new dean next month. I'm surprised at the depth of feeling, to tell the truth."

"You know what they say: emotions in academia run so high because the stakes are so low. Robert explained the Otis process to me. It's a little strange, but I like it." Much about the school was strange. Founded in 1884 by Cornelius Ryan Otis, a manufacturer of farm equipment who turned from unfettered capitalism to a sort of primitive Christian socialism once he made his bundle, its mission was to provide training for students too poor to attend a traditional university. Otis insisted the school be run collectively by the faculty and the eleven-member board of trustees. By design, when the dean retired, as seventy-year-old Raul Salas was doing in eight weeks, the faculty and board would vote on a successor.

"Your husband seems concerned about the outcome. He's been politicking for Howard Zalesky since he got here."

"Well, he's afraid RULA will be disbanded if Karel Jirasek gets in."

"I'd hate to see that happen, of course," Lee said. "But the board would never interfere. People deserve the government they vote for. Even professors. *Especially* professors."

They discussed the election for a few minutes until Lee wandered off to play host. A moment later Robert darted up behind Ann, putting his arms around her waist and kissing her neck. "Hey, back off," she warned. "I'm as contagious as Typhoid Mary."

"Not a chance. The prettiest woman here has me enthralled and I need to come back for my fix."

She laughed and pushed him away. "Edgerton was just telling me you don't have to worry about. D.C. How are you doing pressing the flesh here?"

"Everyone says Zalesky's a shoe-in, of course. But I'm not letting up until—" His eyes widened. "My God, there's Karen Hubbard. I haven't had a chance to talk to her tonight."

Ann lifted her hand in a benediction. "Go, my son. Peace. Love."

"Later with the love," he said and patted her butt. "We have a date."

"Later, I'll be ill." She smiled as he hurried away. Still a handsome man, she couldn't help thinking, with all the thick dark hair he'd had when they met, and a smile opposing attorneys were as helpless against as she was.

Another gust from the ocean made her shiver, and she began to wander again. *Something bad's going to happen tonight.* God, I'm getting irrational. I shouldn't have come; I should be in bed, pumped full of antibiotics and sleeping peacefully while dreaming about... a Nobel? Now that *would* be pleasing. Then she spotted

Luis Teague and smiled. A huge water buffalo of a man at six-foot-six and two-hundred-eighty pounds, he was standing in a group of six or eight men and women, listening to someone talking about the campus election. Teague caught her eye and winked, willing her to join them. Not in the mood for academic chitchat she approached with reluctance.

Luis was one of her and Robert's closest friends. He had known Robert since the two of them were students at Columbia, and now ran the school's Inner-City Law Project where Robert's group was housed, at least on paper. "Ah, Dr. Binder," Teague said with enthusiasm as Ann joined them. "I was just telling my friends here how Edgerton's parties always make me feel like I'm in the middle of a Brueghel painting. All these waiters bustling about with drinks and hors d'oeuvres for the peasants while a pig's being roasted in a pit."

"With a few of the fiends from Bosch's 'The Garden of Earthly Delights' as guests," Maria Bonheur, a Family Law professor, added with a laugh as the lights flickered again.

"Pay your electric bill, Lee," someone yelled, and people laughed loudly.

Maria Bonheur said, "Where's your husband, Ann? I haven't had a chance to talk to him all night."

"Making speeches and kissing babies, I think. He's concerned about the election."

"Oh, there's nothing to worry about. I know my whole department is going to vote for Zalesky."

"Your *whole department* is five faculty members out of sixty-six," Luis Teague bellowed. "Three of whom are not tenured and thus prey to pressure from the Odious Jirasek and the unholy band of merry men who comprise his lackies. If he gets in I'm afraid we can say good-bye to social responsibility and concentrate on turning out an army of Karel Jirasek clones cluttering the judiciary with *trivia*." Jirasek's specialty—product liability, occupational injuries, medical malpractice, what Teague called "attorney enrichment law"—had earned him *Time* magazine's nickname: Class Action Karel.

"I don't see how anyone can support that man," the wife of a faculty member said. "He's a bottom-feeding barracuda making money off other peoples' misfortunes. Have you seen his newest TV commercial? He comes on the screen in one of those ridiculous green and gold sport coats of his, parading a pathetic file of accident victims mumbling 'Karel Associates delivers the goods,' while a huge graphic—$7.2 *Million* or whatever—flashes on and off like a neon light. Put bells on his shoes and he'd look like a court jester."

Teague shook his head in wonder. "He is *amazingly* immune to embarrassment, isn't he?"

Ann smiled as the large man's expressive face seemed to fold in on itself. She knew what he was thinking: *It's Difficult Not to be Outraged*, which was the title of the book he was currently working on. *Yes, it is*, she thought. *Impossible*, sometimes.

Teague blinked away his momentary dissociation. "I imagine Zalesky will manage to pull through. As long as nothing untoward happens."

"Such as?" Ann asked, surprised.

"Haven't the foggiest. But I warned your worthy husband not to get into any sort of argument with Jirasek tonight. Our side has to be above such things."

"I don't think any school topic ought to be allowed at Edgerton's parties," Maria Bonheur said and smiled at Ann. "So—matching my action to my words, as the saintly Jane Austin would say—how's your handsome young John? Is he still going to be the next Pablo Casals?"

"He's 'JG' now," Ann said, happy to be getting away from academic rancor. "He's still attending the performing arts high school in Hollywood. He can graduate next year when he's seventeen and go straight to the Eastman School of Music in Rochester. But I'm not sure I want him to do that. I think another year of master's classes will give him time to mature a bit."

"And Mama can keep him at home one more year before losing him to the evil world," the other woman said with a smile. "I know how wrenching that can be. I wanted Margaret to go to college locally, but she wouldn't even consider it. *Had* to get away. She's at Smith now and actually texts me every month. Or not."

They talked about children and spouses for a while until Ann felt she could wander off. *OK, we've done our bit. Let's get out of here.* At least she hadn't been asked by one of the caterers to bring out another tray of hors d'oeuvres as at last year's party. She was about to look for Robert when she heard raised voices from a group of about two dozen men and women where Karel Jirasek—as always, the center of attention—was histrionically waving over another faculty member. "Damn it, Agnelli, get over here and listen to this. Our esteemed colleague is explaining how the wrong sorts of people go into law."

Ann stiffened as she saw Robert face-to-face with Jirasek. Unlike the other man, though, Robert was smiling. She wandered over, thinking, *Please just walk away. You're not a faculty member. It's not your fight.*

Standing to the rear of the group, she heard her husband say, "Not the wrong sorts going into law so much as the right sorts keeping out. We're seeing a generation of bloodless executive managers—men and women who would be just as happy at Proctor and Gamble as in a courtroom. I think we need to balance this with people who care about access to the law, and the role law has in creating a civil community. As well as upholding the primacy of justice."

"*The primacy of justice.* Yes, yes, rather than attorneys making a little honest money for themselves and their family. Of course, we've heard this from you before. But if by helping the average consumer we manage to benefit ourselves too, what is the problem? Is it not the greatest good for the greatest number?"

"The average consumer, my ass," Robert said with a laugh. "The problem with you New Troglodytes is that you can't make distinctions. To you every position, every plaintiff, every lawsuit is morally equivalent."

Another professor laughed with derision. "Even if there's only a single moral road, Robert will manage to stake out the high ground for himself."

"That's not fair, George!" Robert said angrily and began to argue with the man.

Enough, Ann thought and quickly moved away as the wind came up again and goose bumps popped out all over her flesh.

Come and get me, Robert. Let's get out of here and back to our home before something terrible happens.

2

"THEY'RE all so damnably smug," Robert said in the car on the way home. "Especially that idiot, Jirasek. All he cares about is how he can *use* the law to his own benefit, how he can turn a profit from someone's misfortune. And these supporters of his, these so-called 'New Pragmatists'... They're philistines, all of them. Their single goal in life is to find a 'cause', and if not a cause, a case. If a victim doesn't appear, they'll create one. Not one of them has ever volunteered to work for the Inner-City Law Project or RULA."

His fingers reddened as they tightened on the steering wheel. "Dohr, Haskins, and Poole can keep RULA afloat for a while if Jirasek cuts us loose, but we'd have to find a place to house it. And a new source of funding and staffing. USC or Hebrew Union might give us a home. But Luis's ILP would simply disappear. What a tragedy that would be."

He let out a sigh. "The young professors are the real problem. They have no sense of community. They've been seduced by television and movies to see the law as nothing but the quickest route to a Mercedes and a house at the beach."

Ann's eyes were closed and she held tightly onto the hand grip on the door to keep her body rigid. The motion of the aging Saab was making her queasy, but she tried to bring Robert out of the funk the party had put him in. "Kind of silly calling them 'young', isn't it? You're only forty-six. It's not like you're some tottering old grandfather trying to convince the little ones that things were better in the old days."

"Maybe that's what I *am* doing. Luis was telling me how depressing it is to interview new law school grads for a faculty job nowadays and hear them go on and on about 'eight figure awards' or pushing suits over the most trivial things. There's no seriousness to them. And no *vision* for the school."

"It's difficult not to be outraged." Ann grimaced as they hit a pothole and her stomach lurched, sending bile into her throat. Was it her imagination or had Robert hit every pothole possible tonight? He reached over and patted her knee. "Hell, forget Jirasek. Except for him I had a delightful night. Tell me all the scurrilous rumors you picked up. Someone said—"

"Robert, pull over."

"What?"

"Pull over. I'm going to be sick."

He whipped the car at once to the side of the busy street, and Ann pushed the door open just in time to vomit into the gutter. She sat for a moment doubled up, her feet on the asphalt and her head between her knees as she tried to stop retching.

Robert put his hand on her back. "My God, why didn't you tell me? You didn't have to come tonight. You ought to be in bed."

"I didn't feel that bad earlier. Maybe it's from walking around outside after it turned cold. That breeze off the ocean was pretty frigid." She slid back into the car and shut the door. Almost at once her head fell against the seat-back as her stomach cramped painfully again. *No*, she told herself. *I'm not going to be sick.* She held her breath until the feeling passed.

With the car still idling, Robert grabbed his phone. "I'm calling Doctor Jarrett. He can phone in a prescription tonight. I'll pick it up after I get you home."

"Don't bother. It's probably just the flu. I'll be better tomorrow."

"But you don't want to be up all night, vomiting. At least he can get you something for that." He touched her forehead. "Jesus, you're burning up." He began to tap out the number on the phone as he took his foot from the brake.

Twenty minutes later Robert drew into the driveway of their house in the West Adams section of Los Angeles. A one-time residential area for L.A.'s rich—Fatty Arbuckle and Theda Bara had lived there during the silent screen era, and a number of African-American actors in the thirties and forties—the community was now an historic preservation enclave of Victorian mansions surrounded by the ghetto that South-Central had become. Robert and Ann moved here because the Rural and Urban Legal Assistance program was being run out of a Craftsman-style cottage three blocks away on the edge of Otis Law School. Besides, houses cost a fraction of what a similar home would cost in West L.A. or Beverly Hills. But there had also been the sense of wanting to be in Central Los Angeles, to be connected to the sort of community RULA had been created to represent. "Walking the walk," Jirasek had sneered, "making a political statement..." with their lives. It was the sort of cynicism Robert would not even respond to.

Their five-thousand-square-foot Georgian Colonial had been built in 1894. The two most recent owners had spent years restoring much of it, and the house now looked as it must have to Samuel P. Steward, the railroad executive who had it built. The huge Viennese chandeliers and three authentic Tiffany stained-glass windows with vignettes of the California Gold Rush were still in place, as were many of Samuel P. Steward's leather-bound books (still smelling faintly of cigar smoke) in the formal library.

Robert took Ann's arm as she got out of the Saab. "Can you make it up the steps?"

"I think—"

But she tripped over her feet and he caught her, putting his arm around her waist. "Just lean on me. I'll get you up." The nightlight was on in the large entry foyer but the house was silent. "JG must be asleep already," Robert said and checked his watch. Almost midnight. He clasped Ann even closer as they approached the stairs. "Want me to carry you up like Rhett Butler did to Miss Scarlet in *Gone with the Wind*?"

Ann managed a smile. "Then your back would go out and we'd both be invalids. Anyway, Rhett had something more primal than convalescence on his mind."

"Wise ol' Rhett, a man who knew what he wanted."

In the bedroom Ann hurried into a pair of winter pajamas she'd stowed away in the closet and slipped into bed. "I don't know why I'm so cold if I have a fever." She yanked the covers to her chin and shivered. "Even my bones are freezing."

"I'm going to Walgreen's," Robert said. "Shouldn't take more than twenty minutes."

"If I'm asleep when you get home don't wake me. I'll take the medicine in the morning."

"Of course... Love you." He smiled as he flicked the light out.

Ann was dreaming that she was in an egg-shaped capsule—Robert was there, too—and they were falling , interminably it seemed, through space (or was it down Alice's rabbit hole?) when an annoying buzz seemed to intrude from somewhere. *What? What is it?* She bolted up, feeling her heart pounding out of control. *God, I hate dreams like that.* Then she realized the phone was ringing on the night table. She must have fallen asleep the moment the light went out. It couldn't have been long though. Robert was still at Walgreen's. Then she saw the digital clock: 4:06 AM. How could that be?

She shook her head, trying to clear the cobwebs, and grabbed the receiver. "Yes—"

"It's me, hon. Sorry to wake you."

Robert? Why was he calling her? Was there a problem with the prescription? "What's wrong? Are you at the drug store?"

His voice was strained. "You better come and get me. I'm too shook up to drive." What was all that noise in the background—people talking, phones ringing?

"What do you mean? What are you talking about?"

"Bring JG. He can drive my car home."

"Home from where? Where are you?"

"The police station. Downtown."

"The police? But why? What happened?" And Ann's mind lost whatever clarity and resonance it had as she heard her husband's voice tremble and seem to say, "I just killed someone."

3

"I don't *know* how it happened, it just did." Robert was pacing back and forth in the small featureless interview room at the Police Administration Building while Ann stood with her back to the door.

"But *how*?" she pleaded. "*What* happened? All they told me out front was it was an accident."

He tossed an impatient glance in her direction, as if this were all her fault, or someone else's, *anyone's*, fault, as he kept prowling around the room. "Sit, please."

"I don't want to sit. Just tell me!"

He pulled to a stop and stared up at the ceiling. His face was pale and drawn, his muscles tense, and his body seemed to have shrunk within the suit he had worn to the party. Turning awkwardly, his spine flattened against the wall opposite her. It was a moment before he could begin. "I was coming home from Walgreens... I turned on Normandie for some reason instead of Vermont. I don't know why I did that. Sometimes I just do. I was about to 28th ..."

His lower lip began to quiver. "I saw a man and a woman on the sidewalk fighting. Not just arguing, fighting. He was pulling at her and she was screaming, trying to hit him, to get away. Then I realized there was a van at the curb with the engine running and someone in the driver's seat. It wasn't just a fight, they were trying to kidnap her, trying to drag her into the van. I didn't think, I just aimed the car at them and drove right up onto the sidewalk and got out without even turning off the engine. I yelled at the man to let her go, but he ignored me." His hands flew out in a gesture of angry impotence. "It was like I wasn't even there. I was invisible, or not worth worrying about. He just kept pulling at the woman. She was kicking and screaming and he was dragging her toward the van, the big sliding door on the side open.

"I grabbed his arm and tried to pry his fingers from her, but he wouldn't let go. Then I saw he had a gun in one hand, a pistol of some sort. I wasn't thinking, I lunged at it..." He came off the wall and put the heel of his palms to his eyes. "How could I have been so goddamn *stupid*? This man was probably twenty-five years younger than me and he had a gun, and here I was trying to fight with him. He jerked his arm free and aimed the gun right at my face. It was only inches away, I could see the opening in the barrel and the chamber where the bullets were. Maybe I panicked.

I know I wasn't thinking, I just put my head down and ran right into his chest, butting him like a goat. He was smaller than me, and he wasn't ready for it. When I hit him, he faltered and I grabbed at the gun. It was nightmarish— this poor woman screaming and sobbing while he was yelling at me and holding her arm, the man in the van honking the horn, me shouting at him to drop the gun. And he did." He looked at Ann in surprise, and his voice rose in wonder. "I'd knocked it from his hand. It was on the sidewalk between us. We both looked at it like we didn't believe what had happened. Then I kicked it as hard as I could, but it hit his foot and ricocheted away from us."

He dropped into a chair and propped his head against his hand. "Everyone was screaming, even the man in the van. I dove for the gun and picked it up." His voice had turned frustrated, almost petulant in a childish sort of way. "I don't know anything about guns. I just grabbed it and pointed it at him and it went off. I don't even remember pulling the trigger. But there was an explosion and my ears rang and my hand seemed to jump. Then I saw blood spurting, and the woman made an odd noise, sort of a burp that wouldn't come all the way up, and fell backwards onto the sidewalk." Robert's voice sank so low Ann felt drawn forward to hear clearly. "I'd shot her. This poor woman. Jesus, I shot her. In the neck. She collapsed right in front of us, and blood was pumping out, and I didn't know what to do. I was terrified, I threw the gun away and dropped to the sidewalk, my hands on her neck, trying to stop the bleeding. The man picked up the gun and took a shot at me as he jumped in the van. Then it took off, the side door still open. But I wasn't paying attention, I was yelling at the woman not to die, and pushing on the wound." He held his now-clean hands out, palms up, glaring as though he hated them.

"My God." Ann sank into a chair across from him.

"I couldn't stop the bleeding. I pressed harder but it was shooting between my fingers. I kept yelling at her, 'Don't die, please don't die.' I don't even know how long it was, minutes or maybe just seconds, when this elderly man, he must have been seventy-five, pulled up in his pickup truck and asked me if I needed help. I guess he thought the woman was sick or drunk. I started screaming at him—*of course I need help, call 9-1-1.* An ambulance didn't get there for at least ten minutes. Can you believe that? Ten minutes!" He paused and cradled his head a moment before looking up. "She was dead by then. When the paramedics got there, I was holding onto a dead woman. They had to pry my fingers from her."

Ann felt the breath gush out of her lungs. She sat frozen a moment, then leaned forward and took her husband's hand. "My God... because you tried to help her."

He pushed quickly to his feet. "I've got to go to the bathroom—"

As he pulled the door open a man and woman came in and nodded soberly at him. "Take your time, sir," the man said to Robert, then looked at Ann for perhaps a beat too long. "Mrs. Binder?"

She said yes, and the man turned again to Robert. "No rush. It's been a difficult night."

The woman officer smiled weakly and held out a hand as the door shut behind Robert. "Sergeant Jill Oakley, homicide," she said, then indicated her partner. "The big guy's Sergeant Nick DeFazio. We're going to be the lead investigators on this case."

Ann stood up at once. "Homicide?"

"No need for alarm," DeFazio said gently. "Any questionable death lands in our laps since it has to land somewhere. Why don't we all have a seat?"

Still dazed, Ann sat again and the two detectives took the chairs across from her. Jill Oakley was African-American, in her mid-thirties, with short curly hair, large dark eyes, and a face close to pretty, though hardened by too many years out of doors. DeFazio was in his forties, and indeed large, probably six-three and two-hundred-fifty pounds, with a deep growling voice and a full head of unruly dark hair. There was something vaguely terrifying about him, as if this were someone you wouldn't want as an enemy, but exactly the sort you'd hope was next to you if you had to walk down an alley at three in the morning. She recalled that thought later, the impression he made of barely controlled menace, of being a threat.

Jill Oakley said, "I want you to know that what your husband did tonight was very brave, Mrs. Binder. It's unfortunate it turned out like it did, but it took a true hero to risk his life like that. Not many people would have stopped to help that woman."

Ann's head hadn't stopped spinning. "I'm sorry, I just can't grasp any of this. It's so unreal, so out of the realm of our experience. I don't know how it's going to affect Robert. He doesn't know anything about violence at first hand. I'm sure he's never even had a gun in his hand before."

"There's been a series of rapes in the area," Nick DeFazio said. "You've probably seen the alerts on TV. Six women we know of now. More, probably, that haven't been reported. Always walking late at night, always attacked by two men. Usually they grab the victim from behind and put a hood over her head, so this is the first time we've had a good description of either of them. If nothing else it should help us narrow in on whoever's doing it."

"But that poor woman—"

"Of course, it's tragic that an attempt to help ended like this. But there's no telling what would have happened if those men had taken her away. I think it means they intended to kill their victim this time. Why else add kidnapping to their crimes?"

"Do you know anything about her? Do you know who she was?"

"We have a name from her purse," Oakley said. "We don't know anything else except that she lived nearby. Someone's contacting her family right now."

"We'll catch the bad guys," DeFazio said matter-of-factly. "The point now is to do it before they actually do murder someone."

"Thanks to your husband we have a description of a vehicle," Oakley added. "The men probably live in the neighborhood so—"

"But we live in the neighborhood, too! Is there any chance they might try to do something to Robert? To keep him from testifying?"

"Where exactly do you live?" DeFazio asked. "I left my notebook in the squad room."

"In West Adams."

"Oh—" His surprise was obvious. He glanced momentarily at his partner. "I guess they're not likely to be neighbors, then. And your address won't be in the papers."

"The papers? Oh God. There's no way to keep Robert's name out of the news, is there?"

"It's public information. Is this a problem? You don't have to talk to reporters, of course. It's up to you."

"I'm sure we won't. But Robert's a candidate for an Assistant Secretary's position. In D.C. I don't suppose this will hurt him. It's not a very controversial position. But you never know." Then she thought, *Of course it will hurt him. This is Washington we're talking about.*

"If anyone tries to say he's to blame for that woman's death, you have them talk to me," Jill Oakley said with feeling. "If more people would do what your husband did this would be a far better world. Just because it turned out tragically this time doesn't mean we should consider it any less heroic. I wish we had a world full of Robert Binders."

An hour later in the passenger seat of Ann's Nissan, Robert was still shaking. "I wasn't afraid. Someone's threatening me with a gun, shooting at me, and it never occurred to me to be afraid. Until I got to the police station and it suddenly struck me that I came within inches of being killed. What an idiot. I never should have gotten out of the car. I should have pulled away and called 9-1-1. Why did I have to try to be the big shot? It was stupid, just ego."

"You did what you had to. I'm proud of you. The police are proud of you."

"Proud? I *killed* someone, Ann. That woman would be alive if it weren't for me."

"The police don't think so. They think the men intended to kill her. That's why they were kidnapping her."

"Jesus!" He blew the word out with a gust of air and sank back against the seat, his eyes closed. For several minutes neither of them spoke. Then in a subdued voice he said, "I have to face the fact that this is going to make problems in D.C. There's no avoiding it. RULA wasn't popular to begin with. Now all the people who hate the idea of legal aid for the poor are going to jump at the chance to point at me. The man who wants to expand a program of free legal assistance is himself involved in a killing. What sort of people are these? Et cetera. After twenty years of pushing this program it's all going to go down the drain. Wait until the *Times* comes out: 'DC Nominee Kills Woman'. Or the cable news channels. Wolf Blitzer will be standing on our front yard. Twitter will blow up—"

"You're a *hero*, Robert. The police said so. It might even help when people realize how brave you were." But both of them knew that wasn't true. It was one of those feeble, stupid things we say to buoy someone up, not expecting it to be believed.

Robert let out another long sigh. "God, I shouldn't even be thinking of myself. What about that poor woman's family?" He turned to Ann. "What have I done to them? Because I wanted to help."

4

ANN slowed to ten miles an hour as she noticed eight or ten windowless travel trailers
lining both sides of the street at the intersection
of Vermont and Cody. A dozen or so men and
women were milling about in the early morning gloom, holding Styrofoam coffee cups and
donuts while a policeman set out saw horses,
getting ready to block traffic on Vermont.

"It can't be an accident," Robert said, sitting
up straighter and peering through the wind-
shield.

Ann felt a tremor of annoyance. "No, it's that
movie shoot we were warned about. I guess
they'll be in the neighborhood off and on for
three weeks or so. It'll make it difficult getting
in and out of West Adams."

Robert sank back down and closed his eyes,
uninterested. "What movie? I don't remember
hearing anything about it."

"The one they had that community meeting
about in February. They put fliers on everyone's
door last week saying the filming is about to
start. I've gotten half-a-dozen emails about it

this week. Someone even put up a 'Hollywood Out of South-Central' Facebook page. Access Hollywood and TMZ had a lot of fun with it— Villagers with pitchforks and torches."

His eyes flicked open. "You mean that 1890s railroad barons thing? I thought that idea died a well-deserved death months ago."

"No, it's going ahead. HBO, I think." She gave him a wry smile. "A visionary young director. His point of view will be radical. Daring. A legend in the making."

"God." Robert shook his head. "Why do they have to film it here? People are fed up with movie crews disrupting their neighborhoods. We have enough to worry about with crime and trash and potholed streets as it is."

"I suppose it helps the economy to do it in Los Angeles rather than Canada. And they're going to hire some local people as extras. That was part of the deal with the neighborhood association."

"They'll only do the exterior shooting here. Everything else, including post production, will be done in Vancouver to keep the unions out." His head fell back against the seat. "Suddenly it all seems so trivial, doesn't it? After tonight. After tonight everything seems trivial."

The sun was peeking weakly between hundred-year-old pine trees on the east side of their yard as Ann pulled off Van Buren and onto the long concrete drive that terminated at the carriage house-turned-garage. As they got out of the car she couldn't help but hurriedly look around. Those men in the van lived nearby, the police had said. And they'll know where we live once they hear Robert's name on the news. All they'd have to do is look online.

Robert was already halfway up the front steps. Ann hurried over to catch up and unlocked the door. "Come in the kitchen," she said. "I'll make you some toast. It's practically breakfast time already." Not that she was fit enough to eat anything herself.

JG was slumped at the kitchen table, asleep; Jake, his thirteen-year-old cocker mix, dozed on the floor next to him. They both bolted awake, JG leaping to his feet. "Will someone tell me what's going on? I've been sitting here for two hours."

"I'm sorry, hon. Let me get some breakfast for your dad first. Do you want me to make you some eggs?"

"I ate already. I couldn't get back to sleep after getting the car home. I just want to know what happened." He plowed a hand through the short dreadlocks, like Medusa's angry snakes, he'd taken to wearing in rebellion against the shaved-head ethos of the performing arts high school he attended in Hollywood.

Moving with the deliberate motions of a drunk, Robert sat at the table, carefully putting his hands palms down in front of him. He looked his son full in the face and made his voice go dull. "I shot someone. A woman. Accidentally."

As Ann put two pieces of sourdough in the toaster, she said, "There's been a series of rapes in the neighborhood. West of here, I guess. When your father saw a woman being dragged into a van, he stopped to help. He got into a fight with one of the men and unfortunately the gun went off and the woman was killed. He had to explain to the police what happened. At least they have a description of the men now."

"Only one of them," Robert murmured. "I hardly saw the driver at all." He looked at his son, and spread his arms out, almost as a gesture of defeat, or hopelessness. "I thought I could stop them, but the man had a pistol. When I knocked it from his hand we both grabbed at it. It went off and struck the woman in the neck."

JG's whole body went slack. "And she's dead?" He shook his head as if none of this could be real; this was his father they were talking about, a calm, almost meek, man who seldom lost his temper, and never hinted at violence, had never even been able to spank his son.

"The police are saying he's a hero," Ann said gently, and put a hand on Robert's shoulder.

"God—" JG didn't know how to react. He said, "A hero—" as though trying out the notion, then added, "I guess. You tried to help. Most people wouldn't have done that, would they? I mean, they would have just driven past. Right? You *were* a hero."

Robert was annoyed. "I want it understood that this is not something to make into an act of courage. I didn't think 'I'm going to risk my life for that woman.' I just did it. Instinctively. And bear in mind that someone's dead because of it. I hope you'd be wiser than your old man and call 9-1-1 instead of taking on someone with a gun."

"Even if she'd be raped or dead by the time they got there?"

Ann slid the plate of toast in front of Robert and sat down next to him. She tried to defuse the unexpected emotion she saw in her son. "You'll understand what he means when you're a parent, hon."

"I know exactly what he means. It's OK for other people, or other people's children, to risk their lives, as long as your own kid doesn't. That's it, isn't it?"

"Please, John. We've had a hard night. We don't want to argue. We're just saying everyone has to judge the situation himself. If a man has a gun, what can you do but call the police? That's why they're there."

"What would you do if someone tried to kill me or Dad and you had the opportunity to stop him? What if you had to shoot him? Would you call 9-1-1 and then wait to see what happened?"

Robert raised his voice as Jake pushed laboriously to his feet and looked around, wondering at the commotion. "What are you going on about? We're just telling you to be prudent. It's what we'd tell anyone."

34

"But you weren't, and you're a hero. You ought to be proud. You almost saved a woman's life."

"*Almost* doesn't make much sense in a case like this, does it?" Robert snapped, and added, "She's dead. Because I tried to do something I'm not qualified to do."

"But it was the right thing! That's what's important. You tried!"

"Goddamn it, intentions don't matter. Consequences do." Robert ran a hand over his face, then turned to Ann. "I've got to get some sleep. Will you call the office at nine and tell them I won't be in today? You don't have to explain why. They'll find out soon enough." He turned back to his son. "With all due respect, JG, sixteen is a little too young to be passing judgment on matters of life and death. In a few years you'll agree with me."

"Come on, Dad. This isn't 1950. We live in a violent world. Look at that neighborhood out there—"

"What's wrong with the neighborhood?" Now it was Robert who was getting hot.

"You don't know anything about it," JG shot back. "You didn't have to walk through it every day to junior high. You just stroll over to RULA, or drive an air-conditioned car to an air-conditioned high-rise downtown. Have you ever gone south of 35th or into the ghetto outside our little rich-boy community?"

"I can't believe you're asking that. We moved here *because* of the neighborhood. I'm fighting for the future of RULA *because* of the neighbor-hood. How dare you criticize me."

JG hooted. "You live in a fairy-tale world! Your friends are lawyers and professors and people from Beverly Hills. That's not South-Central, it's not even L.A. Come on down to Manual Arts High School and I'll introduce you to some Crips and MS-13s. You can talk 'the brotherhood of man' with them."

"John!" Ann said sharply. "Leave it for now. This is no time for arguments. Let your dad get some sleep. He's been up all night."

"And do as I say, not as I do." JG stared at her, his face and neck flushed with emotion. "That's the way it always is with parents, isn't it? Talk one way and act another." He pushed away from the counter and stormed upstairs.

Ann's eyes closed. *It's the way it is with families*, she thought with a sigh. *It's the way it is when children grow and stop being children but aren't quite adults and have too much emotion and not enough experience to know how to handle it. It's the inevitable breakdown in every family's social contract. Now it's our turn. We became too smug as a family, too insular and self-satisfied.*

After Robert went upstairs to bed and JG an-grily left for school, Ann sat at the kitchen table with a cup of tea and gazed out the window. She wondered if she should even attempt to get any work done today. Probably not. The Fed didn't seem much interested in her research anyway.

That's why the offer she got several months ago to join a new psychology-econ group at Princeton was looking more and more attractive. Even if it meant re-entering academia. If Robert got the job in D.C., she'd probably take it. It would mean living away from home three days a week, but JG would be at Eastman and Robert could handle three days by himself. It might even be good for them to be absent from each other once in a while, give them time to de-escalate and relax. Robert especially had been on edge about RULA for months. He needed to back off. JG too.

It bothered her that they had gotten so angry with each other this morning. But the last year or so their relationship had begun to unravel as JG sought more and more to assert his individuality, picking arguments merely so he could disagree. Too much emotion. And too little cause. But even before he was old enough for school she and Robert had hints there was something unusual—troubling, even—about their son, his quietness and *intensiveness*. By age six, though, their concerns slipped into the background when they discovered that he was possessed of a genius neither of them expected in a child of their own. Which brought an entirely new load of burdens to their family.

A high-pitched tittering from outside disturbed Ann's thoughts, and brought her to the window, where she could see a blue jay angrily harassing a half-dozen house finches. That area of the yard had been left fallow since a fire seven years ago destroyed the oleander hedge that had been there for decades. The day of the fire RULA had won a civil suit against the LAPD for mistreating a sixteen-year-old named Omar Randall Stahr, who had been arrested for auto theft. A passerby had caught the cops on video just as they were slamming the kid against a brick wall, breaking his nose and fracturing a wrist. Blood hemorrhaged over his face, and he screamed and writhed in pain from the fracture while the camera, safely across the street, recorded everything. The boy had been awarded $3.4 million, and two of the dozen or so patrolmen involved were sentenced to a year in jail, where one of them was later beaten to death by a prisoner. The night the officers were sentenced, someone poured gasoline over the bushes and lawn and front porch and set a match to it. Luckily the fire had been discovered almost at once and extinguished before the house went up. But it had so depressed Ann that she'd left the side garden unplanted until this January, though Beth Sylvester next door had put in a privet hedge some years ago. And now, after all her work this winter, the newly-planted roses were being destroyed by bugs, and Ann just couldn't summon the energy or will to do anything about it. Maybe later this week.

She also had JG's room to paint. Last month she'd stripped off the baseboards and crown molding and bought the paint. *So stop being so lazy and get to it.* But she'd been too

tired or too busy to work up the necessary enthusiasm. The Furious Procrastinator strikes
again. Had she and Robert finally fallen into
the trap marriage counselors called DINS—
Dual Income, No Sex? Husband and wife coming home from work too exhausted to do anything but flop down in front of the TV for several
hours, then go to sleep. She laughed out loud.
Not a chance; we're DIGS—Dual Income, Great
Sex.

Her phone rang, startling her. Day-dreaming
again. She picked it up.

"Midge Colbert, from the *Times*. I'm calling
about the shooting last night. Is Mr. Binder
available?"

Ann felt a tremor that seemed to squeeze all
her muscles at once. She was surprised at the
intensity of her reaction. She should have expected this sort of intrusion into the privacy of
their family. "I'm sorry," she said abruptly, and
felt a tiny stab of regret at sounding rude. "He
has nothing to say."

"But he's a hero. Everyone's talking about it.
I'm sure he'll want—"

She dropped the phone to the counter as if
it were infected. *It's just starting*, she thought
with a shiver. *I don't know why, but it's going to
get bad. It's going to hurt us, our whole family.*

5

"I can't believe how shook up I still am," Robert said when he returned to work the next day. He was sitting in his cluttered office adjacent to the Otis campus, just three blocks from home. The half-dozen century-old Palladian buildings that made up the law school were barely visible through the window behind Luis Teague's massive frame.

His friend twisted back in the wobbly armchair that, like every other piece of furniture in the office, had been rescued from landfills and swap meets. "Good Lord, any of us would feel the same. It gives me chills to even think about it. You were seconds away from being murdered. Liz sends her love, by the way. Wanted to pop over to your place and brew tea or whatever it is people do when friends face tragedy. Bring a casserole, I suppose. I told her to forget it, let the boy get his sea legs first, then we'll bring him a bottle of twenty-year-old Johnny Walker."

Robert stood up and rubbed his bare arms. Why was it always so cold in here when it was so warm outside? "The worst part of this whole mess is that someone died because I tried to help. I was acting on the conviction that we've been a bystander society too long. It's the same message I've been preaching since we were at Columbia. And an innocent person died because of it. What's my message supposed to be now? *Don't get involved, disengage from your community?*"

"Come on, Robert. You did an admirable thing. You stood up for principle, and bully for you. Stop beating yourself up about it."

Robert started to pace around the small room. "I'm the one who has to live with the consequences, Luis. So don't tell me how 'heroic' I was. I've been through that."

Teague raised his eyebrows and Robert told him about yesterday's argument with JG.

The other man waved a dismissive hand. "Don't worry about John. He's just feeling a little conflicted. It has to have been quite a shock to discover his father was caught in the middle of a violent crime. He'll come around. By the way, I ran into the increasingly ethereal Raul Salas a few minutes ago as I was picking up my mail on campus. He slipped up stealthily behind me, giving me quite a shock. I feel strongly that all deans should be required to wear a bell around their neck, like lepers of old. I made such a proposal to the Academic Senate last year and received wide, if not sufficient, support. At any rate, I will miss the man's peculiar sensibility, that late period Henry James lack of engagement with the down and dirty he brought to the Dean's office. He said, 'Luis, did Robert actually shoot that woman? With a gun?' You know how unworldly he can be. He also taxed me on my attitude toward Jirasek. 'I do wish you'd tone it down, Luis. We all know you've never liked him.' 'No, no, that's untrue,' I said. 'For several months this year I experimented with *trying* to like him but was forced to terminate the effort when the results proved unsatisfactory.'"

Robert pushed from his chair and crossed to the window, trying to work off some of the nervous energy that had been welling up within him since yesterday. "The governor called me at home this morning. Just to say he was relieved I wasn't hurt. I thought that was nice of him."

"It was indeed. He's a surprisingly warm man."

"A few others, also. Edgerton Lee, Bobby Stackhouse." Stackhouse was the pastor of an AME church in Central L.A. and president of the Inclusion Coalition, a civil rights organization Robert had worked with in the past.

Teague's voice picked up an edge of tension. "And the amiable Ann? How has she taken all this?"

Robert knew at once where Teague was going and tried to head him off. "Fine. Ann's OK." He turned to stare at his friend. *Drop it*, he willed silently.

42

But Teague wouldn't be put off. "This would be a good time for you and her to talk about Boston, you know. *Past* time."

"Luis, damn it, I *know* that. But I can't. I simply can't make myself do it. I'm sorry. You don't know how sorry I am."

Teague brooded a moment; he was upset and wanted to say more, but finally gave up. Taking another sip of coffee, he asked, "And the firm? No problems with the partners, no arched eyebrows or pursed lips?"

Robert was staring out at the patch of diseased grass that separated the cottage that housed both RULA and Teague's Inner-City Law Project from the rest of Otis. "Maurice Dohr called last night. He was supportive, of course. But not happy to have me labeled in the press as a partner of Dohr, Haskins, and Poole. The old adage that any publicity is good doesn't hold for DHP."

"You probably didn't catch the news last night, knowing your aversion to television."

Robert said he hadn't.

"Legal activist's act of heroism results in unfortunate tragedy, et cetera, et cetera. It definitely bothered me, the way they were playing it out as a litany of clichés: well-known civil rights attorney, vicious kidnappers, innocent victim. Even ten seconds of old film showing you in court on that assault charge." Two years earlier Robert had been arrested for hitting a drunk in a restaurant who had made an obscene racial remark to Ann. Ironically, the same week he'd

43

defended a White Power speaker named Alban Zine who had been denied the right to hold a rally at a public park in the Valley. It had made him hugely unpopular with many RULA supporters, and he still got occasional hate calls because of it. "And D.C.?" Teague added.

Robert sank down on the futon that did the work of a couch in his office. "Haven't heard a peep. I don't know if that's good or bad. Maybe this isn't news back east."

"Even if it isn't, it will be. There's a *Times* reporter literally prowling the Otis hallways as we speak. She wants *quotes, background, color*, any racy bits of *personalia* we can offer about our esteemed colleague in the Rural and Urban Legal Assistance program."

"Jesus," Robert said, annoyed at how he was suddenly becoming public property. "We haven't answered our phones in two days. I thought I'd be safe here, though. Pretty naïve, I guess."

"Actually, it might be a good idea if I rooted out our intrepid newsy to make sure she leaves here with an understanding of just how highly the faculty of Otis Law School thinks of Robert Binder and the Rural and Urban Legal Assistance program."

"Do you think that's a good idea? Maybe it'd be better to let well enough alone."

"Like it or not, chum, Otis and the election are being dragged into your little drama. And as you are very much seen as a partisan of Howard Zalesky, we need to make our position clear. If

not, Karel and the lickers of spittle that consti-
tute his groupies will try to tie you and Howard
and this tragedy together in people's minds."

Robert sighed and stared up at the ceiling
with its mosaic of a hundred years' worth of
water stains. "I hadn't thought about Otis being dragged into this. I suppose I should have
known. God, how I wish none of it had happened."

"Nonsense. It was admirable—courageous,
even. Let the other side try to make of it what
they will, few of them would have taken the
chance you did. Can you imagine the Odious
Karel leaping from his car in his coat of many
colors, and wrestling with an armed assailant?"
His tone abruptly became serious as he remembered another problem that had to be disposed
of. "Did I tell you the ILP's decided to take on
the Transit Authority next year? Assuming Jirasek's not elected, of course. Want to jump on
board with some of your student volunteers?"

And in an instant Robert was retreating into
the quotidian. It was oddly pleasing to be
wrestling with the mundane and the bureau-
cratic again. The normalcy of it all, instead of
annoying him with trivialities as it usually did,
was calming. But in another part of his mind
he was hearing, as he had for two days, the
screams of that woman, and watching in disbelief as blood pumped from her throat while
he crouched helplessly over her body, screaming at her not to die as she stared into his face,
not with fear or hope but a limitless hatred.

"So, John. The semester ends and summer beckons. What are your plans? Music or girls? Or both?"

JG's heart pounded like crazy. He was always nervous when someone in the school hierarchy called him in. Especially publicly yanking him out of class—History, this time—the other kids *ooh*ing and *ahh*ing with deliberate over-emphasis, and yelling "Bus-*ted!*" and, "They found that crack pipe in your locker, Binder!" But this time he knew what it was about, and his mom and dad were going to absolutely freak. Squirming in the folding metal chair, he stared at his Reeboks. "I don't know. My dad has me signed up for Italian lessons with some guy he knows. And the master's class, I guess." He slid to a stop, didn't want to talk about it.

"Italian?" Thick eyebrows shot up.

JG was never sure what to make of this Mr. Wilkerson, his counselor since starting high school. He looked about forty, but weirdly skinny, and always dressed in black. Like a Goth who never grew up. An ancient MP3 player behind the desk had gone from Lady GaGa to some country-western singer JG had never heard of. But the guy seemed to really care about students, not just an act like most adults, so maybe he was OK. He shrugged, flashing a weak smile. "My dad thinks all musicians should speak a little Italian."

"You're not planning an opera career, are you?"

I'm not planning any career, he thought, and began to drift away. It was a trick he developed, being able at any moment to retreat into his protective shell, drawing its contours around him until he disappeared, and nothing anyone said or did could harm him. He'd been doing this since childhood when other kids picked on him ("Hey, peckerhead, macaca, zebra boy ..."), drawing the shell over his body while moving his consciousness outside. *See John disappear, he no longer exists. So go away, leave him alone.*

But Wilkerson's insistent voice found a crack in the shell and wormed its way in. "Opera, John! Is that what you're planning?"

From a distance JG watched himself feign boredom. "I don't know. Maybe." Fade. Fade. Disappear.

Wilkerson tilted back in his chair and hefted his huge ass-kicking Doc Martens onto the desktop with a thud as loud as a pistol shot. "So how's the academics coming along? You've always been one of our stars."

"OK, I guess." JG looked frantically for the crack, trying to pull the shell tighter, blocking out the words, but Wilkerson gave him no chance, raising his voice and pushing pushing pushing until the shell slipped from JG's body.

"How about your social life? You didn't go to the prom, did you? I used to see you hanging with—what's her name? That nice-looking pale girl with the bangs? Sonja something. Hit a blank wall there?"

"Do you have a list of people who didn't go to the prom?" Feeling a little anger—what the hell was this, bugging him about the goddamn prom?

"Hell, that's only part of it, Kid." Wilkerson held up a thick file. "Got reports on everyone who missed the last Jennifer Lawrence flick, and another on people who think they can get away without flossing every night. It's how I got the fancy corner office." His boots crashed to the floor and his wiry six-foot-two body loomed menacingly over the desk. "The reason I'm asking is... I'm starting to get a file on you, too, and that ain't a good thing."

The shell completely vanished, and suddenly JG was alone and vulnerable. He felt a single drop of sweat, icy cold—*Jesus, glacier cold, end of the fucking world cold*—working its way along either side of his ribs.

"And," Wilkerson was sitting drill-sergeant straight now and staring right at him like the truth was there for any idiot to see, "I don't like it when one of my flock messes up. Got my rep to take care of. I'm Counselor to the Stars, the top gun, the Hollywood *capo di capo.* I don't handle footballers, slackers, or kids whose biggest ambition is to work at the Gap. But suddenly JG Binder's on my radar screen as a potential screw up." He shoved his skinny butt back in the chair. "So what's up? And don't say 'nothing'."

The word died a slow death in JG's throat. Instead he said, "How come you're asking?"

"Kid, don't try to bullshit a bullshitter. First rule of life in Holly-weird. I've got the last bunch of progress reports from your teachers here, and for the first time your name's on the 'Deep Doo Doo' list, the 'Call Mom and Dad list,' the 'I wonder if the Army is recruiting' list."

Another two drops of icy sweat dripped and dribbled, making JG bring his elbows in against his shirt to sop up the moisture. "Stuff's getting hard, I guess. Calculus. I hate it. How's knowing that going to help me later in life?"

"Two thousand years' worth of students have made the same whiney excuse, John. You don't have to *use* it, you have to train your mind to accept information, and think, and develop. *That's* the point." He picked up a progress report, waving it in the air. "And don't tell me *History's* causing your brain to freeze up. You've got an IQ of what?" His hand crashed through the jumble of reports in front of him, papers exploding off his desk and onto the floor as he searched for something. "A gazillion and six, or something, right? So tell me what the problem is before all the teachers around here start thinking the Mighty Wilkerson's lost his touch, can't handle counseling any more, maybe ought to be put on the lunch squad."

JG said, because he has to say something, "I'll try harder. There's seven weeks left."

"Five and a half. You can't count any more, either?"

"I'll do OK on my finals. Really."

"Yeah, great, John. Do *OK* on your finals. But I'm locking the door and keeping you in here until I find out what the problem is. What am I supposed to tell your parents when you come home with shitty grades?"

"What does it matter? I'm not going to Harvard. It's a music school. No calculus. Not even History. Just... music."

"Yeah, Eastman. But they want high-school *graduates*, you know. People who've proven they can finish what they start, and not throw in the towel halfway through."

"I didn't throw in the towel."

"Just fell down and can't get up, then. You went from top of the class to what?" He looked at the progress reports and barked, rapid fire, "C, C, D, D minus. All this since March. And that's not giving up? Help me out here, OK? Waz up?"

Silence.

"You getting along with de Santos?" The orchestra leader.

"Yeah. Fine." *She hates me, is all.* He held his breath and tried again with all his might to will the shell back. *Just get me the hell out of here before I explode, leaving scraps of brain and blood all over the office.*

Wilkerson sighed, his voice sympathetic. "Heard about your dad on the news. It was a gutsy thing he did. You've got to be proud of him."

JG smiled as the shell returned. He grabbed hold and pulled it over him. No crack this time, no way for anyone to intrude. Its darkness warmed him, and he felt like a three-year-old sucking his thumb.

Wilkerson stared at the ceiling, frustrated. "That's what I hate about this job: talking to myself. OK, get back to class. But your parents are going to blow a fuse, kid. At both of us."

6

"OK, here's one you should know. What color is Nancy Drew's hair?" Robert tapped the edge of the laminated game card on the table top.

Trivial Pursuit had been Ann's idea, to get him out of the funk he had been in since the shooting and bring a little normalcy back to the family. And maybe even winch her own mind away from the sense of doom that had been hanging over her since Lee's party. As soon as dinner was over she cajoled both Robert and JG (What had gotten into *him* lately?) into joining her at the kitchen table where she had already laid the game out. So far it seemed to be working as Robert offered up the confident look that meant she wasn't going to get this answer.

And she wasn't. "I've never even *seen* a Nancy Drew book. My parents wouldn't allow them in the house. They're ridiculous."

He laid the card face down on the table. "You're delaying, which means you don't know. There's a finite number of possibilities, Ms. Decision-Making Expert."

While she was thinking, JG said, "Have either of you been watching the filming down the street? I was hanging out there for a while this afternoon. They had some actors made up as old-time mounted policemen. All they did is ride slowly down the street on their horses. It took two hours before the director was satisfied."

Ann said, "Did they hire any neighbors as extras like they said?"

"I don't know. But there must have been three or four hundred people on the sidewalk watching. Some of them were pretty pissed off about the streets being closed. Some guys got in a fight with a couple of security people and the real cops had to butt in."

"Do you know what they're going to film on our corner? We got a flier saying it would be next week. They're blocking off the intersections and we won't be able to drive in or out for two days."

"All this is truly fascinating," Robert said with some annoyance. "But meanwhile Nancy Drew's sensibly styled hair is being sadly ignored. You have five seconds." He began mimicking the music from *Jeopardy*.

"Oh, sorry. Red. No, black."

"Blonde. JG's turn."

As JG snatched the die and tossed it toward the center of the board, Robert said, "Did I tell you that Karel Jirasek actually wandered over to RULA to talk to me today? In his amazing Technicolor Dreamcoat, naturally. To offer his *condolences.* It's the only time he's actually shown any interest in what we do. Secretaries and typists were so shocked, they came by to gape. A few were convinced it wasn't Karel at all but merely his stunt double."

"Condolences for what?"

Robert waved a hand. "My getting mixed up in this 'regrettable and tragic situation,' having my privacy invaded by reporters, being forced to deal with the police. There were tears at the edge of his eyes. Actual watery tears! No wonder he's so good with a jury. He could probably make stigmata appear on his wrists, if necessary. Of course, the *Schadenfreude* was thick as peanut butter."

"You've got to ask me a question, Dad. And what's *schaden*-whatever?"

Ann said, "*Schadenfreude* is a marvelous German word with no English equivalent. It means that feeling of guilty delight people experience when hearing of someone else's misfortune."

"Like I felt at the Vivaldi competition last year when that Japanese girl messed up," Robert said.

"Meaning I wouldn't have won if she hadn't screwed up?"

"Meaning I'm a father. I want my child to succeed. Lighten up, it's not a crime. Anyway, I want to play Trivial Pursuit, not defend myself. I've done enough of that recently." He read from the card: "What letter does a cedilla hang from?"

Both Ann and JG said, "A *what*?"

When Robert sat back and smiled, Ann realized it was the first time she'd seen that in two days, and she began to relax. "Ah," he said, "the infinite pleasure of *Schadenfreude*. You have five seconds to answer." He began to hum the *Jeopardy* theme again but was interrupted by the phone, and he reached over to take it off the counter.

"Detective Oakley, Mr. Binder. How are you?"

"Fine—" he said automatically, but something moved deep inside his brain that made him stiffen, a primitive warning system signaling flight that he recognized only later, replaying this conversation over and over as he lay in bed staring at the darkness.

"Good to hear it, sir," Oakley said, and asked if he'd mind coming into the station tomorrow morning. Just to chat a bit. Shouldn't take too long. In and out in a jiffy.

Robert's eyes went at once to Ann, then quickly retreated. His voice turned cautious. "Has something come up? Something new?"

No, no, nothing like that. Just some loose ends. They settled on 10 AM, and Robert hung up, wondering at his unease, but telling himself to relax, that it was OK. Everything was going to be all right.

After JG went upstairs to practice, Ann poured herself some Cabernet and sat down on the couch to read the paper. A minute later Robert wandered out of the kitchen with a glass of the scotch he normally kept for visitors. *How often did he take a drink of hard liquor?* she wondered. *Once a year?* It was that phone call, she decided; it had rattled him. But *why?* Robert put the glass on the end table, moved behind the couch, and began to massage her neck and shoulders. She tilted her head back to smile at him and whispered, "The Incredible Hulk."

Robert's fingers froze. "Words I never expected to hear coming from your mouth."

"I was trying to think who that detective handling your case looked like."

"I don't think that's fair at all. She's a nice-looking woman." He began rubbing again.

"You know who I mean. There's a resemblance. Except for the green skin."

"DeFazio as a superhero? No, I don't think so. He hasn't got the personality for it. Doesn't seem to have any personality at all."

"Why do you think they want to see you again?"

"I can't imagine. She said there was nothing new. So—"

But they were interrupted by the Stones' *Sympathy for the Devil* exploding suddenly from upstairs. One of JG's strange enthusiasms. When he wasn't practicing classical music, he played rap or Sixties-era rock full blast on his phone. "Odd, isn't it?" Robert said. "Our son is fascinated by music even we're barely old enough to remember." He finished his drink and put it down on the table. "I'm going to run up and take a shower. If JG wasn't here I'd invite you to join me."

She patted his hand. "Maybe you can convince him to go to a movie."

Ann smiled to herself as he left, remembering how as newlyweds her pulse would quicken just thinking about sex with him. Supposedly working on her dissertation, her mind would inevitably go to Robert, and *bang*, end of dissertation for another day. It still happened sometimes, twenty-two years later. "When did you first know you were going to marry him?" a friend once asked, and Ann laughed and said from the third date when Robert spent half an hour in a Hallmark store looking for the perfect birthday card for her. "He actually *read* the inside of every card before choosing one. How many men would do that?"

But Ann had decided on marriage long before Robert. He was skittish, having not yet recovered from an earlier marriage that ended in his wife's death from a pregnancy gone wrong. That had been three years before he and Ann met. Robert and Carolyn had been married for just eleven months. Carolyn's father, whom even now they heard from two or three times a year, was financing Robert's law-school studies, something Robert could never have afforded on his own. Ann knew, because he insisted on telling her, on that first date, of the rage he felt at Carolyn's death, the anger that spilled out everywhere because there was no one—no person—at fault. So: anger at hospitals, doctors, the human body. The world.

Carolyn remained a vivid part of Robert's being for years, of course, and when Ann became pregnant, he was panicky for months, insisting on more attentive medical observation than was necessary. You're neurotic, she told him, but his fears seemed justified when two years after JG's birth, an ectopic pregnancy put an end to their hopes for more children. It had been a sadness in their life that even now was with them, though they never talked about it.

Looking around the living room she noticed that someone had vacuumed today. Robert probably. JG hadn't been much in the mood lately. "Shared responsibility and no job descriptions" were the rules of the house. If you see something that needs doing, do it. And no matter how trivial the job, always do your best. It's how you show respect for yourself and your family, Robert insisted. *Hey, we're the Binders*, he liked to joke. *We're special. We soar.* And so they did, working at making their family succeed when it was obvious not everyone wanted it to.

But all was not well now. You're waiting for something to happen, aren't you, Robert? You don't want to tell me what it is. You don't want me to worry. But sooner or later I will. I'll have to. Because this affects all of us.

7

AT ten o'clock the three of them sat on the couch and watched the news. It was the first time Robert had allowed himself to see how the media was handling the shooting, though he had heard from others that the emphasis was on the assailants and not himself. Ann took his hand, holding it in her lap, feeling it tense as they saw a reporter at the site of the attempted kidnapping. "Sharon Chow," Robert murmured when the reporter's name flashed on the screen. "She's called my office a dozen times. I told Luz not to put her through."

"She called here, too," JG said dully. "I hung up on her."

"Speaking of phone calls—" Ann turned toward her son. With so much going on she'd forgotten. "There was a message on my voicemail to call your counselor. He'd already gone home when I called back. What's that about?"

"From Wilkerson?" JG looked at her and shrugged. "Maybe something to do with the fall class schedule." He turned back to the TV, his bare toes pressing deeply into the carpet.

Sharon Chow was saying there had been another rape in the area the previous night, bringing the total to six. The victim had been dragged into an alley and stabbed twice in the back as she tried to run away. The wounds were serious but not life-threatening. At that point two police sketches appeared on the screen. One of the men, based mainly on Robert's recollection, looked to be in his twenties, with a faint mustache and short dark hair. There was no picture of the other man, but the woman said he had a tattoo of a snake on his wrist.

"Not much help," Ann muttered.

"I wasn't really paying attention to faces," Robert said. He knew it sounded churlish, but he'd been defending himself for two days now and was tired of it.

"Of course." Ann squeezed his hand. "It's just unfortunate none of the other victims were able to give a description. But the police must have DNA."

"Sure. But unless it's in the database, it doesn't do any good."

Sharon Chow was on screen again. She began to walk to her left, pointing dramatically at the ground where a makeshift shrine had grown up on the bloody bit of sidewalk where the woman Robert shot had died. Dozens of candles, along with vinyl balloons and bouquets of flowers were heaped against the wall. "Residents of this working-class neighborhood have been bringing remembrances for two days," the reporter said. "Even if they didn't know the

victim they want to show their grief. And support for those left behind."

Suddenly the screen shifted to videotape of
the victim's family, the camera panning the
austere living room of a home just two blocks
from where the woman died. The husband, a
frail, nervous-looking man in his forties, was
identified as Sandeep Chaudhary, an immigrant from India who had been in this country
for two years.

"I had no idea she was Indian," Robert said
with surprise. "I was trying to keep the blood
from pumping out of her neck, I was practically
on top of her, and I didn't even pay attention to
what she looked like."

The camera panned around to show a young
man, the oldest of four children, retreating into
the darkened kitchen with a toddler, and a girl
about fifteen trying to comfort another child
who didn't stop screaming. "Twin boys, four
years old," Sharon Chow said, "suddenly moth-
erless. There has been some help from the local
Indian community, but this has hit the Chaudhary family very, very hard. The wife had been
their main source of income."

According to the reporter, Mr. Chaudhary
has been unable to find work for over a year.
The young man, Rajesh, is a student at a junior
college and working only part time. And now
Mr. Chaudhary finds himself with two young
children about to start kindergarten, as well
as the older girl, a sophomore in high school.

"He's doing the best he can but he's obviously overwhelmed."

Ann felt a rising of compassion. "We've got to do something to help them, Robert. That poor man. And those children without a mother!"

"I'll check with Otis. Maybe there's some way we could find a job for him. Or help with the little ones. It looks like that girl's going to end up doing most of the work."

"I know what usually happens in these cases," Ann said. "There's this huge outpouring of assistance. People send money or offer food or clothing. Then, like a switch was flipped, it stops and the victims aren't much better off than they were."

"I'll call the father tomorrow. The police can give me his number. We'll do something, I promise. Even a GoFundMe page. I'll take responsibility for it."

But later in bed, after Robert had turned off the light, Ann was having second thoughts. "I'm not sure direct help is the right thing to do. Not in this kind of situation. We ought to let someone else take the lead."

Robert rolled onto his side to look at her. "What do you mean? What kind of situation?"

"Well... because of your part in it." She was on shaky ground here and didn't want to make him feel any worse than he did. But she had been thinking about it ever since watching the news. "It might be best if you remained in the background."

"But this is my fault, Ann. It wouldn't have happened if I hadn't made a mess of things. It's up to me to make it up to that family. Me, not some bureaucrat or faceless third party." He took a breath. "Maybe I'm doing it for my sake as well as theirs. But I did something horrible. I can't make it disappear, but I can ease the pain a little. For me as well as them."

Feeling guilty about how this was going to sound, she said, "I guess I don't want that man to know where we live."

"You can't be serious. Do you think he's going to come over here and kill everyone because of what happened?" There was a hint of outrage in Robert's voice that made her feel even worse. Because he was right. What was she afraid of?

Still, *her* feelings were important, too. "I'm not saying it's rational. I'm saying it's how I feel. I'd rather he didn't know." She added, "Maybe we can set up assistance through their temple. They're Hindus, I imagine. Or maybe you can arrange a job through DHP."

"I'll look into it, but we'll have to find out what kind of skills he has."

"He's going to need more immediate aid, too. Those children need help. They didn't look like they had much in the way of food or clothing."

Robert gave her a kiss. "Hey, we're getting too worked up here. I'll handle it. And also make sure no one learns where Dr. Ann Binder, expert on non-rational decision making, lays her lovely head to sleep." He moved closer and put his hand on her hip. "But I think the first course of action is to ensure she doesn't go to sleep quite yet."

She smiled and moved into him, her fingers slipping under his pajamas. "You've heard about what marriage counselors call DINS? Let me explain DIGS to you."

Later, while Robert snored softly beside her, Ann found herself thinking that getting involved with the victim's family was a mistake. Why couldn't Robert see that? He was letting his passions run away with him. At times she loved him for this depth of feeling but at other times it distressed her. Caring mattered, yes, of course, but sometimes he took it too far. Like at Lee's party when he argued with Jirasek even though he knew it was a mistake.

She was falling asleep as she wondered suddenly what that woman had been doing out alone that late.

Why hadn't anyone asked that?

8

Ann went with Robert to the police station the next morning. *A wifely duty*, she thought. More than that—a *friendly* duty, to offer support, though they both forgot what a hassle it was going to be getting out of West Adams as the movie crew advanced to within two blocks of their house. There had been a shrill full-color flier from an ad hoc community group on the door last night announcing a plan by some residents to protest the filming by standing in front of their homes and banging on pots and pans and blowing whistles. It was a technique that had been used elsewhere in the city over the years. But this time there was a degree of fury the studios were unfamiliar with. People were using Twitter and Facebook to stir up emotions. *How Many Studios Are Headed by Minorities?* read the headline on the flier, followed by *What's Hollywood Ever Done for South-Central?* The rest of the page was taken up with a drawing of streets clogged with cars frantically trying to get out of West Adams.

Jill Oakley had been waiting for them on

the fourth floor and led the way to the same sound-proofed interview room they had used previously. There was a maroon accordion folder in the center of the bolted-down table but Oakley ignored it as she waved them to the chairs. "Detective DeFazio will be here in a minute. It's been a rough day. We had a triple murder in Pershing Square last night. We've been here since three this morning."

They sat in silence, Ann clutching her purse, Robert staring blankly ahead, the muscles in his neck and shoulders working. *He's reliving it,* Ann thought. *Because of this room. He's fighting those men, seeing that poor woman... It's something he'll never be free of—the gunshot, the screams, blood and death.* After a few minutes she glanced at her watch.

Oakley frowned her sympathy. "It shouldn't be long. Do either of you want coffee?" They didn't. Oakley began clicking a ballpoint pen open and closed, open and closed.

They're making us wait on purpose, Ann thought suddenly. *They're trying to unsettle us for some reason.* Then she immediately rebuked herself: *Don't be silly. This is a busy place... these officers have a lot to do. We're probably pretty small fish to them.*

Five minutes later the door flew open and Nick DeFazio hurried in, the noisy chaos of the squad room briefly intruding before the door thudded closed behind him. He was coatless, unshaven, a 9mm automatic at his waist. Detective chic. "Sorry," he muttered without looking at anyone, and dropped into the vacant chair. He shook his head wearily and rubbed his eyes, then allowed them to close as Jill Oakley took charge. "Maybe we can wrap up your part in all this today, Mr. Binder, and let you get on with your life. It can't be much fun with both us and a zillion media people bothering you."

"Not fun at all," Robert agreed.

For the briefest moment DeFazio's eyes opened and fixed on Robert with an emotion Ann couldn't read. *What just happened?* she wondered and felt a sharpening of her senses. Because she knew with a sudden unsettling certainty that things were not as they had been three days ago. Or even three minutes ago. Robert, though, appeared oblivious, looking vacantly at the two detectives.

Oakley picked up the maroon folder and drew out the police sketches of the two suspects and handed them to Robert. "I thought you'd like to know we've made some progress based on what you and the others have been able to tell us. We've already had over two hundred phone calls from people who think they might have seen them."

"Already?" Robert said with surprise. "That's wonderful."

"Channel 11 has an 'L.A.'s Most Wanted' segment and they ran the story last night, highlighting the pictures again. Did you happen to catch it?" When Robert shook his head she said, "Too bad. Chief Macklin was on. And he was speaking primarily to you."

"Me?"

"The public in general, but you specifically. His point was that when citizens see a violent altercation, as you did, they should not take matters into their own hands. It's just too dangerous. Policing should be left to the police."

"Our family's debated the same point," Ann said, feeling increasingly uncomfortable. Why had they been made to wait for DeFazio if he was going to sit there catching up on his sleep?

Oakley said, "Actually, the Chief's point was one of the things we wanted to clear up today, Mr. Binder. What motivated you to involve yourself in what was obviously a life-threatening situation? Why not just call the police? That's what most people would have done."

Robert was annoyed at having to revisit a question he'd answered a dozen times. "What if it had been you those men were pulling into a van? Is that what you would have wanted me to do?" Too late he realized that had been JG's point yesterday, the one Robert had argued so adamantly against. *All right*, he silently conceded, *when you're talking about your children, the rules are different.* "No, don't answer. I know you have to follow the party line: citizens shouldn't get mixed up in apprehending criminals. But the alternative would have been certain death for that woman."

"It could also have been death for you," Oakley said. "If the bad guy had been a better shot."

"And that woman would be alive if *I* had been a better shot. Or more careful, or trained in firearms, or wearing a uniform. That's really the message here, isn't it? But you can't sit back in a situation like that and estimate the odds as if it were a sporting event. You act instinctively. OK, it was stupid. But I hope I'd react the same way today."

DeFazio suddenly rumbled to life, his great head lifting from its evident slumber. "Very creative. Very entertaining."

"Sorry?" Robert was certain he hadn't heard correctly.

"And nobody saw any of this?" DeFazio asked. "There's no one to substantiate anything you say?"

"Well... no," Robert said, feeling suddenly uncomfortable.

"Was this some sort of political statement you were making?" The mood in the room had altered suddenly, hardened, and both Robert and Ann felt it. DeFazio's eyes, like Oakley's, bore in on Robert as though the answer to the question was somehow going to be revealed on his face.

Robert's body tensed. "I don't know what you're getting at."

"I mean acting not so much in an attempt to help someone, but from some sort of do-gooder philosophy: we're all members of the human race, brothers under the skin, that sort of thing."

Robert's jaw set. "I suppose that means something but I don't know what. I saw someone in trouble and went to her aid. How did we end up putting an ideological cast on that?"

"Well, sir!" DeFazio's acid tone seemed to sharpen the air around them. "That community you live in, for instance. West Adams. Not the sort of place most people in your income bracket would care to call home. Stately old houses and all, but surrounded by one of the highest crime rates in the city, isn't it? Can't imagine anyone choosing to raise kids there. Unless they were trying to make a point of some sort. And then there's your law firm— Dohr, Haskins, and Poole—which has a well-deserved anti-police reputation, I'm sure you'd agree."

Robert was taken aback. "I don't think that's fair at all."

"I didn't realize until yesterday that you were involved in this Rural and Urban Legal Assistance group. Kind of like a minor league ACLU, right? They're the ones that made a mess of the Omar Randall Stahr case, aren't they?" The kid whose beating went viral on the internet.

Robert stiffened. "I'm in charge of RULA."

The policeman reacted with mock surprise. "You don't say. The Big Kahuna, huh? Well it must be odd then to be cooperating with the LAPD. I mean after attacking the department like you have. 'Out of control,' 'Cops running wild,' 'Cowboys with guns.' That was you, wasn't it? Of course, it wasn't just the

Stahr case. RULA's been making trouble for police departments as long as I can remember. And now suddenly you're Mr. Neighborhood Watch, helping us take a bite out of crime." He shot a look at Oakley. "What did they call that in college psych courses? Role reversal? Shoe-on-the-other-foot sort of thing?"

Robert said nothing but DeFazio plunged ahead, each word set off from the others by a little puff of emotion. "This group of yours is always on the side of the bad guys, isn't it? Always popping up in court to help someone most people would agree belongs in jail."

"I don't know where you expect to go with this," Robert said. "RULA has nothing to do with what happened. If you have two hundred tips, why aren't you following up on them instead of asking idiotic questions?"

"No offense meant, sir. I'm merely trying to understand your motivation for putting yourself in jeopardy. It wasn't your job, and you're not exactly the sort to instill fear in two young street hoodlums. Now my partner here thinks you're a hero. Don't you, Sergeant?"

Oakley didn't look as if she was going to reply, but DeFazio was already moving on. "Were you trying to show that residents are capable of protecting their own neighborhood? That 'cowboys with guns' cause more problems than they solve? We've had these situations before, you see: well-intentioned but naïve people insisting that crime is merely a matter of misunderstanding, and if only we'd *reason* with the hoodlums it would turn them into law-abiding citizens. It's the sort of innocent-sounding nonsense that isn't innocent at all since it can only lead to anarchy."

Robert looked in exasperation at Ann: *What's going on here?*

DeFazio's eyes dilated with mock interest. "Or are you a 'root cause' sort of guy: We can't eliminate crime until we eliminate poverty, boost self-esteem, and create more Boys and Girls Clubs?"

Robert's face was red. "This is bullshit. It doesn't deserve an answer."

"Bullshit?" The policeman's chair scraped on the floor as he turned in surprise to his partner. "Is this bullshit, Sergeant?"

Oakley considered a moment, looking blankly at him. "No... I don't think so."

DeFazio smiled brightly. "There you go."

Robert looked as if he was about to storm out, but Jill Oakley said, "The department's under a lot of pressure to ensure that people don't take crime prevention into their own hands, Mr. Binder. It usually results in some innocent person being killed. As it did this time."

"And of course, *that* always results in a suit against the department," DeFazio added. "Some asshole attorney wanting to slap down the LAPD."

"Come on, DeFazio! You said yourself that woman would have been killed anyway."

The detective waved the comment aside. "I said *maybe.* But with your rather messy intervention it turned into a certainty, didn't it?" He pushed abruptly to his feet. "It never occurred to you to hit 9-1-1 when you saw what was going on? How long would it have taken? One second? Two?"

"I wasn't thinking," Robert said through clenched teeth. "My God, I was trying to keep someone from being kidnapped."

DeFazio's mood again shifted and he smiled as he held Robert's gaze. "This the worst thing you've ever done, shooting that woman?"

There was a stunned silence, no one moving until Robert muttered, "Jesus."

"Hey, I *always* ask. I want to know what kind of person I'm dealing with. Just filling in the blanks. No offense meant."

Hoping to defuse the emotion in the room, Ann said, "Why was that woman alone on the street at that time of night? Didn't she know about the rapes?"

Oakley said, "She had just gotten off the bus from visiting her sister in Cerritos. She only had two blocks to walk. I guess she did it every week or so. There's evidently quite an Indian community in Orange County."

"Then maybe those men were waiting for her," Robert said with feeling. "They might have seen her before and realized she'd be getting home at that time. Did you look into that?"

"We're keeping it in mind. But every other incident seems to be a crime of opportunity, so this probably is also. But our psychologists tell us they've changed tactics, and that's never a good sign, a sort of un-raveling of self-control. Of course, in your neighborhood no one should be out alone at night. And probably not in the day either."

"I know it's none of my business—" Jill Oakley's tentative tone drew everyone's attention. "But since we've come back to it, is there some reason you moved to West Adams? I grew up just a few blocks away and used to ride my bike over there to look at the big houses. I remember stopping a few times and stealing strawberries from a garden in front of this fancy two-story house until some crazy woman came out and chased me with a hoe." She smiled at Ann.

"This is idiotic," Robert said. "I don't have to defend our choice of neighborhood. Do you want to argue about our architectural decisions, also? Or where we work, or the cars we drive?"

DeFazio had stepped behind Robert, out of view but touching the back of his chair with both hands. "Ugly Swedish car, right? Or an electric? Something that says, 'I'm not some mindless lemming. I don't have to drive what everyone else drives.'"

Robert had had enough. He looked at Ann with exasperation. "Ready to go?"

But Ann didn't want to end on a contentious note. "The neighborhood's convenient to RULA. And the houses are magnificent, of course—the sort you can't find anywhere else in Los Angeles. At least at those prices."

"And you want to be part of South-Central," DeFazio said to Robert as though it were understandable. "Makes it convenient for receiving petitions from workers and peasants, organizing boycotts, and issuing communiqués to the press."

Oakley seemed embarrassed. "My partner isn't always this rude. It's his gastric reflux. Bad pastrami last night."

DeFazio laughed. "Not so. I'm always this rude." Then to Robert. "Relax. You're not being accused of anything. Sometimes my interrogation technique gets a bit testy."

Ann said, "We were thinking of doing something for the deceased's family. We saw the husband on television and he seemed overwhelmed. I thought maybe we could see about a job for him. Do you know anything about his background, the skills he has?"

DeFazio again began to pace the small room, crossing back and forth behind Robert and Ann. "*Mr.* Chaudhary, I take it, has been out of work for a year or so. I don't think he told us what he had been doing before that, if anything. I would guess he's not in the country legally and didn't want to get into that sort of conversation."

"He mentioned something about being a security guard at one time," Oakley said. "But that was before he moved to Los Angeles."

"Came here from Cerritos, evidently," DeFazio added as if it were an exotic locale half a world away instead of just fifteen miles down the freeway. "Lived in Singapore before that, and originally India. Quite the world traveler, our Mr. Chaudhary."

"We were also wondering if a fund for donations could be set up for the family. Can the police department do that? That would get it into the media."

DeFazio erupted in laughter. "Not a chance, counselor. Can you imagine how your civil liberties pals would howl if the police handled a victim's donations! But I should think your law firm could get involved—another *victim* to champion, another *cause*." He moved swiftly to the door, grasping the handle to indicate the interview was at an end.

"Actually, that's not a bad idea," Robert said, ignoring the sarcasm. "I'll look into it."

Jill Oakley remained in her seat as Robert and Ann stood. "Before you do anything at all I think you both need to step back a bit and view this incident as a non-participant would. However you look at what happened, Mr. Binder, you killed that man's wife. Personally, I think it would be disastrous to get involved with the victim's family. We don't know what Mr. Chaudhary is going to think about you under the circumstances. Let someone else take the lead. I've worked with enough victims' families to know they'll never be the same. What's done can't be undone."

In the car on the way home Ann watched Robert's arms stiffen as he aimed the Saab up Figueroa. He hadn't spoken a word since they'd left. DeFazio's attitude had shaken him. Robert had thought he could put this incident behind him after today, but now that was unlikely. Why the hell had DeFazio been so deliberately rude? It seemed personal, a fierce hostility that had nothing to do with what happened on Normandie and everything to do with RULA.

The brakes slammed on and she was thrown forward as Robert stopped too abruptly at a red light. His fingers opened and closed over and over on the steering wheel. Outside the car, outside his mind and his memory of last night, the world had ceased to exist.

9

IT was several days before Robert got around to calling Luis Teague about a job for Sandeep Chaudhary. There had been a trip to Sacramento to lobby for RULA with an Assembly committee, then a three-day conference with a consortium of non-profit groups. But perhaps his neglect was really a subconscious desire not to get involved. Of course, he had also been worried about how things were going in D.C. He hadn't heard a word about his nomination to Health and Human Services in weeks. Even Edgerton Lee, once so ardent in his support, hadn't talked to him since the day after the shooting.

But when he finally phoned Luis from home Wednesday afternoon his friend thought it was a marvelous idea. "I'm sure we can find something for the poor fellow. What sort of work has he been doing? I don't think they said on TV."

"I'm ashamed to say I don't know. I asked the police and they hadn't any idea other than possibly a security guard job."

"Well, maybe I can call him and find out. I'd rather get a lead on something first, though, so we don't raise his expectations too much. Ought to find out what happened to his last job, too. Don't want to be responsible for recommending Jack the Ripper. By the way, lad, I just had a visit from two D.C. snoops doing a background check on you." His voice dropped conspiratorially. "Don't worry, I explained about the incident at the park with the two fourteen-year-olds. They seemed to understand."

Robert laughed. "It's nice to have friends. I hope they finish their investigation soon. I've got a thirteen-hundred-page proposal for sending RULA national all ready to go. I want to hit the ground running."

"Attaboy. Dazzle them with your footwork." He paused. "They did ask if there's anything in your background that would prove an embarrassment to the Administration."

Robert was silent. But when his friend didn't go on, he snapped, "Damn it, Luis, we've been through this. A hundred times."

"Yes."

There was only the sound of an open phone line until Robert tried to move on by asking about the election. "Any defections? I worry, you know."

Luis sighed, once again they weren't going to talk about it. "I don't think there'll be a problem, but I've been working the hallways. This has become a pocketbook issue to me as well. The MacDowell Foundation just pulled a hundred-thousand-dollar grant they promised the ILP last year. We can't afford to lose that amount of money."

Robert thought he heard something in Luis's voice. "You wouldn't think of supporting Jirasek for financial reasons, would you?" Jirasek's promise of several million dollars in grants from unnamed "foundations and organizations" loomed large in everyone's minds.

"Good Lord, no. The man is mad, bad, and dangerous to know. Though I'm not at all comfortable with Zalesky's fund-raising skills." Abruptly he changed the subject. "Why don't we go to the Dodger game Friday night? The Mets are in town. As New York transplants we can ethically root for whomever is winning."

"Sure. Maybe John will want to come along, too. In the meantime, there's something you can do for me. Use your contacts in the D.A.'s office to check up on the cop in charge of my case. His name's DeFazio." Robert spelled it for him.

"Rings a distant bell," Luis said, "but very faintly. He giving you trouble?"

"After the Omar Randall Stahr case I guess I can't expect much love from the LAPD, but as soon as DeFazio learned I headed RULA he turned hostile."

"File a complaint. Get him removed."

"That wouldn't be fair. I can't really point to anything but his attitude. I guess I don't care if he vents, as long as it doesn't interfere with the investigation."

"Google News had you as the top three stories in the local section this morning, including a rumor from TMZ that the circumstances surrounding the shooting were being re-evaluated. The reporter made it appear as if the police doubted your story. Was this DeFazio's doing?"

"I'm sure. He wanted to know why I didn't call 9-1-1, then run and hide. Now that I think about it, I wonder myself."

"Well, don't let him get away with any cheap shots. Let him know if he hits you, you'll hit back harder. Meanwhile I'll check him out. It may take a couple of days, though."

"That's fine. I'll—" The doorbell interrupted him. "Someone's out front and Ann's not here. I'll call you tonight. And don't even *think* of supporting Jirasek. Just because barbarians are at the gate doesn't mean we have to invite them in for tea."

Who could it be? Robert wondered as he hurried out of the kitchen. Wednesday was his only afternoon at home and people at RULA knew not to bother him while he tried to catch up on paperwork. But when he opened the door he took a stunned step backward. The man standing there was frail, and slightly built, in his forties, with a three-day growth of beard. His body jerked back abruptly and his gaze only briefly touched on Robert's face before dropping away.

Robert felt his fingers tighten on the door handle. "Mr. Chaudhary."

The man looked at him with an apologetic expression but said nothing.

Jesus, Robert thought, *what are you doing glaring at him?* "Please, come in. My wife isn't here, I'm afraid, she's at work, she works for the government, the Federal Reserve, doing research but—" I'm babbling, Robert chided himself. What's wrong with me?

"Thank you," the man said softly but didn't move. "I don't want to bother you. I just—" He shifted from foot to foot, clearly ill at ease. "I started to come so many times—"

Robert pulled the door all the way open so there was no mistaking his welcome. "It's not a bother at all. Of course you should. I'm glad you did. I hoped to talk to you but wasn't sure where you live. Somewhere nearby, of course—"

They stood a moment in the entryway, looking uncomfortably at each other, Robert feeling his heart thud—*Why am I so nervous?*—before he said, "Let's go in back where it's cool." Wedging his hand under Chaudhary's tensed elbow, he led the way into the formal, high-ceilinged living room. The two huge stained-glass windows on the south wall provided the only illumination as they sent sharpened spires of colored light across the polished oak floor. But Chaudhary appeared unaware of his surroundings as he stood uncertainly, a faint fringe of almost translucent amber coalescing around his body like a saint in a medieval altar piece.

"Please, sit. Is there something I can get you? A Coke maybe? Or orange juice? Or would you like coffee? I have decaf if you're interested."

"No, no, nothing at all. I should not even be here. It's not right." But at Robert's repeated gestures he lowered himself to the center of the camel-back sofa, just beyond the light, and sat with his hands tightly clenched in his lap.

"Of course you should be here. I've been thinking of you quite a bit. I'm delighted." Robert didn't have time to decide if that was true or not as he hurriedly took one of the two wing chairs across from the couch.

Chaudhary was staring into the gloom mid-way between them. "It's just that I wanted to see you." His voice with its distinctive sing-song accent was so soft Robert had to draw forward to hear. "To thank you for trying to help my wife. It was a very courageous thing you did."

Robert's heart sank. "I can't tell you how sorry I am at the way it turned out, Mr. Chaudhary. I wish there was something, anything, I could do to offer some comfort. But—"

"No, no, it was not your fault. You tried to help. I blame myself. I should not have let her come home so late at night. It is a dangerous neighborhood. But I have no car. My son does but he was working. And Nazia had taken the bus before and had no trouble so—"

His voice trailed off. For a moment he sat quietly, tears gathering at the edge of his eyes, then said, "The police talked to me again yesterday."

"Do they have any suspects? I know they were getting a lot of calls."

The man shook his head. "Many phone calls, many names. But still, no one they think guilty."

"I'm sorry," Robert said, and thought, *I have to stop saying that, it sounds so inadequate.* And it only made his guilt that much more real. But it was the limit of what he could do at this point.

"My children—" Chaudhary murmured, and shrugged his shoulders, small brown hands flopping over in his lap.

"Yes, I saw them on television. They're beautiful. Twins, they said. Both boys?"

"Yes, and a daughter, fifteen. My older boy, Rajesh, is twenty. The older ones understand why their mother is not with them, but the little children, we tell them she is away. How can they understand?"

"Do you have relatives who can help? Or is there a temple— Are you a Hindu? I just assumed. I'm sorry if I'm out of line in asking this."

He seemed not to have heard. "Nazia's sister lives in Orange County—Cerritos. She has the little boys now. For a few days. To help, to explain to them maybe."

There was a noise from the front door and Ann's voice calling out.

"In the back—" Robert yelled, and added as a gentle warning, "We have a visitor."

When Ann came in the room she could see her husband's tensed back as he sat in a chair, and another man, small and indistinct, facing her in the darkness next to the cones of colored light streaking through the windows. "Mr. Chaudhary," she said weakly.

"Please, call me Sandeep," he said, scrambling up. There was a moment's hesitation as he took in her dark skin, then tried without success not to show his surprise. "I'm sorry to come into your house like this, Mrs. Binder. I just wanted to thank your husband for trying to help."

Ann looked briefly at Robert, then at Chaudhary. "Oh... well..." Like Robert, she was at a loss for words.

Robert said, "We were just talking about his children."

Ann took the other chair. "I'm sure it's difficult for them. And for you, with two little ones."

He nodded. "Yes, very difficult."

He looked so miserable Ann asked, "Is there anything we can do? Maybe help with babysitting or something like that?"

"No, no. My daughter... It will be all right. It is her duty."

Ann turned to Robert. "Did you hear anything from the school yet?"

Robert said, "I hope you don't mind, but I was going to ask around to see if anyone might know of a job for you. I hope that was all right."

The other man's face seemed to slacken. "I have had no employment since a year ago. I left Cerritos because people told me Los Angeles has better jobs. But—"

"It was difficult to know what kind of work you might be interested in," Robert said, hating himself for not looking into this earlier. "I wasn't sure what you had done so I asked the police. They said perhaps security work."

"In this country, yes. Or work in food store. But in India and Singapore I worked in a bank, the Bank of Asia. Teller, even loan officer. Very good job, very prestigious." His dark eyes darted around as if no one believed him.

"Well," Robert said hopefully, and glanced at Ann. "That's great. So far I haven't heard of anything, but now that we know your background maybe we can find a job in a bank for you."

"That would be good, yes."

Ann said, "Your daughter and older son are OK?"

He turned abruptly to look at her head-on, and Ann felt her body recoil as though she had been slapped. Chaudhary's eyes had narrowed, his lips twisted in a furious grimace, and two ragged vertical grooves, like hatchet marks, deepened between his eyebrows. But a second later his expression eased and he glanced away. *My God, what was that?* she wondered as she stared at him. *What was it I saw in your face?* But it was hours later before she could put a name to it, and even then, it made her spine

turn cold. Despite his attempt to mask whatever it was he was feeling Chaudhary's voice
rose. "*Are they OK?* No, of course not. My son
especially is upset. It's this country, he says,
where people are killed on the street. He grew
up in Singapore, not India. He doesn't know
what it's like in most of the world. But OK?
Neither of them are OK. Their mother is dead."

Ann and Robert glanced quickly at each
other, communicating with their eyes. Almost
at once, Ann said, "How would you and your
children like to come for dinner some night? I
know it's not much, but maybe it would help if
our families got to know each other."

"Of course," Robert said. "It would be good
for everyone, I think, and help us, all of us, deal
with the pain."

Looking as if he had made a terrible mistake
in coming here, Sandeep Chaudhary was suddenly on his feet, his eyes darting around the
room as if looking for the quickest way out. "I'm
sorry I bothered you. It was not right. I think I
better go. Meena will be home soon from school.
I have to be there for her. It is difficult with so
many streets closed."

Both Ann and Robert scrambled up. "Please,"
Ann said, and reached out to touch his arm,
then remembering the look he'd given her,
changed her mind. "I hope we're not inter-
fering, but it's something we'd like to do. For
us as well as you and your family. Think about
it. Then call us."

"Please," Robert said.

An hour later at dinner Ann was still upset by what she had seen on Chaudhary's face. But it seemed too fanciful to talk to Robert about. Anyway, he and JG were arguing politics, leaving little room for her to get a word in. Robert said that the office of Vice President should be abolished as useless. When JG said it was good training for future Presidents, Robert scoffed: Most of them were nonentities who never had any position of power again. Even so, he boasted, he could probably name every Vice President in the country's history. JG exploded in laughter and flicked on his smart phone to check Wikipedia. "Go," he challenged. But Robert only got as far as Jefferson before screwing up. "Clinton? *Clinton?* Mea culpa, mea *maxima* culpa. How dare I forget?"

"George C., died in office, and was never heard of again."

"A well-deserved fate, I'm sure."

So they started talking about more recent Clintons, arguing again just for the sake of arguing. Ann was happy to see that whatever had been bothering JG seemed to have been cleared up. *Welcome back*, she thought. *We missed you, we need you with us.* But while he and his father argued she moved her food around the plate, wondering if she had been reading something into Chaudhary's face that wasn't there. But no, she decided, I saw what I saw.

Later, while Robert and JG were playing basketball in the rear yard Ann tried to get her mind off Sandeep Chaudhary, her concerns about the Princeton job, and everything else that had happened in the last few days by finally taking care of the rose garden out front. Twelve perfect roses that white flies had been feasting on all spring. She was going to have to spray but that could wait until tomorrow. Today she'd peel off all the affected leaves and gather up those on the ground. *And the Furious Procrastinator at last gives in to inevitability.*

Taking her garden shears, gloves, and a plastic garbage bag, she went out front, where the bushes ran adjacent to the six-foot privet hedge that separated her yard from Bethesda Sylvester's next door, and began plucking leaves. "Should have planted berries," a scratchy voice from somewhere admonished. "Hell of a lot less trouble, and you can eat them."

Ann peered through the hedge and saw rapid flashes of color—something that could have been a yellow sun hat, blue shorts, a red-checked shirt—scampering behind it. Seconds later Beth Sylvester appeared with a Tupperware bowl overflowing with moist ripe strawberries. At least seventy years old, Beth was a tense, ninety-pound retired biology professor who never seemed to slow down. "Picking these for you folks, anyway," she said. "Got enough to last until Armageddon. Which all signs point to happening sooner rather than later."

"Oh, that's wonderful, Beth. We love strawberry shortcake. Any kind of berries, actually. Tell you what: next year you plant strawberries and I'll plant blackberries, and we'll trade pies every week."

"You've got a deal," the other woman said. "But you'll have to keep an eye on your berries if you plant out front. Damn kids'll rob you blind. I've been chasing them away for decades. That's why I keep my hoe on the porch." She squinted as a burst of shouting came from the rear of Ann's house. "Someone being mugged? Maybe I should call the police."

"Just basketball," Ann laughed. "The loser has to wash the Saab, inside and out. They don't seem to be able to play without shouting, do they?"

"Testosterone!" Beth shook her head as if it were a disease. She nodded toward the rear yard. "Your hubby holding up OK? Been seeing him all over the news lately."

"Not really, Beth. He's saddened at what happened, of course, but also at how it's being interpreted by some people. It's hard to understand."

"Oh, I know. I wanted to scream this afternoon when I heard some fool radio talk show terrorist say Robert must be the worst shot in the history of the world to aim a gun at a *man* close enough to touch and hit a *woman* ten feet away. I was so mad I grabbed my phone and called in. 'Don't be stupid on purpose,' I told him. 'When you've been attacked by a thug with a gun, maybe you've got some right to criticize. Until then keep your piggy mouth shut.' Then

I slammed the phone down and turned off the radio. Hasn't been on since."

"Thanks for sticking up for him, Beth. I wish everyone was as generous."

"Well, he's helped a lot of folks around here. Time someone helped him. How have the police been? They don't seem any closer to those two men than a month ago. Not that I expect them to worry much about one more woman of color dying in South-Central."

As another burst of shouting erupted from the rear yard Ann told her about DeFazio. The other woman began fuming again. "What is it with people like that? Too much craziness in the world. Of course, you know that from your own family. Your folks still stand-offish, or have they finally realized you and Robert are going to stay married?"

"They tolerate us. There isn't much warmth, though. And my brother has never spoken to us. Traitor to my race, and all that."

"But it's been worth it. You've got a wonderful family. How's John? I haven't seen him much lately."

"JG's doing great—" But she halted abruptly as she saw three men walking past on the sidewalk thirty feet away. They were in their thirties, casually but expensively dressed, and stopping to stare with interest at each house. One of the men was making notes on a clipboard, another had a digital camera and was taking photos.

"Great... White... Hunters!" Beth pronounced the words with mordant sarcasm. "Explorers. Making their way through the uncharted wastes of West Adams."

"Who are they?"

"From that damn movie company." Beth jammed her hands on her hips.

"What are they doing? They're not going to film right here, are they?"

Beth glared at the men as if she could make them disappear by an effort of will. After a moment she said, "I heard they're planning this big scene where some farmers blow up wagons carrying parts of an oil rig. They can't film over by Vermont because the city won't close it, so they had to find some other place. I reckon they're thinking of doing it right here." She added, "Over my dead body, Mr. De Mille."

The men glanced in her direction a moment, then one of them said something and they turned away. Beth spun on Ann, her jaw tight with emotion. "We get *nothing* from Hollywood. They try so hard to make us think they *care* about South-Central. Until it comes to spending money here. Someone told me that little tussle on the street yesterday between bystanders and security people was staged. Can you believe it? A made-for-TV flash mob to create a *buzz* for the film. Want people *talking* about it. Well, it's what we're doing right now, isn't it? Ought to get my hoe and run them out of here."

More people were coming out of the houses and staring at the three men. "No Hollywood," a middle-aged woman across the street yelled at them. The men looked at each other, said something, then began walking over to the woman.

"Oh, Lordy," Beth sneered. "You watch. They'll offer ol' Rosie three thousand dollars a day to film her house. Then probably not use it. Just getting on her good side."

"I guess they see there's no point in talking to either of us," Ann said with a smile as Robert's voice came roaring from the back yard.

"At least you got your family, hon. You don't know how much I envy you. I'm the last of the North Carolina Sylvesters. Not a good feeling, I can tell you. Like watching a little piece of the world come to an end."

It was after eleven as they were getting ready for bed that Ann got up the nerve to talk about what had been bothering her all evening. "I think I was too hasty this afternoon. We both were. We were feeling sorry for that man and acting emotionally."

Robert came out of the bathroom holding his toothbrush. "Too hasty about what? What do you mean?"

"Inviting him for dinner. Maybe that wasn't wise after all."

"I don't understand."

Ann sat on the bed. "We don't know anything about him. Or his family. And we're inviting them into our home."

"But we're trying to help. Where's the problem with that?"

"We don't *know* them, Robert. What sort of man is this Sandeep, anyway?"

"What is there to know? He needs help."

"Why he's out of work, for example. Why can't he find a job after a year if he's as intelligent as he sounds? It's not a language problem."

"I can't believe you're saying this. The man's a foreigner. He has to battle the biases of the community. I hope you're not going to say it's his fault he's unemployed. That's the sort of thing I'd expect from Jirasek. Or the unspeakable DeFazio."

"Robert, we just don't know. All I'm saying is we shouldn't invite him into our home. I don't mind taking them to a restaurant, if you want. Or letting Otis take the lead. Remember what that policewoman said: We don't know how Chaudhary's going to react. What's done is done and nothing you do is going to reverse that."

Robert stared at her, the toothbrush dripping on the carpet. "This doesn't sound like you, Ann. What's really the problem here?"

She took a breath, knowing how it was going to sound. "The way he looked at me this afternoon. You didn't see it, but I could tell what he was thinking. It was like: *You took my wife, and yours is still alive.* It offended him."

"That's ridiculous."

"But I *saw* it, Robert. I saw it in his face, in his eyes. The hatred. Not for you. For me."

"That doesn't make sense. I'm the one that's responsible for what happened. Not you."

"Then it was racial. White man, black wife."

"Come on. He's a minority himself."

"That doesn't mean he can't hate. I'm sure he never saw mixed marriages in India."

"But he's probably been a victim of discrimination. It may be why he can't get a job. He's not likely to be a bigot himself. Anyway, he didn't accept. We left it up to him, didn't we? Maybe you're worrying for nothing." He went back to the bathroom.

In bed an hour later, unable to sleep for the first time in years, she thought, *Why did I really get so upset this afternoon? I couldn't possibly have seen what I thought I did. It was just a momentary expression that flickered across Chaudhary's face and somehow rubbed up against something in my own psyche. It must be me.*

As she was finally slipping into sleep she wondered why he came over on the only day Robert was home in the afternoon. How did he know that? Or did he expect that she'd be there?

10

"**R**OQUEFORT, Roquefort, Roquefort."

Robert was singing softly to himself and sprinkling freshly crumpled cheese over an endive and spinach salad when Ann came in laden with packages from Neiman-Marcus. He gave her a quick kiss, and laughed, seeing how pleased she was with her purchases—a pair of Amalfi shoes and a sensible tan and black "Club Fed" suit for work. "Very patriotic of you to spend time boosting the economy."

"Shopping is everyone's duty," she said as she grabbed a Diet Coke from the refrigerator. "What are you concocting?"

"Wait until the 'reveal'. You know how artists hate to be rushed. But I guarantee it will be restricted to a healthy nine hundred calories. No, no, that's a lie. Let us say no more than three thousand... a serving. And you'll see a key lime pie on the table that the remarkable child brought home. You can help with the steaks, though. My hands are full, and they need to go on the grill."

An iPad on the counter was set to the Channel 7 News where the weather forecast was on. Gloom in the morning, giving way to summer heat. *Plus ça change*, Ann thought, envisioning a cedilla hanging from the c.

"*Une carotte*," Robert announced as though performing a conjuring trick, and grabbed the knife he had been using. He began chopping furiously. "Got a call from D.C. today. The FBI!" He made spooky movements with his hands and lowered his voice. "Letting me know they'll be contacting friend and foe alike as part of their background check. They've already talked to Luis, seeking scandal and skeletons. So if you see someone in a trench coat following you, you'll know why."

"Do you think they'll contact Karel Jirasek?"

"Who knows? Perhaps even the wild man of the LAPD will rush at them with condemnations of anyone pretentious enough to live in West Adams. Which reminds me. I got a letter today from something called the SAFA—Save America For Americans. They want me to join. The only requirement is that you've 'killed at least one illegal immigrant.'"

Ann stared open-mouthed at him. Finally she said, "Sometimes we take freedom of speech too far don't we?" When the phone rang she jumped. "Oh God, I almost forgot. I had a message—"

Robert snatched his phone from the counter. "Yes—"

"Mr. Binder?" The voice at the other end of the line was soft and hesitant, like a child unused to the telephone. "This is Sandeep."

"Oh... yes. How are you, Mr. Chaudhary? It's good to hear from you."

"Sandeep, please. I am fine. Very fine."

When the other man didn't go on, Robert said, "Glad to hear it. Have you considered our invitation to dinner? We'd really love to have your family over some time."

"Yes, yes. I have talked about it to my children—to Meena and Rajesh. Yes. We would be happy to, Mr. Binder."

"And the little boys, too, I hope."

Ann turned the steaks and a burst of smoke escaped the fan and filled the kitchen.

"Of course, the boys. I will have to have Nazia's sister bring them from Cerritos."

"Well then, let's see what would be a good time to have you over." He tapped Ann on the shoulder. When she turned he pointed to the calendar on the wall. She shook her head and frowned. *This is a bad idea, Robert.* But when his eyes narrowed she relented and mouthed, *Sunday?* Robert's voice rose with enthusiasm. "How does Sunday sound, Sandeep?"

Thinking back on it weeks later, Ann realized: This is where it could have stopped. This is where we could have politely backed away from the dinner invitation, parted forever, and no one else need to have died. But Robert was adamant. He had to atone for what he'd done.

"I'm afraid my son plays football, soccer, on Sunday," Chaudhary said. "I have to be there, to cheer him on."

"Ah, well. Would tomorrow do for you? Or is that too soon?"

Ann spun around and scowled. Not tomorrow, Robert.

"Yes. Yes, that would be fine." Chaudhary hesitated a moment, then added in a soft voice, "You were talking about a job, Mr. Binder—" His embarrassment was obvious.

But Robert's discomfort was just as real. "I'm afraid I've heard nothing. Let me ask again at work. Perhaps by dinner I'll have some news." Though in truth he had done nothing since his initial feelers several days ago. Increasingly uneasy under Ann's glare, he turned away. "Would seven o'clock be OK? Or is that too late for the children?"

Seven would be fine, the man told him, and soon after hung up.

Ann was looking at him uncomfortably.

Robert said, "Don't worry. It'll be all right. He's trying to ease the pain, Ann. For me as well as him. This is something I have to do. Even if it causes a momentary disruption in our family."

"I'm not worried about having kids running around the house, Robert. I'm worried about… I don't know." She didn't want to put a name to it because it sounded almost shameful. "I guess I just don't like him. Maybe it's that simple. I shouldn't have invited him. It's not the way to help. He asked about a job, didn't he?"

"I was trying to dance around it, I'm afraid. I still haven't heard anything from Otis. I asked their placement office to see if they had anything and all they came up with was a clerk's position at a 7-Eleven. Can you believe it? For a man with his background? I'm afraid I got a little testy with them. People hear the Indian name and think convenience store. Or cab driver."

"Well, maybe it'd be a start. Better than sitting around the house all day feeling sorry for himself."

"Come on, Ann. The man's bright, you saw that. He used to work in a bank."

"He says."

Robert stared at her. "I don't believe this. It doesn't sound like you at all. Do you think he's lying? What would he do that for? He'd be found out the first day on the job."

"I just don't feel comfortable, Robert. Sometimes we have to trust our feelings and not our intellect. And my feelings worry me. I wish it wasn't so but there it is."

"Look, we'll have them to dinner and if you still feel that way afterwards, that'll be the end of it. But I think after we meet his kids and get to know him you'll change your mind."

"Maybe so. I hope so, anyway. What do you think we can have for dinner? If he's Hindu, will he eat meat? And what about his children?"

"Relax. I'll make something with chicken and something without and let them choose. What were you going to tell me when the phone rang?"

Ann frowned and put the tongs down. "There was another message from JG's counselor. Both email and voicemail this time. He wants us to schedule a meeting with him. Both of us."

"Yikes. What's that mean? I've never been summoned to a parental conference before. It doesn't sound good though, does it?"

"I don't know. I guess we should ask JG. When are you free?"

"You set the time and I'll make sure to be there. Even if I have to cancel something."

"Let's not get worried yet. Maybe it's no big deal." She probed one of the steaks to see if it was done. "Two minutes. I better get John." But instead of leaving she said, "Do you have any idea when your name's going to go up to Congress?" She was thinking of the deadline Princeton had given her for accepting the job offer but didn't want to put any pressure on her husband.

Robert took three bowls from the cupboard and distributed the salad. "No. But Edgerton called this morning to say I shouldn't worry. About the shooting is what he meant." He put the bowls on the table and turned to look at her. "Actually, people have been supportive. Mostly, anyway." He stiffened suddenly as he heard the name Nazia Chaudhary from the television. Ann heard it also and they both spun around to stare at the screen where a middle-aged African-American man was speaking to a crowd from behind a lectern. "...won't let the police cover up this killing like they've done in the past. We demand an investigation of the LAPD's refusal to make an arrest. And we don't intend to stop until justice is done. We'll be out in front of the LAPD every day if we have to." A dozen voices rose in agreement.

Ann was baffled. What was that man talking about? "I've seen him somewhere. Do you know who he is?"

"Bobby Stackhouse. He's head of the AME church on McKinley, and president of the Inclusion Coalition." Robert was beginning to feel sick. "I'm not sure what his—"

Stackhouse brought a fist slamming down on the lectern. He was an imposing figure, well over six feet tall, with thick black hair combed straight back, an intense penetrating gaze, and an unmistakable aura of charisma. He stared into the camera, eyes swimming with emotion. "How many more *lies* are the police going to tell? That woman died on the streets of Los Angeles *because* of her color. You know it, I know it, we all know it. And they're sweeping it under the rug *because* of her color. Just like they've swept these rapes under a rug because they occurred in South-Central."

"Is he talking about Nazia Chaudhary?" Ann asked. She turned to Robert. "Does he think you shot her on purpose?"

Robert shook his head. He didn't know what Stackhouse meant. But surely not that.

As the pastor again raised his clenched fist, the camera drew back to show that he was on the steps of his church less than a mile from West Adams. A dozen well-dressed men and women of various races stood behind him. "Why was there no investigation of this woman's death? We're supposed to believe this was an *accident* by some City Hall insider who just happened to be out picking up medicine at one in the morning and—*poof*—suddenly finds himself in the O.K. Corral? How stupid do these people think we are? If this had happened in Brentwood, the police would be all over it. When it's South-Central, it's just another dark skin dying. Same with these rapists. Why aren't there more police out here looking for them? If women were being raped in the district attorney's neighborhood, there'd be a cop on every corner." The people to the rear of Stackhouse began to applaud and cheer.

Robert put his hand on the back of a chair to steady himself.

The image of Bobby Stackhouse was replaced by the thirtyish anchorwoman. "A spokesman for the LAPD insisted that both the death of Nazia Chaudhary and the rapes in the Central Los Angeles area are being given the full attention of the police department." The camera switched to a male anchor. "Elsewhere today—"

Ann shook her head. "I don't understand. It sounded like he said you shot that woman on purpose."

Robert tried to clear his mind, tried to be calm and reasonable about this because that's what was called for now. "I think what we saw was out of context. He couldn't mean that. His point was the rape investigation, of course. And he's right. If these rapes had been happening in a wealthy area of the city it would be the police department's number-one priority. Around here all we get are posters tacked to telephone poles."

"Well, I don't think it's right to bring in Mrs. Chaudhary's death. The police *did* investigate it. I don't know what more that man wants."

"Let's not worry about it," Robert said. "I'm sure it's nothing."

No, Ann thought fiercely. *It's not nothing. It's something, and it's going to get worse. That man's going to hurt us. But why? Who are we to him?*

Robert clasped her to his body, trying to ease her concerns. "Hey, kiddo, forget all that. And forget Stackhouse. It's not important. Think about tomorrow! It'll be fun, won't it, having kids in the house again?"

11

I T'LL be fun having kids in the house again.

Had Robert really said that? Ann had forgotten what it was like. But perhaps Robert had, too, she reflected, looking at the baffled expression on his face. Of course, there had been only one child to contend with during their own early-parenting years, whereas now there were two. But how could adding just one body multiply the chaos by a hundred? There was no calculus to explain it. But Sandeep Chaudhary seemed oblivious, sitting quietly in the living room as his four-year-old twins chased each other around the house. Poor Jake had decided it was more excitement than he could handle at his age and disappeared. Finally, Meena, the boys' older sister, took it upon herself to retrieve them from wherever they'd ended up on the second floor.

"I have friends from Otis checking with local banks," Robert said over the commotion. "With luck they'll be able to find you something. As a teller if not a loan officer."

While Meena quietly set her brothers on the couch, Sandeep said, "That is good, yes. But loan officer, Mr. Binder, not teller. It is not right I work for ten dollars an hour. I have much experience."

"Yes. Of course. And call me Robert, please." *He's trying so hard to be hospitable*, Ann thought, looking at her husband's forced smile. But Bobby Stackhouse's televised comments yesterday, the implication that the killing hadn't been accidental, had had more of an effect on him than he'd been willing to admit. Robert tried for a note of optimism. "I'm sure we'll be able to find you something appropriate. America has been generous to its Indian immigrants. Unlike our record with other groups, I'm afraid. Here in Los Angeles our greatest symphony conductor was from India."

"Gustavo Dudamel?" JG asked abruptly. He was sitting stiffly in a straight-backed Victorian armchair, his sneakers thrust out in front of him.

Robert hesitated before answering softly. "I guess that was an editorial opinion from our in-house music expert. I was speaking of Zubin Mehta, of course."

JG stared at the floor as a nervous silence intruded. The twins took advantage of the lull to slip off the couch, but Sandeep turned suddenly and snapped at them in Hindi. *Or was it Tamil?* Ann wondered. She didn't know that much about India's languages. Until the crack about Dudamel, JG had barely said a dozen words, and Ann felt for him. Shyness was a curse, not a choice, she knew from her own lifelong struggle. It probably would have been easier if Chaudhary's older boy had been here to give him someone to talk to, but fifteen-year-old Meena was as quiet as he was. Trying to keep some semblance of conversation going, Ann said, "I'm sorry Rajesh couldn't be with us tonight. We were looking forward to meeting him."

"Rajesh has the only job in my family, so he must work when they call. That is his duty. Later he can do other things but now is time for help."

Robert was sniffing the air as if his Chicken Masala might be ready. As he stood, Ann said to Meena, "Do you go to school around here? I guess you're in high school, aren't you?"

"I go—"

"She goes to terrible school, Manual Arts," Chaudhary interrupted. His face tightened with such distaste, rage even, that Ann was reminded of the look he had given her two days earlier. "Gangs of juveniles everywhere. Selling drugs, shooting each other. Why do Americans allow this sort of hooliganism to occur? In Singapore this would never happen."

"But surely the high school is safe," Ann said. God, that reminded her: she and Robert had an appointment with JG's counselor for Wednesday afternoon. When she had asked JG what it was about he seemed baffled; maybe something to do with his final year's class schedule.

Chaudhary turned so he could look at Robert as he headed toward the kitchen. "You are wrong about America treating Indian people well. Americans hate us. This is why no one will hire me. In Orange County I worked six weeks in maintenance department at Boeing Aircraft. Then I was fired so a Mexican man could be hired. This is true—someone I worked with told me this after I left. No one wants people from India. This is why Raj has to work in a market."

Ann said, "I'm sure with all of us looking we'll find something appropriate."

He was becoming increasingly agitated. "You have seen this stupid hatred yourself. Yes? And *you*—" He aimed a look at JG. "As half Negro ... you have been hurt by America. At school, because you look different, people hate you."

Only Chaudhary was looking at JG as the boy replied softly, "Sometimes."

"You are different from everyone, so everyone finds something to hate."

"I'm not different from everyone," JG said.

Ann was upset at how Chaudhary had suddenly fixated on JG after ignoring him all night. But before she could steer the conversation elsewhere he was again talking in a loud voice. "Even Cerritos was like this. Children beat up in bathrooms, money stolen. Blacks, whites, browns all fighting. This should not happen. In Singapore everyone gets along."

"At a cost, of course," Robert said, still hesitating on his way to the kitchen. "Of personal liberty, I mean. Sometimes the cure can be as bad as the disease."

Robert turned again to the kitchen but halted when Chaudhary said, "I do not believe what that man said about you on television."

For a moment there was no sound as everyone looked at Robert. Then he said softly, "Thank you, Sandeep. I don't know why—"

"He called me, this Stackhouse." Chaudhary spit the name out. "He wanted to come and see me. He would bring others. A city councilman, a lawyer. They would help me."

Ann could feel the emotion in the man's voice. It made her arms prickly with tension and she rubbed them. Meena, sitting across from her father, seemed to have stopped breathing. "I told him, 'Mr. Stackhouse, you don't know anything that happened that night. Why do you go on television and lie? Only Mr. Binder knows. And me.'"

Robert's mouth opened and shut. Then he said haltingly, "That was kind of you. It was unpleasant seeing someone trying to make political capital out of a tragedy like this."

When Chaudhary said nothing Robert quickly turned into the kitchen. Ann felt as though she should follow her husband. It had unnerved him to discuss the shooting in front of the woman's husband. But the twins started squirming again and were about to slip away when Meena put a hand on one boy's knee, causing them both to relax. Ann remained in her chair. *How good the girl is with the children,* she thought. She had a stoical nature, unusual in a teenager. She also had the most beautiful black eyes Ann could recall seeing. JG also seemed to have noticed, from the way he kept stealing glances at her when he thought no one was looking. Trying to disturb the gloom that had settled on the room, Ann asked her, "Are you a sophomore at Manual Arts?"

Meena glanced at her father and when he didn't react she said softly, "I am finishing my second year, yes. Only four weeks." She gave Ann a glance that hovered just an instant before shifting to her lap.

"Ah, yes, final exams coming up." Ann smiled. "Your English is excellent, Meena. Were you born in the U.S.?"

Sandeep seemed put out. "English is a school language in India and Singapore. Americans think every immigrant is unable to speak good English, but sometimes it is better than natives."

"John goes to school in Hollywood," Ann said, feeling stupid as she cast about for something to talk about. "He's studying the cello. He'll be going to a music school back east next year."

JG was staring at his shoes and looking as if he wished he was anywhere but here. The twins slipped in tandem from the couch to the floor and started to move toward the stairs. No one said anything for a moment, then Robert's face poked out from the kitchen as he tried for heartiness. "Success. I think it's safe to go into the dining room."

"We made some macaroni and cheese for the boys if they don't like the main dish," Ann said after everyone was seated. "It's the one thing all children seem to love."

"They will eat what we eat," Sandeep replied tonelessly.

"Great." A Vivaldi concerto came from hidden speakers as Robert carefully laid out the meal. "This is my first attempt at Indian cooking, but I think it turned out wonderfully. Be sure to let me know what you think, Sandeep. You too, Meena." In the center of the table he placed the steaming spicy chicken, and next to it a rice and vegetable dish with a curry sauce. "Meena?" He took the girl's plate, and when she said nothing he asked, "Chicken or vegetarian?"

She glanced at her father. "Chicken," she said after a moment's hesitation.

"You cooked this?" Sandeep asked. He was obviously surprised, and his lips pressed together in a tight thin line.

"It's my hobby. Or perhaps vice, considering how much time I put into it. I like the process of experimentation, of adding and subtracting ingredients, and making up new recipes. It's actually relaxing in an odd sort of way. Of course, tonight I followed the recipe to the letter."

Sandeep looked at Ann and started to say something but changed his mind. Handing his plate to Robert he said, "Chicken."

A few minutes later the subject of crime and schools was revived when Robert said, "The law school has a program to intervene with high-school students in problem areas of the city and try to get them out of gangs. Of course, it's difficult when every child in the neighborhood belongs. But I think it's worth the effort. Even if just one child is saved."

"Worth it how?" Sandeep asked. "To try to teach a hoodlum not to be a hoodlum? At sixteen they have fancy cars and clothes and money and you think you can *talk* to them and make them stop selling drugs, make them go to school or get a job? Why should they? They'll never change."

"Oh, come now. I simply don't believe that. Everyone can be redeemed. Even the most vile criminals can be turned around if society cares enough to try."

Sandeep's fork stopped halfway to his plate, and he looked sourly at Robert. "You have no experience of this. You have never been to India, have you?"

"Or Manual Arts High School," JG said, surprising everyone.

There was a silence while Robert restrained himself from turning on his son. Looking at Chaudhary, he said, "Everyone can be brought back into the community, can be taught civil behavior. Even the most brutal criminals. I believe that implicitly."

Chaudhary's fork thrust into his chicken. "The opposite is more true. Each of us at this table is capable of anything, even killing and torturing. Yes? Each of us has a dark place in his heart where evil is always alive. But in this city—this terrible Los Angeles—the dark blocks out the light."

Ann could tell from Robert's tense posture that he was annoyed. But he would keep his feelings under control. It was something he had trained himself to do. JG, on the other hand, was having no luck in concealing his own emotions as his eyes shifted to Meena. Sitting next to Chaudhary and across from the girl, his fork dove in and out of the curry and vegetables without much of it getting to his mouth. Then his gaze would lift slowly from the plate to Meena's face before darting back to his food. *He looks like he's ready to come out of his shoes*, she thought; *He's bubbling like cheap champagne.*

But Chaudhary and Robert were oblivious, arguing again about the nature of criminality —Chaudhary ardent about the danger of the streets, the neighborhood he lived in several blocks away; Robert equally passionate about putting a good face on the city, and the redemptive possibilities of humankind.

Meanwhile the twins said nothing, hardly touching their food, and JG and Meena radiated tension as they ignored each other. Ann felt a migraine coming on. *Seven people at dinner*, she thought, *but only two are even listening to the conversation, and then only to disagree with each other.*

After their guests were gone, Ann and Robert began to clean the kitchen. "Gets a little testy sometimes, doesn't he?" Robert asked as he shoved dishes into the dishwasher with more force than necessary. "A nice guy though, on the whole. An unusual perspective on life. I enjoyed having him here."

Ann gave him a look. "Except for the reference to Stackhouse."

"Kind of a turd in the punchbowl, wasn't it? What could I say? But, yeah, other than that the man's fascinating. Kind of a holy Russian fool, wandering the world and dispensing his own weird wisdom. He's as open and without artifice as anyone I've ever met."

"You two didn't seem to agree on much."

Robert's smile was grim. "Well, he's certainly intolerant from our western point of view. Still, it's interesting having a medieval world view offered up to you from across the table rather than in history books."

"Are you talking about his attitude toward crime?"

"God, that was only a small part of it. Sandeep has an entire *Weltanschauung* that's not just different but antithetical to everything we believe. Didn't you hear him going on about marriage? I don't recall how we got onto it, but it certainly brought out emotions. His own marriage was arranged, he said, as most still are in India. So much better—no need for a man to try to impress the woman, or *woo* her, or act the big shot. In his village marriages are arranged during childhood. It's officially illegal, but the government winks at it. The husband

and wife usually don't live together until they're eighteen, though. All that time they know who they're going to spend their life with. I guess in a way there's a point to it, isn't there? His daughter, by the way, was promised to some-one in India years ago. I think they had an actual marriage ceremony and village feast and so on."

Ann swabbed a sponge across the tile coun-tertop, frowning at the worsening discoloration in the grout. "I'm afraid that isn't going to make JG happy."

Robert slammed the dishwasher shut, turned it on. "Good Lord, is that what was going on in there? Love and lust rearing their ugly heads? On the other hand, why not? Meena's a beau-tiful girl. Stunning. May even be blessed with the gift of speech, though she hides it well. Anyway, I'm all in favor of love and lust." He patted her butt. "Even at my advanced age."

"Don't be mean. She's shy. And obviously her father keeps a close eye on her." She took a bottle of chardonnay from the wine cooler and filled two glasses. "Did you see how she looks at him before answering a question? I wonder how he manages that sort of control while she's at school. Maybe he bugs her school books." She smiled uncomfortably. "Look at us. Five minutes out of the house and we're making fun of our guests. I'm ashamed."

Robert lifted his glass to the light, squinted, sniffed, and took a sip. "Well, I'll put on my pompous Voltaire hat and declare that, despite his antediluvian views, I respect his right to hold them. Anyway, I like him. Very open, I thought. *Authentic.* No bullshit attempts to put on an act or impress the host. It's a nice change from most social events we attend."

"I still don't feel comfortable with him. Maybe it was those comments he made about race. Or the way he won't let Meena talk without clearing it with him first."

"'Ann the Absolutist.' I'm surprised. It's unlike you."

"You were too interested in his ideas to see the emotion behind them. He's a very angry man, Robert." *Of course,* she thought, *Sandeep had been talking to the man who killed his wife.* Which made her wonder again why he had mentioned Stackhouse. Or why he had even come here tonight. And there certainly *was* a reason; it hadn't been just to deal with his grief. In fact, Ann had seen little grief on his part. There was something else on his mind. She wondered how long it would be until they found out what it was. And she wondered if she should tell Robert about the horrible few seconds when they were showing the Chaudharys out and Robert noticed that one of the twins was missing a shoe. As he hurried back inside to retrieve it, Chaudhary, chatting volubly, put his hand on Ann's bare arm, then the small of her back as they stepped onto the porch, and then—an accident, surely—on her butt, where it lingered just a moment, like a lover's touch. But no, it was unintentional; this was the man who had looked at her with loathing, the man whose wife had just been tragically taken from him. An accident only.

"Perhaps he is angry," Robert replied. "Maybe I'm blind about some things. I was certainly unable to see any romantic interest in my son's eyes. How stupid can a father be? Are you sure you're not reading something into rather innocent behavior?"

"Positive. I won't say a woman knows these things, but anyone paying attention would have. Does it bother you?"

"Why would it bother me? She's a nice girl. *Alluring*, in a quiet sort of way. Hints of exotic sexual practices handed down through the millennia, designed to drive men wild. Sounds delightful to me. Seems to be married, though, even if it's not strictly legal. There was that ceremony in India."

"I don't think JG's thinking marriage, Robert. Though I did see testosterone dancing in his eyes." Maybe he, too, was thinking of exotic sexual practices, she decided. She had no idea of her son's sexual musings, didn't want to know. There are some things parents and children needn't share.

Robert stared at his wine glass. "All I saw was that she's a nice but overly shy kid. No need to invent a Romeo-and-Juliet situation."

"Maybe so. But she's also scared to death, Robert. I'm surprised you didn't see that."

12

THE next morning, unable to face breakfast, JG lay stiffly in bed, listening to his parents downstairs in the living room—nothing clear, just a low rumble of muted voices that drifted up the double stairway. Then he heard his dad say something in a pompous, play-acting voice, probably doing one of his imitations, and his mom laughed.

Christ, she's going to kill me. She's going to flat out kill me. He forced his mind away, didn't want to think about it. If he wasn't thinking about it, it wasn't real, more in the realm of "maybe," or "fantasy", or "it won't happen."

The voices eased off and he could barely hear them. So what were they talking about? What did they ever talk about now except Dad's big screw-up out on Normandie? Trouble in River City. The perfect family fucks up big time. *Well, you both fucked up a long time ago and still haven't discovered it.* Though they will in a few days. There was no stopping it now, the locomotive was barreling down the tracks, so get the hell out of the way.

He rolled over and accidentally kicked Jake, asleep at his feet. The dog was so riddled with arthritis he no longer jumped on the bed, but JG lifted him up each night. As Jake grunted indignantly, JG's mind wandered back to yesterday's dinner. And the Indian girl. Smooth tawny skin, small soft breasts, masses of thick black hair falling to her shoulders. Touchable hair. God, yes. Touchable skin. He'd like to have his hands all over her, squeezing a nipple, going to her ass, cupping it, drawing her against him.

"John! Why aren't you up?"

"First two periods were cancelled today. So the teachers could plan the seniors' graduation party." God, the lies came quickly now. It bothered him how easy it was to fool the two people he loved most in the world. Of course, he'd had years to practice. They'd believe anything their perfect son said. But that's because their own parents didn't *force* them to lie, to create a fairy-tale world of illusions only grownups were naïve enough to believe in. All his life he'd had to listen to adults tell him how lucky he was, and how proud he should be of his parents, as if they were something special, extraordinary. *Different*. Hell, could have lived anywhere but chose South-Central, "giving back to the community." OK, that was one way to view it, the adult way. But every time JG heard his folks mentioned on TV he cringed because he knew he'd pay for it the next day, especially back in junior high. *Hey, Binder, your mamma was on*

TV last night. She still doing tricks in that alley by the post office? My brother said your old man got AIDS blowing some dude in West Hollywood .... And in the hallways: *How much money your big shot daddy give you today?* He remembered this one kid, D'Jon Van, already six feet tall at thirteen, grabbing him on the sidewalk right in front of school. *Hey, zebra boy, how 'bout you give us a loan? Whatchu got?*

High school was worse in some ways. JG Binder was separate, apart, with no natural support group to fall back on. He didn't do drugs—well, a little reefer now and then; maybe more than a little lately. He played the cello, for Christ's sake, drove an ancient VW Passat most girls wouldn't be caught dead in. And lived in South-Central.

There were a few others like him at HPA, misfits as pathetic as he was, each alone in his special way, like penguins on their own private ice floes, drifting aimlessly through the leaden sea. Even if he had somehow magically found himself accepted by one group or another, it wouldn't make any real difference. He'd still be under an obligation to be his parents' creation. *Hell, I can't spend all day in bed.*

What should he do all day?

Walking out to his car after breakfast, JG wondered how long it would be before Wilkerson came storming back into his life. Christ, that wouldn't be half as bad as what was going to happen when his mom talked to Mrs. De Santos, the Bitch with a Stick.

When he put the key in the ignition the engine rattled ominously and the frame trembled. Broken motor mount, he figured. Shit, why not? The rest of his world's disassembling, so why not his car? Shifting into neutral and waiting for the engine to warm up, he vaguely heard the demonstrators at the film location two blocks north. He was about to ease onto 26th Street, still unsure how to spend the day, when he heard someone yell, "*John Binder*," making it sound like an accusation. Through the mirror he saw Beth Sylvester standing on the sidewalk in front of her house. He smiled and backed the car over to her. "How you doing, Beth?"

"Need some manly help. Think you're up to it?"

He turned the key off. "Sure. What can I do for you?"

"Got to get this spotlight bolted to the roof right over the gable there." She pointed to the area, an ancient wooden ladder already leaning against the house.

JG's eyebrows shot up as he took in the huge light she was holding. "You going to be playing midnight basketball out here?"

"Pre-riot planning. Don't want to be caught unprepared like I was last time. Anyone comes within fifty yards of me, I want to see them. And vice versa. Especially vice versa."

"You expecting trouble?"

"Listen to those folks down the street. Live here long enough and you learn these things. I feel it on my skin, the way it's making the hairs all jiggly. Lookie here." She shoved her bare arm in his face, but all he could see were age spots. "OK, Mr. Fixit, here's a drill and some screws. Make yourself useful."

It took him twenty minutes. When he climbed down he said, "Did you really sit out here with a shotgun during the riots?" It had the ring of an urban legend. A fancy term for bullshit.

"You betcha. Five nights running."

"Did you use it?" He couldn't picture this tiny woman holding a shotgun, let alone pulling the trigger. The recoil would knock her twenty feet.

"Couple times. Once when your daddy went out to move his car. A half-dozen baby-bangers, maybe fifteen, sixteen years old, came bopping down the street looking for trouble, when they saw him. Damn! You shoulda seen their eyes light up—this dude all alone out here in the middle of a riot. They were on him in a nanosecond, pushing him around, throwing him against the car, talking big about 'white justice' and black victims. I was about to come over and use a little persuasion on them when your mother came flying out of the house. Swore up a storm, putting her hand on her hip like she does." She laughed knowingly. "I didn't hear what she said, but they backed off real quick. Lost their *moral authority* when this black woman jumped on their case. Took away the *raison d'etre* for what they were up to. So they wandered over here, fixin' to do some mischief and recoup a little of the macho they left next door. It was so dark they couldn't see me, so I came off the porch and told 'em to get the hell outta West Adams before something tangibly *bad* and not just philosophically disturbing happened to them. But they still couldn't see me too well, and just laughed and slapped their legs, and started up the walk, saying, Hey, Grandma, whatchu talkin' 'bout? Even the gun didn't bother them. So I sent a load of buckshot over their heads. But not *too high* over their heads. I figure they're still running."

JG laughed. "You're something, Beth. Glad you're our neighbor."

The old woman squinted at him. "So how come you're not in school? Some kind of special holiday old folks don't know about?"

"The teachers are meeting this morning to talk about the senior class party."

Beth exploded in laughter. "Hah! Your folks bought that dumb-ass story? I thought they were smarter than that. So what's the real reason. You're not dropping out, are you? Your folks would be devastated."

"No, no… Just taking a break. Binders don't drop out. They go and go, collecting degrees and becoming famous. It's part of the family myth."

"This doesn't have anything to do with your pop, does it?"

"The shooting? No."

"Hell, that's enough to put pressure on any family. It's got to make for some raw nerves. Families have to fight through these problems, boy. It'll work out. It always does. My God, look at that."

A beat-up old pickup truck rumbled slowly down the street, dragging one of the film company's portable toilets. It banged noisily on the asphalt, but the door must have been locked because it didn't flop open. "Eric Clintock," Beth said, squinting at the driver. "Used to steal tomatoes from me. Let's hope no one's inside."

They walked down to the sidewalk and watched the truck stop at the end of the street and drop the toilet in the middle of the intersection. A minute later a car came by dragging another. Gasoline was thrown on the toilets and someone tossed a match. As the fire burned, people came out of nearby houses to watch and whoop and record everything for YouTube.

"Potty fires," Beth said. "Must be a new form of protest." She put her hand on JG's shoulder. "I think I'm going to go load my shotgun."

"Damn weird weather, isn't it? Hot one day, cool the next." Maurice Dohr, managing partner of Dohr, Haskins, and Poole, stared out the window of Robert's twelfth-floor office in the CitiBank Building, then ambled back to the chair he had been sitting in until a minute earlier, and lowered himself slowly, as if the burden of carrying one-hundred-and-seventy pounds on his six-foot-two frame was too much today. Almost sixty years old, he had been running DHP for twenty-five years, transforming it from a three-person shop set up to assist workers in the downtown garment district to the city's premier public interest law firm, and a major force in local politics. He had also been Robert's hero since the older man recruited him out of Columbia law school with the promise of a salary half what the big firms were offering, no benefits worth mentioning, and the chance to make a difference in peoples' lives. Dohr ran a finger along the crease on his slacks as he asked, "How are things looking for the election over at Otis?"

"About the same. Barring some unnatural disaster, Howard Zalesky should wriggle in."

"Happy to hear it. I assume the confirmation's moving along as well."

Robert gave a grunt. "Seems to be."

"And your problem with the police? Where do you stand there?"

"Where do I stand? And what problem? I'm not a suspect in a crime, Maurice. The police have been quite kind to me." Which was at least half-true.

"Bobby Stackhouse's accusations—'concerns,' perhaps I should call them—are never to be taken lightly, Robert. Particularly those regarding race. Unfortunately, they are repeated in today's papers. Page one, in fact."

"Maurice, you know what he said is complete nonsense. What does he think, that I was driving down the street and saw a brown-skinned woman and said, 'Hey, I think I'll shoot her.'?"

"You follow him on Twitter, don't you? He put up a photo of the death scene today. And a picture of you in front of the law school, #southcentral, #racismLa, #stoptheviolence."

"I know, I know. I've seen it. But I simply don't know what he's getting at, except some gratuitous character assassination. Even if unfounded he knows this sort of talk can ruin a person. If he'd accused me of cannibalism, people would sooner or later forget. Or at least forgive. But to even *hint*—Christ, you've known me for a quarter century. Have you ever heard me make even the mildest racist comment?"

"Naturally, both your career and your personal life absolve you of any thought of racism. Of course, there's the problem of Boston, your history. We can't ignore it."

"Oh come on!"

"Whatever we may wish, Robert, it *is* an issue. And it *is* a worry."

Robert was getting annoyed. "Stackhouse knows perfectly well he's talking nonsense. What the hell's he really after, Maurice? You're on the Inclusion Coalition's board. You must know the man."

"I haven't been on the board in four years. But, of course, I know Bobby. You've worked with him, too, haven't you? He's a steady, conscientious man. Full of *good*, Robert. Not a loose cannon, not someone to speak first and think later."

"Then what the hell's he doing attacking me? Do you call that *good*?"

"I'm speculating, of course, but I'd say he's not particularly interested in you or even Mrs. Chaudhary's death except as it fits into the larger picture. He's concerned about those rapists still being loose. I imagine he's tried everything he can to get the LAPD to assign more officers to the case, to no avail. So he's using this shooting as another example of police incompetence. It's just a stick to beat the department with."

"Maurice, *I'm* the one getting beat."

The older man let out an annoyed sigh. "I agree it's unfair. Still, I'm sure you see that this notoriety hasn't been good for the firm."

"Come off it, Maurice. The firm isn't involved at all."

Dohr clasped his hands behind his head, moving his gaze to the windows. "When you go to D.C. you'll be taking a leave from DHP."

"That's the plan, yes."

A police helicopter shot past the window, dipping suddenly as it headed toward City Hall. Some local officials too self-important to waste time on the freeways like the common people. "There's some sentiment among the senior partners that it would be a good idea if you started your leave early. This week, perhaps."

Robert was stunned. *He* was a senior partner. Had there been a meeting without him? "Do you mean because of the shooting? Or is this because of what Stackhouse said? Either way it's nuts."

"The feeling was to put the firm first. Or more correctly, put the mission and goals of the firm first. It would also give you time to prepare your move to Washington."

"Jesus, Maurice, you know—"

The phone rang and Robert angrily jerked around and pushed the intercom. "*What?*"

"It's a Sergeant DeFazio from the police," his secretary's voice said into the room. "He insists it's important."

Robert gave an impatient sigh and turned to look at Dohr, but the other man had already pushed to his feet and was motioning that they would talk again later in the day. His heart pounding furiously, Robert waited until he was alone before yanking up the receiver. "I hope you've finally made an arrest, Sergeant. It's time we put this affair behind us."

"No arrest, I'm afraid. In fact, things have taken a rather strange turn of events that you should know about since it involves you."

"Involves me how?" *Stackhouse*, he thought; *He's convinced the police to turn me into a villain.*

"Officer Oakley and I were chatting about your hope to get together with the family of the dead woman. It made my partner uneasy—bringing the husband of a woman you killed into your home—so she decided to check with Orange County about this Mr. Sandeep Chaudhary. No need to before, of course, since he wasn't involved in the shooting. Good thing she did. Turns out this is someone you very much do not want to get mixed up with. Quite a dangerous man, I'd say."

Robert's breathing had stopped. "Dangerous in what way? What do you mean?"

"The Cerritos police responded several times to Chaudhary's apartment on domestic violence complaints. Seems neighbors called 9-1-1 when hearing screaming and crying and what sounded like fighting. Bodies hitting the wall, that sort of thing. It was hard for the officers to tell what exactly was going on because there were never any obvious bruises or cuts to indicate the wife was being beaten. Or the kids, for that matter. And no one would speak to the police. The wife claimed not to speak English. One time the department sent a Tamil-speaking officer from the Sheriff's department to talk to her. He got her away from the husband, but she denied there was any abuse. As did the girl. They have an older boy too, I guess. He was pretty hostile, almost got himself arrested."

Robert didn't know what to say.

"At least once Chaudhary was ordered to 'anger management' by the courts. Of course, the police were stunned when they were called to his house a month later. It's probably the first time anger management didn't turn someone's life around."

"I suppose that's what passes for humor in the LAPD," Robert said with annoyance.

"Anyway, I thought you needed to know. For your own protection, if nothing else. One of the responding officers I spoke to said there's no question that Chaudhary's dangerous, probably borderline psychotic. The last time they were out there it took three officers to subdue him. They managed to get him referred to the psycho ward at County Hospital for a seventy-two-hour evaluation, but nothing came it. Since you're at least indirectly responsible for his wife's death, I think it's in your best interest to stay as far from him as possible. And certainly, to keep him out of your house."

Feeling as though the room had suddenly contracted around him, Robert said softly, "We had them over for dinner last night. All but the older boy."

DeFazio didn't react for a moment. "Well. Like we said, even without our new information, that is always unwise in this sort of situation. Especially with Rev. Stackhouse implying the shooting wasn't an accident."

"You're hearing what you want to hear. Stackhouse was criticizing the LAPD, not me."

"Maybe we heard different speeches. Anyway, I've warned you about Chaudhary. You need to take this information seriously. And if you think of any—"

"Wait a minute." Robert had suddenly seen the clouds part, and a strange calm came over him as he realized what was bothering DeFazio. "Let me ask you something, Sergeant. What's the real source of this hostility of yours? It can't be because I tried to help that woman. Or just because RULA was involved in the Omar Randall Stahr case."

"No hostility," DeFazio said. "And no point in making accusations of that sort."

"You were friends with those two policemen who were sentenced for beating Stahr, weren't you?"

"A lot of officers were friends of theirs. They were good cops."

"But you were more than colleagues. You were pals, drinking buddies. Probably went fishing and bowling together, played poker on Saturday nights."

"What's your point, Mr. Binder?"

"More relevantly, what are you expecting to gain by your hostility toward me? Your pals broke the law they swore to uphold. Whatever happened to them, they brought it on themselves. They didn't deserve to be cops."

"I don't think there's any point in going on with this conversation, Mr. Binder. I've warned you about Chaudhary. If you feel some guilt about what happened, I suggest you find another way to deal with it. It's simply not safe to force your way into this man's life. You took his wife from him. You killed her. You can't expect him to forget that."

Robert was boiling as he slammed the phone down. What the hell is DeFazio doing? He's as bad as Stackhouse, with his ugly innuendo and feigned indignation. But maybe he had a point about not getting involved with Chaudhary. *You took his wife from him. You killed her...* Perhaps he hadn't given enough thought as to how that would affect the man, would affect anyone.

A "borderline psychotic," admitted to County ... The phone interrupted his thoughts and Robert angrily snatched it off his desk. "*What?*"

"Good Lord," Luis Teague cried with manic cheerfulness. "What a greeting. Your day must be going as insalubriously as mine. But Robert, lunch is looming. Cheer up. We'll go downtown. I'm in need of a morale break. First, however, I have an observation for you, as well as a potential problem, neither of which, I'm afraid, will brighten your day. The observation to begin with: You wanted some dirt on this detective who's handling your case."

"That's not what I said, Luis. I asked you to check on him, is all."

"Nevertheless, amigo, pay heed: I'm afraid that what we have here is a true believer." Their shorthand for a cowboy cop, a John Wayne or Clint Eastwood who thinks it's his destiny to rid Dodge City of crime.

"Shit."

"Shit indeed. An actual buccaneer, I'm afraid, a *swashbuckler*, and haven't we had enough of *them*! A very spooky fellow, evidently, but a bit of a cult figure in the department. I had someone fax his picture over. Looks like some great river god, doesn't he? Very Wagnerian, very apocalyptic."

Robert's eyes closed with resignation. "Give me some specifics."

"Not much liked by higher-ups, but they give him a lot of leeway because he clears more cases than anyone else in Homicide. I suspect some of them are just plain afraid of him. He has a temper, evidently. Twice investigated by Internal Affairs—"

"Let me take a wild stab at it. Intimidating witnesses?"

"And once for possibly planting evidence on a suspect. I know, I know, you're shocked to the core. I was, too. An officer sworn to uphold the law! Nothing was ever proven, of course. As I stare some more at his picture, he begins to look a bit like the Incredible Hulk. How odd. At any rate he has a reputation of being unusually tenacious. People tell me he's like a guy poking away at a brick wall with a straw. It doesn't seem like anything is being accomplished, but suddenly it collapses in a cloud of dust. So... not a fool, my friend, not someone to be taken lightly. Keep that in mind."

"Yes, yes." Robert was getting annoyed. Everyone wanted to give him advice. "I'll watch my step, Luis. You mentioned a problem."

"Oh God, yes. The hits just keep on coming. There's suddenly rumors all over Otis today that the board's wavering on Howard Zalesky."

"Why would they do that?"

"Who knows? You've been around the school enough to know what it's like: rumors, chaos, anarchy. Just like every other law school. Only more so. If I had to guess, I'd say the Odious Jirasek has been getting to board members, trying to convince them he's a happy combination of William O. Douglas and Ralph Nader. I'm afraid there's also mention of the board's concern about your involvement with the shooting, and some talk that RULA should be cut loose before it causes any embarrassment."

"This is insane, Luis. I tried to do a good deed, I tried to be a Good Samaritan. And I've been paying for it ever since."

"No good deed goes unpunished, huh? Anyway, the most important thing right now for both of us is to make sure Jirasek doesn't become dean and gut our programs. You know how hard it is to stop rumors once they begin. I was going to ask you to get your butt out of the office and do some subtle politicking for Zalesky, but after seeing Stackhouse on TV and all over Twitter last night, I think maybe you should stay in the background awhile."

"Jesus..."

"I know, I know. Stackhouse is a million miles off base. Still—"

"Still, the dirt sticks."

"I know the man. A little anyway. A decent guy, actually. Doesn't usually fly off half-cocked. Do you want me to call him and tell him how wrong he is about you?"

"No, Maurice is going... Yeah, shit, go ahead, tell him this sort of demagoguery does nothing to help find those rapists, or encourage community participation. Who's going to want to get involved when they find themselves being publicly attacked like this?"

"All right, I'll give him a call. You going to be in the office this afternoon?"

"I'm afraid not. I've got a meeting in Holly-wood with JG's counselor."

"Good Lord. What's that about? Surely not trouble in the classroom, not from the boy wonder."

"I don't know what it's about. But it can't be any worse than anything else that's happened to me lately."

After hanging up, Robert thought again about what DeFazio had told him about Chaudhary. He had been wrong, hadn't he? DeFazio *wasn't* trying to annoy him. He was warning him.

13

"IT's twenty minutes to five. Where the hell is he?" Ann was staring through the kitchen window at the driveway. She felt as she had a dozen years ago when JG had taken the school bus for the first time and she'd almost come undone when it was five minutes late getting back.

"Relax. He probably just stopped off somewhere."

She whirled around. "Stopped off *where*, Robert? He didn't go to school today. He didn't even have the courtesy to sit down with his parents and counselor to talk about how he screwed up his life. He just disappeared."

"Can you blame him? Look how upset you are already and he's not even here."

"I have a right to be upset. You should be upset, too. Don't make excuses for him. Don't let him get away with this. He's lied to us all semester."

Robert sat down heavily at the table. "I know. But he's sixteen, Ann. He needs—"

"Oh, Christ!" She put a clenched fist to her forehead. "Don't be so goddamn naïve, Robert.

This is something serious. It will not simply go away if we ignore it. Whatever *it* is."

"You're the second person today to tell me how naïve I am. Maybe it's a fad. If we don't agree with someone, try to make him feel foolish."

When she glared at him, he said, "DeFazio." His hand flopped out loosely. He should have told her earlier, but with the trauma of talking to Wilkerson, it had slipped his mind. "He called me at the firm this morning."

"And?"

"He wanted to dribble out a little more information about Chaudhary. It was like, 'Hey, guess what...?'"

The sound of a car door slamming came from outside and Ann spun toward the window. Robert quickly pushed to his feet. "Take a breath," he said. "Relax. Don't start out angry."

"I don't know what to say, John. I guess neither of us do. You're going to have to help us." They were seated in the semi-darkness of the living room, the afternoon sun lighting up the stained-glass windows behind JG with a panorama of Gold Rush California while the air conditioner hummed unsteadily in the background. Ann stared at her son, feeling the tension in the room squeeze her bones.

JG sat on the couch across from his parents, his feet stretched out in front of him as he tried for the nonchalance every sixteen-year-old thinks is bound into the woof and warp of his soul. "It's no big deal, Mom. One semester of bad grades. Who cares? Really."

"I care," Ann snapped. She felt tiny, as though she was shrinking while the Victorian wingback chair suddenly expanded around her. "Your father cares and, damn it, you should care. Your grades have been going down for months and you didn't say a word to us. Every time I asked you how school was you said 'Fine.'" Her voice rose even as she tried to keep it down. "You lied to me, John. You've been lying for months."

His face was impassive. "It's not a lie. School's fine. What difference does it make what my grades are? Does anyone ever ask you or Dad about your grades?"

"John, damn it—" She felt as though she would explode. *I'm acting like my mother*, she thought with a sudden fury, and it only made her angrier: *A quarter century ago I went through this same stupid scene, staring down my parents, trying to bulldoze them with my cool in the face of their wrath. But they were right then and I'm right now.*

"John," Robert said calmly, "it's not the grades so much as the change in behavior. This isn't like you. What's going on?"

"Nothing's going on. School's just harder this year. Why can't you guys see that?"

Robert glanced briefly at Ann. "Well, yeah, I *can* see that, actually. But usually it gets harder by stages—"

"You don't go from As to Ds and Fs overnight," Ann said. "No one does. Don't tell us that suddenly there's this quantum leap in the difficulty of every class."

JG glared at his mother. "No. That wouldn't be rational."

"That's some sort of slap at me, I suppose. Why is it important for you to do that?"

"Look," Robert said calmly, "no one wants to start pointing fingers or parceling out blame. We just want you to tell us what happened to create this sudden meltdown in what was a stellar academic career."

"Nothing happened. I just got tired. Of everything."

"School?" Ann demanded. "Music? What?"

"All of it."

"Us?" She felt her face flush with heat. *Don't say it's us.*

"I thought I'd like to take some time off. A year, maybe. To travel."

The room went quiet. Ann could hear her heart pounding in her chest.

Finally, Robert said softly, "Travel where, John?"

JG shrugged, pulled his legs up. "I don't know. South America."

"South... America," Ann repeated dully, the words sounding somehow like an accusation. *Calm down*, she thought. *Stop attacking. There's a reason for all this. Find out what the problem is. Then fix it.*

JG's voice was suddenly tense. "I've been to Europe. I've been to Japan. I thought maybe Argentina, Chile, Peru. Someplace I won't stand out like a freak."

Ann's eyes closed, and she felt her jaw go slack as a weariness came over her. "We're talking race now. Is that it? Black mother, white father equals freak son." The elephant in the living room no one wanted to talk about. *OK, now we're talking about it*, she thought, at the same time desperately wishing they weren't. *Let it just go away*, she prayed, knowing it wouldn't. It was with them every day, and the weight of it was wearing her down.

John's gaze pinned hers. "How many others like me do you see?"

"*Millions!*" she shot back. "Go outside, damn it, walk around. Are you suddenly blind too?"

JG's jaw tightened. How could someone so smart be so dumb? But he said, "I shouldn't have brought it up. Forget it. It's not a problem."

"Then what *is* the problem?" Ann demanded. She didn't believe his denial. The elephant was still there, looking around, pleased to see that once again it wasn't going to be disturbed. Her voice shrill, Ann said, "What's this sudden fascination with South America?"

"What's wrong with it?"

"What's wrong with Los Angeles? You're sixteen, a minor, not out of high school. What parent would want her sixteen-year-old tramping around the Andes with guerilla armies and drug smugglers?"

Robert seemed unfazed. "Travel is always commendable. I envy you, to tell the truth. I never did enough traveling when I was young. We'd be happy to finance a year between high school and Eastman. But *after* high school."

"I've got twenty-five-hundred dollars in my own account."

"I'll take it out," Ann said at once.

JG looked at her.

She took a breath, tried to hold herself together. "All right. All right. Like Dad said, travel's not bad. But as a musician you'll get your fill of it. You'll be sick of it—"

"De Santos told me to forget it. I'll never be good enough for even a community orchestra. She told me to think of the future, to try a business college instead."

Ann's mouth hung open. Robert said, "That can't be right. What about Edith Raymond?" The Master's Class. The five years of high-priced special instruction.

JG's gaze moved to take in his mother. "She's been lying to you. What do you expect? If she tells you the truth she loses a lot of money."

"I don't believe it. I know how well you play. You've won competitions."

"I won one second-rate competition, Mom. I've come in third or fourth in the others. Face it, I'm OK, maybe even good. But not good enough to make a living as a cellist. Maybe

I could have a part-time job in a community orchestra someday. But how am I going to live? You've been pointing me toward a career I'll never have. It wasn't realistic; it was a dream. *Your* dream, not mine. So where's plan B?"

Robert tried to lower the tension. "Just looking at the other side for a moment, let's assume you don't go into music. Have you thought about other careers?"

"There *is* no second choice. You've had me pointed toward music since I was four. I didn't take the courses in science and math I'd need for a decent university. I guess I could go to L .A. City College. I might try drafting. I always enjoyed drawing."

Ann put her head in her hands, then looked up. "Look, John, you don't have to assume there's nothing besides Eastman and junior college. Even if you did choose not to go into music, you have a year left in high school to pick up some courses."

His voice was angry. "I need time to think about it, Mom. That's why I want a year off. You two never let me think about anything before. I was on stage all my life so you could prove mixed-race kids were something special. I did what you wanted for twelve years, even when I knew it was stupid. I need to make my own decisions now."

"What are you talking about?" she said, her voice shrill. "Race never had anything to do with this. Talent did."

"Bullshit. I was your zebra boy, your half-nigger show piece. I was—"

In an instant Ann had come out of her chair and struck him. Not a slap, a closed fist punch just below the nose that knocked his head back. "Damn you..." Her body trembled.

JG was on his feet, fingers clenched. He stared at his mother for a long moment before finally sinking back into his chair.

Ann hadn't moved from in front of him. "If you ever talk to me like that again—" Her voice died as the elephant roused itself and began to trumpet in surprise.

Robert let a few seconds pass. "Ann—"

She took a breath. Then another, heart racing. *This is where I'm supposed to apologize,* she thought. *But I'll be damned if I see anything to apologize for.* She threw one more angry look at JG before sitting again. "This *never* had anything to do with race," she repeated. "It was never an issue with you. Never!"

"How do you know what's an *issue* to me? Did you ever ask?"

Robert took a breath, and calmly addressed his son. "From the time you were four your mother and I were bowled over by your gift for music, John. We still are. That's all it's ever been. Honestly."

Ann's head was shaking back and forth. "Don't think we're conceding your music career. I simply don't believe you're not qualified to make a life out of it. I'm calling De Santos. You don't just throw away twelve years of preparation."

Robert said, "This isn't the time to make a decision, John. We'll look into it soon before the semester ends. Then decide. The three of us. Together."

Ann's lips almost disappeared as she pressed them together to keep from speaking out. Sometimes this smoothing over of Robert's, this *conciliating*, infuriated her beyond words. Unable to maintain her silence, she said, "And do something about your grades. You have finals coming up. There's still time to improve. Don't you dare use this as an excuse not to prepare."

Ann was stalking back to the kitchen to get a glass of wine when the phone rang. Grabbing it off the table, she snapped, "*What?*" Her heart was still pounding with emotion, and her voice shrill and angry. But when she realized who it was she forced herself to calm down. "Yes, Sandeep, how are you?"

"Very good, Mrs. Binder. No, not so good, I think. It is very lonely without Nazia."

"I'm sorry. I know it must be difficult." She could hear the *thud thud thud* of JG angrily tramping up the stairs.

"Your husband has not found a job for me," Chaudhary was going on. "I need to look, but I have to care for my sons. It is impossible. If Nazia was here—"

Get off it, you've been out of work for a year, Ann thought. But she tried to remain calm. "I guess if you need someone to babysit when you have an interview we could help."

"No, no. Meena will be here soon. She can watch." Still, the defeated tone remained in his voice, grating on Ann's already raw nerves.

"Isn't your older son home during the day? He works at night, doesn't he?"

"Rajesh goes to school Tuesday and Thursday. Anyway, Rajesh is a man, he does not watch babies. Rajesh will carry on our family. This is important to people from my country."

Ann didn't know where this was going but supposed she was expected to follow up on it. "Is Rajesh planning to get married?"

"Of course. This year. It is time for him." There was irritation in his voice now, as though he didn't want to have to explain the obvious. "Rajesh will help me. After he gets a good job. It is very expensive to raise children in this country. Without a wife."

"I know it's difficult—" She was thinking of a way to get off the phone.

"She didn't deserve to die."

"What?" The words came so unexpectedly it took Ann a moment to realize what he'd said. She added, "No. Of course not."

"It is hard for me. You understand that. I don't blame you. It is because your husband only. The way Nazia died has not— Mrs. Binder, there are things you do not know. About your husband." There was a loud commotion in the background and she heard him yelling furiously at the boys. His tone abruptly changed again. "I am sorry to bother you, Mrs. Binder. It is just that sometimes I feel so sad. We should have stayed in Singapore. Or India. It was not right to come here."

"I know it can be lonely in a new country," Ann said, adding, "I'm afraid our dinner—"

"You have a very nice house. Very big. A nice family. Why do you work?"

"Excuse me?"

"Why do women in this country work? You are rich, you don't need to."

"I can assure you we aren't rich."

"But you don't need money. Nice car, nice house. Your husband has good job. And you are a very pretty woman..." His tone sank into embarrassment, or anger. "This is wrong of me to talk about." He yelled at the twins again, a long harangue in Tamil, before turning again to English. "Sometimes I just miss her too much. I am sorry."

There was a dial tone in her ear.

"He's a violent man," Robert said with feeling. He was pouring himself a drink from the newly-opened bottle of Cutty. "That was the point of that idiot policeman's call this morning. Or maybe scaring me was the point. He seemed to revel in letting me know. *Borderline psychotic*, he said in that annoying, tough-guy way of his. Can you believe it? And I don't find out until today."

Ann sat down and rubbed her forehead with her fingertips. She didn't want to worry about Chaudhary with her son's future suddenly in peril. "I'm not comfortable with him either, but I'm not sure 'psychopath' is justified." Though she wasn't sure where Chaudhary had intended to go with his "you are a pretty woman" comment.

"You were right. We never should have invited him over here. He's after something. Are you sure he didn't ask for money? Was he hinting around at it?"

"I think he's just lonely, Robert. He misses his wife. And he's at his wit's end from taking care of the twins. I offered to babysit while he looks for work—"

"Christ, Ann, don't offer to do anything. We'll do our helping from a distance. Like you and everyone else has been warning me. What was I thinking, getting mixed up with someone whose life I messed up so much? I knew absolutely nothing about this man. Other than I caused him a great hurt. Then I invited myself—*forced* myself—into his life." He swallowed half his scotch in a gulp. "According to DeFazio he just flies off the handle and strikes out at people. But you saw it, you were the one who noticed how cowed his kids are. I should have listened to you."

"And now you're jumping to the other extreme and turning him into some kind of monster. I don't know how real that is." She put her wine glass down so abruptly half of it spilled onto her hand. "I'm calling Edith Raymond. I don't believe De Santos. She doesn't like John for some reason."

Robert put his hand on hers. "What was all that race stuff? That can't still be a problem in *high school*, not like it used to be. I mean, with Obama, and mixed-race marriages on TV—"

"School's no different than the rest of the world, Robert. Maybe worse. Of course it's a problem. But it shouldn't have any impact on his music."

"It bothers me hearing him talk like we've been trying to prove something with him—"

"Haven't we? Isn't it always there, in our minds?"

"I hope not. I want to think of him as my son, not a symbol of the races coming together. I sure hope he doesn't believe it had any role in our marriage."

But Ann's mind was elsewhere. She grabbed the phone. "Damn that woman. I'm not giving up on my son. I want to know what the hell she has against him." She was punching out Edith Raymond's phone number when she heard Robert shout, "Christ, now what?"

Something out the kitchen window had caught his attention. Ann turned to see Jill Oakley and Nick DeFazio stepping from a nondescript white Chevrolet. They glared over at the house as DeFazio said something and Oakley nodded glumly. A sick feeling went through Ann as she realized this terrible day was about to get worse.

"What the hell is he after?" Robert asked bitterly. "Why won't he leave me alone?"

14

THE two detectives stood woodenly in the entryway, DeFazio giving off the same dark aura of barely-controlled hostility as the last time they'd seen him. "Took an extra twenty minutes getting here because of all the damn road blocks. This has got to be the only city in the world where the police close off streets so someone can make a movie about how terrible the police are."

Robert shoved his fists in his pockets. "Is that the point of the movie? I didn't get that impression."

"That's the point of all movies." He jerked his head toward the door and the neighborhood beyond. "Awful lot of angry people out there. Getting stirred up by not-so-social media. Maybe they ought to get an attorney and take their streets back."

Neither cop was smiling, and no one offered to shake hands. Ann rubbed her bare arms, wondering what the hell was going on. Finally, she said, "We may as well go into the living room," and led the way to the rear of the house.

The moment they entered the large Victorian space Jill Oakley's mood lightened. "My God, look at this! It's like we've been swept back in time." She stepped into the center of the room, her head thrown back, and pivoted slowly around, taking in the decorated walls, beamed ceiling, and stained-glass windows. "Look at that fireplace! You could roast an ox in there." She hurried over to it, running her fingers over the carved mantel and wrought-iron fire screen. "Where did you find this screen? And those andirons! Did they come with the house?"

"There's a restoration firm in Palms that carries a lot of Victoriana," Ann said. She was trying to sound accommodating though she felt anything but, her mind still on JG. *One crisis at a time*, she wanted to scream. But she smiled weakly and added, "We found a photo taken in this room about 1890 and tried to recreate everything just as it was."

Both Robert and DeFazio were looking annoyed, but Oakley ignored them. "Ever since I was a kid I wondered what these houses looked like inside. Now I know. I could swear the house next door with the gables is where that witch chased me with a hoe."

Everyone had found a seat, the detectives on opposite ends of the couch like kids on a see-saw—*or two people who didn't much like each other*, Ann thought—and the others on chairs. Robert's anger about DeFazio's call had been festering all day. "I can't believe you waited two weeks to check up on Chaudhary. If I'd any inkling of what he was like I wouldn't have had anything to do with him."

"As I explained to you, Mr. Binder, there was no reason to check on a non-participant. It was my brilliant partner here who decided to push a little beyond our normal bounds, and then only because she was worried about you inviting the husband of the woman you killed into your home. I would think you'd be thankful rather than belligerent."

"Cut the bullshit, Sergeant. Your negligence has put my family in harm's way, no matter what kind of spin you try to put on it. He just called Ann and threatened her."

The policeman looked at her. "Yes?"

"Not exactly a threat," Ann replied. "He's been at loose ends, I guess, since his wife died. And seems to blame Robert."

Robert didn't try to hide his annoyance. "So what else did you find? That he's an escaped madman from Madras? An ax murderer, perhaps? A suspect in a thousand crimes?"

"Actually, it's about his wife," Oakley said. "Since Mrs. Chaudhary was the victim, we again had no reason to check on her, beyond our normal run-through with L.A. county records. But after finding out about her husband, I thought I'd also check her out with Orange County, since she used to live there."

"Turns out she was arrested near Disneyland last year," DeFazio said. He hesitated just a moment before adding, "For solicitation."

"She was a prostitute?" Robert's voice was louder than he intended.

DeFazio's eyebrows lifted. "You're surprised?"

"Well, yes. Of course."

"The D.A. didn't bring charges so there's always the possibility it was a mistake. The Anaheim police were making one of their periodic sweeps along Harbor Boulevard, where tourists and hookers congregate. Our victim claimed she was merely walking back from visiting a friend at a motel."

"At one AM," Oakley added.

"Rather like the night you encountered her, Mr. Binder. A strange set of coincidences, is it not?"

"Yes..." Feeling mildly confused, Robert looked at them, slack-shouldered, wondering what was next. Because something had to be.

"Well, sir," DeFazio continued, leaning forward, smiling, almost friendly now, "knowing this tiny tidbit of information, is there anything about your story you'd like to change?"

"Sorry?"

"Any little fact you want to reconsider?"

"I don't follow."

"I think you do, sir."

Ann felt herself stiffen at the policeman's tone. A sound came from the kitchen, JG getting something from the refrigerator.

Robert was stunned into rigidity. *You think I was picking her up?*

DeFazio smiled as if it were obvious. "That's what the facts point to."

"*Facts?* What facts?" Robert's face had flushed with sudden fury, and he had to fight to remain seated. "You take a disputed arrest in Anaheim, then without any reason or logic turn it into a completely different scenario a year later in Los Angeles. Tell me where the *facts* are."

DeFazio resorted to a notebook he carried in his pocket. "According to your statement you told the passerby to call 9-1-1 at 1:40 AM. How long would you say this altercation with the two men took? Two or three minutes?"

Robert shrugged. "About that."

"You picked up the prescription at 1:06. We checked. Walgreens is only a mile away. So how do you account for the missing thirty minutes?"

"Your time is off. I got the prescription about 1:30. I know, I looked at my watch."

"The time and date are automatically stamped on every receipt, sir."

"Then *they* made a mistake. Or their clock is off. Or I was wrong about when the man in the truck came by. Are you trying to say I was having sex with that woman?"

"Happens all the time, doesn't it?" the policeman said, as if revealing a sad fact of modern life. "Nightly even. Hooker and john argue over money, the john gets angry and they start to fight. Or the hooker pulls a gun and tries to rip him off. Usually ends up bad for the hooker, of course, as it did this time."

Jill Oakley said, "We've checked for two weeks in the area around the killing and can't find anyone who heard the screaming you told us about, or heard gunshots, or saw a blue van. That's unusual, given how busy Normandie is. And, of course, the neighborhood is known for prostitution."

With an unnecessary flourish DeFazio flipped to a page he had marked in his notebook. "Did the man you claimed to be fighting actually use the weapon?"

"What the hell do you mean 'claimed'?"

Jill Oakley said, "Please, Mr. Binder."

"For God's sake, it was in my statement. He took a shot at me as he ran to the van."

"And you took one shot at the kidnapper," De-Fazio said. "Killing the woman. Then where are the shells, sir? That, too, has been bothering us.

"It was a revolver, damn you. There *were* no shells."

The large man seemed surprised. "I thought you knew nothing about pistols." He rapidly flipped a few pages, then began to read from the notebook. "*I don't know anything about guns.*" Your official statement the day of the shooting."

"I know revolvers hold their shells. Christ!"

"And there's no slug from the shot the man allegedly took at you. We looked. In fact, there's no physical evidence of a crime at all, except the victim's blood. It's almost as if the scene had been tidied up."

"The slug could be anywhere. It could be half a mile away. I was standing on the sidewalk, the bullet went past my head, down the street."

"So Detective Oakley and I thought we'd take another look-see at the area. We've found it helps put us in the picture to actually re-en-act the shooting. Then, since we were in the neighborhood, we thought we'd pop over here and do a show-and-tell."

"There's a dumpster about thirty feet from the spot where the woman fell wounded," Jill Oak-ley said. "A place where someone might have tossed a gun."

Robert was beside himself. "Is that what you think? I shot her and then tossed the gun in the dumpster?"

"They're emptied weekly," DeFazio said, "so we didn't find anything. Of course, you could have tossed it in your car knowing we'd have no reason to search the vehicle of a Good Samari-tan who'd risked his life by stepping into a very dangerous situation."

"Look, I told you what happened that night. Why would I throw the gun away?"

"Why indeed? Unless there was no proof any-one else had handled it. By the way, where was your son when all this gunplay was going down?"

That startled everyone. Robert looked at Ann and muttered, "Home in bed." Ann nodded, and said, "Why would you ask such a thing?"

DeFazio shook his head as though embar-rassed by his own weakness. "Obsessive-com-pulsive. I have to know where everyone was or I get a headache."

Robert came out of his chair. "This is insane. I tried to help that woman, for Christ's sake. I tried to be a good citizen, and you come in here, firing from the hip with these idiotic questions. It's no wonder people don't want to get involved with the LAPD."

"Well, sir, let me be absolutely clear that we are not accusing you of anything. But you must see the difficulty we face: you're angry because you think we should leave you alone, and the Inclusion Coalition attacks us because you're not in jail. Damned if we do, damned if we don't. So we'll take our time and go by the book. But we are definitely going to solve it, even if it leads us to people whose influence and self-importance makes them feel untouchable."

"That's it. I'm not answering any more questions. If you want to charge me with a crime go ahead. But don't think I'm going to allow you to railroad me because you don't like civil rights organizations, or attorneys, or can't find the men terrorizing this neighborhood. Get the hell out of my house. And you damn well better have a warrant for my arrest if you come back."

"As you wish." DeFazio rose on his thick wrestler's legs and stared around at the elegant surroundings. "Not exactly *la vida loca*, I'm afraid."

"*What?*"

"This house. And West Adams. You're not living the life of a Central American immigrant, are you? I thought you moved here to be part of the community. You were going to hand out condoms, register voters, and offer reasoned alternatives to gang life. But it's all a pose." His eyes wandered critically around the room. "This place is an adult fairy tale, a museum for your illusions about the city and the LAPD. It's narcissistic: Look at me, courageously sharing the discrimination and poverty of Central L.A. while collecting antiques and dining on lobster and Kobe beef."

"Get the hell out of here." Robert was within seconds of striking the man.

"I think we already agreed on that, sir. No need to show us the way out. I think we remember. Through the parlor, past the library and conservatory to the south entrance hall, right? Just like Downton Abbey."

Robert's face was convulsed with fury as he turned to Ann, who was staring at him as though the ground beneath her feet had fallen away.

15

Ann didn't move after the front door shut. As Robert stormed into the kitchen she sat frozen in the chair, feeling the tension in the air sharpening around her. It was as if all the molecules in the room had been rearranged in some way nature hadn't intended. She rubbed her arms against the icy chill prickling her skin.

A cupboard door slammed and a moment later she heard Robert swear loudly to himself. When JG's voice, angry and loud, also came to her she rose to her feet with a sigh that went through to her bones and headed toward the kitchen.

Robert was splashing Scotch into a glass as JG stood behind him, his voice trembling. "You were with a prostitute when you were supposed to be getting Mom's medicine? That's why it took so long?"

Robert spun on him. "That's *not* what happened."

"Why were you even talking to a prostitute? Why did you stop unless it was to have sex with her?"

"I wasn't talking, for God's sake, I was trying to keep two men from kidnapping her."

"Oh, please!" JG took an angry step away, and Ann could see his face was flushed, sweat standing out on his forehead like drops of shellac. "What two men? Even the police don't believe that. Was her pimp there? Is that who you were fighting? Did you refuse to pay, or did they try to rob you?"

"That doesn't even deserve an answer."

"Did you know she was a hooker when you stopped?"

"If I had does it mean I should have driven by? Are only certain people deserving of help?"

"Then you did know!"

"That's not fair, John," Ann said from behind. "Your father was trying to do the right thing."

He swung on her. "Mom, he went out to get a whore. Don't you care?"

"That's not what happened, John. That policeman has been hostile to us since the beginning. But that's his problem. We can't let it upset our family like this. If we do we're letting a very ignorant man control our lives."

"And she *wasn't* a prostitute," Robert added. "That also is DeFazio's strange fantasy. She was a woman alone on the street who was being threatened." He tried to put a hand on his son's shoulder but the boy jerked away, close to tears.

Ann was alarmed. "This isn't fair, John. You're over- reacting. You know your dad would

never do anything like the police were implying."

"How do I know that? How do you know it?
You're just protecting him because he's your
husband. Do you know what he does when
you're not around?"

"That's enough, John."

"*Go to your room.* That's next, right? Go
practice, stop asking questions, get out of here
so the adults can talk." He stormed from the
kitchen without looking at either of them, and
Ann wondered again what was going on with
him. Was all this emotion because of what De-
Santos had said? She felt a sudden fury toward
the woman. Even if she was right about JG's
future in music she could have found a better
way to tell him.

Robert swallowed his scotch, then filled the
glass again. He was staring at the refrigerator with a blind rage. "If this gets in the papers... if they let it be known she might have
been a prostitute, it's going to ruin me with D
.C. And RULA will be finished, dead. It won't
last a month. Can't you see what people will
say? Binder's using government money to pay
for his hookers." He slammed the glass down
on the counter.

Ann stared at his back. *It's not true, is it?
That woman wasn't a prostitute. It's not why you
stopped.* But she couldn't bring herself to say
the words. She had to trust her husband. He
wouldn't lie to her, couldn't lie to her. It was
how he was.

"It'll be trouble for you, too, won't it?" Robert asked, turning to look at her. "Belasino will have you in his office wanting to know why the spouse of a Federal Reserve employee is up to his armpits in a murder investigation. One involving a hooker at that."

She gave him a wan shake of the head. "Well, we're supposed to be invisible as we pull the strings of the nation's economy."

But Robert didn't even smile at the joke. "They won't dare go public. They have no proof at all. Not even that she was a prostitute. It's all that crazy DeFazio with his weird hatred of RULA. 'Narcissism!' Jesus, did he bone up on Freud before coming here? Is he going to tell me I'm still in my phallic stage and suffering from castration anxiety? Are we supposed to be impressed?"

"Policemen read, too, Robert. He's allowed to use big words."

"Yeah, yeah, tell me how I'm stereotyping. What a terrible person I am! Christ, this is a fucked-up world." He took a gulp of scotch. "I'm going to ask Dean Salas to talk to the Chief. This is nothing but harassment." He sank down in a chair. "Lot of good it'll do. The whole police department hates attorneys, hates Otis and RULA and the ILP." Suddenly he was on his feet again. "How dare those people come in my *home* and accuse me of... of *what*? They never actually said, did they? But the implication was I murdered that woman. Murdered her! Wait until Chaudhary finds out!" Anger suddenly gave way to depression and he stood immobile, staring at the floor. After a moment he said, "Why the hell did I stop the car? Why can't I have those few seconds back? I'd do what everyone else would have done and close my eyes to the entire incident. *I didn't see it, I didn't see it, I didn't see it.* Let her die. That's how most people would have handled it. Let her fucking *die!*"

A burst of heavy metal music rumbled down the stairs like a cannonball hitting each step, and Ann shuddered. Robert seemed not to have noticed, and she looked at him and realized he was oblivious to everything but what was happening to his world, shattering all around him. RULA, the Assistant Secretary's position, his law practice. His family. All breaking apart because of a split-second decision that could never be reversed. It made her angry, made her feel the same indignation that fueled so many of Robert's passions over the years. But she also felt something she couldn't identify, wasn't sure she wanted to identify: some partially concealed fear that there was much about this she still didn't understand. *That's what I was feeling that night at Edgerton's, the same night you shot that woman. It was as though something was waiting for us, out there in the darkness, waiting like an assassin, for our family. Waiting to pull the trigger.*

16

BUT the sense of dread that had plagued Ann for so long passed as two weeks went by with little happening, other than being repeatedly put off by Emily DeSantos when she tried to find a time for a meeting between her, JG, and the orchestra instructor. She finally got through one day while driving home from work.

"Of course John has talent," the other woman said. "But not enough to be a member of any decent symphony orchestra."

Ann's fingers squeezed the phone. "I don't believe it," she said, picturing the fiftyish, painfully thin woman with her humorless Napoleonic demeanor as she stood on the podium, furiously hacking the air with her baton as though she was dismembering a chicken. "John' has been in master's classes for years—"

"You've been taken," De Santos interrupted. "You're throwing money down the drain."

"You recommended a private class last year," Ann said. *Taught by your husband*, she remembered.

"Last year John's deficiencies weren't so evident."

"He's gotten an A in orchestra every year."

"Everyone gets an A in orchestra. We wouldn't have a program if I graded honestly. As it is, most American kids won't come anywhere near classical music. Two-thirds of my students are foreign-born. All my better string players are Asian. Maybe it's genetics or finger dexterity. Whatever the reason, JG just doesn't have it."

"Do you want to run that by me again?" Ann said with determined calmness. "Are you saying cello playing is *racial*?"

"I'm saying look around. Yo-Yo Ma—"

"Jacqueline du Pré."

"Well... she's dead, of course."

"Pablo Casals, Kathleen Ruth, Mstislav Rostropovich—"

"I'm not saying non-Asians can't be superior. It's just less likely. Anyway, John is... different. Well, you know what I mean."

"I guess I don't, Mrs. DeSantos. How is John different?"

"He's such a loner. Quiet. Almost pathologically so. How many friends does he have?"

"What does *quiet* have to do with playing the cello? Or is it race? Or isn't he sufficiently deferential to your special insights as a judge of human nature?"

The woman's voice was sharp. "You're not qualified to judge his talent or my expertise. Just as I'm probably not qualified to judge whatever it is you do."

"But Edith Raymond is. She's been in the L. A. Philharmonic for years."

"Edith Raymond is bleeding you. You just aren't ready to accept that a famous father and a mother with a Ph.D. can be the parents of a mediocre child. But that's the—"

Ann didn't hear the final words as she threw the phone on the floor of the car, and almost banged into the SUV in front of her.

That night she called Edith Raymond, who said, "That's baloney. Of course he can have a career in music."

"In music! What does that mean? As a performer, or selling trumpets behind a counter somewhere?"

"I fully expect John to develop into a competent performer. But he's only sixteen—"

Ann felt sick. "What exactly is a competent performer?"

"I think he could be a studio musician. Or an instructor in a college."

"But not as good as you. He could never be a member of an orchestra."

"He's young, Ann. My God, he's not even shaving regularly. Send him off to Eastman. But stop pushing him. Let him give another two or three years to music, then make a decision. He'll only be nineteen. That isn't the end of life, it's the beginning."

"I'm not *pushing* him. I'm helping." Why did people act like you're some kind of crazed stage mother when you sought your child's success? JG was a bright, talented kid. She wasn't going to let him end up like so many young people today, thirty years old, still living at home, working part time while spending ten years in college, Ann and Robert wondering if they had done a disservice to their son, had deceived themselves concerning his skill. Wondering if everything bad that could happen to their family *had* happened.

The answer came when Maurice Dohr accosted Robert one morning as he came through the door at the office.

"You knew this was going to happen and said nothing to me?" The older man was livid as the two of them began striding rapidly down the hallway to Robert's office.

And the two weeks of waiting for the other shoe to drop after DeFazio practically accused Robert of murder were shattered. *It's all going away*, Robert had thought with relief the day before; *it's going to be all right.*

"Are you trying to drive a stake into your chances in D.C.? Is this some sort of perverse death wish?" Dohr demanded.

"I assumed it was behind me." Robert struggled to keep up with the taller man's furious pace. He nodded at a colleague walking in their direction and staring at Robert's face as if there was something to read there.

"Did you see that?" Dohr asked with disbelief. "Herington was looking at you as if a murderer was a senior partner in the firm. Jesus!"

"Look, Maurice, I wasn't keeping anything from anyone. The police came to talk to me a couple of weeks ago. They wanted to know if I knew the woman was a hooker when I stopped to help. But that was it. I haven't heard a word since."

Until this morning.

Robert opened his office door and waited until Dohr stormed in, then gently shut it behind him. Dohr threw the first section of the *Los Angeles Times* at him and snapped, "Page three," as he dropped into a chair.

"I know, I know. I read it." *Five times*, Robert thought, looking at the paper, crumpled where Dohr's sweaty hand had been gripping it. "That reporter called me last week. I probably shouldn't have taken the call, but I wondered what she was up to so long after the shooting. The first thing she said was she heard the victim was a prostitute and wondered what my reaction to that was."

Dohr grabbed the paper back. "Your reaction?" He began to read. "'Woman Shot By Savior May Have Been Prostitute. In a strange turn of events, police sources yesterday confirmed that they are now looking at the shooting death of Nazia Chaudhary late last month from several different angles.' Meaning—" Dohr's eyes jerked angrily up from the newspaper—"you shot your whore rather than pay her. Jesus, Robert, did the reporter know you were a candidate for an Assistant Secretary's position in HHS?"

"Of course she knew. That's what makes this a story. The subtext here is 'Another attorney fucks up; aren't the rest of you happy?' That so-called 'police source' is the lead investigator on the case, a homicide sergeant named DeFazio. He hates Otis, hates attorneys, hates me. He was pals with the two cops who were convicted of beating Omar Randall Stahr. He leaked this to the *Times* to get back at RULA."

Sweat stood on Dohr's forehead like rain on a window. "What did you tell this reporter? Are there any more revelations about to spring into the public eye?"

"I told her the truth. Just as I've told the police, and you, and everyone else. I didn't know who that woman was, and what difference did it make anyway? She needed help. Why does the rest of this, this dressing-up of the story with make-believe scandal, matter?

"Is it true? Did you not know she was a prostitute?"

"Come on, Maurice."

"Don't give me that long-suffering look. After the police told you she was a hooker you chose not to inform anyone at the firm."

Robert threw his hands out. "I thought it would go away. It's a non-issue. Why would anyone care?"

"That's absurd. How could you think that? And trying to cover it up just makes it worse. People are talking about it in the hallways now, in the restrooms, in the dining room. Emails are buzzing around the building, if not the world. Robert Binder—a senior partner in the —" He grabbed the paper back and read, "—politically-connected law firm of Dohr, Haskins, and Poole." He crumpled the paper. "Every story printed about you—and they now number seven just in the *Times*—has identified you as a partner in DHP and the founding director of RULA. This is not the sort of publicity we want. RULA may have been your child, but it's outgrown you and me and every other single person. If you bring scandal to the program, if people think its director is using public funds to hire hookers—"

Dohr jerked into a standing position, looking as if he wanted to kick something. "I spoke to a deputy police chief yesterday. The attitude there has grown decidedly chilly. They want this case wrapped up." He half-turned toward Robert. "It's because of Bobby Stackhouse, of course. His involvement creates a whole new dynamic—one nobody wants to face. Have you seen his latest tweets? Another South-Central killing, another case of police incompetence, another immigrant killed. It's not good for any of us, Robert. We can't have any more negative attention. It's as simple as that. Talk to the police. Bring the investigation to a close. Now! Or take an immediate leave of absence. Those are your two options." He threw the crumpled-up newspaper at the wastebasket and watched it land on the floor. "There's a third option, of course, but I won't consider it now."

"Resign?" Robert felt hollow inside.

"I'd never ask you. You've meant too much to the firm. To me, as a friend. But damn it, I don't want any more surprises." He sank down on the couch again. "Tell me the truth, Robert. The truth! Are there any more secrets out there waiting for me?"

Robert was staring dully at the window. Twenty-two years he and Maurice had been friends. Outside of his family and Luis Teague, Maurice was the oldest and closest friend he had. For the past eight years the two families had taken a house together for a month in Tuscany. Last year they spent Christmas in Yosemite, the year before in El Salvador.

"Robert?"

He shook his head, clearing away the cobwebs. "No. No more surprises."

"You're not going to be indicted for murder?"

"Jesus, Maurice."

"Yes or no?"

"No!"

"You're a man of your word so I'll accept that." He paused, settled back in the couch and his tone eased. "How's Ann holding up? It's got to be rough on her."

"Ann's not the problem. JG's not handling it at all well. He skulks around the house, has hardly spoken to me in two weeks. He's upset with orchestra, angry at me about the shooting, his grades have gone to hell. It's eating me up. He and I were always so close. I was never embarrassed to have my son as my best friend. Proud, for God's sake. Now—"

Dohr tried to put him at ease. "Hell, maybe it doesn't have anything to do with you. It could just be typical teenage angst. Girls! No appetite, right? I seem to remember that from high school. Girls can do that to you. Especially when they say 'Go out with you? You gotta be kidding.' I heard that a lot. Still hear it. Only now it's my wife."

Robert shook his head. It wasn't girl trouble, more likely just the cumulative effect of too many things coming down at once. But later that afternoon he was still thinking about it when he suddenly felt like hitting himself. *Jesus! How could I have been so stupid?* Ann knew, didn't she? But he hadn't paid attention, even though it was right in front of him, as bright and clear as a giant neon sign. He grabbed his sport coat. *God, what an idiot I've been.*

A few minutes after two o'clock Ann put two unopened gallons of paint on JG's desk and stepped back, gazing around at the room. I'm not snooping, she told herself. I'm getting ready to paint. I just need to tidy up a bit first. I'm not snooping.

Anyway, he was her son, damn it. And this was her house. She had a right to look around. Because she didn't believe JG's sudden academic breakdown had anything to do with music—no, no, it was more than academic, it was behavioral, a splintering apart of everything he had been. There was something else. Though in a distant part of her mind that was hurriedly pushing itself forward, she feared finding out what it was.

And with that a little bit of Ann-rationality took a stand against her growing hysteria: What do you do with mysteries? You solve them.

Maybe she should wait, though. JG's been coming home from school at odd hours. If he discovered her searching his room she'd never get over the shame. Then she thought, *No, damn it, it's now or never. But hurry, before he gets here.*

Fighting against a black cloud of guilt, she pulled open the top desk drawer and looked inside. Dozens of school papers, two old cell phones, an MP3 player she hadn't seen in years. Loose paperclips, an old nail, two Snickers wrappers. A jumble, a disordered mess, like his life had become. She sat in the chair and tried each of the side drawers. School exams from last year, paperback books, ancient video games, half a ream of printer paper. But nothing out of the ordinary.

Standing abruptly, she glanced at the shelf over the desk. His iPad. Last year's high-school yearbook. There was also a video yearbook, but he hadn't wanted it. On impulse she took the book down and flipped to the picture of John. Good-looking kid, especially with those sexy dreadlocks. But he hadn't had his picture taken this year, had he? He hadn't attended

173

any school functions either, especially since the breakup with Sonja.

Was that the front door? She froze, holding her breath. *No, it's nothing. But hurry, you don't know when he'll return.*

Her heart racing now, she put the book back and crossed to the closet. At the rear of the single high shelf where he kept his ski boots and gloves, she found two copies of *Hustler* and a magazine called *Black and Stacked.* Well, he's sixteen. She didn't like it, but what can you say? In the inside pocket of a raincoat she discovered a baggie of marijuana, probably an ounce. OK, it wasn't that big a deal. She stuffed it back and picked up an old pair of sneakers, running her fingers inside the toes. *Nothing there,* she thought, feeling relief, then a greater sense of guilt. *I can't believe I'm going through my son's things as if he's a criminal.*

Sensing something moving behind her Ann spun around to see JG frozen in the doorway, eyes darting from his mother to the open closet door. Her first impulse had been to say, "It's not what it looks like." But he could see right away that it was exactly what it looked like. She said, "You didn't have your junior picture taken this year."

He began to tremble. "Why are you here? What are you doing?"

"I brought the paint up. Then I saw your yearbook."

He glared at her as if the lie were too blatant to respond to. *Even my mother,* his expression said. He came inside and slammed the closet door. They stared at each other—the boy taller than the mother, and the air between them vibrating. Fighting the urge to flee, Ann said, "John, what's really been bothering you this semester? It can't be just the music."

"Nothing's bothering me. I'm fine. I'm great."

"Please—" She tried to put a hand on his shoulder, but he jerked away and sank heavily onto on his bed.

"Is it Performing Arts? Do you want to transfer to another school?"

"What difference would that make now?" he asked angrily.

She took a breath, sensing that this was one of the crucial and irreversible moments in both their lives, something she had to handle correctly or things would never again be right between them. But she was baffled at how they had ended up here. "Is there something your dad or I did to upset you? Are you angry with us? If you are we need to talk about it."

"Maybe I'm just tired of being the prize exhibit in your marriage."

Ann's body stiffened with the effort to remain calm. "Please, John. We told you: race was never an issue. Your talent was."

"Do you think I'm stupid? I've heard you and dad talking about how both your families were against your marriage, how people said your kids would never fit in anywhere, how your brother told you mongrel pups can't even get into the dog show, let alone win a ribbon."

"John—"

"That's why you're always pushing me. I've got to be better than everybody else's kids, smarter, a musical genius. For *you*. So you can hold me up to your brother and people like that."

"That's not true, John—"

"I'm sick of being paraded around! 'Look at our John. Isn't he beautiful? And smart! Gets all As. Did you know he's going to Eastman? We're all so *proud*.' Why did you even have to have a kid?" He had lost control, and it was all spilling out now, all the things he'd never admitted even to himself. "Why couldn't you and dad fight your battles without making me a part of it? You should have adopted. But you wanted your fifty-fifty, your half-this-and-half-that baby to prove your brother and all the others wrong."

"John, we're proud of you, proud of—"

"*I don't want people proud of me.* I just want to be left alone." He closed his fists and drove them slowly into the mattress. "I don't want to live here anymore. I hate this place."

"This house? Our family? You can't mean that."

"*Everything!* Why do we have to live in West Adams? I heard what that cop said. He was right. This is your fantasy world. But you and Dad didn't have to walk through two gang territories to get to junior high. You and Dad weren't threatened every day for three years. The only thing I learned in that school was to control my bladder, because there was no way I would ever walk into a bathroom. While you were off at UCLA and Dad was at Otis, I was getting the shit beat out of me."

"John, I'm sorry. You should have told us."

But the instant the tears came he was on his feet.

"John, please—"

He raced from the room, and Ann stared at her hands, at the yearbook, at the illusions of the past sixteen years and a life she never understood.

Robert could feel the throb of his pulse as he sat in his car at ten minutes to three and stared at the 1930s façade of Manual Arts High School half a block away. *Idiot!* he told himself. So wrapped up in his own problems he couldn't see what was happening right in front of him.

His gaze shifted from the school to the non-stop flow of traffic on Vermont. The closer it got to three o'clock the thicker it became, with at least two dozen cars double-parked in front of the school now. A few minutes later the first trickle of students began to wander out of the main building, on their way to bus stops or walking home. So what exactly had drawn him here? he wondered, again going over his conversation with Maurice Dohr that morning. Maurice's flippant remark about teenage girls had started a cascade of thoughts, culminating in a sudden and surprising fusion of meanings as Robert gathered together the strands of a dozen conversations and events over the past few weeks, ranging from JG's moodiness, to his increasingly argumentative nature, to his distraction during dinner. *Girls do that to you*, Maurice had said. But how had Robert noticed none of this when it was going on right in front of him?

He glanced in the rearview mirror just as a familiar dung-colored VW Passat came down the street. Luckily JG was staring at the school as he drifted slowly by. Robert turned the key in the ignition as he watched the VW draw up in front of the gymnasium entrance while another flood of teenagers streamed from the buildings and onto the sidewalk. He couldn't make out faces at this distance but saw JG's brake lights flash red, and a moment later someone hurriedly climbed into the car. With an angry screeching of tires the VW shot down the street, as though hoping to disappear as quickly as possible.

Robert pulled into traffic, keeping his distance. Two blocks from the school JG slowed, and seemed to be going nowhere, cruising along Vermont and Central as far as Watts, then up to Exposition Park and the Coliseum, as if lost. After half an hour the car headed north past West Adams, then abruptly turned into an area of nondescript prewar houses near the Santa Monica Freeway. Almost at once it eased to the side of the road as if to park, and Robert was forced to pull into a driveway. He watched for two minutes as JG's car didn't move. *What the hell are they doing?* A moment later Meena Chaudhary stepped out, hurriedly looked both ways, then bent through the open window and said something before rapidly walking away, her head down, staring at the sidewalk.

17

"You followed me?"

JG looked at his father in disbelief, his face red with rage.

The three of them had just started dinner —Ann's turn tonight, ravioli, spinach, French bread, nothing fancy—and Robert realized at once he should have waited until the meal was over. But he hadn't been able to restrain himself. Three forks sank to the table at the same time, and there was a deafening silence as JG and Ann stared at him.

Weakly, he tried to explain. "I wasn't spying. I was talking to someone today and it just struck me that you might be seeing Meena. I'm not objecting, John, I just want to know what's going on between you two."

"How do you call it 'not spying' if you were following us for an hour?"

Robert kept his eyes from Ann but he knew she was looking open-mouthed at him. Feeling his body grow warm, he said, "Are you seeing her or not? And if so, why the secrecy?"

JG slammed his fork onto his plate, tiny bits of ravioli flying across the table. "It's not secrecy. I don't *have* any secrets." He tossed an angry look at his mother. "I just didn't want to talk about it. I knew you wouldn't understand."

Robert reacted with disbelief. "What's that supposed to mean?"

"Robert, please," Ann said. "This isn't the time."

"No, no. I want to know what he means."

JG said quickly, "All I hear every day is how crazy her dad is, how you don't like the whole family, don't want anything to do with them."

"The man's a psychopath. Didn't you hear what the police said?"

"So the whole family's bad?" JG's jaw trembled as he stared at his father.

Ann felt a flash of alarm. Too much emotion, too much over-reacting.

"Anyway," JG went on, "we're not *dating*, so what's to tell? She's just a friend. Someone to talk to." He looked at his mother, then back at Robert, holding his gaze. "She needs a friend. Her mother was just killed."

Robert dropped his head; there was nothing to say to that. But Ann wondered why John had brought it up if not to hurt his father. And why that had suddenly become so important. She said, "If she's a friend why not bring her over here? There's no need to keep it a secret."

Robert's head bobbed up at once. "Again, you both know what we've learned about the father

—his temper, the police going to his house, the time he spent in a mental ward. Does he know about you two?"

JG shook his head. "He can't know. He'd beat her. He already beats her. And the boys, the twins. He hits them. He hits everyone."

Ann said sharply, "Then we should report it." "No," JG said in alarm. "That'd only make it worse. Don't do anything. I wasn't even supposed to tell you. Now she won't trust me."

Robert said, "How do you know it's true? Have you seen him hit them? Have you seen any injuries?"

JG blew out a sarcastic laugh. "Always the big-time lawyer, huh, Dad? No, he never invited me over to watch. I'm not even allowed at their house. No American kids are. Just another girl from India who goes to Manual Arts and wears a sari and hardly speaks English."

"Then you don't know for sure what's going on."

Ann shook her head. "Robert, don't—"

"*He burned her with a hot spatula.*" JG's voice shook. "Last year. Grabbed it off the stove where her mother was cooking and beat her with it. The skin on her arm and back is all scarred. He never even took her to a doctor, just let it heal. Do you want to see what it looks like a year later?" Tears stood in his eyes.

"The girl needs to talk to a social worker," Ann said firmly. "Surely there's someone at school."

"No, Mom, please. Her father told her if they ever have any trouble with the police he's taking the family back to India. As bad as it is for her here, at least she can be free of him when she's eighteen."

"Does she want to be free of him?"

His head dropped. "I don't know." He stared at his plate for a moment, then became aggressive again. "She's not even allowed to have friends at school. Her brother saw her talking to a black kid in Cerritos and they made her sit on a stool in the center of the living room all night. Her dad hates blacks and Hispanics. He thinks they get all the breaks in this country!"

"Are you certain he doesn't know about you?" Robert asked. "It sounds like it would be trouble if he did."

JG nodded. "I think he'd kill her. They don't trust her at all. It's like something out of medieval days. They don't even let her go to movies or watch television. It's like they're hiding her in a tower and won't let anyone near her."

"Maybe they consider her married," Robert said, and felt uncomfortable bringing it up. "I guess there was that ceremony in India."

"Come on, Dad. It's not legal, even in India."

Trying not to sound judgmental, Ann said, "It sounds like you're more involved than just being a friend."

"You should be supporting me, both of you. Her father's nuts, he abuses his kids, he treats her like she's three years old. In Orange County he even kept her out of school for a year because there were too many Americanized Indian kids and she started complaining about how she was treated. She's only in school now because Social Services found out about her."

"I'm sorry, John," Robert said. He put his fork down and sat back in his chair. "I wish we could help. It's an impossible situation. But no one can intervene unless she complains to the police or a counselor. And that would probably just make matters worse. The county isn't likely to take the man's kids away."

"Besides," Ann said, "we can't just tell Sandeep he's wrong because he's strict. It's simply a more traditional culture than ours. I'm sure he feels we're as bad as we think he is. If you had been born in Madras or Mumbai, you'd feel the way he does."

"Mom, branding your kids with a burning spatula isn't being *strict!*" He stabbed his ravioli and watched tomato sauce hemorrhage around his plate. "Anyway, her mother wasn't a prostitute," he said in a weak voice. "Meena told me. It's not true. The police picked her up because of where she was, but they let her go the same night."

"Well, finally the truth comes out." Robert looked at Ann with forced enthusiasm. "That's a relief to hear. Not that I ever believed it. Now if only someone would tell DeFazio. And a retraction in the *Times* would be nice."

"Do you think it's safe to keep seeing her?" Ann asked. "If her father finds out, she's the one who will suffer, not you."

JG seemed not to have heard. "There's something going on in that home. Something I don't know about. She won't tell me what." He looked up, his face tortured. "But Meena's scared to death of something. It's more than her dad. Worse."

The doorbell rang and Jake began to bark half-heartedly. Ann rose with a sigh. "Magazine subscription," she guessed, and gave JG a smile. She wanted to go to him, give him a hug but wasn't sure how he'd respond. Trying to sound hearty, she said, "Eat, boy. Mother's orders. Maybe later we'll have time to get even with you in Trivial Pursuit."

JG was looking at his dad with renewed anger. "What are you really upset about? That she's foreign? Or that she wears clothes from Goodwill and speaks with an accent and doesn't know anything about Vivaldi or the Federal Reserve System?"

Robert was striving for a response but something about Ann's expression when she came back made him stiffen. "It's those detectives again," she said finally. Her eyes went to her husband's face as though looking for something she had missed before, some sign or signal that she should have seen. "They want to talk to you. They sound upset."

Robert was on his feet at once. "Jesus, why can't they leave me alone?" His face was red as he stormed out of the kitchen.

Ann thought, *This is it, isn't it? This is what you had been expecting, what you wouldn't tell me about.*

18

Nick DeFazio and Jill Oakley were in the living room, DeFazio's large unkempt body radiating hostility and taking up half the couch, while Oakley sat on a chair, her hands stiff in her lap. Robert and Ann's discomfort was growing by the second as they seated themselves on the Victorian wingchairs while JG stood near the kitchen door.

DeFazio looked at Robert with an expression Ann wasn't able to read. But neither of the cops was in a good mood. Something's wrong, she knew, something's happened in the two weeks since their last visit.

DeFazio's raspy voice filled the room like an icy wind. "So, Mr. Binder, we're back again. Won't be able to play *Antiques Roadshow* this time, I'm afraid. And we're going to have to ask your boy to leave us for a bit." His thick head bobbed around toward JG. "You don't mind, do you, son? Shouldn't take us long."

Everyone turned to look at JG, whose eyes were already dark with vitriol. He glared at the policeman a moment, then stalked into the kitchen. *I'm sorry, John,* Ann thought as she watched him, though she wasn't sure what she was apologizing for, only that her son had been subjected to too much in too short a time, and for that she wanted to make amends.

"Well, sir." DeFazio smiled with unexpected enthusiasm and rubbed his large hands together. "Now that you've had time to think about things, is there anything in your story you want to change?"

"I beg your pardon?" Robert's body gave a little twitch and jerked forward at the waist.

"About how everything happened that night. You coming home and taking a wrong turn—"

"It wasn't a wrong turn. It was something I don't usually do but it wasn't wrong. Just a spur of the moment thing."

"And you saw these two mysterious men."

Robert's face froze. "What's the point of this visit?"

"To ask questions." DeFazio's eyebrows shot up in surprise. "That's what we do. We're detectives."

Oakley stepped in with an explanation. "It's been three weeks since the shooting and we still can't find anyone who saw or heard anything that night." She glanced at Ann with what looked like sympathy before turning again to Robert. "We keep looking. But there's no corroborating evidence at all for your story." A moment ticked by before she added, "Nothing."

"There are eight million people in L.A. county," Robert said. "You talked to all of them?"

"We canvassed the neighborhood," DeFazio replied, rearranging his bulk on the couch. "Took out ads in community newspapers, put up posters, even had our Explorer Scout troop knocking on every door within half a mile. You'd think *someone* would have seen or heard something. Gunshots, screaming, a van racing away. That's reasonable to assume, isn't it?"

"Reasonable? You're talking to me about 'reasonable'? If you people were doing your job instead of putting up posters maybe we'd be done with this madness."

"And what might our job be, Mr. Binder?"

"Finding those men," Robert said through clenched teeth. "They're still out there, for Christ's sake! Why aren't you looking for *them* instead of trying to implicate me in this weird fantasy you've concocted?"

"Well, sir, thank you for reminding us of our duty. Actually, we, the department that is, all the usual experts, have come to the conclusion that these men you say you saw are not those responsible for the rapes. Which, by the way, have stopped."

Robert's jaw dropped. "What are you talking about?"

"Put it another way: you saw no men. There was just you, the darkness, and a prostitute. Who you got in a fight with. She probably tried to rob you and you ended up shooting her. You had to think quickly to provide yourself with an alibi, and what better story than the rapists who had so frequently been mentioned on television."

"That's it," Robert said. He began to lose the tenuous hold he had on himself. "End of discussion. Arrest me or get out of my house."

Ann's eyes were glued on her husband. She could see the muscles in his neck tighten like a suddenly knotted rope. She understood none of what was happening but saw the two detectives watching Robert also. They're not done, there's something else, she realized. They're anxious for something to happen, like people waiting impatiently for a show to begin. She felt her back stiffen and wished she could make time stop, to keep the next few minutes from happening. But she sat dumbly as a cloud drifted in front of the sun, dimming the light in the room.

Oakley's voice was almost apologetic. "The District Attorney has asked the department to devote more resources to this case. He's assigned it to an Assistant DA named Lyndall Scaggs. They'd like to wrap it up by the end of next week."

"There is suddenly a great deal of pressure on the department," DeFazio added with annoyance. "Political pressure. Not just Stackhouse but the professional rabble-rousers and Department bashers that hang out with him. People you would know, I'm sure, sir. Not what you'd expect from a crime like this. But it seems our industrious Mr. Chaudhary has hired an attorney to advance a claim of wrongful death."

Robert had to keep himself from gasping in surprise. "An attorney? How can he afford that? He doesn't even have a job."

Jill Oakley said, "It turns out he's getting some pro bono assistance from the Inner-City Law Project."

"That's associated with Otis Law School, isn't it?" DeFazio asked as if he really didn't know the answer. "In fact, I believe it's run out of the same building as your Rural and Urban Legal Assistance group."

Robert was stunned. He opened his mouth, but the words died as Ann said, "That's Luis's group. Why would he do that?"

Robert's mind spun dizzily. This couldn't be right.

DeFazio smiled, enjoying the moment. "So we thought we'd drop by, see if you'd like to make any adjustments to your recollection of events that night. Going up against the ILP, that's a pretty heavy-duty group of legal do-gooders, isn't it? They win most of their cases. Even when they're wrong."

"*What case?*" Robert demanded. He looked wildly from face to face. "Why is everyone twisting this around? I was *helping* that woman. How the hell can I be considered culpable? This is madness."

DeFazio settled back in his seat, affecting a surprised look, and Ann thought, *This is it, this is what they came here for, what they want us both to see. But why am I a part of it?* Jill Oakley was tensed but trying desperately to appear calm, and Ann realized: She's forcing herself not to look at me. I've become a participant in this drama of theirs; they want me on stage, ready to take my role.

"Strange how things work out," DeFazio went on as though making an announcement. "Even after many years. For example, what happened out there on Normandie is remarkably like what happened in Boston, isn't it? Funny you never mentioned that to us. Maybe 'funny' isn't the word. But it makes me wonder when people keep things from the police. Never would have heard about it at all if someone in the ILP hadn't been diligent enough to dig it out."

"It's not the same at all," Robert said indignantly. "That's absurd."

Ann was looking from the detectives to her husband. Boston?

Robert was on his feet, outraged. But there was a looseness to his body that softened his tone. "There was never any doubt about that. It was an act of great courage. Everyone said so. Why are you even bringing this up?"

Ann had to fight against an urge to jump up also. "What are you two talking about?"

DeFazio ignored her, looking at Robert as if they were the only two people in the room. "As my grandmother used to say, once is unfortunate, the second time, it begins to look like carelessness."

Jill Oakley gave her partner a look and muttered. "Come on, Nick."

"This is evil!" Robert said, as if to himself. His body was twisting about as though he couldn't hold himself steady. "There's no other word for it. A citizen tries to help someone in need, risks his life, and suddenly the whole weight of the LAPD comes crashing down on him. It's wrong, it's vicious. How do you expect people to become involved in their community when this sort of state-sponsored terror is the consequence?"

"Would someone tell me what's going on!" Ann shouted.

DeFazio's voice came to her with its own charge of electricity as he said, "Didn't he tell you? Turns out this isn't the first time your husband's killed someone."

19

"**Y**OUR first wife? Carolyn? Is that what he's talking about? You didn't kill her, she died in childbirth—" Ann was almost screaming. She listened to herself—the words sounding scratchy and shrill, as if from a defective and distant radio—and thought, *This isn't me, this woman who's lost control of herself. It's someone else, someone I don't know, don't want to know.*

Robert sank into his chair as though his bones couldn't support him anymore. "Of course I didn't kill her!" His hands twisted in his lap, then flung forward as if tossing everything into the light. Tears stood in his eyes, and through her confusion and anger Ann found herself wondering: *When was the last time I saw that? When John was born? The last time you were moved enough to cry?* His voice was slack with emotion. "I couldn't explain it to you, Ann. I tried. A thousand times I tried. I just... wanted it to go away. But it didn't. I still dream about it, twenty-four years later."

"Dream what? What are you talking about?" she heard herself shout.

He looked at her, his lower lip quivering as he realized that for the first time in a quarter-century he was going to have to give voice to the images that tortured him every night. It would belong to everyone again, giving them the right to walk around his private tragedy, to poke and probe and question, and watch as his life bled out in front of them. He should have been honest with Ann years ago, of course. He thought this every day, carried the guilt like a huge burden on his back, while some distant, little-visited region of his brain sought desperately to reverse time, to go back to Boston and un-do everything that happened that night.

"Mr. Binder." DeFazio was impatient. But Robert didn't even hear him. He was alone in the room with Ann. As his eyes went to hers, any hope he had for the future—his or his family's—died. Simply died. He sank further into the chair. And the words he should have spoken to his wife years ago finally formed in his mouth, drained of all emotion because that was the only way he could confront them...

Newlyweds. Married just eight months in one of those ostentatious 1990s wedding ceremonies. He was still embarrassed by the memory of the waste and frivolity of it all. Dozens of stretch limos lining the street in front of the First Congregational Church, seven hundred guests (who even knows seven hundred people?), a reception that didn't end until dawn at Boston's ritziest country club. Followed by three months in Europe, paid for by Carolyn's grandparents, owners of New England's "Largest and Finest" furniture manufacturer. Then their first home, a townhouse leased for the school year and paid for by her father (a wonderful man, and still alive after all these years; Robert and Ann had chatted with him on the phone just last Christmas) while Carolyn finished her senior year at Wellesley and Robert took some time off before law school.

Eight months later, early May but unseasonably hot, they had dinner at a neighborhood restaurant, then watched TV at home for a while before finally going to sleep, leaving a window partially open. When something heavy dropped to the floor they both jerked awake. Robert, more curious than concerned, was about to turn on the lamp when a man's voice from across the room said calmly, "Don't."

They both saw him now, a looming but vague presence moving in the almost total darkness, like black painted on black. As their eyes adjusted they could see he was wearing a ski mask and standing next to the bed with a gun. Carolyn let out a screech and Robert started to jump up when the man said loudly, "You move and the lady dies first." Robert froze, thinking: *This is a dream, it has to be, this sort of thing doesn't happen to people in real life.* At the same time his mind was desperately searching for a weapon, an advantage, anything he could do to get the upper hand.

A pair of handcuffs landed with a dull clunk in front of Carolyn. "Stay calm and everything will be OK. Cuff his hands behind his back, then take off your nightgown. Don't give me any shit and maybe everyone'll get out of here alive." Then to Robert: "Hey, rich boy, you get to watch. You might learn something."

But Carolyn started screaming.

"Goddamn it, shut up!" The man struck her with the gun, but it just made her scream louder, and he began to panic. Robert could see he hadn't expected any resistance and didn't know what to do. Carolyn was hysterical, throwing her arms about, trying to climb out of bed.

The intruder struck her in the sternum, knocking her sharply against the headboard. "Stop, goddamn it, shut up!" He struck her again, and when she didn't quiet, the small room filled with the sound of a single gunshot. On purpose? An accident? A warning? Robert wasn't even thinking about it. He was out of bed, grabbing the heavy brass lamp from the night table and swinging it like a baseball bat, striking the intruder on the side of head. The man faltered and Robert was on top of him at once, throwing him against a dresser. Both men tumbled to the floor, grappling with each other, but Robert, an athletic twenty-two-year-old, wrenched the gun from his hand. The man swore, lunged at him, howling furiously, and Robert pulled the trigger.

Then he turned around and saw Carolyn slumped on the bed and began screaming. He was holding her when the police arrived minutes later.

Robert was sobbing, his body rocking gently back and forth. "That's why I got out of criminal law. I wasn't able to defend anyone accused of a violent crime. No matter how much I thought them innocent, I just couldn't stand up for them in court. Every time I tried, I'd see that man pointing the gun at Carolyn and pulling the trigger. My stomach would start churning and I'd break out in a sweat. That's why Maurice let me set up RULA. If I couldn't appear in court myself, at least I could find and train other attorneys who could."

"Maurice Dohr knows?" Ann said in disbelief. "Who else did you tell while keeping it from your wife?"

Robert's shoulders slumped. "Luis and I were friends at the time, Ann. He knows." He looked pleadingly at his wife. "I can't tell you how sorry I am. About all of this."

She sank back in her chair and put her hand to her forehead.

"Well, well, well, Mr. Binder—" DeFazio's voice came to Robert and Ann like a giant fist dragging them back from the private world they had inhabited for the past five minutes. "Two times now. Both accidents. Both involved alleged rapists. Both resulted in a woman dying. And you becoming a bit of a hero. Strange, is it not?"

Robert didn't even look at him. "That's absurd."

"Just on a whim, you might say, I contacted the Boston police." DeFazio straightened on the couch. "The officer who worked the case is retired now, of course. But still alive. Owns a tavern called the Last Call. He remembers it. *Vividly*, he said. Because he was never comfortable with your story."

Robert came out of his stupor. "What are you talking about? Do you think *I* shot Carolyn? My God, there was an investigation, there were people on either side of our townhouse who heard the whole thing. They're the ones who called 9-1-1. There was never any doubt about what happened. The man had gunshot residue on his hand, his prints were on the gun and on the window sill where he forced his way in. He had handcuffs and restraints for my feet. What are you trying to do?" His voice was near hysteria.

DeFazio waved a hand as if none of this mattered. "No one doubts he killed your wife, Mr. Binder. It's the *story*, this fanciful account of your heroic bedroom confrontation that the police never accepted. After all, the intruder was shot in the back. Five times."

"We were *fighting*." Robert looked as if he was going to come out of his chair. "We were tumbling on the floor, I pulled the trigger and he got up again. I thought he was going to attack me, but he spun away at the last second. I panicked and shot until the gun was empty. I probably pulled the trigger a dozen times after it stopped shooting." He slumped back in the chair. "You're trying to make this into something it isn't. It was in and out of the newspapers in two days. There was no scandal, no one doubted me. What are you trying to do?"

Ann's eyes squeezed shut. She was in a daze, unable to process anything but the fact that Robert had killed someone twenty-four years ago—Robert!—and hadn't told her. Two of his friends knew, but his wife didn't. A movement to the side caught her attention and she turned toward the kitchen to see JG standing, white-faced, and staring in disbelief at his father. She felt alarmed and wanted to go to him. But she couldn't move, couldn't make her body function as Robert's words floated in the air above her.

Nick DeFazio and Jill Oakley were also staring at Robert. As DeFazio's face eased into a smile Ann thought, *My God, he's enjoying himself. He's watching Robert fall apart in front of his family, and he's enjoying it!* "Well, sir, it troubled the police that you knew the rapist. A friend of yours, wasn't he?"

Robert was livid. "I didn't *know* him—"

"The way they figure it, you hired him to kill your wife, then shot him to keep him quiet. There were well-known marriage problems between you and the lady, of course. She was going to get a divorce, wasn't she?"

"Of course we weren't going to get a divorce. Her sister started that nonsense. We had the sort of problems all newly married couples have. Do you think her father would still be talking to me if it were true? My God, he put me through law school. And I didn't *know* the killer. He was a waiter at a restaurant we used to go to. He must have followed us home one night and learned where we live. When the police showed me his photograph I remembered him trying to flirt with Carolyn, but she wouldn't have any of it. It must have angered him."

Ann was going to be ill. Bile was forcing itself into her throat, but she couldn't leave for the bathroom. She tried to stand, but her legs simply wouldn't obey. She sank back in the chair.

DeFazio's voice kept going. "I'm surprised you're allowed to practice law in California. Doesn't the bar association do background checks anymore?"

"They *did* a background check, damn you. I don't have a criminal record. I've never been arrested, nothing but a parking ticket two decades ago."

"But you *have* killed two people. Not many folks can say that. Including police officers. Even the 'out-of-control,' the 'cowboys with guns.'"

"Come on, Nicky," Jill Oakley muttered to her partner. She was embarrassed at his manner.

Or—Ann thought, because she didn't trust either of them now—*was this an act they'd agreed on?* At any rate, DeFazio paid her no attention. He bent forward, his thick wrestler's forearms braced on his knees. "This ILP the law school runs, it always takes the criminal's side rather than the victim's, doesn't it? This will be a change for it, helping Mr. Chaudhary in his case against you."

Robert's hands began to jump on the arms of the chair. "This is crazy. They're not going to go against me. It must just be informational —Chaudhary wants to know the details of his wife's death. It's only normal under the circumstance. There's no crime, no crime. Nothing to prosecute. You're trying to make a case based on something entirely different that happened twenty-four years ago. It's irrelevant; it's idiotic to tie them together."

"We don't make cases," DeFazio said with complaisance. "You know that, sir. We merely turn information over to the DA. They decide what to do with it. But I doubt they'll let this one slide. Not with your history. Not with the ILP and Stackhouse and the *Times* and a hundred social media sites worked up."

Robert's back straightened and his tone suddenly hardened. "If this gets out, I'll sue you. Do you understand me, DeFazio? Not the department. You, personally. I don't know what you have against me, but it's obvious you're trying to ruin me."

"How am I doing that, Mr. Binder?"

"I know it was you who told the *Times* Mrs. Chaudhary was a prostitute. It wasn't true, but that doesn't bother you at all, does it? Mere facts can't be allowed to interfere with this vendetta you have against me and RULA."

"If you have a complaint to make, I suggest you talk to the Internal Affairs department. A diligent and hard-working group of officers. I've dealt with them before. We're practically pals."

Ann had had enough. What was she supposed to do, sit here and listen to him abuse her husband? Fighting to keep calm, she came to her feet. "You need to go. This is nothing but harassment. If you had any basis for these accusations you would have made an arrest."

Robert was also on his feet, his body rigid as a dead man's. He turned stiffly toward the kitchen, surprised to see JG staring at him. When Ann put a protective arm around Robert's waist, JG spun on his heel and disappeared through the doorway.

It was still early, only shortly after nine, when Robert and Ann went upstairs to bed. JG was in his room, 50 Cent making the walls vibrate with angry emotion. From the moment the police left Robert had desperately wanted to explain to Ann about Carolyn's death, about why he had been unable to talk about it for so long. But Ann said no, wait until we've both had a chance to calm down; it was still too much to process. Maybe in a few days. But when he shut the door behind them he started talking, and he couldn't stop.

"Of course I should have told you. I should have explained the first day I met you. *Don't go on with this relationship until she knows what happened*, I told myself over and over. Even Luis hounded me to tell you. But I couldn't do it. No matter how much I wanted to. I'd think, *Tonight, goddamn it, tell her, because if you don't she'll hear from someone else*. I must have tried a thousand times, but there weren't any words. I'd open my mouth and my brain would freeze. Later, when I finally felt I could talk about it, it was just easier not to, easier to pretend it would all just go away. I'm sorry … it was cowardly and I knew that. But I was powerless to do anything about it."

Ann sat on the bed to take off her shoes. There was a fireplace across from her with an intricately-carved white mantel with bas reliefs of cavorting porpoises and palm trees and conch shells. She kept her eyes focused on it now to keep from looking at her husband. "Please don't do this, Robert. Wait a few days. We'll talk then."

"DeFazio acts like the police thought I was involved somehow, but that's bullshit. Why's he doing this? I had one interview with the Boston PD—one!—and they confirmed my story. That was it, damn it." He squeezed his eyes shut until they stung. "I've thought about that night every day of my life. I even saw a psychologist for a while." He turned to look at her. "Right after JG was born. The dreams and insomnia were killing me. I started going to this guy in Beverly Hills. I didn't want you to know. I went every Friday morning for eight months. What a crock. I'd sit there and talk and he'd—I don't know what he did. Think about fishing in Colorado or what kind of Porsche he was going to get with the money I was paying him. I might as well have been talking to a wall for all the good it did."

He turned to the mantel, seizing it with both hands as if he was going to rip it from the wall. "Every night when I turn out the lights, I relive it: that man coming through the window, the handcuffs, the way my ears throbbed when the gun went off, the blood everywhere when I went to Carolyn. It's *there*. Not a memory, Ann— the *experience*, forcing me to relive it, to *feel* it again."

Then you should have told me, she thought with fury. *Anything that important should have been shared. For my benefit, if not your own.*

"You can't imagine—" His voice was shaking as he twisted around to look at her. "No one can understand what it means to see someone you love die like that, practically while they're in your arms. That's why I had to help Sandeep. Don't you see? I'm responsible for what he's going through. He's where I was twenty years ago. And I'm the one who *caused* it."

Unable to keep silent any longer Ann looked up at him. "How does this happen two times in a person's life?" Almost immediately she regretted both the tone and the words. It wasn't fair. And Robert was instantly angered.

"You're the expert on randomness. It happens twice to one person, once to a few, and never to millions. Isn't that the definition of the process? It's like getting hit by lightning or winning the lottery. Even when the odds are astronomical, it has to happen to someone." He sat next to her on the bed, his thigh touching hers, making her flinch and move away. "I wasn't hiding anything except my own pain, Ann. Believe me. There's nothing else to hide. It's not like it was a secret, it was in newspapers all across the country. DeFazio's using it to get at me for his own reasons, the Omar Randall Stahr case, I guess. Everything the department does now is because of Stahr. But those implications of his are bullshit and he knows it. I had that one interview with the Boston PD, they cleared me, and that was the end of it."

He sat silent a moment, his head thrown back and his palms pressing against his eyes. "DeFazio is my punishment for trying to be a hero. Next time I'll know better. Disengage. That's the moral. Every man for himself. Nihilism triumphant." A sour taste rose in his mouth and his eyes snapped open. "I was thinking a few minutes ago about Chaudhary, his volatility, how he's convinced the ILP to take his case, the way we're all afraid of him now, and I thought: here this goddamn *illegal* sneaks into the U.S., takes my tax money, and then uses it to *target* me because I wasn't able to save his wife's life. I was outraged at the unfairness of it all. *This is my country, goddamn it, who the hell is he to attack me like this?* Then I realized what I was doing, how I needed to demonize him to validate my rage."

As he gazed at her, his face pale and helpless, Ann could feel herself getting warm. *What am I supposed to say, Robert? I'm not a priest. I can't give you absolution. I'm not even sure you deserve it.* "I guess I'm surprised you could slip into that kind of thinking so easily. It's frightening how quick it can happen, isn't it? But then you did grow up in a house full of phony Mayflower descendants, lording it over their Puerto Rican maids and Mexican gardeners like medieval noblemen. They send off a check to the NAACP every year to show how enlightened they are but refuse to meet their daughter-in-law's parents."

"My family? What about your precious brother with that bogus 'Afrocentric' education he forces down kids' throats? He won't even talk to us."

Ann was on her feet at once, her face burning. "Don't start in on my family, Robert. That's an argument you're not going to win." Quickly crossing to the dresser to get her nightgown, she yanked open the top drawer. Robert was going on about his parents, but she couldn't hear him for the fierce buzzing in her ears. For a long moment she didn't move. The nightgown she wore last night was scrunched up and shoved to the rear. That's not how she left it. Her winter flannel nightgowns had been moved to the front. She slammed the drawer shut and opened the next one. Her panties looked as if they had been pawed over. Or had she just shoved everything in here after doing the washing yesterday? It was possible, as upset as she had been. But no, she was too much a creature of habit to do that. She spun around. "Robert, someone's been in here."

"In the bedroom? What do you mean?" His voice was still angry.

"This dresser isn't the way I left it. Did you rummage around in here?"

"Of course not. Are you sure? Could you be imagining it? What's not the way you left it?"

"My God." She hurried into the bathroom. "I can't believe this is happening," she whispered, remembering again the unmistakable feeling of dread she had while staring into the darkness at Edgerton Lee's party; the way it made the skin on the back of her neck crawl. "What's going on, Robert? What's happening to us? What haven't you told me?"

"What's that supposed to mean?" He followed her into the bathroom.

I don't know what I mean, she thought as she yanked open the medicine chest and glanced at Robert's shaving supplies. *I don't even know how much I understand the man I've been married to for twenty-two years. I just know it's going to get worse.*

"There is no more," he went on weakly as she began pulling the half-dozen bottles of prescription drugs off the shelves and looking at them. *What if they had been tampered with? How could she tell?*

"Just hang on a few days, Ann. This is all going to go away. The police don't have anything to charge me with. It's just this madman DeFazio. He's obsessed, trying to get back at RULA because of his friends. But it'll be OK, like it was, like we want it to be."

Filled with fury she whirled around, felt her arm fly up as though she was going to strike him. "No, Robert. No. It will never be like it was."

She spun back to the medicine chest. *Was it all like she had left it? Had someone rearranged things?* She felt like screaming.

20

ROBERT couldn't help feeling dragged down by his own despair as he drove in to Dohr, Haskins, and Poole the next morning. Ann had scarcely spoken to him at breakfast, and JG stayed in his room long enough to make it plain he had no intention of going to school. Or seeing his father. *I'm a pariah*, Robert thought, at the same time sensing that feeling sorry for himself was a fool's game. But he couldn't help it. This was something new and frightening, becoming the monster no one wanted to be with. Why were people always so eager to think the worst? Ann, DeFazio, Stackhouse. Even John. They had already convicted and condemned him. But there was no denying it was his own fault. For twenty-two years he'd lived a lie because he had been afraid to tell Ann the truth.

Then he heard his name on the car radio and his heart stopped...

"...another bizarre development in the death of Nazia Chaudhary, the woman killed when two men allegedly tried to force her into a van last month. Police sources indicate today that Robert Binder, the passerby whose intervention resulted in the death of Ms. Chaudhary, was involved in another shooting twenty-four years ago..."

A black wave of fury rose up in front of his eyes. *DeFazio again. He's going to push and push and push until... what? What does he expect to get from this harassment? Does he think I'll suddenly come running into the police station, begging to be arrested?*

He couldn't let them do this. If he had learned anything in his twenty-plus years as an attorney, it was to fight back. Starting with Luis and the ILP. He pulled abruptly off Figueroa and aimed the Saab toward Otis just as his cell phone rang.

"You could have warned me," Edgerton Lee bellowed from Washington D.C. "How long have you known this was going to be in the news?"

"I'm as shocked as you are," Robert shot back. "That idiot policeman was out at my place last night to crow about the ILP digging up this little piece of character assassination. He also promised he wouldn't tell the press. So much for the LAPD's alleged integrity."

"It's true, then?" Lee's voice leapt up. "You shot a man twenty-four years ago and didn't tell me?"

"Edgerton, I didn't see the need to tell anyone. It was a lifetime ago, old news. For Christ's sake, I wasn't hiding anything. It wasn't a crime. There was an intruder, I tussled with him, I shot him in self-defense after he murdered my wife. I was considered a hero, for Christ's sake."

"Not exactly the story the Boston police gave out."

"Wrong. Edgerton! *Exactly* the story the police gave out. Somehow DeFazio managed to rustle up a retired cop who claims to remember what happened a quarter-century ago. He's an old man, he runs a bar. He probably can't remember what happened last week."

"And the Inner-City Law Project is responsible for this? I thought these people were friends of yours."

Robert blew out a long sigh. "Yeah." *How do you explain that?*

"You should have told me, Robert. You should have told me when we first started talking about an appointment in D.C. I've already had calls from three reporters wanting to know what I planned to do about your appointment."

"Edgerton, it was a quarter-century ago. I wasn't arrested. I wasn't a suspect. There's no police record anywhere in the world with my name on it. If my wife hadn't died I'd have been given a medal, for God's sake." He paused, feeling the blood pulsing in his neck and chest and the very tips of his fingers. "I didn't think anyone would ever hear about it, to tell the truth."

"There aren't any goddamn secrets any more, Robert," Lee bellowed. "We live in a society gorging itself on disclosure and public embarrassment. If you were disciplined in kindergarten, someone's going to find out." He took a breath. "My immediate thought when I heard this was to wash my hands of the appointment, and RULA, and especially you. But what RULA does is too important. Frankly I don't give a damn if you bleed all over the network news. I don't give a damn if your law firm sends you packing. But I do care about getting this project through Congress, and like it or not it's associated in everyone's mind with Edgerton Lee and Robert Binder."

"I could take my name out of the nomination process," Robert said, feeling both sick and combative, though the tiny portion of his mind that remained dispassionate was warning him not to let emotion destroy the rest of his life. In a few weeks this would all be old news.

"Too goddamn late for that. The hearings are scheduled. RULA *is* Robert Binder, and both are going up to the Hill to be judged in front of the nation. You're going to have to convince people that your model for legal aid for the poor is more important than anything that happened in your personal life." Lee's voice suddenly sank. "What race was he?"

"What? Who?"

"The man you killed in Boston. What race was he?"

Jesus. His heart seemed to sink to his knees. "White, Edgerton. Just like me."

"Thank God for that. Can you imagine what Bobby Stackhouse would do if he hadn't been?" He hung up.

Hurrying through the law school's paneled corridors on the way to Dean Salas's office, Robert saw Luis Teague deep in conversation with Karel Jirasek outside the copy room. *What the hell...?* Luis looked up abruptly, color rising in his cheeks when he noticed Robert bearing down on him. But before either man could speak, Jirasek stepped between them.

"I don't believe it, Robert. Not a word. No one does. Just more of the attack by innuendo America has become so enamored of."

Ignoring Jirasek, Robert said to Luis, "What the hell are you doing helping Chaudhary? The man's trying to ruin me. He's probably trying to work up a civil suit for damages. All because I tried to protect his wife."

Embarrassed, the large man shoved his hands in the pockets of his baggy trousers. He tried for heartiness and failed because he knew he was at fault, and there was no way he could avoid it. "I meant to alert you, but it was all so sudden I didn't have a chance. I was going to call you at DHP this morning. This is your day downtown, isn't it?"

Robert couldn't control his fury. "Now you have the LAPD persecuting me because of something that happened twenty-four years ago. Something you more than anyone knows

I wasn't at fault for. What are you thinking, Luis? What's the point of this?"

"I'm sorry, Robert. I'm not all that sure what's going on. I felt because of our friendship I couldn't get involved when Chaudhary came to us for help, so I turned it over to a team of interns. I told them they'd have to use law-school professors, rather than the ILP, for any courtroom work, if it came to that. I didn't want to know anything about it. I wasn't even in the loop until last night. But I couldn't very well turn the man away. I think one of the interns decided to check with the Boston and New York police departments. It's what they've been trained to do. But you know that. Hell, you've trained some of them."

Two professors, a wiry, white-haired tax attorney, and a young woman who had been hired this past fall to teach administrative law, squeezed past them in the hall, averting their eyes but soaking up every word.

"What about that parking ticket I got in Manhattan when we were at Columbia? Did you tell the interns so they could mention that to the LAPD, too? Christ, Luis, you went back twenty-four years to take an act of self-preservation and turn it into something horrid. It's completely irrelevant to what happened with Chaudhary's wife and you know it."

"Robert, you're an attorney. You know everything's relevant. That doesn't mean it's legally meaningful, of course. I agree this was unfortunate—I wish it had never come to light. Hell,

I wish Chaudhary had never come to the ILP. But once he did, we couldn't turn him away."

"*I was exonerated, Luis!* Did that fact get mentioned in the news reports that are all over the city by now? Or would that merely get in the way of the anti-RULA, anti-Binder sentiment that's driving this madness?"

Karel Jirasek put a hand on Robert's shoulder. "Please, you must see that this is not personal. The ILP was set up to help those who couldn't afford legal representation. The fact that you or anyone else has a connection to Otis doesn't mean you should be excluded—"

"Don't get cute with me," Robert snapped, pulling loose from Jirasek's hand. "If you were dean RULA and the ILP wouldn't last a week. You detest everything we stand for. You've never done a minute's worth of pro bono work in your life."

"Actually," Jirasek said softly, "everyone in my office gives half a day a week to pro bono work. Including me. And I was just telling Luis that when I'm dean I'm going to make a concerted effort to boost ILP funding by at least a million dollars a year. I'm sure I can raise that from just two or three philanthropic organizations I have ties to."

Robert spun on his friend. "Is that what he's promising? Money for the ILP? He's buying votes?"

"I don't think that's fair," Luis said uneasily. "Just because you or I don't agree with his views on some issues doesn't mean the man is wrong about everything."

"In fact, Robert," Jirasek said, "since my practice is separate from both Otis and the ILP, I could represent you without any conflict of interest."

"*What?*"

"I'm offering you my services. Gratis, of course. As a colleague. And a friend."

Robert felt like laughing. "You're nuts."

"You can't represent yourself. I'm a disinterested party. I would be proud to help."

"I don't need help. I'm not going to be charged with a crime. I didn't *do* anything, goddamn it. I was *helping* that woman. Can't anyone see that?"

"But certainly it's the *perception* of what happened you need to be concerned about. Please —"

"Maybe you ought to let Karel represent you," Luis said. "I'm in charge of the ILP so I can't get involved. But as Karel says, he's disinterested, and offering to help."

This is madness, Robert thought. *It's goddamn crazy, the world turned upside down.* He didn't know what to say. He shook his head repeatedly as he tried to clear his thoughts. Then he remembered Raul Salas. Maybe the dean could get the LAPD to back off.

"I'm afraid he's not in," Diana Charon, his secretary, said. "Going to be gone all day."

"His car's in the parking lot. I saw it."

"He left with someone. I think they're down-town."

"Jesus," Robert said with an angry sigh. "Is he that leery of me?"

Diana Charon, loyal servant, frowned. "Sorry?"

"Forget it." Robert spun on his heel and headed out of the building. Halfway across the quad he saw a gaggle of reporters and TV cameras hurrying in his direction. They hadn't noticed him, or perhaps didn't know what their quarry looked like. But he was taking no chances. Spinning around he walked swiftly back into the building, and all the way to the rear where a stairway led down to the basement and another door that opened onto a series of narrow tunnels connecting the library to each law school building. Known as the Catacombs, they had been designed to expedite the transfer of heavy law books and records from one building to another but now were seldom used.

Trying not to breathe in the stink of decay and rot that seemed to surround him as he hurried through the underground passageway, he felt a surge of fury toward Luis Teague. What the hell was he conspiring with Jirasek for? Because the man promised him increased funding? Of course money to keep programs alive was everyone's main concern at Otis, but there was no way Jirasek would keep his promise once he became dean. There was only so much pie to cut up, and if he knew Jirasek he'd probably promised 150% of it by now.

Jesus, it stank down here, like an old Roman mausoleum. You could practically feel water bleeding through the walls. Somewhere ahead of him he heard a rat hiss with fury and clatter away. No wonder everyone kept out.

A ramp at the end of the dark passage led to the rear of the library. Robert hurried up, pushed on the door, and found himself in a rear corridor of the large building. A dozen library offices led off to the right and left. He strode at once to the door leading to the parking lot and exited into the sunshine. Blinking at the sudden bright light, he was almost to his car when he saw someone waiting for him. Realizing who it was he wheeled around, hoping to escape, but it was too late.

21

JG's shyness was painful to watch as he said, "Hi, Mom. Meena Chaudhary is here."

Ann had come out of the kitchen when she heard the front door open and close. Seeing Meena and JG, she went through a range of emotions: surprise, concern, and finally a mother's pleasure as she saw how proud and excited JG was to be displaying his new girlfriend. "I'm delighted to see you again, Meena. Come on into the living room where it's cool."

The girl smiled, beautiful white teeth sparkling against the intense cocoa color of her skin, and held out her hand. *Both pretty and polite,* Ann thought, *and not nearly as cowed as she'd seemed when her father was here.*

"We just stopped by for a minute, Mom. We might go up to the mall and hang out for a while, maybe get a juice or cinnamon roll or something."

Meena was wearing sneakers, faded jeans, and a white and blue top, all very American school-girlish. "Why don't you have dinner with us tonight?" Ann asked. "Robert's doing something with lamb, I think. We'd love to have you." Then she thought, *Maybe not. Robert wasn't going to want any of that family around here. Chaudhary wouldn't permit it anyway.*

But the girl was already declining. "Thank you, but I can't. I have to watch my little brothers now that Raj works."

"I'm going to get us a Coke," JG said, and hurried into the kitchen, coming out almost immediately with two cans. He opened one clumsily, spilling some of the drink on his hand, and gave it to Meena. *God, he can't help himself,* Ann thought, and felt a rush of warmth for her son. *Bless you, boy. For feeling, for love. And bless you, Meena, for enchanting this too-reserved child who has had enough bad times lately.*

"We can't stay, Mom. Is Dad here? I thought we ought to say hi. You know—"

Of course. After the blow-up. After the distrust and shock and anger. "He's still at the office. I'm sorry." Later, when she could see JG privately, they would have to talk about this relationship. After seeing how happy he was, she didn't want to tell him not to see Meena, but maybe they better keep things low-key for now. She said to the girl, "Does Raj work around here somewhere?"

"On Wilshire Boulevard at a supermarket. He stocks shelves at night."

"And your father hasn't found anything yet?"

She shook her head, her lips tightening.

"We better go," JG said. "Meena has to get back soon."

Unable to stop herself, Ann quickly asked, "Does your father know that you and JG—"

"It's OK, Mom!" JG interrupted. He held her gaze for several seconds until Ann said softly, "Don't be late for dinner, hon."

JG's face relaxed. His mother wasn't going to give him any trouble.

As Ann watched them walk out to the car— Meena almost as tall as JG—she saw him take her hand and not release it until he opened the passenger door. *God, he's lost,* she thought with a smile. *Lost in her beauty and exoticism. Our little intellectual is, after all, merely human. And she's clearly entranced with him also, the way her eyes keep going to his face, and her smile lingers when he looks at her. Good for them. Keep that feeling as long as you can, both of you. But the girl's also frightened to death. All the while she was in the house she had hardly been able to keep her hands from shaking. Had JG seen that, also?*

Left alone again Ann sank down on the couch. *Yes, keep that feeling, both of you. Let it lift you. Because it will fade someday. Or die. The inevitable casualty of the day-to-day interaction of any two people who live together. Like Robert and me.*

With most people it was the accumulation of a thousand or a million small hurts over the years that brought the relationship down. What Ann was experiencing, though, was the sudden devastation of an earthquake; one minute everything's OK, the next the ground falls away and you find yourself treading air.

But then, how many people neglect to tell their spouse they've murdered someone? Not murdered... *killed*. That distinction was important. If real. *Is it real, Robert? What were you thinking that night twenty-four years ago when your finger squeezed the trigger? Then repeated. Again. And again. And again. While that man lay dying at your feet. What was going through your mind as he died? What were you feeling?*

And Robert very much did feel. He was a man of emotion more than thought. *Heart over head*, her mother said after meeting him for the first time, just weeks after they began dating. Thinking back on it later, Ann realized it was pure chance that she and Robert had even met, let alone married. Her parents had opposed it from the beginning. "Think," her father said softly, inquisitively, "what your life will be like in twenty years. What will it be like for your children?"

Well, chalk one up for Pop. Twenty years on, things had become pretty bad. Though not for the reasons he had meant.

Ann's brother Harvey, a junior high-school principal in Baton Rouge, where they'd grown up, refused even to meet Robert, and he hadn't spoken to Ann since the engagement. But her sister Ginny's eyes glittered with excitement when she heard the news. She took Ann's hands in hers and said, "I think it's wonderful.

Show the world you don't give a damn what people think."

But Ann had never wanted to show the world anything. She wanted to be in love.

Years later she discovered Robert's parents had also opposed their marriage. Race, again, though they never explicitly mentioned it. They were embarrassed by feelings they didn't know they had until that moment. ("Leakage," Ann called this sort of unacknowledged prejudice.) Robert was furious with them, but he'd been furious with them all his life—angry at their wealth and pride and lack of family feeling. But he talked them over to his side. He could do that, convince people of anything. *Ah, the Art of Persuasion*, he liked to joke, as though he were writing a book on the subject. But he enjoyed that part of his life—arguing, cajoling, convincing.

Yet how different is that from lying, tricking, fooling? *For twenty-two years you lived a lie with me, Robert. And I never even suspected.*

When the phone rang she jumped in surprise. "Thought you'd like to know someone's been lurking around your house, hon," Beth Sylvester said.

"You mean hiding? Or watching?" Ann went to the front room and stared out the picture window.

"Sitting in a car down the street for ten minutes. Finally walked over to your place. I thought I saw him looking in a side window. Soon as I got my phone he came clickity-clack out of your rear yard and be-bopped out to his car. Not a friend of yours, I take it."

Ann was still staring outside. "What did he look like?"

"Early twenties. Dark. Dirty jeans and faded T shirt. In a ratty-looking blue Honda held together with spit and duct tape."

Ann said it probably wasn't important, but she'd keep an eye out for him. And keep her doors locked. "Let me know if you see him again."

She headed toward the back door but was stopped by a glimpse of the rose bushes. She had wanted to spray them with an organic insecticide Beth had brought over in an ancient Tupperware pitcher. She wondered if she would get to it before they were destroyed by whiteflies. She wondered when she'd finish painting JG's room. And where JG and Meena were... if they were as happy as they seemed. If they talked about Meena's mother.

"How much time do we have?" JG asked as he aimed his Passat south along Vermont.

"Forty minutes." Meena glanced hesitantly at him, then turned toward the front of the car.

Feeling the joy of the afternoon, JG flipped the radio to an oldies station. Bob Marley singing about "...burnin' and a lootin' tonight – burning all illusions tonight." *Tell me about it,* he thought, but said, "Let's go to that shopping center on Jefferson."

"What are we going to do there?"

"I want to buy you something."

She smiled, sending his heart soaring. "A cinnamon roll?"

"You'll have to wait. It's a secret."

Pulling into the left-turn lane, he stopped at the light, tapped his fingers on the steering wheel in tune to the music. He still couldn't believe he was here alone with this marvelous girl. *It's a miracle, there's no other explanation.*

Out of the corner of her eye Meena caught him staring. "What are you doing? Watch the road."

"You're beautiful. I'd rather watch you."

She smiled again, but uneasily now, and turned toward the passenger window so he could only see the back of her head. JG laughed. Any part of her was worth staring at, even her neck, which was suddenly flush with embarrassment. *Bliss it was to be alive, but to be young was heaven.* Words from some poet they'd read in his English class last year. And suddenly he understood. Bliss, yes. Heaven, yes.

They'd been seeing each other almost daily for three weeks now, since the day after their families had dinner together. JG had shown up at Manual Arts after school the following afternoon, and when Meena and another Indian girl exited the school he maneuvered himself in front of her, tried to keep his knees from knocking together, and said, "Hi. Remember me?"

She looked shocked, then smiled, and his heart went at once to two-hundred beats a minute. It had hardly slowed since.

So how is this so different from Sonja or any other girl? he wondered now. It just was—night and day. Sonja was attractive and popular and he could remember too well losing his heart to her, as well as the terrible darkness that came over him when she broke it off. Even so, he'd felt vague and stupid around her, as though he was going to say something idiotic, or trip over his feet, making her laugh in that sarcastic way of hers. But Meena wasn't like that. He never felt tense, never afraid she was going to make him feel klutzy. Everything about her was bright and new and *magical*—the gentle hesitant sing-song of her voice; the black, knowing eyes at once so innocent yet sensual; the nutmeg-colored skin, not so different from his, and soft as a cloud. She was like a gift unexpectedly and undeservedly yielded up from the earth and offered to him.

Still staring out the passenger window, Meena said, "I got an A in our Geometry quiz today. I think I'll get an A in the class. Not in Science, though. I wouldn't cut up a frog and the teacher gave me an F on the assignment."

Making conversation. Grades! Like adults talking about the weather or sports. *Hot enough for you? How 'bout them Dodgers?* Shit, he didn't care. Whatever she had to say was OK by him. He felt her eyes on him, but when he looked over she turned away with a smile. She didn't wear lipstick, or use any kind of makeup, as far as he could tell. Probably not allowed to. But she didn't need it. *She's perfect.* Especially the bow-string tautness of her body, the sweet ripe taste of her tongue and mouth, the suppleness of her flesh. He moved his mind away, embarrassed at what was happening beneath his jeans.

Meena smiled suddenly, touched his arm, enthusiastic. "I want to meet your friends. All of them. I want to know all about you, where you like to go, the movies you like, the music you listen to." Her eyes glowed, seeking a connection, and this touched him deeply. Without even trying she'd slipped under his defenses. Then he realized: the shell was nowhere to be seen and it didn't bother him at all. For the first time in his life he didn't need it.

"I don't have any friends," he said honestly. "Not really. Just kids from orchestra."

"Good!" she said as though it was the answer she was hoping for. "I'll be the only one." Still smiling, her voice turned somber. "You're my only friend, too. The kids around here don't like people from India. They think we study too much. Or they say we're stuck up." Her voice dropped to a whisper. "And my father—"

"I know." She wasn't allowed American friends. Black friends especially, from what she'd already let drop.

He turned suddenly into a 7-Eleven parking lot. "What do you want to get here?" she asked, looking at the run-down stores.

He switched off the engine and reached over, taking her in his arms. When he kissed her, she frightened him by drawing back, as though repelled. Then her mouth partially opened and she responded with a tenderness that excited him more than he could believe. He felt there was enough electricity in the car for it to spontaneously combust.

After a moment she said anxiously, "Someone might see us."

"Your father doesn't have any friends, does he? He doesn't even know anybody in L.A."

"I'm not sure. Sometimes he goes away for hours. I don't know what he does or where he goes."

"Well, he doesn't hang out in 7-Eleven parking lots. He doesn't even have a car, does he? What does your brother drive?"

"A Honda Civic. An old blue one with dark windows so you can't see inside."

"I'll keep an eye out for it. But this is stupid. Why does anybody care? This isn't the eighteenth century."

Her body tensed but she didn't say anything. She never said a negative thing about her family. JG took her hand, felt it tense beneath his touch. "My father—" His voice broke and he hesitated. He knew it would be difficult to do, but this was why he pulled in here and he was determined to finish. "My father feels terrible about what happened, Meena. It's hard for him, too." Christ, what a stupid way to start. How could he compare what his father feels to what she and her family were going through?

He could tell she didn't want to talk about it either. "I know."

Forcing himself to go ahead, he said, "It's changed him. He has all this shame and it's eating away at him because he doesn't know what to do about it."

Meena's tone remained neutral. "In India people are killed because someone feels shame. Even now. Honor killings. Raj and my father tell me stories."

JG felt sick as Meena stared down at their entwined hands. He wanted to hold her, feel her body next to his. But he could sense her stress and knew this wasn't the time.

"My father hates your mother." The words were so abrupt, yet so soft, JG wasn't sure he heard correctly. His *mother*? Meena looked into his face. "He told Raj it wasn't right. He was shouting at him last night. He said why should your father have a wife after what he did?"

This made no sense to JG, but he said, "He's upset. I understand that."

"No, no, no. It's more than that. Different. I can't explain. He just... He doesn't think like you and me. He blames everything on your family now. Not just what happened to my mother, but being out of work, and Raj having to take a job—"

"You mean it's like a feud to him? He has some idea for revenge on my dad? Or mom?"

"I don't know. He doesn't talk to me about it. I'm a girl. Only Raj. And Raj won't say anything. But it scares me."

"He wouldn't do anything violent, would he? He's not like that." He knew what the police said about Chaudhary, but he wasn't about to tell Meena.

She hugged herself. "He calls her 'whore' and 'nigger.' Your mother. I don't know why he hates her so much. She didn't do anything to him." Her voice sounded small.

JG put his lips on hers, felt the heat of her. "Come on, relax. He won't do anything. This is Los Angeles, not Madras. Let him be angry if he wants to. What our parents think doesn't affect us." His mom was obviously upset at seeing him with Meena, but it didn't matter. They didn't need to involve their parents. Meena would be the single thing in his life that was his alone, the first time he'd done anything without some adult hovering over him.

Meena went rigid in his hands, and her lower lip trembled. Frightened at the changes he saw, he kissed her, at first tenderly, then passionately as she responded. Suddenly she wrapped her arms around his neck, holding on like a child. "I love you," she whispered, her voice urgent and cracking because it was the first time she'd said these words to him, maybe the first time she'd said them ever.

A tremendous calm settled over JG, a feeling like he'd never experienced. *This was the way we should always feel*, he thought, wanting it never to end. "I know." He kissed the tip of her nose then broke away and turned the key in the ignition. "We have to hurry. I need to get your present."

"What is it?" She was smiling again, excited, happy.

"A cell phone. You're the only person in California without one."

"But my father—"

"He won't know. We'll get a tiny one you can keep hidden in your purse. I'll never call you. But you can use it to call me. Or the police. Whoever. It's for safety. Really. You ought to have one. After all, Manual Arts—" He couldn't tell her the real reason was that she lived with a crazy man.

As they pulled into the shopping center parking lot she said in a trembling voice, "Before we go in... I need to tell you something."

JG switched off the engine, feeling the elation of just minutes ago vanish. His body turned cold and the world outside the car faded to black. "I'm not going to like this, am I?"

22

THE moment he saw Sandeep Chaudhary standing by his car, Robert wanted to hurry back to the library. But Chaudhary's insistent voice reached out to hold him. "I have been waiting for you, Mr. Binder."

Embarrassed, he turned back. "Hello, Sandeep. How are you?"

"I wanted to see you."

Robert looked around, hoping someone else was nearby, but there was no one. Then he thought, *What the hell, the man wasn't going to assassinate him. He just wanted to talk, to try to intimidate.* Anyway, maybe Robert could find out what the hell Chaudhary expected to get out of the ILP. "Yes. Well. Nice to see you again." He forced a small smile as a drop of sweat dribbled along his ribs.

"I waited two hours."

"And here I am. What can I do for you?"

Chaudhary was dressed in worn blue slacks, leather sandals without socks, and a tattered long-sleeved white shirt that was several sizes too large. He seemed frail and weighed down by grief. His eyes went to a spot on the ground half-way between the two of them. "My wife is dead, Mr. Binder. I keep wondering why."

Robert aimed the remote opener at his car and felt a ray of reassurance as the lock shot up. "I hope you understand how sorry I am about that, Sandeep. I would give anything to make that night just disappear."

"Now I have to take care of my children in this terrible city without any help. How am I supposed to do that?" His dark eyes rose to Robert's. "Tell me, sir. How am I supposed to do that? This was not a mistake. You did this on purpose."

"You know that isn't true, Sandeep. I was trying to keep her from being kidnapped."

"It is your responsibility to help my family now. What are you going to do?"

Robert felt a warming burst of fury but tried to tamp it down. "I'm trying to find a job for you. I have the law school working on it." *If you're really interested.*

The small man turned abruptly away and began to stride back and forth along the row of cars, his head bobbing up and down. He seemed disoriented with emotion. Sorrow? Anger? Robert wasn't sure, so mercurial were his moods. In the distance—it couldn't have been more than three blocks away—an ugly plume of black smoke was rising into the sky. A home burning? Where were the fire trucks? Then he realized with a sigh that it was just the film company, burning for make-believe.

Chaudhary's voice rose sharply as he continued pacing in front of Robert, his sandals slapping angrily against the asphalt. "Nothing good has happened since I came to this country. Nazia is murdered, Meena is acting like American trash, my little boys yell and scream and never stop running around when I'm trying to think. Only Raj is good."

"I know it's difficult being an immigrant, Sandeep. But I'm hoping a job will turn up soon."

"How do you know what it is like?" Chaudhary stomped up to Robert, close enough for Robert to see the perspiration trembling from his mustache. "Tell me that. How do you know?"

"I've spent a lifetime trying to—"

"It is your responsibility, your fault. You! My life is ruined." The man's hands tightened into fists, and he was almost jumping off the ground in rage.

Robert's hold on himself began to loosen. *Don't blame me for everything that's happened to you. You've been out of work for more than a year. How am I at fault?* His angry tone matched the other man's: "Why did you go to the Inner-City Law Project? What are you really after?"

Chaudhary looked at Robert with surprise, and a sudden calm seemed to come over him. The tiniest of smiles appeared on his unshaven face. "They are here to help the poor. You told me about them yourself. Yes, yes, you did. Remember? 'Go to the Inner-City Project for help,' you said. These young people are very nice. They told me how you killed Nazia because she was Indian, she was immigrant. What does it matter if she dies, this woman with dark skin?"

"No one told you that. Her death was an accident."

"They are very smart, these young people, very active and concerned. They know I have been mistreated. This happens all the time, they said. This Los Angeles is evil, very hateful to people like me. But they will help me get justice."

"Justice? Or money? That's really it, isn't it?" Of course. Everything boiled down to the essentials, Indian or American.

Chaudhary turned slowly away and stared at the plume of black smoke now dominating the sky, then looked at the Saab as if for the first time. He ran his fingers slowly over the polished surface of the fenders, and seemed to be regarding his reflection in the glossy yellow paint. "You are rich, Mr. Binder. My family has nothing. That is not right. Nazia worked in a restaurant to help us. Now there is no money since you killed her."

"She was a prostitute!" Robert blurted out. A law school professor was heading to his car twenty yards distant. He halted a moment to look at the two men arguing, then continued on his way but moving more slowly than before.

Go ahead, listen to us, Robert thought angrily. *Get some gossip for the faculty lounge.*

Chaudhary's body straightened and he stared at Robert with eyes that were preternaturally calm. "How would you know that, Mr. Binder?"

"The police told me!" *Don't do this,* a voice in Robert's head warned. *Stop right now, get in your car and drive away.* But he was somehow held by the man's gaze, the way his dark pupils had dilated with a sudden intensity. He really *is* insane, Robert realized. He had never seen true madness before, only on TV or in the movies. Now it was just inches from his face.

Chaudhary turned again to the car, fascinated, it seemed. He touched the surface, so highly polished it looked wet, and watched as his fingerprints formed on the paint. "She was not a whore."

"She was arrested, damn you."

The smile was suddenly confiding and intimate as he turned again to face Robert. "How much did you pay her that night?"

"Don't be ridiculous."

"It wasn't your first time." Chaudhary's voice was an anxious whisper that seemed to reach out and grasp Robert by the lapels. "She told me, Mr. Binder. For weeks she told me about you. I followed you to your home once. The rich attorney who paid Nazia for sex. I know all about you, for weeks I've known. I've told no one. Only you and I know. I have kept your secret. I have helped you. Now you have to help me."

"This is absurd." Robert reached for the door of his car but the small man pushed in front of him, his face trembling with rage. "Do you know what it is like for my children to see their mother called a whore? It was in the Hindi newspaper in Hollywood. Raj brought it home and showed me. Even Meena saw what it said. What shame this brings to us! Why would the police do this, put this where everyone can see it?"

"I don't know why they did it. It was wrong of them. But we can't keep things out of newspapers in the United States just because it upsets someone." Fleetingly he remembered his own anger at seeing his name in the *Times*.

Chaudhary grunted bitterly, and wheeled around, stalking away, then hurrying back as if he was going to strike Robert. "How is my family to eat? We have no money. No one will hire me to work in this country. They don't want people from India unless for taxi driver or work in convenience store. But I am educated man. I read Jane Austin, E.M. Forster, Nabokov. What am I supposed to do, put my daughter on the street? Or—" A sly look came over him, and his voice became confiding again. "Is that it? Do you want Meena now? Shall she come to live in your house? How much will you pay? Fifty thousand dollars?" He seized Robert by the arm and whispered urgently. "Fifty thousand and you can have her, my friend. That is not too much money for you. Think how *young* she is. She will be good to you. I know this. Only fifty thousand—" Suddenly he began to sob, and dropped his hands to his sides. "I am lying, I'm sorry, I don't mean it. I am desperate, there is no one for me to turn to."

"That's simply not true, Sandeep. I'm trying to help you find work. Others at the law school are trying. But these things take time."

Chaudhary ran a hand across his face, wiping away his tears. "Nazia told me she had a man in the neighborhood. A man who worked in the fancy law school. He liked her, he came to her five times. Five times he stopped in his car and drove her to the alley, Twenty-fourth Street, by Vermont. Behind the Exxon station. He gave her a hundred dollars each time. That was you, Mr. Binder. I waited and followed you home last month in your yellow car. Does your wife know? I will tell her."

"This is ridiculous."

"It was you. Nazia told me. She *laughed* at you. She said next time she was going to make you pay two hundred dollars. 'He will,' she said, 'he'll do it because he likes me, he likes what I do for him.'"

Robert pulled open the car door and started to climb in.

"*You owe me!*" Chaudhary screamed and grabbed furiously at him with both hands.

Quickly slamming the door, Robert yanked his wallet from his pocket and drew out all the bills he had. It was two or three hundred dollars, he knew. He buzzed the window down. "Take it, Sandeep. For food. Until we can find you a job." When Chaudhary didn't move, Robert stuffed the money in the man's shirt pocket, then turned the key, and the engine hummed to life. As he started to back up he saw the law school professor still staring at them from fifty feet away.

In a rage Chaudhary snatched the money from his pocket and threw it at the car, and they both watched as a gust of wind lifted the bills, sending them back toward the library. "You owe me for killing my wife," the man shouted. He could probably be heard all over the parking lot. Three or four other people were nearby now, also watching. "You did this to me, to my family. I want one million dollars, Mr. Binder. That makes up for what you did. One million dollars."

Robert's heart was racing wildly as he slammed his foot on the accelerator and shot backwards out of the parking space, almost hitting a Jeep behind him. Chaudhary was still yelling as he aimed the car out of the lot, the sky now black with smoke. The man was insane. Or was he? *Conniving* was a more likely term. He was laying the groundwork for a wrongful-death suit. Or out-of-court settlement. One million dollars! *You owe me!* Is this what the ILP had taught him?

Robert's fury abated sufficiently for him to realize he didn't know enough about Chaudhary to tell *what* he was after. He was clearly unbalanced, but was he really as dangerous as DeFazio said? *A borderline psychotic.* De-Fazio had enjoyed that, hadn't he? Maybe it was true. Or was this all an act? *Do you want Meena now? Shall she come and live in your home?* He had to be crazy. Still... He needed to find out about the man's history. But how? Then he remembered Asha Vatsyayan—a sociologist at UCLA, a lovely woman, and a scholar well-known for her articles on the Indian Diaspora. He'd helped her last year when one of her students was threatened with a slander suit for what he said about an L.A. councilman's real estate dealings in Watts. Even if she didn't know Chaudhary, she would know someone who did. He grabbed the phone from his jacket pocket and quickly dialed Information. A minute later he was leaving a message on her machine. "I need some background on this man, Asha. Whatever you can find out. Please..."

Robert was convinced Chaudhary wasn't going to be content with yelling at him. He would do something. Robert had seen it in his eyes, the way he threw the money back. He would try to redress what he saw as the terrible wrong that had been done him.

23

"CAN you believe it?" Robert's heart hadn't slowed since speeding away from the law school parking lot, Chaudhary's voice following him as he passed the half-dozen faculty members who had gathered to watch their confrontation. "He was waiting for me. Waiting! He stuck his face right in front of mine. I could see his brown teeth and smell the ginger and coriander on his breath."

Robert and Ann were in JG's room. Ann was perched on an ancient wooden ladder, finishing painting the ceiling a dull red, the original color as far as they had been able to tell. *Keep working,* she had told herself all day. *Don't give yourself time to think.*

Unaware of her mood, Robert sank down next to Jake on JG's bed. "A million dollars! What does he think I'm going to do, write him a check? But it's nice to see he's assimilated our American values so well: the first thing he thought of was suing somebody."

"Of course, that's his right," Ann said, and regretted it at once. Robert was seeking sympathy, not an argument about rights versus opportunities. But she was finding it difficult to empathize, her own emotions numbed into lifelessness since discovering that he had been living a lie for all of their twenty-two years together. She wasn't sure things could ever be the same between them. Once broken, how do you repair trust?

Robert seemed scarcely to know she was in the room. "It's like he's stalking me. Waiting two hours at the parking lot so he could make a fuss in front of my colleagues, siccing the ILP on me, even pulling out the race card to toss in my face." He ran a hand through his hair, then looked up as if suddenly realizing he wasn't alone. "I'm sorry to put you through all this, Ann. Especially if it's created problems for you at the bank. I don't suppose Belasino is pleased to see the husband of a Fed employee held up to public ridicule."

"Forget Belasino. I don't care what he thinks." Scarlatti began drifting from the iPad she had been listening to, and she felt an additional twist of annoyance. Scarlatti always rubbed her the wrong way, made her want to scream. But everything made her want to scream today: Robert's dishonesty, JG's moodiness, Chaudhary and his absurd demands. *At least things can't get any worse*, she told herself. *We've hit bottom.* Then with a rising sense of superstitious dread, she thought: *Of course they can get worse. No matter how bad the world looks, there's a mathematically feasible chance that something else is waiting out there to fall on you like a safe dropped from the second story.*

Robert was saying, "...anyway, he knows better than to make trouble for an attorney. There's no way he can intimidate me. I'll keep him wrapped up in court for years if I have to. Even the ILP will give up on it when they realize how expensive it will be."

Balancing herself on the top step of the ladder, Ann turned sharply to glare at him, suddenly looking for a fight, wanting to scatter her anger like seeds in front of them both. "That's the sort of personal twisting of the law you always used to deplore."

"Ann, he threatened me! He's not interested in *justice.* He's not even interested in a job. Weren't you listening? He wants a million dollars. He sees this upper-middle-class white guy and thinks he'll play the guilt card. Only this time it's spelled g-i-l-t. This woman's death is like winning a lottery to him. Where else is he going to get money like that?"

"That's idiotic, Robert. Do you think he'd really rather have his wife dead so he could collect some money?"

"You didn't see him! He offered me his daughter, he was selling—" He stopped suddenly and asked, "Where's JG? Or do we ask anymore? I suppose he sees it as none of our business."

"Where do you think?"

"With the girl?"

"I imagine. It's only to take her home from school. Why, does it bother you?"

"Of course it doesn't bother me. Why should it? As long as Chaudhary doesn't find out."

"You're not upset that she's Indian? That her breath smells of ginger and coriander?"

"What the hell's happening here? Why am I suddenly suspected of something in everyone's eyes?"

"What about Chaudhary's wife? A nice-looking woman, according to the picture in the *Times*. Alluring. Was that important to you? Or her olive-colored skin? Are you attracted to dark-skinned women? I think it's a fair question, under the circumstances."

"Jesus." It came out as a whisper of disbelief.

Ann steadied her hand on the wall. She could feel the fierce pounding of her heart as the room began to fill with the toxic black cloud that hovers in the background of all twenty-year relationships, a compendium of everything said and not said, the hurts and angers and furies that never quite go away. "Look at the *Times*, Robert. It's on John's desk."

He reached over and snatched it. "Yeah? What?"

"Inside. You'll see it."

Feeling dizzy from the paint smell, he began to turn pages, then stopped at a half-page ad with a small photograph of his perplexed face, surrounded by masses of white space. The three-inch headline said, "ROBERT BINDER. WHY DID YOU STOP ON NORMANDIE AT 1:11 AM?" Small print at the bottom said "Paid for by the Inner-City Labor Project."

He crumpled the paper in his fist.

"What does it mean, Robert?"

"It doesn't *mean* anything. It's supposed to intimidate, to make me worry about what they might do next. Next week they'll come to me with some sort of out-of-court deal, involving money, of course." He put the heel of his hand against his forehead and pressed at the pain behind his eyes. "I've spent my life helping others. How has everything suddenly turned around to where I'm automatically the bad guy now?"

"Maybe there's a reason, Robert. Maybe if you had been more honest with everyone none of this would have happened."

"Honest about what? You mean Carolyn? I explained that. I didn't lie to you. You knew she was dead. That was the most terrible experience of my life. I was a wreck for months. OK, you're right; I should have been more open. You don't know how sorry I am that I wasn't. But once I didn't explain it to you, every day it became more and more difficult to change course. But I didn't lie, Ann. To you or anyone. You know that. I simply can't."

"And the prostitute?"

"For Christ's sake, she wasn't a prostitute! Or maybe she was, I don't know. Maybe that's just Chaudhary's latest scam. When he heard what DeFazio leaked to the press he must have thought he'd stumbled over a pot of gold. *A prostitute! That'll make Binder squirm.* But you heard what Meena said! It's not true. And even if it were, it wouldn't matter. I stopped to keep a woman from being kidnapped. Period!"

"You should have told me about Carolyn, Robert. Whether it was difficult to talk about or not, it was a part of you, something essential to who you are, something that needed to be shared. And you didn't do it. You made a conscious decision not to. Every day for the past twenty-two years you made a decision to lie to your wife."

Robert's head fell back and his eyes squeezed shut. He couldn't continue to go over this again and again. But Ann could, and had, for hours online with the *New York Times* and *Boston Globe*, reading twenty-four-year-old accounts of the break-in and shooting. The stories confirmed Robert's version of what happened that night, but it was a symptom of her mood that even that made her anger grow. "Why did you shoot him like that?"

"Like what?" Robert's head jerked forward. "What are you talking about?"

"In the back, Robert. How many times was it? Five? Six?"

"For God's sake, he was going to kill me. He had murdered my wife. What would you have done? Reason with him?"

"But in the *back*. After he was dead. What were you doing?"

"It was rage, Ann. Emotion. I was so filled with rage I couldn't help myself." His body rocked back and forth. "Ann, I'm the same person you married, the same person you've loved for twenty-two years. I haven't changed; I haven't somehow become a monster. Sometimes I think everything that's happened—Chaudhary, RULA, Otis, digging up this story from a quarter-century ago—is too much to be a coincidence. Someone's behind it. Someone's trying to ruin me."

Ann looked at him incredulously. "Who would do that?"

"Jirasek. Or Stackhouse. I don't know—"

"Why not both together? And maybe the two major political parties along with the Veterans of Foreign Wars and Girl Scouts. You're getting paranoid. These are *your* problems, Robert. Don't try to blame someone else." She snatched the brush up and turned away from him. "Someone tried to break into the house today. Beth saw him coming out of the backyard and called me. I found a tire iron by the porch. He may have been planning to pry open a window and got scared away."

"Chaudhary? What time was it?"

"Early afternoon. Beth said he looked young. Dark."

"His kid."

"I called DeFazio. He wasn't very helpful, but then there was nothing to report. Just that I found a tire iron. He isn't going to help us anyway. I suppose Chaudhary could just be trying to frighten us."

"If so he's doing a damn good job of it." Robert began to massage the back of his neck as Jake roused himself enough to jump off the bed and pad slowly into the hallway.

"He's obsessed," Ann said, staring at the wall. "It's a sickness, this fixation."

"Of course he is. I've been telling you he's psychotic."

"I don't mean Chaudhary. DeFazio. The way he's grabbed onto you and won't let up, like some modern-day Javert stalking Jean Valjean." She lowered the brush as she took in the ceiling. What had she done here? Even the thick crown molding wasn't going to be able to cover the blood red splotches she had somehow splattered all over the wall.

"I called a professor at UCLA," Robert said in a defeated voice. "A Hindu woman I know who teaches anthropology. She's pretty tuned into the Indian community here. I'm going to talk to her tomorrow about Chaudhary. Maybe she has some idea of how to handle him."

"If he's got the ILP backing him it doesn't much matter what she says. If you weren't an attorney I'd say you need a good lawyer."

He looked at her with a bleak smile. "Karel Jirasek offered to represent me. This is how screwy my life has become—the world turned inside out like a sweater so all the knotted-up confusion is on the outside for everyone to see. A sleazy ambulance chaser wants to protect me from a psychopathic Indian who acts like this is a blood feud from the Middle Ages."

Robert's phone rang and Ann began painting again, the swift, angry strokes of her arm making the paint leap across the ceiling. Robert didn't move, thinking he'd be better off not answering, but then he couldn't help himself.

"Barbara Parrini with Fox News in New York, Mr. Binder. How are you doing?"

When he said nothing, she hurried on. "We're very interested in having you appear on Hannity tomorrow night. To give your side of the story? It's a—"

Robert almost laughed. "You're kidding, right? Hannity?"

"You should want to defend yourself, Mr. Binder. All America seems to have convicted you of something—racism, lying, patronizing prostitutes, if not worse. Reverend Stackhouse is going to appear and—"

Feeling as if he had suddenly found himself sleepwalking, Robert clicked off the phone and let it drop to the bed.

24

LEAVING his office the next afternoon, Robert glanced warily around the parking lot, expecting to find Chaudhary waiting for him, but the man was nowhere to be seen. Nor was he the following day. Perhaps he'd had a change of heart and was through trying to intimidate him. *Don't kid yourself,* Robert thought. *People like that don't give up their obsessions. They pound away at them.* Especially now that the complexity of his grief had been reduced to a simple common denominator everyone could understand: "You owe me, Mr. Binder. I want one million dollars." *Nothing like putting a price on your sorrow.*

Even if Chaudhary wasn't lying in wait, the press was. Robert's problems had become the trough at which the media now gleefully gorged. The coincidence of two violent encounters with crime and death, though separated by almost a quarter-century, was too much for the topic-starved talk shows to ignore. *How could this happen twice to one person... Obviously a dangerous man to know... A hypocrite with his anti-*

police views. No wonder RULA always jumps in on the criminal's side.

Reporters swarmed the sidewalk in front of their home, aiming telephoto lenses at the windows. Ann couldn't even water the garden without having cameras pointed at her and questions hurled across the lawn: *"Did you know about the first Mrs. Binder?... Do you worry about your safety?... Is your husband a violent man?...*

Still, Robert felt a welcome wave of relief when he left school without incident. The instant he turned onto 26th Street, however, his heart sank. There were at least four or five hundred people, mostly college students, across the street from his home, exploding in rage the instant they saw his car. They were carrying signs and chanting something that sounded like "Can't hide here... Can't hide here..." A handful of policemen stood in the street, looking bored as TV cameras took it all in.

He could feel himself stiffen with anger. There was nothing spontaneous about this supposed outrage. It was theater. Twitter. Facebook. Instagram. Contrived passion. And the ILP was behind it. Who else could muster a crowd like this so quickly? A girl with a sign that said "Stop the Violence" ran screaming in his direction but was intercepted by a cop. Someone else threw something heavy that bounced off the rear fender of the Saab as he turned into the driveway. But the crowd remained on the other side of the street, content with chanting, "Murderer... Murderer... Murderer..." in a slow lugubrious dirge that sent chills down his spine.

The scent of blossoms was heady in the air of a delightful Southern California afternoon as JG and Meena walked through the formal rose garden in Exposition Park, just a mile from West Adams. Holding Meena's hand, JG felt its warmth and smallness and *promise* against his palm.

"I wish I could go to your school," she said in her soft, shy voice. "I hate Manual Arts. Every day there's trouble. This morning a girl set her boyfriend's car on fire because he was talking to another girl. So policemen and fire trucks came, and no one was allowed out at lunch. I usually just sit in the library anyway, so the boys won't bother me."

"It isn't any better at my school." He didn't tell her about his own problems, afraid it would make him look like a fool. Motioning her to a bench he said, "I want to show you how to use your phone." After she took it from her backpack he said, "Do you know how to text?" She didn't, so they played with it for ten minutes. Facebook she knew about from school, so he showed her his page and his parents', and RULA's, and finally the Eastman School of Music.

She stared at the pictures of students rehearsing. "My father hates all American schools. He thinks girls and boys shouldn't be together."

Her voice faltered and she turned to him. "I think he saw us together. I heard him talking to Raj. They were really mad about something. You're lucky. Your parents don't watch you like you're a little kid or yell at you all the time." She smiled shyly. "And your mother can help with homework, she's so smart. Your dad, too. No one helps me—"

JG dropped her hand. "Why are you talking about my parents? Talk about you. Or me. Or roses... or Manual Arts. Anything else!"

"I'm sorry. I didn't mean—"

"I'm sick of always having to be their son. Why can't I just be me?" Angry with himself, JG shook his head, slipped his arm around her waist, and they began to walk again. "Forget it. I'm just fed up with people telling me how lucky I am. *Your mom and dad are so nice, so smart, so perfect.* Who wants to live with that all the time?"

Silent now, they strolled past a score of rose beds, each a different variety and in a different stage of blooming. In the center of the garden a huge fountain sprayed water into a pool. Finally, JG said, "I'm sorry. But we don't get much time together. I don't want to spend it talking about my parents." His voice tightened. "Especially after what my dad did."

"Even though he didn't kill my mother?"

"Even though." He felt sweat prickling his back.

They walked on, sharing a secret. But also a new fear. It drew them together, made them closer. But it had a cost, JG knew, and soon it would have to be paid.

Just inside the front door, Robert stopped to gather the mail that had spilled through the slot. Politicians wanting money or help on election campaigns. A group of academicians doing studies of Title IX of the Civil Rights Act. And a letter from the Office of Representative Edgerton Lee in Washington D.C. He ripped it open and took out the embossed sheet of paper with its imposing seal of the United States House of Representatives. "Dear Robert, I'm sure you'll appreciate the sadness I feel at having to withdraw your name from consideration for..."

Robert's body went cold all over. Lee hadn't even had the courtesy to call first. Damn him! Forget HHS. Didn't he realize the damage this would do to RULA? Robert had spent twenty years on this project and now it was going to come crashing down because Lee didn't have the guts to stand his ground in the face of grossly unfair criticism.

But nothing had been released to the press or he would have heard it on the radio. There was time, then. He'd call Lee. They could talk, there was still a chance. But he'd have to do it now. He took out his phone and started to call when angry voices intruded from the living room.

Ann and...?

Robert dropped the phone and raced toward the voices. The moment he entered the large formal room, Sandeep Chaudhary leapt to his feet. "Where is my money, Mr. Binder? You said you would have it. You promised me. I want it now. This minute!" He was shouting and gesturing wildly, his spindly arms flying awkwardly about as though swatting hornets. In a pocket of his baggy trousers Robert saw one of Ann's small garden claws, only the pointed metal tines protruding.

Robert's gaze shot to the couch where an obviously shaken Ann was easing to her feet, her eyes silently warning him of the claw. Thank God she was OK, but why had she let the man in the house? Before Robert could react, Chaudhary bounded across the room, his eyes flashing like tiny chips of flint. "Why did you lie to me, Mr. Binder? You said you would get the money. We have no food in the house. What are we supposed to do? Is my family to starve because you killed Nazia?"

Robert tried to keep his voice calm. "Sandeep —"

The small man whirled around to look at Ann. "As I told you, one hundred dollars he paid to Nazia for sex. Each time one hundred dollars. We needed that money to live. Do you think I'm proud to tell you this? I am the man of the house. It is up to me to take care of the family but I cannot get a job. Only for that Nazia had to do what she did. It was how we eat, how we pay the rent. Only Nazia made money because Raj was in school. Now Raj has to work, and still it is not enough to feed five people."

It was time to put an end to this. "Sandeep, that simply isn't true. It's no good trying to intimidate me. I'm not giving you any money. And if you don't leave me and my family alone, I'm going to get a restraining order against you."

"A man from the law school!" Chaudhary was having little luck controlling his fury. "A stupid yellow car with many books in the back seat. Always late at night. Five times. He liked Nazia very much, told her how pretty she was. *Beautiful Nazia.* Someday, he said, he would get an apartment for her so she doesn't have to be with her family." His body froze and his eyes fixed on Ann, stunned at the audacity of it all. "My Nazia he wants all to himself."

"This is absurd," Robert said. He could feel his body getting warm. He had to get Chaudhary out of here and call Lee before anything about the appointment was released to the press.

But Chaudhary stepped in front of him, and poked Robert in the chest, leaving faint smudges that looked like blood on his shirt. "It is no good, Mr. Binder. You see, I followed you." Sweat prickled the small man's forehead and his muscles tensed, as if he was about to strike Robert. "Do you want me to tell the reporters about you? They call me every day. 'Mr. Chaudhary, what do you think of the man who killed your wife?' 'Mr. Chaudhary, why did Mr. Binder stop that night?' A supermarket newspaper offered me fifty thousand dollars just to *talk* to them. But I don't want their money. I want my wife's killer to pay."

"In America we have laws against libel and slander, Sandeep. I hope for your sake you remember that."

A sly look suddenly replaced the anger on Chaudhary's face, and his voice moderated. "Maybe we find Nazia's fingerprints in your car, Mr. Binder. What do you say to that? *Inside* the car. Or her hair? I watched you wash your car after you and your boy played basketball. I know what you were doing. But the police can find a single hair even after you vacuumed. I think I tell them."

Robert had turned stony. "Do as you wish. But leave my house. If you come back I will be the one to call the police."

Chaudhary stood frozen in a darkened square between twin shafts of brilliantly-colored light from the stained-glass windows. His mood again shifted and he sank into a truculent silence. Then his body began to tremble. "There's another way to get justice, yes? My way."

Ann came forward. "Please, Sandeep, what happened is terrible, but Robert was only trying to help. What you're doing now isn't right."

He turned to her with contempt but also, it seemed, a sense of deepened intimacy, of embarrassed but shared emotion. *We have this in common*, his eyes said; *we've both been betrayed by this man.* "Five times. Always late at night. Think, Mrs. Binder. What does your husband tell you when he is gone at night?

Does he have 'meetings'? Does he tell you he has to shop?" He paused as he looked into her eyes. "You know I'm telling you the truth. I see it in your face. You know!" He spun toward Robert, the garden claw suddenly in his hand. Traces of dirt and—what? blood? hair?—flew from the metal tines as his arm rose. "You are killing me! You ruin my family, you keep me from getting a job, you throw money at me in the parking lot so I have to crawl on the ground like a dog. I am a man, Mr. Binder, as good a man as you. I don't crawl in the dirt for dollar bills."

As Robert moved protectively in front of Ann the man seemed to lose all control over himself. He let out a low, anguished howl, his hand trembling high over his head, about to strike.

"Don't," Robert said more calmly than he felt. His arms came up protectively, but Chaudhary had reeled away and was stomping around the room, still wailing pathetically. "Why do you do this to me? Why do you hate my family?"

"Sandeep, I don't hate anyone..." His phone was in the entry hall. Before he could call 911 Chaudhary would be gone. But he could file a report and get the man arrested for threatening him, if nothing else.

Chaudhary suddenly whirled around again, facing him. "You think your money protects you. But you will never be rid of me, Mr. Binder. Not as long as you live." He moved toward Robert. As Ann screamed, "No—" Chaudhary's arm again flew up, the claw about to strike.

"You've done this to me." He was almost in tears. *"You've done this—"*

Robert lunged forward but Chaudhary yanked up his shirt with his left hand and brought the claw down like a hatchet on his own chest, raking the flesh. Ann gasped as a dozen spots of red blossomed in three parallel rows. "*You* did this," he repeated in a quivering voice. Again, the claw came down, harder this time, ripping more flesh. "*You* make me bleed. You are killing me. Do you understand? *You!*"

Robert's arms fell weakly to his sides. And as the two men locked eyes, Robert did understand; everything that was happening to this man was because he had stopped his car that night. But he stared dumbly now, unable to reply, his stomach sick. Within seconds blood covered Chaudhary's chest and belly and dripped onto the polished oak floor. Chaudhary dropped his shirt and immediately it clung to his flesh. "You owe me, Mr. Binder. And you will pay." Still grasping the bloody claw, he whirled around and stalked to the back of the house. A moment later they heard the door slam.

Robert started for the hall and his phone. "Did you notice how careful he was not to harm us? He's not going to risk jail when he can frighten us into paying him off."

"Robert, he *mutilated* himself. He doesn't know what he's doing. He's in agony over what his life's become. I don't think frightening you even entered his mind."

"And all this pseudo *indignation* of his, his little shared confidence with the aggrieved wife. *Think, Mrs. Binder. What does your husband tell you?* Goddamn it, why the hell did you let him in the house?"

"I didn't. I'd just come home. He was just sitting on the couch."

"*He broke in?*"

"I don't know. I haven't looked around yet. Maybe the back door wasn't locked. I saw the claw in his pocket, but he didn't threaten me. He looked as if he had been crying. Before I could say anything, he started talking about how he and I were alike, both outsiders, both mistreated by America. He said we should be friends. It was frightening to me, the way it seemed almost seductive, sexual in a creepy way. But when he started in on you and..." Her voice faltered. "...his wife ...how often it happened, and where, and what you paid her."

Robert began to pace, the phone at his ear. "Goddamn it, Ann, this is a scam. You know that. He's using it to destroy my family."

"Of course." In twenty-two years of marriage she'd never seen him come undone as he had in the past few days. A month ago she wouldn't have thought it possible. She asked softly, "Does he really think you'll pay him a million dollars?"

"Your first mistake was to use the word 'think.'" He pounded out the LAPD number on his phone. "Sergeant DeFazio or Oakley, please..."

When DeFazio's low rumble sounded on the line, Robert told him what happened.

"Did he take anything? Harm anyone?"

"Other than himself? It doesn't matter. He had no right to be here. He threatened us. He harassed my wife. He tried to convince her I'd been paying that woman for sex."

"So at least now we can agree she was a prostitute."

"Don't be an idiot," Robert snapped. "She was a waitress. You were the one who insisted she was a prostitute, so Chaudhary jumped on it. Anything that makes me look bad he's going to use to beat me over the head."

"Don't you think you're over-reacting Mr. Binder?" The voice of reason, of logic, the enemy of wild emotion, of cops running wild and cowboys with guns. "We're a nation of laws, Mr. Binder. What exactly would you have us do?"

"Talk to him! Let him know there's a law against breaking and entering. As well as extortion."

"If you wish you can come down to the station and file a complaint. But you should bear in mind that without proof to the contrary, it is not you but Mr. Chaudhary who is the aggrieved party here. It's his wife you killed."

"Meaning you'll do nothing," Robert said flatly. His heart slowed to a dull thud, and he stood rigid and alone in the center of the large room, feeling the sun like an icy hand on his back. "What if I hadn't been involved in the Omar Randall Stahr suit?" Stating the obvious now. "Would your willingness to help be improved?"

"Tell you what. We can set you up with a wire. Tell Chaudhary you've reconsidered and will pay whatever he wants. Maybe you can get him to say something incriminating. Of course, if he decides to frisk you there's no telling what he'd do. If he's as dangerous as you think."

Robert was silent.

"Sir?"

"I'll think about it," he said, though he wasn't sure how serious DeFazio was. But there was no way it would fool Chaudhary; the man had endless reserves of cunning and wasn't likely to be tricked.

Robert clicked off the phone and immediately punched out Edgerton Lee's home number. No answer, not even a voice mail. Damn the man! He tried Lee's D.C. number as he heard JG come through the front door. Lee's office was closed but a recorded voice asked him to leave a short message. "This is Robert, Edgerton. Don't release anything to the press about my appointment until we have a chance to talk. Call my cell phone, any time day or night. Please. I don't deserve to be treated this way."

Ann was staring at him as he slammed the phone down. "Later," he said as he saw JG standing in the doorway. His voice went slack as he said to his son, "Chaudhary offered Meena to me. He was *selling* her. His own daughter. For fifty thousand dollars."

JG's face seemed to drain of blood.

"I'm sure he didn't mean it," Ann said quickly. "He's upset; he doesn't know how to deal with this. Imagine yourself in his shoes. He's a stranger, an outsider, from this male-oriented, macho culture. Suddenly he's a failure as a breadwinner. On top of that his wife was killed."

JG said softly, "She wasn't his wife."

"What?" both Robert and Ann said at once.

JG shifted his weight from foot to foot. "I'm not supposed to tell anyone. I shouldn't have said anything."

"If she wasn't his wife, who was she?" Ann demanded.

JG looked as if he were about to bolt from the room. "Chaudhary's wife died in Singapore before he came to the U.S."

Ann's voice was shrill. "Then who was that woman?"

"Someone he met in Cerritos. She lived there, in his sister's house. Meena said she wasn't even Indian, she was from Bangladesh. She came to this country as a maid for some rich Indian family but ran away when the husband raped and beat her. Chaudhary's sister took her in, then Chaudhary made her come up to L .A. She helped pay their rent and food. I guess they needed her money."

Ann shook her head. "I don't understand, John. Why the secrecy? Why didn't they tell this to the police?"

JG stared at his feet; then his head bobbed up and he held his father's gaze. "She was a prostitute. She'd probably been a prostitute back in Bangladesh. She hadn't worked as a waitress for a year. Anyway, waitressing didn't pay enough money. Sometimes hers was the only money the family had."

Robert looked as though he had been kicked in the stomach. "I don't believe it."

Ann said, "Meena told you this?"

JG nodded.

"What else did she tell you?" Her voice was strained. There was more, she knew; he was holding back.

JG waved a hand—nothing. But color was rising in his face.

Robert looked at Ann. "I don't believe it. Chaudhary's trying some kind of con. He knows what DeFazio thinks, and that the newspapers said she was a prostitute, so he's going to use it somehow, make something out of it. It's just another way to harass me."

"But Sandeep didn't say it, Robert. Meena did. Isn't that right, John?"

JG nodded. "No one's supposed to know. Chaudhary's afraid he'll be deported. None of them are here legally. He doesn't even want to talk to the police because he thinks Immigration will get involved. That's why Meena lied about it earlier."

Ann turned to Robert. "How was she dressed that night? Like a hooker?"

"I don't know! This is ridiculous. It doesn't make any difference. Someone was attempting to kidnap her. I tried to help. I don't care if she was a hooker or a bank president. She didn't deserve what was happening to her."

"You're right," Ann said while a part of her mind said it made a hell of a difference. She added, "The effect on Sandeep is the same, no matter what she was doing to make a living. She was his only source of income. He wasn't able to support himself in America. He was living off a woman and now he can't even do that. His world's shattered. He must think it's come to an end. No job, no money. And alone with all those kids in an alien environment. If he were in India or Singapore it might be different, he'd have family for support. But here there's no one. He's a failure."

"What about me? Everything I've worked all my life for is being stolen because of an act of kindness. Even my family's safety. What else do I have to lose?" He put his head in his hands. "In India his family would insist on revenge. He'd call out a score of brothers and cousins and we'd all be dead." *Jesus*, he thought suddenly, *Edgerton's home phone!* He could get hold of him that way. He grabbed his phone. The phone at the other end of the line was ringing.

Lee's phone kept ringing and ringing. Suddenly Robert turned toward her. "Why didn't Jake bark?"

Her head snapped up. "What are you talking about?"

"If Sandeep came in through the back, Jake should have been going crazy when you got home." He said to JG, "Have you seen him?"

"No."

They hurried to the rear yard. The twenty-foot rope attached to Jake's collar to keep him from running away had been used to hang him by one leg from an orange tree. His chest had been ripped open, three parallel claw marks, and he'd bled to death.

JG screamed and rushed forward, tearing at the knot, and clutching the bloodied dog.

Ann felt her stomach knot. "My God..."

Robert went inside and called an alarm firm. They told him it would be a week before they could come out. Six other firms told him the same thing. Evidently people in Los Angeles were suddenly concerned about urban unrest. Gun sales were up also. "Folks are tired of being victims," one man said.

25

No crowd in front of his house this morning. But Robert knew it wasn't because the so-called "fury" of the mob had abated. They—whoever *they* were, the ILP probably—were planning something else, another "spontaneous" flash mob to get attention. Or something worse.

But there was already something worse when he walked into his office at nine AM. Immediately he sensed that something was wrong, was —*out of synch* was the only way he could phrase it to himself. He froze as his eyes raced past the aging futon and stuffed chair, the wall of photos, the end table and desk and windows, then abruptly back to the papers and reports on top of his desk. Everything was neat, orderly, and precise, and not in the least as he had left it. Hands shaking, he punched the intercom button for the secretary he shared with Luis. "Was someone in my office this morning?"

"Yesterday afternoon three men from Otis came over. Is that what you mean? They said you knew about it, it was an audit."

"Audit? What kind of audit?"

"I don't know. They took three boxes of stuff from your desk and file cabinet. And the account books from my desk. Also, your computer. But they gave you a new one."

"What? Why didn't you call me?"

"I did. But your voice mail was full. Anyway, they said you—"

Robert swore as he slammed down the phone. This was madness. Did the whole world expect him to just sit here and become everyone's willing victim? What was the name of the Deputy D.A. assigned to his case? *Scaggs*, he recalled Oakley saying, as he began punching in the number.

"To tell the truth, I don't think I should even be talking to you," Lyndell Scaggs said after Robert told her about Chaudhary's threats. She sounded about twenty-five but had already perfected the weary condescension that characterized the prosecutor's office. "We've been discussing you around here for several days now and haven't decided what to do."

"What to do? What to do about what?"

"Your creepy obsession with the husband of the woman you killed. None of us have ever seen anything like it. What are you trying to achieve by persecuting him? He's a victim, Mr. Binder. My God, you're responsible for his wife's death. Why don't you leave him alone?"

"He's a psychopath! Don't you and DeFazio ever talk? I want him arrested before he kills me or someone in my family. Is that so hard to understand? If nothing else, turn him over to Immigration so—"

"That's really the crux of the matter, isn't it?" That *knowing* tone again. "You want to use the man's undocumented status as a threat against him. You should know that sort of thing doesn't work with us, Mr. Binder."

"Stop being so damn self-righteous. The man threatened to kill me. He was in my home yesterday. *He killed my dog.*"

She almost laughed at the accusation. "Please, Mr. Binder. Sandeep Chaudhary is a Hindu. You should do a little research before you slander someone. Hindus do not kill, not even a mosquito or fly."

"Have you really not heard of the Pakistani war? Or honor killings, or the religious violence all over the country? What sort of closet have you been living in?"

Her tone turned cold. "I understand you're the attorney for Alban Zine." The White Power speaker who had been such a thorn in the side of the city.

"What's that got to do with anything?" There was a sharp knock, the door opening at the same time, and Luis Teague came in without being asked. Robert felt a surge of irritation, remembering their last encounter in the Otis hallways. But his friend smiled and held up a calming hand as he took a chair and whispered, "Be of good cheer, my son. I bring tidings of comfort and joy."

Lyndell Scaggs was saying, "You should look into your heart, counselor. Why are you so hostile to Sandeep Chaudhary while honoring a racist thug like Zine?"

"I can't believe you said that. But your department was embarrassed in the Omar Randall Stahr debacle too, wasn't it? I guess I shouldn't be surprised at any attempt to make me or RULA look bad."

"We've come to the end of our conversation, Mr. Binder. I advise you to stop harassing Mr. Chaudhary. And you may want to think about engaging an attorney. We haven't decided if we'll file charges on Mrs. Chaudhary's death but, speaking off the record, if I were you I'd be prepared. For reckless homicide if not murder."

"On what grounds?" he shouted. "What proof do you have? This is nuts."

"Oh come now. Do you really need me to lay it out for you? The woman was a prostitute. Her husband says you were a regular client. He was able to identify you and identify your car. After weeks of looking we can't find a single witness to anything you say, including the blue van. The crime scene was tidied up, there's no gun shells, no slugs, nothing but a dead body. You can't explain where you were for the thirty minutes preceding the shooting. Your past history of killing someone under similar circumstances, which you withheld from us. Like I said, you'd better get an attorney," she advised, and then she hung up.

Robert sank into a chair. "God save us from the D.A.'s sanctimonious underlings. Someone named Scaggs. Do you know her?"

Luis didn't.

"She thinks she has enough to charge me."

"Nuts."

"My word exactly." Robert stared hard at his friend. "So surprise me. Tell me your news is actually something I can be grateful for."

Teague's eyes glittered playfully. "Indeed it is. I received a visitation by the Federal Bureau of Investigation yesterday. A woman from the headquarters office in D.C., no less. It turned out to be a most enjoyable interlude in an otherwise dreary day, which concluded happily in her confiding that, news reports notwithstanding, the investigation into Robert Binder's background was complete, and that Congress would not be receiving a negative report."

"Congress doesn't need a negative report. Lee withdrew my nomination."

"He couldn't. He wouldn't. It's not possible."

"Nevertheless."

"Has he announced it?" An atypical shrillness sharpened Luis's voice.

"I don't know. I don't think so. I can't get him to return my calls."

Luis braced his feet, ready to get up. "Then I'll call him! I'll have Raul Salas call, too. We can't let this happen." His eyes locked suddenly on Robert's, and he froze in his seat. "Why now? Why at this late date? Has there been any news I'm not aware of?"

"Nothing," Robert said carefully, "except the intervention of the ILP."

Luis sank back and breathed out a remorseful sigh. "Robert, really, I'm devastated at how this has played out between you and the ILP. You don't know how much I wish Chaudhary had never come to us. But we couldn't turn him away merely because you're my friend. That's the sort of thing the ILP was set up to fight. There was no alternative but help the man out. At least to some extent."

Bullshit, Robert thought, the muscles in his neck tightening. *You could have told him you didn't have the resources... you could have told him he had no case. You could have simply said No!* But he was too tired and too upset to argue. Instead he asked about their other area of concern, the impending election. An accommodating dean might be able to keep RULA afloat until the next session of Congress, when Robert's troubles would be old news.

Teague's fleshy face worked into a scowl. "Things are a bit dicier than last week, I'm afraid. The Odious Karel is proving his mettle as a stretch runner. Of course, the finish line is just two days away. I'm not sure he has the time or stamina to actually move ahead. It would take changing several more minds."

"Which is why he's throwing money around like a Chicago alderman."

Teague turned serious. "I'm afraid I didn't make myself clear about that earlier, Robert.

Obviously, I support the man's attempts to increase funding for the ILP. It would be idiotic to turn money away. But I have no intention of helping him in his electioneering. In fact, I told him I was committed to Zalesky and couldn't support him even if Howard were to pull out."

"What did he say to that?"

"What could he say? He wept copiously, he rent his garments, he begged and pled. All to no avail, of course. But since it has pleased God to put him within the compass of our tiny world, we should try not to unnecessarily antagonize him. He has a peasant's primitive cunning and nose for revenge. Neither the ILP or RULA can afford an entrenched foe."

"*If* RULA survives. That is now highly questionable."

"You are too pessimistic."

"Realistic, Luis. Not pessimistic. We need to ensure its future. Independent of me." And with that, he made a decision about something that had been on his mind since yesterday's letter from Lee. He came to his feet and reached for the phone. "I'm going to call that woman from Channel 4 who's been after me for weeks. If I'm going to save RULA I can't let the *Times* or Bobby Stackhouse or social media dictate the tenor of the debate."

Luis was stunned. "Good God, Robert. What's come over you? *Never* invite trouble from the press. The FBI investigation is complete. I'll get hold of Lee this morning. I think I can convince him to back off and allow the process to work itself out. I'm sure that when the truth is known, Congress will do the right thing."

Robert almost laughed. "That's undoubtedly the stupidest thing you've ever said."

Teague was adamant. "You have little experience with television. You will not come out of this looking good. Don't do it."

"I've been on television any number of times, Luis. I know how to handle myself."

"In an interview, not an interrogation. I know the woman you're talking about. Her specialty is public humiliation. She'll crucify you. It's absolutely out of the question."

"Luis, I'm drowning. My side of the story isn't getting out—"

"There is another way. We'll have you take a lie detector test."

"You've got to be kidding. Not a chance."

"Why not? Even if it's not admissible in law it's vital in the court of public opinion. It'll set peoples' minds at ease about what happened that night. As well as in Boston."

"Come on, Luis. Lie detectors are hocus pocus, not science."

"It depends on the skill of the tester. I know the owner of Encore Investigations. They're sound, reliable people. They'll—"

"I'm not turning my future over to some warlock with an electronic dowsing stick. Forget it."

The air seemed to go out of Teague, and his arms hung loosely. "I'm disappointed."

"It's the way it has to be."

The other man pushed to his feet and began to pace. Suddenly his mood brightened and his face was transformed by a broad smile. "Well, sir, if you insist on holding a public lynching —" He waved his arms skyward, the old Luis Teague again. "We'll do it right. Not a one-on-one with Channel 4's resident gorgon but a full-bore press conference, peppered with friendly reporters as well as Buzzfeed and Huffington, and all the social media mavens. It'll be Come to Jesus time, your life as an open book. I'll set it up, since I've been doing this sort of thing for years." Luis the Impresario, the Master of Revels, was once more in his element, practically rubbing his hands together with anticipation. "We'll have Raul Salas there to bless the proceedings in person and add the imprimatur of the prestigious and progressive Cornelius Ryan Otis School of Law. And the marvelous Ann, of course. All our guns on deck, driving the doubters back into the hills. Let's say tomorrow afternoon at two. You can do that, right? Prepare your comments tonight, my boy. Absolutely no off-the cuff extemporizing. You will be facing piranhas, just waiting for the first drop of sweat to appear on your upper lip."

Robert was uneasy. "You're sure this is the way to go?"

"Absolutely. Give an exclusive interview and every other reporter in town will declare you anathema. They'll find ways to make Robert Binder look responsible for every depredation to happen in America since and including the

Great Depression. And this way I can plant some softball questions to make you appear not only innocent of all the rumors but the sort of man who would happily lay down his life in the pursuit of justice."

"You've got to be the most cynical person I've ever met."

"We live in cynical times, my friend."

Robert put his head back and let out a sigh. "All right, Luis. But no Ann."

"Trouble in that area? Please tell me no."

"No, no, we're fine. But she has her own career at the Fed. I don't want to drag her into this."

"Regrettable, but if you insist, we'll live with it." He began to prowl around the room, thinking things out. "Again, I want you to understand how important it is to actively prepare tonight. Think of every hostile question anyone might ask about the incident with Mrs. Chaudhary, as well as what happened in Massachusetts. I won't remind you that I several times begged you to talk to Ann about that. Give her a list of questions to fire at you—bang, bang, bang, with no time to think" He pulled to a stop behind Robert. "It's difficult not to be outraged." He let his hand fall comfortingly on his friend's shoulder. "How about lunch? I was planning to go downtown to The Pantry and stand in line with their very *odd* clientele."

Robert waved him off. "I'm afraid I'm not in the mood. Anyway, a friend from UCLA is supposed to call and explain Chaudhary to me. If that's possible."

26

Iᴛ took all the courage Ann had to pick up the phone and make the call. She had been working up to it since breakfast.

"No bother at all," Maurice Dohr said. "Just going over some notes for a speech to the L.A. Press Club this evening. It's a chance for me to plant a few subversive notions about downtown redevelopment in the collective unconscious of people who matter."

Her voice was determinedly toneless. "I'm calling confidentially, Maurice. I don't want Robert to find out. Is that OK?" In the twenty-two years she had known Dohr she'd never spoken to him like this.

But he didn't hesitate. "Of course. What is it?"

"I want to know about Boston."

This time he did hesitate.

She said, "You knew him then, didn't you?"

"I met Robert somewhat later, when he was at Columbia. But Luis knew him in Boston. Why not ask him?"

"Because Luis is loyal to a fault. And I don't think you could lie if your life depended on it." Of course, that was what she had thought of Robert, too. She added, "I want to know what happened that night. Until the police told me, I knew nothing about it."

"I'm sorry to hear that. I assumed Robert had told you everything."

"All I knew was that Carolyn had died."

"I see." He took a breath and became business-like. *His courtroom voice*, she thought. "The story as it appeared in the paper is what you're referring to? The attempted rape?"

"Yes."

"Well, of course I was aware of it when I started thinking about hiring Robert. I had only two associates at the time and he was going to be the first new graduate I hired. So I wanted to be extremely careful. Over a period of months, I talked to him quite a bit, and to people who knew him, as well as to some people in the Boston Police Department. I even hired a detective firm to do a background investigation. And everything checked out. I wouldn't have hired him otherwise. So you can put your mind at ease. This stranger broke in, panicked when Carolyn screamed, and he shot her, and was shot by Robert after a tussle. End of story. Or it should have been the end. What we are seeing now is an attempt to engage in the popular American pastime of enjoying the embarrassment of a public personage."

"Schadenfreude."

"Indeed."

Ann felt her pulse relax. "Thank you, Maurice. I needed to hear you confirm it."

But she had known the truth all the time. You can't be married to someone for twenty-two years and not know what he's like. It's just not possible.

JG couldn't help but smile when Meena stepped from the 1930s-era school building facing Vermont Avenue. *My God, she's beautiful. Look at her!* She saw him at once, waved happily and tilted her head toward the Indian girl she usually walked home with. They whispered and giggled a moment before she hurried over to where JG was standing in the shade of the school's theater-style marquee—BASEBALL THUR JEFFERSON, STUDENTS OF MONTH R RAMIREZ S KIM. JG started to put his arm around her, then reconsidered as he nervously looked around. She held her books waist-high in front of her with both hands, very school-girl-ish, and blushed. "I didn't expect you today."

"She won't say anything, will she?" He indicated the girl Meena was with, now walking north on Vermont.

"No. Of course not. She's my friend. She won't tell anyone."

"I'm not worried about me. It's you."

She nodded but said nothing, and they began to walk toward his car while all around them kids were coming and going, fumbling with phones and talking with friends. The air seemed alive with joy. Fifty yards away on the other side of a chain-link fence a group of girls began to practice an elaborate cheerleading routine, bending, kicking, spinning around and jabbing their arms in the air. Meena glanced at them wistfully. "I'm not allowed to do any after-school activities. I can't even stay in the library to study."

Halfway to his car JG tensed as he realized they'd have to pass a group of seventeen- and eighteen-year-olds in baggy jeans and hooded sweatshirts. *Crips?* he wondered. *MS-13s? Bloods?* There was an embarrassment of riches, and he'd met them all. The boys suddenly became attentive when they saw Meena.

"Hey!" A tall kid JG recognized from junior high, D'Jon Van, stared in disbelief. "Someone's finally got the Indian bitch."

"No, shit. Lookie there." They started whooping and posturing, making animal noises, enjoying themselves.

JG took Meena's hand, felt it go cold.

"Thought no one was gonna pop that cherry," a kid said, then added to JG, "Way to go, bro."

But Van recognized JG, too. "Goddamn, it's the *cello player*. Remember him, Dre? Little half-breed faggot from Byers with the big shot da-da."

"Lives up in the *mansions*," Dre said. "Yeah, I remember the motherfucker. Used to buy lunch for us. Hey, faggot, you buyin' us dinner today?"

JG and Meena ignored them, tried to walk by, but the group closed around them.

Dre's voice turned ugly. "Little shit used to kiss up to the teachers, tell everyone how important his mommy and daddy are. Binder, right? Binder the blow job. Binder the asshole." He stared hatefully at JG. "You need to be buyin' us dinner, asshole. You fuckin' *owe* us. How 'bout you loan us your Visa card? We'll bring it back after we eat." A weird sort of excitement surrounded them. Anticipation, electricity. Like children set loose at Disneyland. JG's muscles tensed up and Meena, sensing him about to explode, whispered, "Don't, please. I'm used to it."

An older kid—man, really, about twenty, and a hundred pounds heavier than JG—stepped in front of Meena, blocking her way. "This cello player don't know how to satisfy a bitch like you. Let's go to my place while my homies dump this chump in a trash barrel."

JG grabbed Meena's elbow as two of the others seized his arms and began to move him away from the group. He felt his feet leave the ground, and his heart raced. "Hey!" He tried to struggle free but his captors had too tight a grip on him.

Just then a male teacher stepped from in front of the administration building where he'd been watching and walked over. "Someone got a problem here?" African-American, wearing a sharp-looking dark suit and tie, he seemed more like an ex-football player. There was silence, then someone said, "Just goofin,' Mr. Muncey."

"Actin' fools is what I see." He stared at JG. "You don't go here."

"No, I'm—"

"Then get out, both of you. And don't be hanging around here again or I'll have you arrested for trespassing." Then he turned to the others. "And you fools—"

As JG and Meena walked away, Raj Chaudhary, sweaty from sitting in his car fifty yards down the street, started the engine. He didn't know what it was he was feeling because never before had he been nearby when someone chose death. It gave him a tingling sensation—awe, almost—like he had as a child when he was forced to view the lifeless body of his grandfather.

Still feeling the humiliation of his encounter at Manual Arts, JG stood at the shopping mall Panda Express, paying for teriyaki chicken, egg rolls, and Cokes while Meena was in the restroom. Why did he act like such a wimp when those guys harassed them? He looked like a goddamn cello player, not a man. His face burned with shame. Turning quickly with the tray of food, he collided with a thin dark-complexioned young man standing just inches from his back. JG struggled to keep the drinks upright but the man didn't move, just stared furiously at him.

"Sorry." JG started to step away, but the man moved with him and again the tray tilted.

JG offered up an embarrassed smile and apologized again, but instead of moving the young man seemed to reach out to take the tray. Some weird misunderstanding, JG figured. Or perhaps the guy's retarded. But there was such hostility in his eyes JG felt his arms tense defensively. Just then he spotted Meena and he stepped quickly aside, heading to the rear where she'd chosen a table.

"It's not your fault," she said when he apologized again for not being able to protect her. "There was nothing you could have done. They weren't going to hurt me anyway. They were just showing off."

JG wasn't reassured. Even worse, once again an adult had been forced to intrude in his life to set things straight.

Meena said, "I used to walk home in Orange County. But when I got here I was afraid to. I'd put my head down and go as fast as I could. I wish there were some Indian boys in our school. Then maybe the others would leave us alone."

JG smiled faintly. "A few days ago my dad, who everyone thinks is so damn smart, said 'Race can't still be an issue in high school, can it?'"

"Just every day." She brooded a moment. "Adults don't want to know. Parents especially. It's easier to pretend."

"A museum of illusions," JG remembered. When she looked at him inquisitively he added, "Something a cop said to my dad." He shook his head. "Are you going to be OK tomorrow? Those guys—"

"They're not in my classes. I'll be fine."

"But after school?"

She shrugged. Like everyone else, she'd figure a way to survive. "Hang on," JG said valiantly. "Only two more years. Why doesn't your brother help? He could pick you up before he goes to work, couldn't he?"

Meena made an angry stabbing gesture with her fork. "He never—" She stopped, her lips tight and her head still as she seemed to move something around in her mind. "*I hate him!*" she said with such vehemence the Vietnamese kids at the adjoining table stared at them. "Sorry." She lowered her voice. "He says your father... The killing? He says he did it on purpose."

JG was tired of hearing it. "You know what happened." He took out his phone and began to check his messages while he played with his teriyaki. Wilkerson wanting to know why he was still missing school. His mom saying don't be late for dinner. "Does Raj have a Facebook page?" Meena shrugged, unsure, but he found it. Not much on it, and what was there was mostly in Tamil.

"They were talking about you last night. Raj and my father. They call you 'nigger boy' and your mother 'Aunt Jemima.' I told them not to talk that way but Raj just said to shut up. Even in our village he would not be so rude. But in America..."

284

JG shifted in his seat and tried to move her away from thoughts of Raj and her father, and the numbing dreariness of her life since moving to L.A. "Do you remember much about the village? You were only three when you left, weren't you?"

She shrugged. "My grandmother's house, I think. Smells. Little statues of Lord Krishna and Shiva, I think. Noisy streets. Bicycles and motor scooters. But some of it I probably remember from pictures, or things people have said." She hesitated, thinking, staring into the plate without seeing it. "I think my father killed someone there. Raj says he did, someone who insulted him."

"And he wasn't arrested?"

"No one could prove it. They just found the man's body by the well, stabbed over and over in the chest, blood everywhere. The family moved right after that."

JG leaned back in the chair. The young man he'd seen earlier dumped his trash in a container twenty feet away, turned and glared at JG before sitting down again, his back to them. JG said, "Do you think it's true? Maybe he's just trying to frighten you."

"No. I don't—" Her hand suddenly shot out, taking his, squeezing tightly, and her voice cracked. "What I told you before, JG, about Nazia—"

"Being a prostitute?"

"Yes, yes. That was true. But it was only part of the truth." She dropped his hand, sagged back in the chair and began to cry. "I can't say it. I can't tell you."

Pain wrapped itself around JG's heart as he fought back tears and put his hands on top of hers, giving strength, holding on. "You don't have to. I figured it out yesterday."

"I cannot tell you how upset I was when I heard about the shooting," Asha Vatsyayan said into the phone. "That poor woman! Then when you called about her husband, I'm afraid it rather unsettled me. It's not what you'd expect, given that it was an accident."

Robert strode over to the windows and closed the Venetian blinds with a loud snap, plunging the room into darkness. "He's somehow convinced himself that I'm responsible for everything bad in his life. I simply don't know how to deal with him, Asha. It's like being stalked by a lunatic."

"And you say your son is seeing his daughter?"

"I'm not sure Chaudhary knows about it. But he definitely wouldn't approve."

"Well, I'm not going to be much solace. I called around as you suggested. People in Orange County and Hollywood. Everyone, it seems, knows *of* Mr. Chaudhary, but no one admitted to being a friend. A very disturbed man is the consensus. Violent, very much not someone you want to know, OK? I'm afraid you invited a devil into your home. A very regrettable move. Are you paying attention?"

"You're scaring me, Asha." He dropped onto the futon. On the other side of his office door he could hear phones ringing, people talking, everyone else's life going on as normal. It affronted him, this normality, as if his own life was unimportant to the world.

"Listen, Robert, I think you were looking for a sociological rationale for this man's behavior, right? You expected the answer was India. Or America. But that is not the case. *Pathology*, not sociology. He's a volatile personality; he's lost everything. His world is crashing all around him and he thinks someone has to be responsible. Unfortunately, that's you."

"Damn it, this just isn't fair. I tried to help a woman being threatened and became the victim of a madman."

"Interestingly, more than one person said they thought that woman wasn't his wife. She was too young to have a twenty-year-old son. People also say those who know Mr. Chaudhary cross the street when they see him. A man from his village who owns an Indian video store told me Chaudhary emigrated to Singapore because he was suspected of killing a man. That was years ago. These are just rumors, but still. People say that's why he left Singapore, also, though there the victim may have been a woman. A sexual crime, very bloody, the way her chest was ripped open. But it's how he deals with problems. Killing.

"I saw him on television with his children. He seems a dull dog, doesn't he? So quiet. Shy.

We don't expect someone like that to be mad. We think madness is the realm of the extravagant, the out-of-control. Not the dimwitted, the plodder. One other curious fact emerged from my questioning, Robert. Please pay attention."

"Yes?"

"Mr. Chaudhary has no daughter. Only three sons."

Robert was stunned. "Then who is Meena—"

"I don't know. But I imagine your son does, don't you?"

Ann was too unnerved from Chaudhary's visit the day before to be in the mood for cooking, so she drove to the supermarket and picked up two rotisserie-roasted chickens, wild rice, and a quart of spinach salad. Better get a bottle of wine also, she decided. Or maybe two, the mood she was in. She was placing an Australian Semillon in the cart when a fist plunged like a knife into her back.

"He *promised* me, Mrs. Binder. One million dollars he would pay. He lied to me and lied to you. Five times he was with my Nazia, five times he paid for sex in his yellow car and..." Chaudhary's voice raced and his sweaty unshaven head bobbed back and forth. He was wearing a black t-shirt, but she could make out bandages beneath it, wrapped mummy-style around his torso. "...you have to tell him. *You!* He's your husband. He *lied*—"

Ann spun around and began to wheel the cart rapidly toward the front of the store.

"No, Mrs. Binder, you cannot run away. You have to do what's right." Chaudhary seized her elbow. "*Listen to me!*" he yelled as other shoppers turned to watch the slightly built man in baggy trousers and sandals screaming now in a mixture of English and Tamil. "Your Robert paid for sex, now he *owes* me, he—"

Ann wrenched her arm away and tried to remain calm though her heart was pounding so hard it was making her dizzy. "Leave me alone, Mr. Chaudhary, or I'll call the police."

"The police?" He seemed genuinely startled. "Mrs. Binder, your husband murdered my wife."

"Not your wife," Ann shot back with quiet anger. "She was a prostitute and you were her pimp."

Chaudhary blinked, then an almost gentle look came to his face. "How is your pretty dog, Mrs. Binder? Does she protect you now? What happened to the dog can also happen to your son, this stupid black boy who tries to defile my family."

Ann shoved the cart at him but Chaudhary caught it and rammed it back as hard as he could. It missed Ann, hitting the shelves next to her. Dozens of bottles tumbled down in a deafening cacophony of breaking glass, sending a sticky sea of wine flowing over their shoes. Ann spun away and marched quickly toward the front of the store as Chaudhary's words raced after her. "Your *boy*, Mrs. Binder, steals our Meena. This is the family you have. Your husband kills Nazia and your son steals Meena."

A wine bottle flew through the air, exploding at her feet, and then another as Chaudhary followed her.

The automatic doors flew open and Ann hurried out, trying to keep her composure while everyone stared in a sort of stunned immobility as Chaudhary ran across the parking lot. "Your husband pays for sex, your son rapes my daughter. What kind of family do you have?"

When he tried to grab her arm as she opened the car door, Ann jerked the phone from her purse. "Leave me alone, Sandeep, or I'll call the police. A hundred people have seen what you've done to me."

Chaudhary's head abruptly ceased bobbing, and his hand shot to the back of her neck. He jerked her head toward his, his lips close enough to kiss. "It is too late for the police, Mrs. Binder. If you do not help me I will kill your boy. Then I will kill your Robert. Then I will kill you. Do not think I am kidding."

She got into the car, slammed the door and immediately locked it. Chaudhary whirled around, grabbed an empty shopping cart and rammed it as hard as he could against the side of the car. *"You owe me, Mrs. Binder!"* As she hurriedly backed out of the parking space he slammed the cart into the car again and again. *"You owe me. All of you. You owe me. I will collect."*

Driving home, Ann couldn't still her pulse. *Take deep breaths. Relax... Relax... Because it's not over. Chaudhary won't give up until he gets what he wants. But what is it he wants? A million dollars? Would that really satisfy him?* She didn't think so. *Something else then. Something involving Meena? Could that be it?* She felt like screaming. There was simply no way of knowing. The man was insane.

This was the secret of the mad, wasn't it? To abjure rationality. To make a world none of us can understand. To force the impossible.

27

"THEN who is she if she's not Chaudhary's daughter?" Ann asked. She had been in the kitchen looking for the Advil when Robert came home. Seeing the agitation on his face she decided to wait before telling him about her supermarket confrontation. Maybe tomorrow, if he was calmed down by then.

"Asha doesn't know who she is, but she's going to keep asking around. She also said Chaudhary's probably killed before. A 'very disturbed' man, she said. Very dangerous. Isn't that lovely? Like an idiot I invited a mentally deranged killer into our family, *begged* him. Everybody told me not to, but I thought I knew better. Where's John? He ought to hear this."

"I don't know where he is."

"You don't know? What the hell does that mean?"

"It means I don't know. He doesn't tell me these things anymore, Robert. He doesn't tell either of us."

"Christ—" He put a hand to his head. "Has Edgerton called?"

"No one but reporters on the machine. I finally unplugged it."

"Did anyone mention my appointment being rescinded?"

She shook her head. She hadn't heard anything, she couldn't listen to the news anymore, couldn't even use her email or social media accounts because they'd all been hacked by Binder haters. Even her Fed page and Wikipedia entry had been hacked. Robert grabbed his phone and dialed Lee's cell phone but there was no answer. And no answer at his house or D.C. office either. "Hiding out, goddamn it. He hasn't the guts to face me. Or stand behind someone being slandered. What a perfect definition of a politician."

"Forget Edgerton, Robert. Call DeFazio, tell him what Asha said. Maybe Chaudhary's wanted in India or Singapore. The police can check with Interpol. This is more important than your appointment."

"Nothing's more important than my appointment. I don't want any dinner—I feel like shit." Still holding the phone, he went into the living room and sat in front of CNN for three hours, repeatedly calling Lee, until finally going to bed early with a headache.

Ann waited until Robert was upstairs, then sank down on the couch with a bottle of Merlot, staring at the stained glass of the Tiffany windows, watching them ease from the golds and greens of Sutter's Mill to a dull indigo and finally an aggressive, angry black that sucked the last light from the room. She still had no idea where JG was. And she no longer knew what to believe about what happened that night when Robert stopped his car. *Was I not good enough for you? Did you have to go out and pay for sex? Did your wife no longer please you?* Not once in their marriage had she been tempted to seek sex elsewhere. Though the opportunities were certainly there.

Wine sloshed in her glass.

Don't put your hopes in Lee, Robert. You've lost him. Your friends are going to fade away next; you're going to wake up one day and find yourself alone. And it wasn't just the press enjoying his fall. Half of Congress was cheering from the sidelines, along with officials he had annoyed or antagonized at City Hall, and virtually everyone in the police department.

She stared at the windows, now only a darker shade of black against the night.

Where are you, John? Are you OK?

"Such hopes we had," she whispered aloud before the wine finally blotted out all thinking. "We were the Binders. We were special. We were going to soar."

"You must do it tomorrow at the law school." Sandeep Chaudhary's voice shook with outrage as he stared at his son across the kitchen table. "Find a bucket. Meena will help you, she will prepare it. It must be from all of us. Do you

understand? The radio says the press conference will be at two o'clock. You will be ready."

"Press conference for what? What is he going
to say?"

"What is he going to say?" Chaudhary seized
the boy's hands. Did he have to explain everything? "What does this man ever talk about?
He insults us, he lies about our family. He
wants us sent out of the country. He kills
Nazia, now he wants Meena for his son."

Raj tensed but kept quiet; it was better not to
talk when his father was like this. Instead, he
focused on the twin splotches of color that had
burst from around the older man's bandages
and now stained the front of his shirt like owl's
eyes. "Do you want this to happen?" Chaudhary demanded. "Do you want this Binder to
insult us, to lie to everyone, to make you look
the fool?"

When Raj shook his head Chaudhary said,
"Then you must show America what he is like.
It is up to you. Do not disgrace us. Two o'clock.
But wait for the cameras. Everyone must *see*
his shame." He sank back in his chair and
his eyes began to pulse. "They are evil, these
Binders. This woman is as bad as her stupid
boy. She uses her *sex* to make fools of men
... she is a vixen." He had known women like
that in India, whores who entice men with their
looks, their bodies so alluring, only to fool and
torment and laugh at them. Women need to be
controlled, like Nazia, like Meena. Otherwise
they will poison you. They will laugh and make

monkeys of you. "Why too is she alive, this vixen?" he wondered aloud. His body was heating up, and his hand squeezed Raj's so tightly the boy winced. "Why too is she alive?"

Ann was already dressed for work when Robert came down for breakfast. "Did Lee call yet?"

"No, but it was on the news. He withdrew your nomination. Funding for RULA is expected to go next."

Robert's temper flared at once. "If Lee thinks I'm going to accept this without a fight he's nuts. I'll tell the reporters he's—"

"You're not going ahead with the press conference, are you?"

"Of course I am. The election's tomorrow. I need to clear the air. Anyway, it's too late to back out." He had called Luis before going to sleep last night. The small "Mexican Garden" with its brightly colored bougainvillea and lush palms was reserved for two o'clock. All the television networks would be there, along with Yahoo and the Huffington Post and a dozen radio stations and newspapers. Though it was probably too late for it to make a difference. But whose fault was that if not Robert's?

Ann stared at him in disbelief. "What do you mean it's too late? Just call it off. How hard can that be? Do you think you're the only person to change his mind?"

They had argued about the press conference last night also. Ann thought it a monumentally stupid idea. "Luis's folly," she called it, all

smoke and mirrors to impress the police and reporters. And not the sort of stage where Robert
was used to performing.

"I'm sinking, Ann," he had said plaintively. He
felt lost, like a child who had just experienced
something until then unthinkable. "The job in
Washington, RULA, my position at the firm, all
the crap going on at Otis, a possible murder
charge. Everything's coming apart because I
went out to pick up a goddamn prescription."
Your prescription, she knew he meant. "I can't
just sit back and let it happen. I have to *do*
something."

"But not *this*, Robert. Let Maurice Dohr talk
to the press. He's not emotionally involved like
you are. He's got a reputation for integrity. He
can present a more reasoned defense without
sounding whiney or self-justifying."

"*I* have a reputation for integrity!" he shot
back, then thought, *God, how pompous that
sounds.* But he was right. He did have a reputation for integrity. At least until recently.
Now even that was gone. "Anyway, Maurice
has practically told me to take a leave from the
firm. I've been with him twenty-two years—I
was the third attorney he hired. And suddenly
he's embarrassed to be associated with me."

"Then let Karel Jirasek represent you. You
said—"

"You're joking, right?" He stared at her, feeling his temperature rise.

She was exasperated. "All right, all right."
She took a deep breath, let a moment pass,

then kept her voice steady and reasonable: Ann Binder, master of rationality. "Luis can meet the press if he thinks it's so important. But not you. It'll just look like you're guilty of *something* and trying to weasel out of it. What do you think the TV talk shows will make you look like? Every redneck in the country is already calling up to tell them what a hypocrite this do-gooder attorney is."

"What are you worried about, anyway? Your job at the Bank?"

"You know that's not fair."

He did, and he told her so. But that was where it stood when he'd gone up to bed. Things were no better at breakfast. Ann bolted up from the table and swiftly cleared her plate away. Robert dropped two pieces of sourdough in the toaster and poured a cup of coffee, waiting for the bread to pop. "Luis wanted you to be at the press conference," he said, his back to her, "but I told him to forget it. You have enough problems at work without adding silent-but-loyal wife to your repertoire."

A night-time's worth of wine-fed fury burst out as Ann said, "Did you pay that woman for sex?"

He spun around. "What are you saying? You know better than that."

"Then how did Chaudhary know so much about you? How did he know where we live or that you have a yellow car with books in the back? *Five times*, he said. I've thought about it, Robert. A lot. Five times in the weeks leading up to the shooting. Every week for a month you were gone at least once. One time to go back to DHP, once to pick up some wine—"

"Come on, Ann. You know me better than that."

"No... I don't, Robert. I don't know you at all. You've kept yourself from me. You created a façade and let everyone believe it was you. Answer the question. How did Chaudhary know where we live? How did he know about the car?"

"We're in the phone book, for Christ's sake. And online. Anyway, the Saab was out front when he came to dinner. He passed by it when he came up the walk and looked inside and saw the books. There's no mystery there."

But she wouldn't let up. "Why can't the police find anyone who saw those two men. They went door to door asking people, Robert. It doesn't make sense that no one saw them. Not then, not before, not later."

"It was after one in the morning. The whole thing didn't take but three minutes. And right now they're trying their best not to be seen, aren't they? What would you do if you had been featured on *L.A.'s Most Wanted*?"

She was dizzy, dissociated, her thoughts freewheeling recklessly as though some other Ann had taken possession of her mind. And this other person said, "Did you shoot her on purpose? Tell me the truth, Robert. Was this murder?"

"God, Ann." When the toast popped he turned back to the counter.

Ann saw the tautness in his back and neck as he grabbed the toast and buttered it. *Do it,* she told herself. *Now! Before you chicken out.* She took a breath and forced her voice into a dead calm. "I've been thinking I need a break. We both do."

Robert slowly turned around. "A break from what? What are you talking about?"

She waved an arm weakly, feeling the pulse in her temple begin to throb. "The past few weeks … Everything." *Your dead hooker, if that's what she was. The intruder you killed and neglected to tell me about. The police. Chaudhary and his dysfunctional family. My work. Our family's make-believe life.*

Robert put the toast down. "I guess I don't like the sound of that."

Ann shrugged. She knew she wasn't handling this well but was at a loss how to talk to him about all the things bothering her. Last night, alone in the darkness of the living room, she had begun to cry and was still red-eyed when she got up at four this morning. She had gone into the kitchen, sat at the table, and, to her shame, drank two glasses of wine as she waited impatiently for the sun to come up.

The blood began to drain from Robert's face as he stared at her. "Don't do this, Ann. I couldn't stand it if you left."

"That's not what I said, Robert. I said taking a break, letting things settle."

His head was shaking back and forth. "That's not what you mean. Please. I need you. I'm not a strong person. I can't handle DeFazio and Chaudhary and Lee and everything else by myself." He began to blink, and his body seemed to go rigid. "I need you, Ann. I need to hold on to you."

Unwillingly, compassion rose, and she wanted to go to him and reassure him that this was all a minor hiccup in their life—that everything would soon return to normal. But she didn't move. *My suitcase is packed and in the car*, she thought. *I made a reservation for a flight to San Francisco for after work today. Cool weather. Fog. I'll go out to dinner by myself. I'll drink in my room at the St. Francis. I won't turn the television on. I won't hear a word about Robert Binder. I won't have to think about what's happened to my family. And when I come back, everything will be better.*

Robert was sunk in despair as he looked down at his toast. "None of this madness would have happened if Chaudhary hadn't been an immigrant. The police are so afraid of Stackhouse and the *Times* they gave him a Get Out of Jail Free card. Even the D.A.'s office treats him with kid gloves. The whole city thinks 'Poor Sandeep, getting beat up by America.'"

"Robert, that's idiotic. The police don't care where he's from."

"Of course they care. If that woman had been white—" He stopped.

"What?"

"Nothing. Forget it."

"No. I want to hear where you were going with this."

"I wasn't going anywhere. I'm just frustrated. And scared." He stared sullenly at his feet.

She said abruptly, "Someone from the D.A.'s office came to see me about you yesterday."

"The D.A? What the hell did they want?"

"She asked me what time you left to get the prescription at Walgreens."

"Did you talk to her?"

"Of course. What do you expect?"

He jerked away from the counter. "Don't. Don't cooperate. Tell them you won't talk unless your attorney is present. Don't make it easy on them."

"Easy?" She couldn't believe what he was saying. "What does that mean? Do you want me to lie?"

"No, of course not. But what have they done for us? The police and D.A. are trying to create a case where one doesn't exist. Don't help them. If they want to talk to someone have them contact Luis. He can handle things for me. For now, at least. What else did she ask?"

Ann put a hand to her forehead. She could feel a tightening behind her eyes, a renewed pounding in her temples. She stepped abruptly away from the table and started for the living room where her purse was.

"Don't go," Robert said in alarm, following her. "Please. We can talk tonight. Running away isn't going to solve anything."

"After the press conference," she murmured. *After you make a fool of yourself in front of the world. After I hear you tell the world you've lied to me from the day we met.*

"Yes. After." His jaw hung slackly, as though he could tell what she was thinking, and what was left of his self-respect drained away.

Ann's eyes closed. She could feel the pulse raging in her neck, the muscles in her shoulders and back tighten.

"And we need to talk to JG. About Meena. Who is she if she's not Chaudhary's daughter? Why is she at that house? Please, Ann."

JG hadn't come home last night until everyone was asleep, so they hadn't been able to tell him what Robert had learned from Asha Vatsyayan. Considering the mood he had been in lately, they didn't know if he would even take the time to talk to them. He had such anger in him. Some of it directed at them. Some at himself. Ann took a breath, held it. "I don't know, Robert... I can't think." She went into the living room and snatched up her purse, then sank down on the couch.

Ann was still on the couch when Robert left for Otis. The wine was slowing her movements. She closed her eyes and felt hrself start to doze. Then her phone rang and, like an idiot, she picked it up. It was a producer for the *Today* show. They wanted to interview Robert and... Ann slammed the phone down. *Damn you*, she thought. *Instead of focusing on Robert you ought to be probing the real story here, the senseless rage everywhere today—Chaudhary hates me and JG, DeFazio hates Robert, people in the community hate the police who seem to hate everyone. Why aren't reporters investigating that instead of trying once again to topple a statue?*

A sound interrupted her thoughts and she turned to see JG hurrying down the stairs, wearing only shorts. He was startled to see his mother still home. "Why are you sitting here? You're all dressed up." He looked at her as if he knew something was amiss.

Well, of course, she thought, *everything is amiss, including your life. More than you know.*

She tried a smile, hoping to disarm him as she ventured into dangerous territory. "Dad talked to a woman yesterday who knows something about Mr. Chaudhary."

JG's face closed down.

"She said he doesn't have a daughter."

The boy looked at her, his eyes desperate, but he said nothing.

"John, what's going on?"

"She doesn't want me to talk about it. She's afraid."

"Afraid of what? Who is she if she's not his daughter?"

His voice was unwilling. "His niece. She's only lived with him since they moved from Cerritos. He said if she told anyone she'd get deported back to India. Her family's not here legally. She was born over there, but she's lived in the U.S. since she was three."

"I don't understand. Why the secrecy? And why is she living with her uncle?"

A distancing look came into his eyes and his tone deadened. "I don't know."

She stood so rapidly it made her dizzy. "John, don't keep secrets. There's been enough of that in our family. What's going on?"

"Mom, I promised not to. I'm not going to betray her. I gave her my word."

"I'm not going to Immigration. I'm not going to tell the police. But Mr. Chaudhary has threatened all of us. Yesterday he attacked me in the supermarket. I need to know what's going on."

He stared at his mother for a long time, his face gaining color and his muscles tensing. *He's going to clam up*, she thought. *He's going to turn around and walk away*. But after a moment the words dribbled out, tight with anxiety. "There was a ceremony in India when she was a child. With Raj. She wasn't even there, but they call it a marriage. She's his 'wife.'"

"Oh, John. I'm so sorry. But it's not legal. She's only fifteen. It doesn't have any validity in this country. It doesn't even have any real validity in India."

"They're going to get married here next year when it's legal, as long as her mother gives permission."

Ann sat down. "How does Meena feel about it?"

"How do you think she feels? She didn't have any choice, she was forced into it."

Ann shook her head.

"You can't tell anyone, Mom. Even Dad."

"You need to, John. There are people at RULA who could help her. They deal with immigration problems all the time."

"She's a juvenile. They'll put her in a foster home. Or a county home with gang members and runaways. You know what those places are like."

She felt another wave of dizziness. What had she been thinking, drinking through the morning? She held her body steady. "I have a meeting at the Fed today with Belasino and some economists from MIT. After it's over we'll talk. OK? You and me and Dad. And Meena. Invite her over. Please, John. The four of us. Can you do that?"

For a long moment he stared at his mother before finally agreeing. But when Ann asked where the Chaudharys lived he froze up again. He could think of no good reason for her to know, and a hundred bad ones. She put a hand on his shoulder. "Relax, John, I'm not going over there. I'm just uncomfortable not knowing." Reluctantly, he told her.

"Thank you." She gave her son a hug, holding him close, at last feeling the tension leave his body. "We'll talk tonight, hon. We're going to solve this problem. OK?"

He nodded dumbly as she reached down and grabbed her briefcase. Her plane reservation was for 4:10. But there was no way she could leave with this facing her family. "I've got to get downtown. I'm already late." She met his gaze. "Take care today, John. You know how dangerous this man is. Don't do anything stupid."

He hesitated, looking at her oddly.

"I'm serious. This is no time for emotionalism. Make your Mama proud. Make decisions you'll be proud of next month and next year."

He smiled uneasily. "I'll be left-brained as hell." Then, worried about what his mother was planning, he said, "You won't go to the police?"

"I promise."

His eyes reddened and his voice lost its timbre. "I don't want to lose her, Mom."

"I know."

As she drove away Ann thought, *OK, the meeting's at one.* She'd leave by two, done or not. And whatever the hell her boss thought. She had something to do now, and it was more important than her job. But Robert couldn't know about it. No one could know. *Make decisions you'll be proud of.*

But as Asha Vatsyayan, trying to comfort Ann, said days later, "Of course what you did was very stupid. But don't beat yourself up about it. It's not your fault. Once this man decided on killing he wasn't going to be stopped."

"What do you mean he's in a senior partners' meeting?" Robert had called Maurice Dohr to

give him a heads-up about the press conference, but Hannah Avril, Dohr's administrative
assistant, was giving him the runaround.

There was an intake of breath on the other
end as Hannah realized her mistake just as
Robert was saying, "I didn't get a notice..."
Then he knew what was happening and his
mouth went so dry he could barely form the
words. "They're meeting about me, aren't they?
They're pushing me out."

"I... I don't know what—"

Robert hung up, feeling a little more life drain
away. But it rang almost at once and he clicked
it on. Obviously there had been a mistake and
he had been invited to the meeting after all.
"Yes?"

"We have a secret, don't we, Mr. Binder?
About you and Nazia. In your car, the back
seat."

Robert bolted to his feet. "Damn you—" His
heart was beating so rapidly he put his hand
on the desk to steady himself.

"Why did you have to kill her? Fifty dollars
more is all she asked. Was that reason to shoot
a beautiful woman?"

"Listen to me, Chaudhary. If you don't stop
harassing me I'll—"

"No, you won't, sir. You'll do nothing. Because you don't want the world to know. The
shame, the disgrace. Better to be dead. But
your wife understands, she *knows* the truth,
Mr. Binder. She tries not to, but she *knows*—"

Robert slammed the phone down. As he did so his gaze went to the window. A thin, dark young man was striding rapidly across the street and onto the Otis campus. Raj? He'd never seen him so he couldn't be sure. But why would Raj be here? And what was he carrying?

28

AFTER his mother left for work JG stormed around the house, wondering what to do between now and three o'clock when he would pick up Meena. Finally, he sat down, took a deep breath, tried to calm himself but couldn't. He'd fucked up bad today, telling his mom about the "marriage." Now she'd tell Dad, and God knew what he'd do, the mood he'd been in lately.

But JG had been on edge ever since he and Meena sat in his car in front of the phone store and the world outside faded to black. *"Rajesh... says we're married.... I have to do whatever he tells me. I have no choice. My parents arranged everything, it's my duty. He's my husband, JG. Please try to understand..."*

Overcome by shame, she could hardly form the words. It wasn't right for this man—a stranger she hardly knew except as a cousin, and who had always been both rude and dismissive—to force himself on her, to demand her instant obedience. She had been through the same state-mandated school lecture as JG, and knew the laws about sexual harassment, rape, and child abuse, had been warned about how often family members were to blame. But her case was different—her mother had agreed to the arrangement, *demanded* it, because everything had been settled years ago. The only question had been the passage of time. There was no way for Meena to now oppose what others had decreed. She had been taught that since childhood; it was woven into who she was and always would be. Family. Submission. Fate. This was the way things were and always had been in India. There was simply no room for argument.

And so at fifteen her life is effectively over, John thought. She was little more than a commodity, bound over to Rajesh till death.

"I hate him," she'd said through tears, and choked on the words. "I dream about killing him. Every night when he is with me I want him dead, I hope he will sleep and never wake up."

The rage in JG's heart was unquenchable. *This wasn't a marriage*, he railed at her. *It's kidnapping, rape. Raj and Chaudhary belong in prison for the rest of their lives.*

But Meena panicked: "No, no, please. They're doing what they think is right, this is all they know. It is how my parents and grandparents and their parents, back to the beginning of time, married."

JG couldn't settle his mind. How was he supposed to worry about his own future now? But guilt also assailed him because Meena made him promise not to tell anyone, and already he'd betrayed her. Maybe it didn't matter. She couldn't oppose her "husband", she told him, but she could leave him. And only JG could make that happen. She could run away, live in one of those abandoned buildings in Hollywood that teenage squatters had taken over. She'd heard about them at school, dozens of kids living together, almost like a family. A real family.

Then she had broken down in tears. *He hits me every night. He tells me I have to do anything he says. We are husband and wife, we will raise his children.*

JG realized there was no reason to talk to his parents tonight as he promised. They were too wrapped up in their own problems to worry about him. It was up to JG alone. *The second generation of Binders to "help" Chaudhary's family,* he thought wryly. So he stayed home, sitting nervously in front of the TV—Judge Mathis, Jerry Springer, *I Love Lucy.* Then the noon news. But he was only vaguely aware of the voices and faces flashing in front of him until Sandeep Chaudhary filled the screen with his jittery smile and faux innocence.

"...he *threw money* at me in the parking lot. Ask the people who were there! 'Mr. Binder,' I said, 'why do you do this? I don't want your money. I want justice.' But he screamed at me, he called my wife whore, she *deserved* to die, he said. Why does he say this?"

Someone off camera asked a question and Chaudhary's eyes exploded with outrage. "She attacked me! I was buying milk for my children —all I had was five dollars—when she threw a wine bottle at me. It missed my head by *inches*. The whole family is like this, their money makes them above the law. The son, too, this hooligan who follows my daughter wherever she goes."

JG sat up. The weirdness of seeing himself talked about on TV receded enough for him to think, *Following his daughter? What the hell was he talking about? And did he mean Mom threw a bottle at him?*

The anchorman's bland handsome face replaced Chaudhary's. "Attempts to reach Mr. Binder were unsuccessful, but we'll have a reporter at today's press conference. Be sure to watch the five o'clock..."

JG threw the remote at the television. None of this made any sense, but none of it mattered. He and Meena had already decided what to do when he picked her up after school today. She'd have extra clothes in her backpack, and he'd take five hundred dollars out of his savings account. But instead of going to a Hollywood squat, he'd check her into a motel a mile from here, prepay for a week, give her the cash and his Visa card. And he'd tell no one where she was when they asked. Not Chaudhary, his folks, the school, the police, Social Services, though he knew they were going to fall on him like a wall collapsing.

So he waited impatiently until 2:40, then drove to Manual Arts and parked across the street. Windows down, he sat in the stifling heat, unaware of anything except the door Meena would come through. *Chaudhary's going to absolutely freak when she doesn't return tonight.* But hell, he'd been freaking since JG first saw him. Meena had been living with them for six months by then—Chaudhary insisted on it. Or had Raj insisted? They wanted her out of Orange County and put with her "husband" so she could relearn the old ways. But Meena didn't know any old ways, hardly spoke Tamil. Or had that been their real reason? Was Meena a sex toy for Raj, just fourteen years old when he'd first brought her to his house. And only for Raj? JG wasn't sure. From comments Meena let slip he thought Chaudhary could be forcing himself on her when Raj was at work. But Meena was too embarrassed to talk about it.

He heard a bell and quickly started the engine, staring toward the boat-like main building. Seconds later doors flew open and students exploded out like bees from a hive. Within minutes the street was a noisy confusion of cars as parents and boyfriends stopped only long enough to load up, then take off up Vermont, engines roaring and tires squealing.

No Meena.

Three-fifteen. He wiped his palms on his jeans.

The Indian girl Meena sometimes walked with came out and headed north. *OK, Meena's still inside. She's making sure Raj isn't around before she leaves. Good girl. Smart.*

Three-thirty.

Damn it, did she go out through the back? Stepping from the car, he looked up and down the street, then trotted over to the main building, looking around at the few stragglers. Not knowing where to go, he opened a door into an office; half a dozen men and women inside looked up suspiciously, so he immediately closed it. Moving quickly now he went out to the athletic field. Boys on three different basketball courts shooting hoops and yelling at each other, but no Meena. He ran first to the Art Deco auditorium, glancing quickly at the lifeless gloom inside, then into a dank green-tiled hallway, hurrying past a row of vacant classrooms. *Jesus, almost four o'clock.* He sprinted back to the front of the school, took the phone from his pocket and checked his messages. Nothing. Maybe she's out at the car, waiting for him. Running again, he went back to Vermont—but no one was near his car.

He looked around, trying to catch his breath as his head spun. The terrible dream-like *normality* of everything—people calmly walking around, buildings still intact, cars rolling down the street—nothing registered. This couldn't be right. His world was falling apart and no one cared, no one offered to help. His body tensed, all his muscles tightening at once.

"Well, I must say, this is not what I envisaged. Looks like you're promoting poverty, not fighting it."

Howard Zalesky, nine years on the faculty at Otis, had never been to the RULA office before and seemed taken aback by what he found. It was less than an hour before the scheduled press conference, and one day until Zalesky's anticipated election to the deanship. Annoyed at this unexpected intrusion, Robert said, "When we set up RULA we decided not to put money into *things*. We're here to provide students with hands-on public-service experience. And we cross-train with the ILP, as well as provide a great deal of publicity for the School."

"Well, publicity cuts both ways, of course. I understand you have a press conference coming up."

"In forty-five minutes." Robert squirmed uneasily. He wanted to have some time to himself before meeting the reporters.

"It's been a difficult time for you, I'm sure. But it's difficult for Otis also, of course. The negative press coverage—"

"What coverage was that, Howard?" Robert couldn't mask the annoyance that crept into his voice, though he knew it was unwise. Without federal support Zalesky was going to control the major source of RULA funding beginning July first.

"Bobby Stackhouse called me a few days ago. He heard that I was to be the new dean and wanted to set up a meeting with the administration. "He asked me about you, about the incident."

The incident! *Jesus, was that what it was now? It was beginning to sound very Dreyfus-like. The incident, the Affair.*

"He's concerned the police and press are going to let this slip from the public's consciousness. He feels"—Zalesky's eyes briefly met Robert's—"there's more to the shooting than has been made public."

"Is that why you're here, to ask questions for Stackhouse?"

"If the woman was a prostitute—"

"Come on, Howard. *If!* If she was a Martian or a mermaid or nine feet tall perhaps there'd be a story. But none of those 'ifs' happens to be true."

Zalesky sat back heavily and blew out a sigh. "And there you have what bothers me most about this whole business—this arrogance of yours, this contempt, this 'I'm above answering' attitude of yours."

"Howard, I'm holding a press conference in a few minutes. How is that 'above answering'? Why don't you show up and ask your questions there?"

But Zalesky was heading off in a new direction. "It's a tense time for this city. Did you know the governor has put National Guard troops on alert? Social media seems to be stirring things up—Twitter and so on. Of course the community is already upset, what with these Hollywood people exploiting the poverty around here."

Robert was about to get himself a cup of coffee when the other man said, "I want this press conference moved off campus. And as of the Fall semester I want you and RULA out of this building and as far from Otis as possible. Beginning with tomorrow's election, RULA no longer has any connection to the school. Is that understood?"

Robert wondered at the calm, almost spiritual serenity that had suddenly come over him. Like a drug, it soothed him. His voice was mild. "No, Howard. To both things. Go back and tell Bobby Stackhouse I won't be intimidated and I won't be threatened. By either of you. I'll go down fighting first. Starting with today's press conference."

He stood up. Like it or not it was time to meet the press.

As he glanced toward the windows he wondered again about the young man he'd seen earlier. Something in his gait, the determined way he strode across campus bothered him tremendously.

JG's panic spun out of control as he drove slowly up Vermont, looking at the kids walking home or hanging out, then over to Hoover, and all the way to Venice Boulevard. Meena wasn't anywhere. Maybe she hadn't gone to school today. Maybe Chaudhary made her stay home. Or she was sick. Of course! She was sick and didn't go to school. But why hadn't she called him? Grabbing his phone, he checked his text messages again. Nothing. And nothing on voice mail. *Jesus!* Should he call the phone he gave her? No, not yet. Chaudhary or Raj would go nuts if they found out about it. But the moment he tossed the phone on the dash it rang. He lunged forward, slammed on the brakes and almost collided with the car in front of him. "*Where are you?*"

Meena was crying and whispering at the same time. "My uncle—he won't let me go anywhere. I have to stay in the house."

"I can hardly hear you. Are you home?" He buzzed the window up.

"I'm in the bedroom. My uncle just went out to the garage. Raj isn't here. He went somewhere this afternoon, he wouldn't tell me where. But it has something to do with your father. Something bad—"

But JG was only half paying attention. "Why won't they let you out?"

"Raj saw me with you yesterday. When I came home he started hitting me. He said he had the right to kill me because of what I did. They called my mother and told her I was a whore. She said I can never leave his house again. I can't go to school. I can't go anywhere." She began to sob louder.

"Did he hurt you? I'm calling the police."

"*No, don't tell anyone.* It will just make it worse. Please."

"Are you hurt?" His heart beat so fast it seemed to burst through his rib cage.

"No, I'm OK. He just... hit me and... the other ..." She was too embarrassed to say it.

"I'm going over there. I'm going to talk to him."

Her panic boiled over. "No. Please. They'll kill me if anyone knows. They will! Don't come here. Ever!"

"But they can't do this. You don't have to let them. The police will—"

"He's my uncle! This is my family, JG. They love me. I *have* to do what they say!"

"You don't have to put up with kidnapping and rape. You don't have to be someone's victim. Please let me help."

"Oh, God, I heard a door." Her breathing was rapid and uneven. "He's in the house."

The dial tone buzzed in his ear.

JG dropped the phone. Panic raced his heart. *Where to go, what to do?*

Robert was hurrying across the Otis campus on the way to meet the press when his phone rang.

"Where are you?" Luis Teague demanded.

"I'm on my way. Relax."

"I tried to catch you at your office but you'd already left. I thought I should tell you this personally."

Robert's pace slowed. "Tell me what?"

"There have been rumblings from the D.A.'s office."

Robert said nothing.

"I think they're going to file a murder-one charge. You could be arrested any time within the next twenty-four to forty-eight hours. I've already contacted Temple Bail Bonds.

"As soon as you're processed they'll show up. You shouldn't have to spend any time locked up."

Robert halted. When he didn't respond, Luis said, "Are you still there?"

"In two minutes I'll be in front of a dozen TV cameras."

"I'm sorry about the timing, but I felt you needed to know. Surprises are never good."

Robert shoved the phone in his pocket and started walking quickly. He could hear an angry rumble from the reporters on the other side of a line of trees. They were tired of waiting in the heat. They wanted to get this over with.

Twenty-four to forty-eight hours, he thought.

29

THE stench of the Mexican Garden was overpowering. It was everywhere, making Robert's stomach cramp with disgust. Had something died? His head twisted quickly from side to side as he stood on the podium and stared around.

Then he felt the blood roaring in his ears, the warm sweat swimming on his forehead and hands, and realized he had imagined it in his fear of meeting the press. *They're hoping to see me make a fool of myself, they want me to die in front of them.* He should have listened to Luis—he'd had more experience with hostile environments like this. Robert remembered somebody years ago telling him if you're going to live in the public eye you better be ready to put up with public disapproval. But what about blatant hatred? Or the morbid national compulsion to be present, to assist, in a public dismemberment? How did politicians stand it?

He took a deep breath, and then another, felt his knees wobble as he stared toward reporters he could only vaguely see behind the blur in his eyes and the heat waves bubbling up in layers from the lawn as the afternoon sun beat down. For a moment he thought he saw the young man he'd noticed earlier walking onto the Otis campus. But he blinked and the man was gone. Get going, he warned himself. *They're not going to wait forever.* "Thank you all for coming—"

Christ, he'd already thanked them, hadn't he? He had meant to say something about RULA first, but he'd forgotten what. Now he sounded like an idiot, sounded like someone fearful, someone with something to hide, as his words tripped anxiously over each other. Another deep breath. *Once you start talking the anxiety disappears*, he'd learned long ago. But not this time. Sweat was pasting his shirt to his ribs.

"Let me begin with a few words about the Rural and Urban Legal Assistance group and the urgent need to provide direct legal representation to those who can't afford it. More than twenty years ago we set up the first test program here in Los Angeles..." And suddenly his heart slowed, the words came out clearly and forcefully. This was something he could talk about.

The spot Luis had chosen for the press conference—the garden supposedly planted by Cornelius Ryan Otis himself in 1899—was encased in a lush tropical forest of coconut palms, blood-red bougainvillea, and exotic colorful lilies. A humid and blisteringly hot rainforest, incongruously wedged deep in the heart of hundreds of miles of gritty industrialization and urban decay. In addition to the ancient podium

the school used for its own press conferences—
lawsuits joined, gifts received, faculty honored
—here was a lectern that threatened to teeter
over under the weight of a dozen microphones.
And how many reporters, he wondered? *Forty?
Fifty? What difference did it make?* Even one
was enough to annoy him because he knew
they weren't here to learn about RULA. They
wanted to see a man, shamed and beaten down,
try to justify himself. They wanted a comeup-
pance. *See, these big shots are no better than
you and me. Watch him burn, watch him shrivel
and die in the midday heat.*

His throat tightened and he felt faint. *Go on,
keep talking.*

"As you know, my nomination to Health and
Human Services has been rescinded. I can't tell
you why because Congressman Lee refuses to
return my calls. Given the current climate of
the country and the city, I realize that's not going to change, I'm not going to HHS. So be it.
But there's no reason for the program we've begun here to suffer..."

He spoke for five minutes on the importance
of keeping RULA alive. Then got to what the reporters wanted to hear: "Due to what I think
is an honest misunderstanding, my reputation
is being impugned because of what happened
more than twenty years ago when an intruder
broke into my home and murdered my wife."
Patiently, his anxiety gone now, he led the reporters, minute by minute, through that night
—the dinner out with Carolyn, the window left

partly open on a warm evening, the intruder, the struggle, and the gunshots.

"Despite what's being alleged now, there was never any doubt that I acted to defend my wife and myself. The newspapers and police called me a hero. To put any other interpretation on it a quarter century later is not just misleading but malicious.

"If, because of this, or because I tried to help a woman being threatened here in Los Angeles, I have to give up my position in Washington, it's unfortunate but something I can live with. If I have to give up my association with Otis Law School, I can accept that also. But for the Rural and Urban Legal Assistance group to suffer because of this unwarranted character assassination is unconscionable."

He wiped his brow and realized his hands were beginning to shake again. *It's my future you've taken from me, damn you. My job, my program, my family...* He took a breath, let it slowly out, as though from the mouth of a balloon. The sun was beating down unmercifully and he became aware again of the terrible stench in the air. It must be from the garden, tropical plants decomposing in the heat. The stink of rot and decay was making him dizzy. Flies darted overhead, and something, a rat or a dog, was rustling around in the undergrowth behind him. His shirt was soaked with sweat. A sudden urge came over him to run. It was overpowering, a panicked voice screaming in his ears to get out of here *now*, to run and run and run until he ended up somewhere where no one knew him. Then he thought, *There's one thing left to do.* His gaze settled on the reporters, now completely obscured behind his heat-blurred vision, and he heard a voice—it had to be his—asking for questions.

And they came at once: Why did a Boston policeman say you'd been a suspect in the death of your wife? Why didn't you tell Congressman Lee about the trouble in Boston? Why do the police say they don't believe your story about two kidnappers? What happened during those missing thirty minutes?

For fifteen minutes it went on. Sweat dripped along his neck to the small of his back as he tried to keep up with the questions. What Ann and JG must think of him now! He was being made to look petty and shameful as everything he'd devoted his life to came apart, piece by piece, in front of the cameras, in front of America.

Then there was a murmur, an unexplained parting of the crowd as reporters leapt nervously aside, letting the lanky olive-skinned young man he'd seen earlier advance determinedly toward the podium. Robert's legs started to give way as he saw the next few minutes present themselves with perfect clarity. Everything that would happen, everything he would feel. *No*, he prayed hopelessly. *Please* ... But whatever force gave him the power to see the future also kept him frozen in place.

The young man began to shout at Robert, and at once the cameras spun away from the podium to take in this tall intruder with his flushed face and angry sing-song voice. "You are evil man, Mr. Binder. *Evil!*" The word rang thrillingly above the on-lookers. They stood on tip toes, listening, watching, waiting. "You ruined my family—"

I did, Robert thought as the man continued screaming furiously and advancing toward him with ungainly, awkward steps. *But I didn't mean to. It was a mistake. I shouldn't be paying for it now.* But he would, Robert saw. For now, forever. Because he was fixed to this spot, because he could not think, because his future had been fated since he stopped his car on Normandie.

"You should die. You killed. You don't deserve to live."

Robert's face felt as if it were on fire. The young man was approaching with the sun to his rear, burnishing his wild unkempt hair and shadowing his relentless movement toward the podium. He could see that the man was holding a bucket at his side. Rousing himself too late, Robert tried to move but couldn't, his legs frozen with panic and resignation. *I did a terrible thing. I know, I know.* He opened his mouth to the youth but couldn't say anything. His eyes clouded, so he didn't realize until he felt the moisture and took in the horrible odor that he had been drenched in urine and feces. It stood in his hair and dripped from his head and shoulders, across his chest and down his slacks to his shoes as he stood alone, and the man yelled at him, and the cameras took it in for all time.

30

THE air in the conference room was warm and murky and thick as Jell-O. Sitting at the elaborately carved table, Ann felt she was drowning, sinking beneath the surface and helplessly gasping for breath.

"...*real* growth in Ukraine we project at closer to three percent. Once you factor out the bullshit increase in petroleum production they keep talking about, and factor in..."

She was going to scream. If she didn't get out of here, she was going to scream. She twisted uncomfortably in her leather club chair, her arms accidentally brushing the printouts and monographs in front of her onto the deeply-carpeted floor.

The MIT economist stopped in mid-sentence, looking over his half-glasses at her while she bent to pick up the papers. The other dozen people in the room were also staring in a sort of stunned disbelief as she hurriedly put everything back on the polished mahogany tabletop in front of her. "Sorry. Go ahead. Bullshit petroleum production..."

Belasino glared as though she had just insulted his mother. "Please, Doctor Binder."

Ann looked at him. *Please? Please what? Please sit here and listen to this jerk from Boston rehash what everyone in the room already knows, while we pay him an eight-thousand-dollar daily "consulting" fee? I can't take this. I have things I have to do. And this meeting should have ended an hour ago.*

"And factor *in*," the MIT professor continued in an aggrieved tone, "the underground economy. We estimate that at a *remarkable* twenty-two percent of GDP."

Ann stood up. "I have to go. I'm sorry. I'm... not feeling well." Her voice was over-loud, over-strident, but she couldn't help herself. Again she was the center of attention, everyone staring at her as though her nose had fallen off.

Belasino was livid. "I don't understand. You're *leaving*?"

"I told you. I don't feel well. I'm going to be sick."

"But our meeting—"

"You want me to be sick here?"

"No. Of course not."

"I'm sorry." She snatched up the papers and reports. "I'll talk to you tomorrow."

Belasino scrambled to his feet so quickly he had to steady his thin body against the table. He wanted to say something but seemed not to know what, not with all these guests present. Above all else he mustn't appear not in control of his own staff. His hands shook as humiliation roiled through him.

Ann paid no attention. Clutching the papers, she hurried from the room with one final angry look in his direction. *Fire me, goddamn it.*

Twenty minutes later she was sitting in her car in front of Sandeep Chaudhary's home on 22nd Street. Her stomach tightened as she stared at the single-story clapboard cottage, one of thousands that had been hurriedly thrown up in the 1920s as the city spread west and south. It hadn't been painted in decades and burglar bars covered the windows. An ancient Big Wheel and soccer ball were baking in the dead grass of the front yard. No car in the driveway. Maybe he wasn't home. Maybe he's looking for a job. Or attacking cars with shopping carts.

It didn't matter. If he wasn't here she'd wait. She wasn't going to let a madman destroy her family.

She got out of the car and walked up to the house. But as she approached the front door her knees gave way and she realized how stupid this was. After what she'd seen of him the past few days, there was no doubt the police were right. *A psychopath. A dangerous man.*

As she turned back to her car the house's door flew open and an angry Sandeep Chaudhary stood barefoot in the opening wearing worn slacks and a yellow T shirt that said LAKERS in bold purple letters. His eyes swept over her head to the street, as if expecting someone to be there, then angrily back to Ann. "What are you doing here, Mrs. Binder?"

There was still time to return to her car. But she heard herself saying, "I want to talk to you."

Chaudhary's face screwed up—it was the same expression she'd seen in her home and at the supermarket, the pure, unalloyed fury that she was still alive—and he started to slam the door. *Good!* she thought. *He won't talk to me, I won't have to go through with it.* Then he had a change of heart, muttered, "Wait," and disappeared inside. Thirty seconds later he yanked the door open and allowed her to pass inside, their bodies almost touching. He hadn't shaved in days, his thin hair was uncombed, and Ann could now see the quarter-sized splotches of dried blood on his shirt. "Talk about what?" he demanded as they stood in the small living room. There was only a couch, a television on a card table, and two folding metal chairs in the room. The house wasn't air-conditioned, yet the windows were closed, making the air intolerably hot and foul with a dozen noxious smells.

Ann wiped perspiration from her forehead. "I want you to leave my family alone."

Chaudhary was clearly surprised, then furious. "Alone? Your husband, Mrs. Binder, killed my Nazia. He should have left *us* alone. And he gets away with it. Because Nazia was Indian he can kill her and nothing happens to him. This is not right." He began to stride rapidly around the room, picking things up from the floor: an

Indian newspaper, socks, a toy truck. "I talk to Reverend Stackhouse, very nice man. He tells me this is wrong, this is not the way it should be in America. He is helping me. We will have justice."

"Sandeep, Robert was trying to help. Honestly—"

"No, Mrs. Binder. He lied to you." Chaudhary hadn't stopped moving, bending and snatching things up. Grabbing one of the metal chairs, he folded it with a *snap* as loud as a gunshot.

"That's not true. Those men—"

In a fury Chaudhary flung the chair at the wall. Suddenly he was next to her, glaring at her. "Mrs. Binder, there were no men. Your Robert paid Nazia for sex in his car. Many times. *This* is true. He gave her one hundred dollars. Then Nazia did stupid thing. She said if he didn't give her more money she would tell you. She knew where you live. We followed him, Mrs. Binder. How do you think I came to visit you? Nazia asked for another fifty dollars only. For this your husband killed her. Fifty dollars!"

"Please don't do this, Sandeep. Whatever happened, don't destroy my family."

Chaudhary's arms shot out, clawing at the air between them like a man falling from a cliff. "*Your family!* Your family is evil. Your husband kills Nazia, now your son, this nasty one, is trying to steal Rajesh's wife. He should die, your son, for what he does."

"John isn't trying to steal her, Sandeep. He likes Meena. He just wants to be friends."

For an instant she thought he was going to hit her. His fists flew up in a rush, then fell to his side. "Meena is married to Rajesh. Do you understand? Married! In India she would die for what she's done. Your son is to stay away from this family. Your husband is to stay away. All of you. It is dangerous for you to be here." He picked up the chair he had thrown and slammed it against the wall.

Ann's head was spinning. "This isn't right, Sandeep. Can't you just leave us alone? Robert's professional life has been ruined. He's lost his position in Washington, he's in danger of losing his job at Otis. Even his law firm wants him gone. Isn't this enough? Stop trying to get him arrested."

Chaudhary glanced at the hallway and the bedrooms beyond, then looked at Ann. "Mrs. Binder, your husband is an important man so people listen to him. But he is telling you lies. I am telling the truth. People like me have no chance in the world against someone like your husband. But I will keep on. I am in the right." His voice was almost gentle. "You know that, Mrs. Binder. *I* am in the right. Not your Robert."

"I'll give you one hundred thousand dollars to stop what you're doing and go away," Ann said abruptly. Her voice raced. "It's my money. I don't want Robert to know. I can have it for you tomorrow. If you leave California."

A startled look came over Chaudhary. "And go where, Mrs. Binder?"

"I don't care. Back to Singapore. Or New York. Anywhere."

His voice sank to a whisper and sounded almost disappointed. "You would do this for your husband? This money?"

Ann saw again the madness in his eyes that she had seen at the supermarket. She shuddered and stepped back. "Yes. For my family."

"You love them."

"Of course."

"But your husband went to Nazia for sex. Why did he do that? You are good with sex, yes? You like men, I know this. You like me. I can tell."

"Please, Sandeep. A hundred thousand dollars. Cash. Tomorrow." Though in the back of her mind, trying desperately to break through to consciousness, was the knowledge that no amount of money could appease the man.

He turned away. "No." His gaze darted to the hallway again, then back to Ann. "How much money do you have?"

When she hesitated, his voice became a scream. "What bank? Where is your money?"

"Angeles National. It's a small bank downtown."

"Call them. I want to know how much."

No, she told herself. Don't do it. Get out of here. She turned to leave but Chaudhary shoved the receiver of his landline at her. "Call!"

Ann looked at him but didn't move. He seized her wrist, squeezing painfully, and forced the phone into her hand. "I will listen when you ask."

"I don't know the number."

He was becoming increasingly agitated. "*Now! Call!*"

Her hand trembling, Ann dialed Directory Assistance, and when the number was given she had them make the connection. Seconds later she listened to a recorded menu of choices, then pushed the number 3 on the handset, waited, and punched in her pin number. Chaudhary grabbed the phone from her as they heard the computerized voice say, "The balance is... two hundred... twenty-two thousand... one hundred-forty-six dollars... and nineteen cents."

He swung the phone so hard against her temple it broke the skin. "I want it. All of it."

"Sandeep, that's for John's college. We have been saving it for him for years."

"All," he repeated.

Ann pressed a hand to her head to stop the blood flowing onto her cheek.

"Tomorrow," he demanded, and began to pace again, taking rapid, fury-fed strides around the over-heated room. "In cash. Then I will leave. You will do this for your family." When tears appeared he quickly moved closer, putting his hand on her shoulder. A tenseness had come to his eyes but Ann didn't see it, her mind churning too violently to think of anything but the menace facing her family. Only gradually did she become aware of Chaudhary's bobbing face, the hand moving around her, jerking her forward against his body. Her heart jumped and she took a step back, then another, until her spine flattened against the wall. Chaudhary put a hand on her breast, the other to her neck. "It is only your Robert I hate. And this stupid boy who—"

Ann broke the embrace as her mind cleared, and she attempted to step aside. *I could kill him*, she thought, surprising herself, but instantly recognizing its truthfulness. *I could kill him right now and not feel a moment's remorse.* But she said, "I'll have the money transferred to your account. It's too much cash to take out."

"No!" Furious, he rammed her head into the wall. "Cash, Mrs. Binder. Tomorrow."

Suddenly there was someone else in the room. "My son," Chaudhary said proudly, and smiled at Ann.

The thin young man staring at her from the front door was frightening in his silent fury. He said something in Tamil and Chaudhary jerked his head toward the bedrooms. Rajesh nodded, said something that caused Chaudhary to smile, then turned to Ann. "I will kill your JG if once more he talks to Meena. I will kill them both."

There were sirens in the distance when she left for home, more as she neared Vermont. A moment later, still shaken from her encounter with Chaudhary, she had to pull to the side as four police cars and a SWAT van surged past. Hoping to discover what was happening, she turned on the news station and caught the tail end of a report from the movie location. Evidently a group of actors, incensed that filming was being held up by chanting and bell-ringing residents, started heckling them. When a middle-aged actor shouted, "Don't you people have welfare checks to pick up?" fists started flying. "Just a minor flare up," the reporter said, though angry shouting could be heard in the background. "As a precaution the Mayor has ordered in specially trained riot police they were holding in reserve. Everything should soon be getting back to normal."

As she switched off the radio, Ann wondered what the hell normal had become.

31

"I know she's not his daughter. She's his niece."

JG was sitting on his bed, near to tears as he unburdened himself to his father, standing in the doorway. Robert said, "Then where are her parents?"

"Her father's dead. Her mother lives in Cerritos. But Meena was promised to Raj when she was three. They had that stupid ceremony, so her mom says they're married. She made Meena move in with them." He bolted to his feet, threw his head back, and pressed his arms to his sides as though forcing himself not to come apart.

Robert was at a loss for words. He had been in the shower, washing urine and feces from his hair and skin, when he heard JG running up the stairs. But Robert didn't think he could face him, his humiliation was so great. When he heard sobbing, though, he put on shorts and a T shirt and came to his son's room. The instant he saw the anguish on his JG's face his own problems receded and he wanted only to go to the boy, to put his arms around him, hold and comfort him like he'd done when JG was four. But he held back, frightened at the despair he saw.

JG's head sank onto his chest. "Raj..." His voice was brittle with emotion. "He rapes her... every night. Hits her. Forces her if she doesn't want to... Sometimes he just hits her anyway."

"I'm so sorry, John." The feebleness of his response was like a weight on Robert's back. *Both of us,* he thought in despair. *Both watching helplessly as our world shatters. Because of Chaudhary. Because this madman has targeted our family.*

"She's afraid they're going to kill her. They tell her stories about what it's like in their village. Her uncle was screaming at her that she brought shame to the family by seeing me. Even *talking* to a boy is forbidden. In India her own *brothers* would kill her to bring honor back to her relatives. They'd *have* to kill her, he told her, or *they'd* be killed." His head tilted up and he stared at his father, seeming very small suddenly, a child asking for the impossible. "We have to *do* something. We can't let them do this to her."

Robert felt helpless—felt again the shame and humiliation he had brought to his own family as he stood on the podium and let Raj drown him with shit and piss.

"I think Chaudhary heard her talking on the phone," JG went on. "If he did they'll do something bad to her. I know it."

Robert's shoulders slumped. "I don't know how we can help, John. There hasn't been a crime."

"The police ought to be able to do something. She's not his daughter. She shouldn't even be living there."

"But her mother approves. It's a family affair. And Chaudhary is family."

"She's being *raped*! She's only fifteen. That's not legal... they'll do something. They have to. Or he's going to kill her."

Robert was remembering what Asha Vatsyayan told him about Chaudhary killing before. Maybe it was only a rumor, but people who knew him believed it.

"We can't just sit here, Dad. Can't we go over to his house, the two of us, and take Meena away?"

"Is she locked up?"

"I..." His voice wavered. "I don't know. I think they have her in a bedroom most of the time. I don't think she's chained to the wall, if that's what you mean."

"Then if she wanted to leave she could. Right?"

John's gaze dropped to the floor. "I don't know. Maybe."

"We can't kidnap her. If she actually tells you she doesn't want to stay, maybe we can bring in the police, see what they can do. At the least they can look into how she came to be living there."

"What's that going to prove? It's not important now. What's important is keeping her from being murdered."

Robert stared at his son. "We'll think of something." But what? They were powerless. Not believing his own words, he said, "We'll get her out of there. I promise."

32

THEY made Ann wait for an hour in the bank's small conference room after trying and failing to talk her out of her withdrawal Finally she was called into the manager's office where the money had been assembled into stacks of fifty- and hundred-dollar bills.

"I think you should let me call the police, Mrs. Binder. I know you don't want to talk about it, I won't ask anything, but please—"

"No," she snapped. She was going to come undone right in front of them if they gave her any more trouble. "Just give it to me! Now!"

Carlson Tang, whom Ann had known for twenty years, was clearly distressed. "Is there *anything* we can do? Is someone waiting for you outside? Are they watching you? I can have the police send plainclothesmen to follow when you leave. No one will know."

Ann's body almost exploded with the effort to remain calm. "Carlson, this is not a kidnapping. Believe me. I just need the money. Please stop delaying and let me have it."

He sighed and stood up. "If you'll sign the receipt, I'll count it out for you."

She grabbed the paper and scribbled her name without reading. "I don't want it counted. Just put it in an envelope and let me out of here."

In the car on the way home she was listening to the all-news station when she heard about the press conference. "The ongoing saga of the law school professor and the woman he shot keeps getting more and more bizarre..." She felt tears suddenly pressing against her eyes, then anger took over. *No! One of us has to be strong.*

Staring at the iPad on the kitchen counter Ann watched for the third time—the five o'clock news, the five-thirty news, and now the six o'clock news—as her husband stood in front of a backdrop of fiery tropical flowers while two gallons of urine and feces dripped from his hair and shoulders, sliding down his torso and slacks to his shoes and onto the podium. Her voice sounded to her like the voice of a stranger, some hideous alien who had been hiding inside her body, as the angry, disbelieving words filled the kitchen. "How could you let him do that, Robert? Didn't you see him coming? Couldn't you get away?"

She knew she shouldn't criticize. It wasn't fair. Especially after he had experienced this public humiliation. But she had no control over what she said now. This other person inside her was speaking, this stranger with the angry, disbelieving words.

Robert sat at the kitchen table with JG, the air conditioner rattling in the background. No one was interested in having dinner. JG was staring into space, and Robert's fingers tapping on the tabletop made Ann want to scream. Without looking up, Robert said, "I couldn't move. I saw him coming, but I just... froze." His head hung low. "What have you got to be upset about? I'm the one who looks like an idiot."

"The whole idea of a press conference was asinine. I *told* you that. Why'd you have to humiliate yourself in front of the world? Who were you trying to impress."

"Christ, Ann, I fucked up. OK? Is that what you want to hear? Or are you afraid I made you look bad, too? Is Belasino going to *tsk tsk* tomorrow because your husband's a fool? It's not exactly news, is it? Lester Holt and David Muir have already made it official."

Ann's eyes closed and she arched her back as an angry sigh roared through her. *Don't answer. Don't make it worse.*

At the mention of Robert's name everyone turned to the TV again. William Macklin, Chief of the Los Angeles Police Department, wearing his heavily-starched navy-blue uniform with four perfect stars on the lapels, was standing at a microphone, the Mayor and a dozen other people behind him. Macklin was saying, "... this commission will look into how the

Nazia Chaudhary killing was handled by the Department. We take any crime seriously, but especially crimes of this nature. Everyone deserves a city safe enough to walk in, no matter what the hour."

"Will Reverend Stackhouse be part of this commission?" someone asked. Or more correctly, challenged, since anger and defiance were obvious in his voice.

"Of course."

"Will Robert Binder be questioned?" Another reporter, another burst of pious hostility.

"The commission has no subpoena power, but naturally he will be asked to appear."

Someone said, "Why do hate crimes have such a low arrest rate? Statistics show that..."

As Robert angrily turned it off, JG bolted up and jerked open the refrigerator, grabbing a can of Mountain Dew. Eyes closed, he pressed it against his forehead for a moment before slouching down again at the table. No one spoke until Robert said, "I'm talking to the Trustees tomorrow. The dean's election is in the afternoon. I said I wanted to talk to them first. About RULA. They owe me that after all these years. Maybe we can figure a way to save it."

Ann said waspishly, "Zalesky already told you he's kicking RULA out. What's the point?"

"Maybe the board will overrule him. I don't know. I have to try something. I can't just let it die because he's afraid of a little bad publicity. Anyway, Zalesky hasn't been elected yet."

"You'd support Jirasek? Knowing what he'd do to the school?"

"I don't have a vote, Ann! I'm only talking to the board. They said I could have five minutes."

"To try to save a program you've run for twenty years. How magnanimous of them."

"It's how it is. I'll do what I have to. I'll beg or grovel or whatever they want." He stood up, angry, embarrassed, tired of justifying himself.

"Beg or grovel," she repeated dully as JG popped the top on the Mountain Dew can. Her thoughts were on the press conference again. "Did you watch yourself on TV? Did you actually *see* how you looked to the world?"

His head moved slowly back and forth. He wasn't going to watch it. He didn't have to.

"You looked pathetic, Robert. You looked stupid. You looked like you were guilty, like you deserved to be covered in shit." *Why am I doing this?* she wondered. *Why am I taking everything out on him while at the same time trying my damndest to save my family?* Upstairs in the bedroom, in two large brown envelopes she'd hidden in the closet, sat the two hundred-twenty-two thousand dollars that would make their troubles go away, make her family whole again. And someday, a week or a year from now, when everything was back to normal, she'd tell her husband and her son what she'd done.

But she still felt her fury at him growing. Who else was there to blame? Everything they had as a family was being threatened because

Robert had stopped on Normandie to... what? No, that wasn't fair. If she had not asked him to get her medication none of this would have happened. It was her fault, too. *But I didn't ask,* she realized; *he volunteered, he insisted, after making sure I went to sleep.*

Robert stared at her, his face red. "Why are you getting on me like this? I'm the victim here, I was attacked in front of millions of people. But you need me to be the bad guy for some reason. What does that do for you? Make you feel superior somehow?"

"*What about Boston, Robert?*" The anger had gotten away from both of them now and was racing through the room on its own, like a snake that had escaped from a box and was snapping at whatever it saw. "What really happened in Boston? Are there any other little revelations you want to tell your wife and son? More secrets you haven't found time to reveal in the last twenty-two years? Come on, Robert. Be honest for once. Do it for us, for the family you love so much. We're the Binders. We're special. We soar."

He looked as if he was about to hit her. "Damn you!"

Soda exploded in the air as JG slammed the can on the table and leapt to his feet. "*Stop it, God, stop!*" He was trembling, his face red and fists clenched at his sides.

Ann looked at him and felt the fury drain from her heart as her son's eyes began to flood with tears. She opened her mouth to apologize, but he said loudly, "I'm going out," and pulled the car keys from his pocket.

"You're not going to Chaudhary's are you?" Ann hurried after him as he stalked from the kitchen.

"Of course not. It would just make things worse." He stopped at the front door, trembling, trying to keep the tears at bay.

Ann put a hand on his shoulder, and flinched when he twisted away. "Things will get better, John. Tomorrow. I'm sure." They *would*, she was certain of that. But only because Chaudhary and his sons would leave California forever.

JG's body sagged against the wall. "How can they treat her like this? She's only fifteen. She's a kid. It's not right. She ought to be with her mother."

Robert had also come out to the hallway. His voice was weak with exhaustion. "Chaudhary's from rural India, John. He doesn't think he's doing anything wrong. He's just acting the way his own parents or relatives and friends would. He has to set right anything that might shame him or his family. Including you seeing Meena." But Asha Vatsyayan had thought otherwise, hadn't she: *pathology, not sociology*. "We'll talk to the police tomorrow," he added feebly. "Maybe Child Protective Services can get involved. I'll *make* them get involved. I promise."

"John," Ann pleaded, "be careful. Please don't do anything stupid tonight. Let's not—"

"Be irrational?" he whispered with such fury she stepped back as though slapped. His body uncoiled and seemed to shrink toward the floor. In a small voice he said, "She's pregnant."

"Oh, John."

"Chaudhary doesn't know. Raj doesn't know."

"I'm so sorry. How does she feel about it?"

"How do you think she feels? She was raped."

"She can get an abortion," Robert said.

"He'll kill her first. Raj. Or Chaudhary. They'll kill her before they'll allow that. They might kill her anyway. They have their *honor*. Their *pride*."

"John—" Ann began but stopped when he grabbed the door handle.

"I know, I know. I won't do anything stupid."

"Tell me," Sandeep Chaudhary said softly.

"Killing her is not enough. This stupid *boy*—" Rajesh was speaking Tamil, as he always did at home. The rage he felt was almost too much for him and his breath caught in his throat.

"The shame is unbearable. Unbearable."

"And the woman who insults you with money."

Sandeep Chaudhary was watching his son's eyes, searching for hints of doubt. After all, Rajesh had lived away from India since he was a child. So, a test: "Meena is very pretty. A strong girl. She would have given you sons. You would have been proud."

The boy said nothing.

"Rajesh."

"Yes!"

"But we should have returned to India. These girls in America are all whores."

Raj agreed, but with his eyes only, his face a mask now.

Chaudhary's voice hardened as he added, "American girls mock you. They have no respect. They have sex with a hundred men."

Raj started to respond but changed his mind, pressing his lips so tightly together they seemed to disappear. Sandeep thought maybe there was a ghost of a doubt after all. Perhaps the boy wasn't ready. Feeling anger rise but keeping his tone calm, speaking as a father should, brooking no dissent, he said, "Tomorrow, Rajesh. When they die all will be right."

But the boy surprised him with his fury. "It is only this JG I want, Father. I don't care about the others."

Chaudhary understood, and touched his son's hand, sharing his anguish. "But Meena also. She is your responsibility. She is the one who brings you disgrace, makes you look the fool." Chaudhary had told him many times about his nephew in India, how he restored pride to the family by killing his sister after she shamed them. He added, "The others I will take care of. The whole family will pay for what they've done."

But this Ann Binder was most important. She stormed through his thoughts every minute of the day and night. This woman who made a fool of him in front of a hundred people at the market, who tried to buy him with her bags of dollars and used her sex to mock him. She should be made to bleed, he said to himself. Like Nazia, she should bleed onto the ground.

Meena would be necessary to accomplish all this. He was not sure why this was so, but believed it implicitly. Before she died Meena would bring about everyone's death. First, though, he had another job for her.

When Chaudhary focused on his son again, however, he could see Raj regarding him with suspicion. Chaudhary felt himself grow warm, but he forced himself to remain calm. This was something new, the child doubting his father. *It's because we left India,* he knew. *Because we tempted fate.* Was that fear in the boy's eyes? Fear of the father? Or hatred? It was hardly to be believed, but Chaudhary saw it, *saw* it. *Because we left India.* A mistake that could be rectified in only one way.

At 2:16 AM the phone woke Robert. He sat up, his heart charging though he was half asleep, and thought, *Lee? Finally!* But when he grabbed the receiver the tortured voice on the other end was hard to make sense of. "Meena? Meena, is that you?"

The soft whispered words seemed to hover seductively, puzzling his mind while sucking the last bit of self-respect from his soul. "That was my shit and my piss on your body, Mr. Binder. For calling Nazia a whore, for insulting our family, for all that you and your son do, I cover you in my waste."

33

JG bolted awake—heart racing and sweat flooding across his forehead—when he heard his phone go off. What time was it? He looked at the bedside clock through frightened eyes: 8:10 AM. Jesus, he should have been up two hours ago, but he'd driven around until three in the morning, going out to Malibu, immediately turning around and following Pacific Coast Highway all the way to Orange County, then heading back to central L.A., somehow holding himself together as he drove past Chaudhary's house a dozen times. Finally, he'd parked across the street, staring for an hour at the darkened windows as his head swam with fears too horrible to picture, but which hummed in the background of his mind even now.

Gulping down his panic he leapt from bed and grabbed the phone off the desk where he threw it last night. "Yes. What?" Knowing it was Meena.

He could hear the shower down the hall. Probably his mother. His dad was going into

Otis this morning. *Pop's Big Day*, he remembered. The day his professional life—RULA, Otis, DHP, everything—would crash and burn.

Meena's voice sounded strained, like she'd been crying. "Raj is at school. He took the cell phone away and broke it. They won't let me leave the house. I can't go anywhere." *Ever*, she meant.

"What about your uncle?"

"He went to Cerritos to get the little ones."

"I have to see you."

"I know." She began to weep. "But not today. We can't—"

"I'm coming over there. Now."

"No. Please, JG."

"Five minutes." He pulled on his pants.

"When will your uncle be back?"

Meena stood in the middle of the cramped living room, looking small and terrified in the dim light that made it around the edges of the old-fashioned blinds. Trembling, she wouldn't look at him. "I don't know. An hour. More. Raj will be here at eleven. Please go, you can't stay."

"We have to talk. Come with me, I can't stand it here. We'll be back before anyone returns."

"No, JG. Please."

"Have you had breakfast?"

She shook her head, a hand flopping weakly in the air as her body went slack.

"Look at you. You're scared to death. Come on, we'll get a Coke or something. You'll be back before Chaudhary gets here."

Her head wobbled back and forth, back and forth as she struggled against her upbringing. "I can't. I promised."

"Break it."

Ten minutes later they hurried through the drive-up window at McDonalds, getting Cokes and fries, then headed aimlessly down Vermont, only vaguely aware of the other traffic on the busy street.

"Something's wrong with my uncle," Meena whispered, forcing herself to say aloud what had been frightening her for months. "He acts crazy, screaming all the time. Not just at me. On the phone to his sister who has the twins, at some friend he has in Hollywood. Even at Raj. I think he threatened to kill everyone in your family last night, but it was in Tamil and I couldn't understand it well enough. I don't know—" The McDonald's bag sat unopened between them. "Sometimes he looks at me, just *looks* and says nothing, and it scares me so much I think I'm going to be sick."

"You can't keep living there, Meena. It's not right. No matter what your mother tells you. It's wrong."

"Raj is my *husband*, JG. I can't disobey. If I don't do what he says—" She cringed back against the passenger door as though hoping to disappear.

Something caught JG's eye and he reached out with his free hand, grabbing her shirt at the neck and yanking it down. Huge welts and black-and-blue marks covered her shoulder and upper chest. He let her go and she slipped back against the door.

"My uncle said he can kill me if he wants. That's his right." Her voice trembled. "Girls who bring disgrace on their family have to be killed to restore honor. He told me his brother in India stabbed his own daughter to death because she was seen outside with a man after she had been promised to someone else. And the family was *happy* he did it."

Overcome by emotion, JG pulled into the post office parking lot on Vermont and killed the engine. "You can't let him do this, Meena. Doesn't he know this isn't India?"

"I don't think he does know. He acts like we're living there, like nothing's changed from his childhood. Sometimes he talks about people he knew in his village, but talks like they live next door."

Suddenly a blue Honda Civic squealed around a line of cars, its front end loudly colliding with the VW, knocking it sideways.

"Raj!" Meena shrieked.

The lanky young man burst from the car, a pistol in his hand and shouting in Tamil. As he reached for the passenger door, Meena screamed and pushed down the lock, panic overtaking her. While Raj pounded on the window with the barrel of the gun JG turned the key, jammed into reverse, and the VW shot backwards, just missing an SUV exiting the parking lot. Slamming into drive, he floored the accelerator and the car exploded out of the lot and onto Vermont as half a dozen horns honked furiously.

"Stop!" Meena screamed. "I have to go to him. I have to."

JG paid no attention, turned unexpectedly into a neighborhood of eighty-year-old tract homes. The sidewalks and yards were crowded with kids and mothers and toys, everyone stopping to stare at the car racing by, some of the women yelling angrily at him to slow down. JG looked in the rearview mirror, saw the Civic just coming into view, and spun right at the first street, tires squealing loudly, heading toward a park where boys were playing soccer. Turning suddenly, he aimed the car over the curb and onto the soccer field. Kids shrieked and scattered as the VW kicked up dirt and grass, shooting diagonally across the park. At the far end he was forced to turn abruptly to miss a collection of playground equipment where children were screaming in terror. The car skidded wildly on the wet grass before JG was able to regain control, then bounced sharply, metal rattling against metal as it roared off the sidewalk and onto the street.

"You have to stop," Meena begged. Then, remembering, she screamed, "No, don't. He'll kill you. He told me if you see me again he'll kill you."

JG didn't know the neighborhood but figured there must be a police station nearby. Maybe he should head to Watts, he'd be sure to find a cop there. When the Civic appeared again in the rearview mirror, he spun hard left, racing north, then left again. Ahead he saw a three-story office building surrounded by a parking lot, and had an idea. Making sure Raj wasn't in his mirror, he pulled into the lot, looked for an empty space, and hurriedly parked, lost in a sea of cars. "He didn't see us. We'll wait a minute, then—"

But the Civic roared up behind them, crashing into the VW, sending it hurtling into the Jeep in front. Raj shot backwards, then rammed into the VW again and again. Meena screamed as JG slammed into reverse, but the car's bumper was hooked under the Jeep's rear end. The radiator spewed steam as the engine loudly turned over but the cars wouldn't disengage. Raj was at the passenger door, the gun in his hand, screaming at Meena. She sobbed but opened the door. He grabbed her by the hair and pulled her to the Civic. JG's door was jammed from the collision and wouldn't open. All he could do was sit there, screaming and pounding on the door as the Civic disappeared.

34

"I'M not asking for anything for myself," Robert said. "I want that understood from the beginning."

His back stiffened as he looked around the conference room table, taking in each member of the Otis board of trustees as they stared silently back at him. These dozen men and women—minus Edgerton Lee, who hadn't bothered to show up—weren't going to do anything for him, no matter what he said. It wasn't that they were hostile, more like embarrassed at being associated, even tangentially, with yesterday's press conference. The humiliation of Raj's attack, in their eyes, tainted the entire school. They wanted to forget Robert, pretend he never existed. He could accept this; he was beyond trying to protect his career. But he was desperate to save the Rural and Urban Legal Assistance program and would do whatever it took to do that. Including prostrating himself in front of the business executives, attorneys, and politicians who ran the school.

"I've been working with the poor all my life," he went on. "RULA is the culmination of this work. It is the only program of its type to offer direct assistance to the sorts of people this school was created to help. Otis has been generous in the past. I want to encourage you to continue this tradition. If that means I have to sever my connection to the program I will. If I —"

"Why did you choose to have that press conference on the school grounds?" a trustee Robert knew only vaguely, a lobbyist for a government-employees union, interrupted.

Robert stared at the man, then at the darkly-paneled room they were in with its dozen Old Master paintings collected by Cornelius Ryan Otis before his abrupt and unexpected conversion to the tenets of social activism. Suddenly everything he was attempting to accomplish seemed ludicrous. How could these people understand? During the twenty years of the program they'd never asked a single question about RULA. He kept his voice calm. "It was the logical thing to do. The Garden is where press conferences are usually held."

"But *school* conferences, certainly..."

Just then the door popped open, a burst of light and noise from outside briefly intruding, and Edgerton Lee walked in, apologizing for being late. As the heavy, carved door slowly swung shut, Robert could see Howard Zalesky seated in the hallway beyond, waiting to make his presentation to the board. Robert knew he had only three more minutes to save his life's work and tried to hurry on. "I wasn't trying to bring any embarrassment to the board or the school."

"Well, you certainly succeeded in doing so," Lee said as he slid his chair closer to the table. "It was almost as if that was your purpose. What the hell were you thinking?"

"If I could just speak about RULA a moment ..."

Ann dropped the two large brown envelopes onto the card table in Sandeep Chaudhary's stifling hot living room. "It's all there. Count it." She had to force her hands not to tremble.

Chaudhary was clearly agitated about something. He paced nervously in front of her and scarcely glanced at the envelopes. "Yes, yes, now go!"

"You said you'd leave California. I want you gone today."

His two small boys were running through the room, yelling, and kicking a soccer ball. One of them fell and started crying but Chaudhary seemed not to notice. He rubbed his eyes, glanced at the envelopes, and abruptly grabbed them, hurriedly ripping the tops off and letting hundreds of bills flutter onto the table. His gaze lost its focus and he stood as though drugged.

"Mr. Chaudhary," Ann repeated forcefully. "You promised."

His head snapped angrily, and he glared at her. "It is all taken care of. You leave now."

He seized her elbow and propelled her out the front door just as Raj came in, grasping Meena by her upper arms. The girl looked like a Raggedy Ann doll, stumbling over her feet as the young man dragged her at his side. She was sobbing, and an ugly smudge of blood streaked across her lips and chin. Raj was beside himself with fury, and he stared hatefully at Ann before hurrying the girl inside.

Out on the sidewalk feeling increasingly uneasy, Ann turned back to look at the house. Chaudhary waved threateningly, as if flinging rocks at a dog. "Go!"

"You promised to leave," she said in a weak voice. "Today."

A scream came from inside, and the sound of something breaking. "I will do what I said," Chaudhary shouted, and disappeared inside. As the door slammed another scream escaped from the house, and she could hear the twins begin to wail.

Her phone was buzzing as Ann came into her kitchen ten minutes later. As soon as she answered Belasino was shouting at her. "Ms. Binder, you are expected to adhere to certain standards of professionalism. Since that seems beyond your abilities—" She hit "end call" and was fumbling with a bottle of Advil when the shrill ring of the house phone made her jump. She lunged for it. *Something's happened to John*, she knew with a mother's instinct. He hadn't been here when she got home. Where had he gone? He wasn't at Chaudhary's. And certainly not at school.

But it was Meena, sobbing uncontrollably, her voice so faint Ann could barely understand her. "I'm in my uncle's bedroom. Please, Mrs. Binder, listen to me. Raj and my uncle are planning to kill JG. I hear them now. They say it's their right, they *have* to do it. Because of the shame. Because of what I did. *It's my fault.*" She quickly told Ann what had happened at the parking lot.

"No—" Ann whispered. Just minutes ago, Chaudhary had promised to leave. But in the back of her mind, because it was too alarming to bring to consciousness, she knew that trying to bribe him had been incredibly stupid. Money was the wrong inducement, an insult to this proud man.

"Raj has a gun," Meena said in a frightened voice. "He hit me with it. He said now he will kill JG and his father. *He'll do it! He will, I know he will!*" Meena was screaming and whispering at the same time as she tried to make Ann understand.

"But I gave your uncle money to leave. He *promised.*" She paused, knowing how ridiculous this now sounded.

"He threw the money on the floor," the girl cried. "He never wanted it. You were the one who made him take it. He's going to burn it, burn the house down. He took it to hurt you because he said money is what you love more than all else. Not family, not honor, not what's *right*. He thinks—" Suddenly there was a scream, and a banging noise, then a louder scream that made Ann shudder. She heard Raj shouting, the sound of the phone hitting the floor and bouncing away, followed by the maddening calm of a dial tone.

Her body trembling, Ann tried to hold her fingers steady as she punched in DeFazio's number. "OK," he said. "I guess we need to see what the hell's going on over there. I'll have a patrol car stop by Chaudhary's and check things out. We can have them keep an eye on your house too, maybe drive by every hour or so—"

"Thank you," Ann whispered, but thought: *It's too late for Meena, they can't get there in time.*

"But let's be realistic, Mrs. Binder. All we've got is a hysterical girl's accusations. If the patrolmen don't find any evidence of a crime there's nothing they'll be able to do."

"They threatened to kill my husband and son, for God's sake."

"I understand that. But we can't arrest anyone because of what the girl says. We can't even go in their house without probable cause. They have their rights too, you know."

Ann bit her tongue to keep from saying anything.

"I'll tell them to talk to the girl. But don't expect her to make any accusations to the police. Kids don't like seeing their parents arrested."

"She's not his daughter. She's his niece. She shouldn't even be living there."

"But the mom agrees with this set-up, right? It's a family decision."

"The girl's being raped, for God's sake. She's only fifteen and her cousin is keeping her like she's some kind of sex toy. They have this bizarre marriage agreement—"

"No more bizarre than your own marriage must appear to them." Evidently thinking he may have gone too far DeFazio quickly added, "If the patrol officers think she's in any danger they'll contact Child Protective Services. CPS can come out there in the morning and take a report. But there's a lot going on in your neighborhood right now. I'm not sure we'll have the resources for a while."

"Take a report!" Ann was stunned by his stupidity.

"Look, Mrs. Binder, the law is set up to protect people from unreasonable harassment by the police. What they do at home is their own business. From what you've told me you couldn't even get a restraining order."

"*I don't want a restraining order*. And don't lecture me. Robert's the one with an exaggerated respect for the law, not me. These people want to kill my husband and son, and you're talking about knocking on the door and asking them if everything's all right."

"What would you suggest?" The voice of reason... speaking to the voice of hysteria.

"Arrest them. They've made threats. They have a gun."

"The girl says."

"Damn you," Ann screamed. "Damn you!" She slammed the phone down then snatched it up again and punched in JG's cell number. She let it ring until it went to voice mail, then, her voice cracking, she repeated what Meena had told her. "They're serious, John. Come home! Now! *Do you understand? Now!*" Then she called Robert.

The phone went off as Robert was trying to explain that RULA's arrangement with Otis was unique in the degree of autonomy it allowed students in assisting with high-level court cases that had a real impact on society. His face reddened when he heard the beeping from his sport coat. He thought he had turned the it off before coming in here but must have been too nervous to remember. He grabbed the phone from his pocket, checked to see who the call was from, then switched it off.

Edgerton Lee's eyebrows arched. "We keeping you from something?"

"I'm sorry. How much time do I have left?"

35

Pacing back and forth in the kitchen, Ann kept the phone in her hand, hitting redial every few seconds. But both JG and Robert must have turned their phones off. She could sense herself coming apart, pieces of her mind spinning off into space as she slipped deeper and deeper into hysteria. But she had to keep at it. The police weren't going to help. It was up to her. But, my God, where to look? She tried Wilkerson. No, JG hadn't been to class in weeks, was he planning—? She hung up, called Robert again and got voice mail.

The instant she put the phone on the counter it began ringing. She lunged for the receiver. "John?" Blood was pounding so hard in her ears she wasn't sure she could hear anything on the other end.

There was a pause, beats of terrible silence, before a woman's voice said, "Mrs. Binder?"

"Yes, yes—"

"This is Asha Vatsyayan."

"I'm sorry. I don't have—"

"Robert's friend. From UCLA."

"Oh—the sociologist.

"Is he there? I must speak to him."

"No. He's at Otis, I think."

"Mrs. Binder, it is vital I talk to him. I think someone is trying to harm him."

"Sandeep Chaudhary..." The words slipped out in a whisper.

"An Indian friend in Hollywood just called me. He said Mr. Chaudhary phoned him a few minutes ago and rambled on about Americans using money to cover up their crimes. He was very agitated. Just like India, he said, the rich can do whatever they want, and he—Chaudhary— was going to deal with it just like he did in India. He's planning to kill Robert, Mrs. Binder. He is not just making a threat. Do you understand me? He's not well, he's—"

"Mrs. Vatsyayan, do you have any idea where my son might be? Chaudhary is after him too."

"Your son?" She was surprised. "No. I'm sorry. Do—"

But Ann had already clicked off and was trying Robert's number again. Nothing. Nothing for JG. *I can't just stand here, I've got to do something,* she screamed inwardly. But what?

The only thing she could think of was the car. She ran out to her Nissan, started the engine, jammed it into reverse and shot backwards out of the long driveway. She quickly slammed on the brakes as she became aware of noises coming from somewhere, an indistinct rumbling that touched some frightening aural memory stored so deeply it hadn't risen to consciousness in years: the riots from several years ago, bands of angry young people and enraged adults, and the terrified, outnumbered cops and poorly-trained National Guard troops with their tanks and armored personnel carriers, the buzz and hum of chaos everywhere as buildings burned and people died. Then she relaxed as she realized it was from the movie site two blocks away. Residents venting their anger, shouting and blowing whistles and banging on pans as they tried to disrupt the filming. Suddenly it seemed so petty. Someone was trying to kill her husband and son and these people were complaining about a *movie!* But as her foot slammed down on the gas pedal she wondered if JG could be with the demonstrators. He'd been hanging out there lately, hadn't he? It wasn't likely, but she couldn't chance missing him. She switched off the engine and hurried out of the car, leaving the door open. Running as fast as she could she maneuvered between the barricades and police tape at the intersection and raced down the middle of the empty street, the confusion and noise and sense of madness—of something terribly wrong, fissuring apart and breaking everywhere—growing with every step.

Even from a block away she could tell there must be several thousand people massed in front of another set of barricades. They had been brought there by Facebook and Twitter, members of dozens of activist organizations, fueled by rage, real and assumed. Or by only a need to be a part of something. The massive police presence meant to ensure order had done just the opposite, causing the protest to metastasize, and it was creating its own energy and hatred now as more and more neighborhood residents were drawn in by its force. They were shouting angrily toward the trailers where the film crew had evidently taken cover. As she got closer she could see glimpses of armor-clad policemen nervously holding their nightsticks in a two-handed grip as though expecting to be attacked at any minute. A dozen mounted patrolmen, their horses high-stepping and snorting nervously, were at the patrolmen's rear. She was immediately swept up by the crowd and carried forward in its surge. Then a group of women started chanting "Hollywood out!" and it was suddenly all around her: *Hollywood out... Hollywood out... Hollywood out...*

"John?" Ann screamed the name as she pushed through the mob. *"John!"* My God, where was he? She cried out, noticing a few faces she recognized, but not her son. Twenty feet ahead she saw a half dozen young people wearing the black Guy Fawkes mask that marked them as members of the group Anonymous. Another group wore blue bandanas covering their faces. Everyone yelling, pushing. Chaos. Chaos. She would never find John amid this chaos. Spinning around, she began to force her way back, fighting the rush of bodies moving against her. The demonstrators had worked themselves into a frenzy, chanting, hating, ready to explode. She had to get out while there was still time. She was almost free when someone called her name. Whirling around she saw Beth Sylvester waving at her.

"Not leaving are you?" the older woman yelled. She was carrying a cow bell that she had been clanging loudly.

"I'm looking for JG," Ann shouted. "Have you seen him?"

"Not today." Beth maneuvered around a large man with a bull horn and worked her way to Ann. "What's wrong? Something's happened, hasn't it?"

"It's that Indian man. I think he's going to try to hurt Robert and JG."

"My God—"

The mounted policemen were fumbling in backpacks for gas masks as the other cops began moving barricades aside as if ready to force the crowd away from the trailers and mobile homes. "I can't stay, Beth. If you see JG tell him to go home and lock the door."

She didn't wait for an answer, breaking free of the crowd and racing down the street, arriving at her house just as a police car pulled into the driveway. Ann screamed and sprinted forward as Detective Jill Oakley stepped out. "Oh, my God. It's John—" Her knees weakened and she almost collapsed.

"Your son? No, I just wanted to let you know a patrol car's been to Chaudhary's. There was no one home so—"

"No one home? But I saw them, they were there. All of them, even the girl."

"The officer knocked and no one answered so he went around back and tried that door. He'll try again every hour or so if he's not tied up elsewhere. Of course, God knows what's going to happen with this movie shoot. Those people are pretty upset. I don't blame them. But still —" Oblivious to Ann's hysteria she looked down the street. "I'll drive over to Chaudhary's tomorrow and have a talk with him. It'll all work out. I promise."

"Damn you, they're going to kill my husband and son. If they're not home it means they're looking for them."

"Nicky told me what you said. But we can't do anything just because someone talked about what might happen. If he comes over here with a gun, of course, it's a different story."

"Of course. I'll call the police and thirty minutes later someone will show up. Then he can call the coroner."

"We have a car coming by every hour. You'll be all right."

"Do you know how incredibly stupid that sounds?" She stomped back to her car.

"Look, Mrs. Binder... Ann." Oakley came up to the Nissan. "People make threats all the time. I guess it makes them feel better. But they almost never actually do anything. It's all talk. It's a way to blow off steam. If they didn't threaten they probably *would* do something."

Her body trembling so badly she could barely stand, Ann climbed in the car and slammed the door without responding. She knew what she felt may have been irrational, may have been nothing but a mother's panic, but she was certain something bad was happening right now as they spoke. As certain as she had been at Edgerton Lee's party when she felt something rustling in the darkness, waiting to destroy her family.

Once again she jammed the car in reverse and shot backwards out of the driveway. Holding her phone in one hand, she hit redial and heard it ring and ring.

36

Tears streaming down his face, JG tried desperately to disengage the two cars, pulling furiously and kicking with his feet. But they wouldn't budge. Finally he jacked up his car and accelerated backwards, sending the jack flying under the Jeep as the cars tore apart with a loud ripping and crunching of chrome and steel. The damaged radiator sent an angry plume of steam shooting into the air, but he ignored it and threw the gearshift into drive. The transmission made a grinding noise and hesitated, then lurched forward. He floored the gas pedal and raced out of the lot.

Turning onto 22nd Street, he saw a police car backing out of Chaudhary's driveway and he pulled to the curb to watch it disappear to the east. What the hell was that about? Did someone see Raj struggling with Meena and call the cops? He took his foot from the brake and let the VW drift past the house, staring uneasily as he went by. If the cops had taken Raj or Chaudhary away there would be neighbors clumped in groups on the sidewalk, wondering what they'd done. But there was no one around, and the house looked abandoned. JG felt panic spreading through his body, making his pulse jump and eyes cloud. Where'd they go?

He circled the block again, pulling up fifty yards down the street and killing the engine. His heart racing, he waited, fingers opening and closing on the steering wheel as he watched the house. But no one came or went. No movement at a window. No sign of life at all.

Ten minutes later, not able to take it any longer, he started the engine—*Fuck it!*—and pulled right into Chaudhary's driveway, still with no idea of what he'd do if they opened the door. Force his way inside, grab Meena, rush her to safety like some comic book hero? *Why not, aren't we a family of heroes?*

Sweat streaming down his body, JG stalked up to the door and knocked. No answer. More knocks, then hammering with his fist, jabbing the doorbell furiously with his thumb. Nothing. *Where the hell are they?* Hurrying around to the back, he pounded on the rear door, tried the handle, then kicked as hard as he could but it wouldn't budge. He couldn't even look in a window with the blinds pulled all the way down.

Without a second's hesitation he ran to the garage and yanked up the door, feeling it almost come apart as it slammed noisily against the frame. It looked like no one had been in there in decades and it reeked of damp and decay, cat piss and dead rats. Flicking the light on, he pawed through a jumble of lawn equipment until he saw an ancient sledge hammer on the floor and grabbed it. Back at the rear door he swung the heavy hammer like a baseball bat. On the second attempt the door shattered and he kicked it open, hearing screams from inside.

JG rushed to the living room and saw Meena sitting stiffly in an arm chair in the middle of the room. Currency was everywhere, great heaps of fifty- and hundred-dollar bills, but he barely registered it.

"I didn't know who it was, I heard the noise. I was scared." Meena sobbed, shaking her head wildly back and forth.

JG's pulse began to slow. "Where are they?"

"Looking for you and your father. They went to the law school. You have to leave, you have to warn him."

"Come on, we're getting out of here."

"I can't go, John. Please, I told you. It was wrong for me to be with you." She paused only a second and her voice cracked. "I have to stay with my husband."

"Meena, if they want to kill me, they want to kill you, too." She seemed so tiny and oddly formal, sitting stiffly in the chair in the middle of the room like a child in "time out." Then he noticed blood on her face and a bruise on her cheek. "My God."

"It doesn't matter! I can't leave them."

"Goddamn it, you act like you're brainwashed. Hurry up, we're going to the police. When they see what he did they'll help you. But hurry, move!"

She shook her head, tears streaming from her eyes. "No. Just go! Please!"

"Come on!" He seized her arm and the chair almost tipped over. Releasing her, he stared in disbelief. "Jesus, you're tied to the chair," he whispered. Wire was wrapped around her wrists and ankles, then to the chair. She couldn't move. JG dropped to his knees and tried to unwrap the wire, but it was wound so tightly to itself he couldn't unravel it. He jumped up, remembering the piles of tools in the garage. "I'll be right back."

But as he turned he noticed three two-gallon gasoline cans, and all the air rushed out of his lungs. He tried to lift one, felt its weight, and stared at Meena, feeling dizzy and nauseous. "He's going to burn the house down. With you in it."

She turned her head and closed her eyes.

"And you'd let him?"

"JG, *go*—"

Nothing made sense. He wanted to scream, throw things—wanted to hit *her* for some rea-son. This didn't fit it into any realm of rational behavior, any experience he'd had before. Then he remembered the wire and ran out to the garage. Moments later he was back with nee-dle-nose pliers. He forced his trembling hands under the binding on one of her wrists, cutting her skin in his haste, and snapped the wire, freeing an arm. Then the other wrist. Meena lifted her hands, sobbing so loudly she could hardly control her muscles. As JG freed her ankles and pulled her to a standing position, she sagged against his body. "Come on," he said. "We've got to get out of here."

"He has a gun. You have to tell your father. He'll kill him—"

"We will. Let's go." Then he saw a child's plastic boat on the floor. "Where's the twins?"

"He has them in the car. He's bringing them back here."

JG's mouth went dry but he forced the words out. "He's going to kill everyone, isn't he? You, the kids, Raj. Himself."

She didn't answer.

He grabbed her arm. "Come on, we've got to find my dad."

"*I can't!*" Meena screamed, breaking free and fighting him.

"You can't stay here. I won't let you!"

Again he seized her arm, but she was hysterical and kicked out at him, clawing at his face. He wrapped his arms around her and pulled her outside where her shrieks drew neighbors to their doors and windows. JG threw her in his car and hurried in after her. When she screamed that she hated him and lunged for the door handle, he grabbed her by the neck and pulled her against his body. With his left hand he held the steering wheel and raced away while Meena fought and yelled to be let free.

37

"WHAT happened in Boston isn't relevant to why I'm here today. The point is to save a very important program that might die because of this board's reluctance to take a compassionate stand in favor of the disadvantaged." The five minutes Robert had been promised had stretched to ten, then fifteen and beyond. But the trustees were less interested in RULA than the other baggage he brought to the meeting. How much was real concern for Robert and how much prurient desire to see someone bare his soul in public, he wasn't certain, but their attitude was making him angry. And he was worried about the phone call from Ann. What was so vital that she would interrupt him now?

Edgerton Lee glared down the carved and polished nineteenth-century trustees' table at Robert. "How can we divorce RULA from you, especially since you allowed yourself to be humiliated on national TV? And did so while appearing on the Otis campus and as a representative of the school?"

"I did not represent myself as connected to the school. That's nonsense." *Don't*, Robert warned himself. *Take a breath. Relax. You need these people.*

"Then why *this* campus, *this* lectern with the Otis shield visible to all the world?"

This is ridiculous, Robert thought with a quickening of emotion. He had to get out of here, if only long enough to make a phone call. He rose unsteadily to his feet. "I'm sorry... but I have to use the bathroom. I won't be long."

But Lee held up his hand like a policeman stopping traffic and looked around at the other trustees. "I don't think the board ought to be responsible for making a decision this impor- tant, considering that a new dean will take over as of July first. He's the one who will have to live with the consequences."

"What are you suggesting?" a woman asked.

"Let the faculty decide. They can do that at the meeting this afternoon before the election." He turned to Robert. "How does that sound?"

Like you haven't the guts to make a decision yourself. "Fine. OK. A vote." He reached for his cell phone and started to leave.

"Howard Zalesky and Karel Jirasek will be giving presentations to the faculty in forty min- utes," Lee said. "From what I gather this will be crucial to the election since attitudes toward the candidates appear to have shifted in the past week or two. And since this is such an important issue, I think it would be appropriate to give you ten minutes before the presentations to offer your vision for RULA and how it might fit into the school as we begin the new era with new leadership. If you are truly serious about saving the program, rather than your own neck, you might consider RULA continuing on without you."

"That's very generous." Even Robert wasn't sure if his words were meant sarcastically. Or if Lee knew of Zalesky's intention to jettison both Robert and RULA.

"You'll give your side of the picture during the open forum; the dean candidates will make their presentations; then an up-or-down vote: Otis keeps RULA, yes or no."

Robert was squeezing his phone. "Fine."

"Forty minutes," Lee reiterated, looking at his watch. "You'll be up first."

Robert was dialing as he hurried down the crowded hallway. No answer at home or at Ann's cell phone. He called JG with the same result. Now what? He started for the basement auditorium to do a little pre-meeting politicking before he had to make his presentation to the faculty. At the head of the stairway he thought, *Screw it*—after yesterday's humiliation he couldn't face any of them, couldn't tolerate the searching looks and phony sympathy. From the stage he could probably pull it off, but not face to face. Thirty-five minutes until he had to start. Time enough to get home and back if he hurried.

He began walking, but by the time he was to the sidewalk he was running. As he neared 26th Street he saw yellow police tape blocking the way and heard the chanting and howling demonstrators two or three blocks distant. There was an ugliness to it now, an anger that hadn't been there earlier. An LAPD helicopter appeared suddenly overhead, and three patrol cars raced down the street, lights on but sirens off. *That goddamn movie,* he thought with fury. *It's been hanging over us, threatening us, for weeks.*

OK, he'd have to go around the back way. He started running again and was covered with sweat by the time he got to his front door. "Ann!" He was yelling at the top of his voice. "John! Ann! Who's home? Is anyone upstairs?" But there was no response. Hurrying inside he took out his phone and again tried Ann's number. Just then he heard a car pull up outside.

38

THE door flew open and Ann shouted, "Where's John?"

Robert started to answer but she wasn't paying attention, her eyes racing around the room. "I've looked everywhere—school, parks, friends. No one's seen him."

"I just got here. I have to get back to Otis. What's going on? Why did you call me?"

"Did you look upstairs?"

"I called out for him. He's not here."

"*Did you look?*" she screamed, and when he said he hadn't, she ran upstairs. A moment later she was back in the kitchen, breathing heavily. "Meena called an hour ago. She was terrified. She said Raj and Chaudhary are looking for John. And your friend from UCLA called —"

"Asha?"

"They want to kill both of you, Robert. They're serious."

His knees weakened and he sank into a chair. "That's just talk, Ann. They wouldn't—"

"You don't understand." How could he be so damn naïve? How could any of them have been? "Meena's *married*, at least in their minds. She's disgraced the whole family by seeing JG. The only way they can deal with both problems is by eliminating their cause. You and John."

Robert struggled to his feet, his mind following a maddeningly predictable track. "All right. All right. I'll call the police." He reached for his phone.

"*I called the police*! They don't know where Chaudhary or Raj or any of them are." Vaguely she thought, *They've left California. He changed his mind and took the money and left.* But how likely was that? Chaudhary's world was fracturing; he needed to reestablish his family's honor, and money wasn't going to do that. Only JG's and Robert's death would. She seized Robert's arm, trying to shake some sense into him. "Do you understand what I said? They're after you, too. Because of what you did to Nazia!"

He felt the burden of this unfairness once again, like a weight pressing down on his shoulders, pushing him into the earth. "Ann, believe me. I stopped to help her. That's all it was. I didn't know she was a prostitute." His eyes implored her.

"Robert, I don't care. But you have to be careful. You can't leave the house until these people are caught."

"Who's going to catch them? No one's even looking. They haven't committed a crime." He looked at his watch. "I've got to get back to Otis. They're going to vote on RULA."

She wasn't paying attention. "Damn it, think! Where could JG be? You're closer to him than I am. Where would he go when he's upset?"

A helicopter flew so close to the house it rattled the windows, startling them. Ann's mind cleared momentarily, and she stared outside. "It's bad out there. Those people got so rowdy the police moved in to break them up. You'd think they'd know better by now."

More sirens could be heard in the distance, coming closer. As Ann turned from the window, the front door banged open, and a second later JG and Meena were in the kitchen. Ann shrieked when she saw her son. "Where have you been? I've been looking all over for you."

JG was breathless with panic and grasping the girl by the arm. "You've got to call the police, Mom. Chaudhary's going to burn down his house. With Meena in it, and Raj and the twins and probably himself. He's completely lost it, he wants to kill everyone."

"I've talked to the police, John. They're not going to do anything, they can't—" Then the girl's presence struck her. "I thought they wouldn't let you out of the house."

Before she could answer, JG said, "I took her."

"Took her?" Robert said loudly. "What does that mean? Kidnapped her?"

"Didn't you hear what I said? Her uncle wants to kill her."

"Do you think taking her out of the house is going to stop him? Now he'll come over here and ..." He fell into his chair as the full implication of what his son had done hit him. "God, John! What were you thinking? This is kidnapping, you could go to jail."

Ann said at once, "Meena, did you want to come here?"

"She was going to be burned alive, Mom. I had to do something."

"Meena," Ann repeated, "did you come here willingly?" JG was still holding her arm. He let it go as Meena shook her head but said nothing.

"Now we can't even call the police," Robert said. "You're more likely to be arrested than Chaudhary is. Do you know the penalty for kidnapping?"

"Calm down," Ann said, sounding not at all calm. "No matter how she left she's here now of her own accord. Aren't you, Meena? We're not keeping you here against your will."

Her voice was a whisper. "I don't know. It's OK—" She started crying softly.

"She's a juvenile," Robert snapped. "She doesn't do anything voluntarily. John's at risk here. He forced her from her house. Did anyone see you? Did she make a fuss?"

"Robert—" Ann was trying to keep from screaming. "Would you stop being so goddamned legal. No one cares about that now."

"I care! The police care. Chaudhary sure as hell cares."

"Dad, listen to me. He has a gun, he has gasoline all over his house. He's going to murder those little boys and Raj and Meena, and probably himself. All to keep her from seeing me. Why can't you understand that?"

Robert's body jerked, and he let out a sigh as JG's words finally penetrated through to consciousness. "Yeah—" he said softly. "A grand gesture. *The* grand gesture. I guess I *can* see it. With him."

"We have to do something," Ann said. "Meena can't stay here. But we can't send her back to her uncle either."

"Yes," the girl said at once. "I must go back. I have to. I can't be here. It will be OK. He won't hurt me. JG, listen!" She faced him and forced her body not to tremble. "I love Raj. He is my husband. We are having a baby. I don't want to be with you. I don't want to!"

JG's arms hung loosely. Tears clouded his eyes, and he couldn't speak. Robert quickly said to Meena, "You want to be married to Raj? This is your idea?"

"It doesn't matter..." Her voice was gently pleading.

Ann touched the girl's shoulder. "Would your uncle really burn the house down? It's not just a threat?"

Her head nodded slowly, up and down. Yes, yes, yes. He'll do it.

Robert said, "We're going to have to try the police again. Now that we have everyone together we'll explain it all and they'll take the necessary steps to protect her. You'll talk to the police, won't you, Meena? You'll tell them what you've told us? About Raj and Chaudhary?"

The girl was sobbing, but she didn't answer. When she spun around and started to dash out of the kitchen, JG grabbed her as more helicopters rattled the windows. "Can't you see what you're doing to her?"

Ann agreed at once. "We haven't time to argue. We've got to act."

"OK," Robert said, trying to calm everyone while he thought this out. "Meena can spend the night here. Tomorrow—"

"*No!*" the girl shrieked. "I can't! I have to stay with my family."

JG's voice was desperate. "She can't stay in the same house with a man who's not in the family. Everyone she knows would turn against her. Even her mother. She'd never forgive us, Dad. Honestly. We have to think of something else."

"All right," Robert shouted. "All right!" He began to stride around the kitchen. "This is what we'll do, then. I'll call Child Protective Services. We'll have Meena put in a group home. Only for as long as it takes to sort this out. Then the police can talk to Chaudhary, maybe get the courts to order counseling. And we can think about getting Meena made a ward of the court. Perhaps we could take care of her as guardians.

Not necessarily here but we could be financially responsible. In fact, I'll talk to the District Attorney about it tonight, to cut the red tape. Not one of his assistants either, the DA himself. I've met him a few times, been to his house socially. I'm sure he'll see me. This will be handled at the highest level. It'll be all right. I promise."

Ann was beside herself. "Robert, try thinking clearly. There's no way to protect her or our family if Chaudhary wants to do something. Counselors aren't going to get him to give up three thousand years of culture because you and I don't like it."

Robert was still holding his phone when it sounded shrilly. "Why the hell aren't you here?" Edgerton Lee demanded.

Robert's fingers squeezed the receiver. "Edgerton, I can't talk now. Maybe later." He turned it off, a vague feeling of destroying his life's work moving through him. "We can't stay here. Chaudhary's sure to show up when he finds out Meena's missing. We'll go to the D.A.'s. I'll call CPS on the way. They'll know how to handle this. Anyway, if we don't get out of here now we may not be able to, from the way it sounds outside." They could hear sirens again, and had the sense of things happening nearby without knowing what those things could be.

Moving quickly, Robert shepherded everyone out to the Saab. They could see more police helicopters, and pillars of black smoke rising from just two blocks away. Meena was reluctant but

JG put her in the back seat, where she sat quietly, hands to her face and trembling. Robert was about to pull out when a police car, its light bar flashing, roared up behind him, blocking his way.

39

Robert and JG climbed warily from the Saab as a heavy-set black policeman, followed by a clearly furious Sandeep Chaudhary, exited the patrol car. Chaudhary immediately began waving his arms and yelling in Tamil at Meena, who started to get out of the car, but Ann put her hand on the girl's arm. "Wait, hon. Let's see what the police do." When Meena shrank back against the rear seat and began to shiver, Ann put her arm around her.

Chaudhary started at once toward the Saab but the policeman restrained him. "Hold on. Let me talk to these people first."

Another black-and-white—siren and lights on—raced up, and a male and female officer walked over to the little group. The woman glanced at the Saab. "Dispatch said it might be a kidnapping. Is there a child involved?"

"A teenager, from what I gather." The black cop told the other officers what little he knew—most of it gleaned from Chaudhary—while the middle-aged patrolman had his head cocked, listening to the radio pinned to his shoulder.

His companion looked as though she'd done this sort of thing a thousand times. "I'll see what the girl says. You talk to these folks."

Her partner nodded toward two police helicopters in the sky several blocks away. They had been joined by several news choppers from local TV stations. "Downtown's thinking of calling a tactical alert. If they do, this whole part of L.A.'s going to be shut down and we'll be on duty for the duration, so you can forget about watching *Jeopardy* tonight."

She followed his gaze. "How bad is it?"

"Getting out of control, I guess. Dressing rooms and outdoor toilets tipped over, fist fights, rock-throwing, a couple of cars on fire."

"All right," she said impatiently. "Let's get this over with. One way or the other." She went over to the car and opened the door to talk to Meena. The black cop told Chaudhary to wait where he was and took JG and Robert aside. "Before we do anything, I'm going to read you both your rights."

"We know our rights," Robert said.

"You have the right to remain silent..." He went through the memorized spiel, then said, "Let me tell you two what you're looking at. It ain't pretty, so I don't want any bullshit, you understand? Neighbors of this man called 9-1-1 when they saw the boy here dragging that little girl from her home. She obviously didn't want to go. 'Kicking and screaming,' is what they said. So at a minimum, what we're looking at is kidnapping. Worse if we find out there's been a sexual assault."

JG shook his head, but said nothing, staring at the ground. Robert could tell he was close to losing control and put a restraining hand on his son's shoulder. The cop said, "I got to Mr. Chaudhary's house just as he was driving up with his twins. He's understandably upset. He left the boys with a neighbor so he could come with me, but he wants his girl home. She's only fifteen. Either she was forced to leave or she's a runaway—"

"She's not his daughter," JG snapped. "She's being held in his house against her will. They're the kidnappers."

"Not true," Chaudhary yelled from several feet away and raced up to them, his baggy trousers flopping against sandaled feet. "Meena is my daughter. This boy lies. He tries to steal her when she will not go with him. He tries to rape her. Arrest him!"

"Hannah," the cop yelled at the woman officer. "Ask the girl if she's this guy's daughter."

Chaudhary immediately began shouting at the girl in Tamil. The woman turned to them and yelled, "She said she is."

"The neighbors already told me that," the cop said to JG. "So why don't we start over and try the truth this time? Why'd you drag her over here?"

"Look at her," JG shouted. "She's scared to death of him. She's his niece. His son has her a prisoner in their home, *he's* raping her, Chaudhary probably is also. They're the ones who belong in jail." JG was breaking down. "She's just a kid. You can't let this happen."

"He's telling the truth," Robert said. "The girl's a juvenile. He has no legal right to keep her against her will."

"You a lawyer?" the cop asked sarcastically.

"I am."

The cop stared a moment, then an "oh, shit" look passed along his face as he seemed to recognize Robert. He yelled out again, "Ask her if she's being kept against her will."

The woman yelled back a negative.

"Looks like you over-stepped yourself, counselor. Or over-stepped yourself *again*. You and your boy. By now you should know what happens when civilians take the law into their own hands. That's why we have cops and courts."

"I want her back in my house!" Chaudhary shouted. "You have no right to keep her."

"Don't do it," JG yelled in alarm. "He's going to kill her. Did you go in his house? He has cans of gasoline in there. He's insane. He's going to burn it down with all of them inside."

Chaudhary's eyes grew large and he almost laughed. "This boy is the one mentally sick, officer. He is dreaming bad dreams."

"Looks to me," the policeman said to Robert, "that you two need to do a little work on understanding other cultures. People from India are very family-oriented. They certainly aren't going to be killing each other."

Robert's own panic was spiraling out of control. "You don't understand. This man has been mistreating that girl for months. He has some idiotic notion she's brought shame to the family by seeing my son. He thinks the only way to deal with that shame is to kill her. If you make her go back you're sending her to her death. We were on the way to Child Protective Services when you stopped us. This is something they should be involved with."

Chaudhary scoffed, throwing up his hands. "You know nothing." He turned to the Saab and shouted, "Meena, get in the policeman's car. We are going home."

The cop said to Robert, "Let me tell you how it's going to be. That girl's going back to her father. I'll have CPS look into things tomorrow. And I'm turning over this possible kidnapping to the detective bureau. They'll be in contact with you, but my guess is the boy gets charged. In the meantime, you both stay away from this family. Understood?"

Chaudhary was at the Saab, yelling over the policewoman's head at Meena. The girl glanced hopelessly at the officer, then climbed unsteadily from the car. Chaudhary seized her roughly by the elbow and dragged her toward the black-and-white.

JG was frantic. "Tomorrow she'll be dead! You have to arrest him!"

"Look, kid, you're the only one here I might arrest. Now just relax and let the law take care of things."

Just then there was an explosion from some-where, and everyone whirled around to see a huge cloud of smoke rising from several blocks away. "That's it," the cop said. "We're outta here." He twisted his head to say something in his walkie-talkie, then shouted, "You take the girl and the dad home, Hannah. I'm going to see what the hell's going on over there. Soon as you drop them off get your ass to 25th and Hoover. We're on alert."

As the police car drew away Robert saw Chau-dhary smirking triumphantly at him through the window. He turned to JG. "I don't know what's going to happen around here, but it's getting out of hand. Stay with Mom. She's go-ing to need you. I'm going to see the D.A."

"I'm coming with you."

"Stay here, damn it. If it looks like the house is in danger, don't try to fight a mob. Get your mother and get the hell out. Do you under-stand? Whatever you do, don't leave her alone."

Ann was upstairs half an hour later gathering up the flash drives where her research data was stored. The house was replaceable, her data wasn't; losing it would set her back a decade. She was listening to riot reports on the radio—the governor was sending in police from San Diego and San Francisco—when an unfamiliar sound outside drew her to the bed-room window. Smoke from fires was getting closer and closer to West Adams. According to the radio the demonstrators had appeared to be calming down, but when the police tried to arrest a young man who had driven his car around barricades on 29th Street, all hell broke loose. And now, like a forest fire, it was feeding on its own energy. Helicopters swooped overhead with loudspeaker announcements that all South-Central was under a curfew, anyone on the streets would be subject to arrest. Which meant Robert wouldn't be able to get back. He was trapped on the other side of the curfew line.

Across the street she could see neighbors turning on lights and standing on their porches to show that they were home. Three houses down a man from one of the universities—a sixty-year-old Iraqi immigrant—stepped onto his porch with an M-16 automatic rifle.

My God, my God, my God.

When Ann heard a noise at the front door she thought immediately of rioters forcing their way in. But before she could turn from the window she saw JG running to his car.

"John, no!" she yelled.

But he was gone, the VW racing south, away from the tanks.

40

JG's hands shook so much he could barely hold the steering wheel. Turning too quickly onto Hesperia, the car spun out, fishtailing wildly, side-swiping a station wagon and barely missing a parked motorcycle before he regained control. But none of it registered. He only knew he had to get Meena away from Chaudhary. What he would do when he got there, he didn't know. It didn't matter. He'd do something.

Then he was startled out of his fog when he realized there were half a dozen squad cars up ahead, jammed in every which way and blocking the street, red and blue lights spinning madly in the darkness. Smoke billowed and helicopters *thumped* just a few feet overhead, loudspeakers blaring something he couldn't decipher, but dozens of people were running in his direction now, mostly young but some middle-aged, even older people, like the whole neighborhood was moving out. They were yelling or laughing and darting up to houses and cars and down the middle of the street. *Having fun!*

he decided. *Enjoying themselves.* Damn them, damn them, *damn them.*

Throwing the car into reverse, he screeched back six feet, spun the steering wheel, and jammed into drive just as the front part of the crowd caught up to him, enveloping him in its surge, making him a part of it. Suddenly people were everywhere, and he couldn't go forward or backward. A few of them banged on his car, yelling, "Hey, get the fuck outta our neighborhood... You a cop? ... Looks like a fucking reporter..."

JG had no idea what to do. He wanted to step on the gas, but too many people were in front, more to the rear. Others saw the excitement, the car being pummeled—hell, he was the only idiot trying to drive tonight—and rushed to join the fun, pounding on the windows and hood and yelling at the poor sucker inside. *What's he doing in our neighborhood? Get outta here, asshole.* But they wouldn't let him go.

When a dozen teenagers started rocking the car, JG became petrified. "Stop it, stop, what are you doing?" His heart pounded through his rib cage. *Christ, I've got to get to Chaudhary's.*

The engine was running in neutral, *pruuum pruuum,* and he was afraid they'd push the car over, or it would jump forward, hitting someone. He looked at the young men as they popped in and out of focus, but he didn't know any of them—shit, this was *his* neighborhood, not theirs. "Leave me alone, I live here," he yelled, but they were having too much fun to care and kept rocking the car back and forth, lifting it off the ground on two wheels, letting it tumble down with a bang.

JG turned off the engine and suddenly felt weightless as the car lifted up and, seemingly in slow motion, hung in the air for a moment before crashing all the way over onto the passenger side with a loud mangling of steel and shattered glass. Trapped by his safety belt he hung like a marionette from the door as the young men laughed and cheered and slapped hands. Frantic, he slipped out of the belt just as the car flipped over on its top to the cheers of hundreds of people and another loud crunching of metal. He was the evening's entertainment, more fun even than setting fire to portable toilets. He tumbled onto his stomach, again to the roar of the crowd, and landed on his arm, possibly breaking it. Vaguely, the sound of sirens and helicopters expanded around him, a larger reality, but he could think of nothing except how to get out of there before Chaudhary...

The door noisily wrenched open and hands angrily grabbed at him, seizing his sore arm. "Hey, fucker, get out here."

"Leave me alone!" He tried to fight back but they pulled him from the car, jerked his body into a standing position, then shoved him violently against the upended auto. His head bounced off the fender and he fell forward but was slammed back again. Pain and dizziness shot through his brain; blood gushed from his mouth. *They're killing me.*

"What the fuck you doing here?" Images shifted and faded in front of his eyes. He guessed there were six or eight of them, yelling, grabbing, pushing, taking turns, while the crowd cheered and urged them on. *Do it... Waste the fucker... Torch him...* He was jerked forward, feet lifting off the asphalt, and struck in the stomach, someone else hitting him in the back of the head. He tumbled forward, clutching at a shirt to keep from falling, felt someone grab his hand, bending his fingers backwards, breaking two of them. He groaned and sank to the street but was instantly yanked to his feet again.

A cry went up from the crowd, its tone different this time, deeper, and a new emotion —panic—suddenly took over. *What's happening? Why's everyone yelling?* The young men spun away, cursing with anger, disappointment, fear. JG's knees buckled and he crumbled to the asphalt as the crowd roared off down the block—a middle-aged woman taking the time to stop and kick him in the back as she went by.

The ground rumbled and shifted under his body as though an earthquake was roaring beneath the city. Through bloodied eyes he sensed headlights moving unsteadily in his direction as a column of police cars rolled toward him. At first distantly, then more clearly, a loud amplified voice ordered the crowd to disperse, get off the streets or be arrested. A moment later he saw the black fatigues and boots of a

SWAT officer who was pulling him to his feet. "You OK, kid?" the guy asked. "Your car's pretty well trashed. Jesus, you look like shit. Going to have to get to a hospital on your own, though. No ambulances available."

JG looked north through the confusing images blurring his eyes and saw barricades, fires, police cars everywhere, smoke. Chaos. He began to run.

41

By the time Ann had raced downstairs and grabbed her keys, JG had vanished. As helicopters swooped and buzzed and sirens sounded and people screamed in the distance, she stood in her driveway, unable to calm her mind enough to think what to do.

"Looking for John?" Ann whirled around to see Beth Sylvester standing on her brilliantly lighted porch, holding a twelve-gauge shotgun in both hands.

"Did you see him?" Ann had to scream to make herself understood over the pandemonium.

"Took off toward Hesperia. Seemed to be in a hurry."

As Ann yanked open the door of her Nissan, Beth yelled, "I'll watch your house," but Ann didn't hear, already screeching out of the driveway, barely missing a group of young people running past.

Hesperia, she thought, getting to the intersection just as dozens of people looking both frightened and elated raced in her direction from the north. She stared up the block trying to see what was happening, made out what looked like armored vehicles of some sort, and a few immobile police cars, sirens ineffectually blaring and roof lights spinning sparks of red and blue into the darkness. Suddenly one of the cars went up in a ball of flame. A group of teenagers, laughing, raced past, slapping her car as they shot by.

OK, I can't get out by going north or east. I'll go south then, and get to Chaudhary's the back way. Where else would John have gone?

Even Raj! Sandeep Chaudhary thought with a rising of emotion. He could trust no one now.

I can't, his son had told him twenty minutes ago. Pleading! *Not Meena, father... You can't make me do it.*

"You will *not* defy me," Chaudhary said aloud now, and repeated it again and again, a chant that became almost hypnotic as he sat alone in the stifling room. "We need but wait," he calmly told his son's corpse. "Just wait... It is the way with Americans that they will run and run and run to get to the place they had no choice but to be at anyway."

It was necessary to have both families together, of course, all of them to die at the same time. Otherwise, what was the point?

How many in all? Meena and the twins. Himself. Three Binders. Seven. And Raj. Too many to round up alone—outside, this terrible city burns—so let them find him.

But not where they expected.

"Yes, yes, Raj. The boy is most important. Do not worry. He will be here within minutes. Meena will bring him to us with her tears." His pulse raged as he thought of these Binders. This Robert who did not have to kill Nazia but did so because he *wanted* to. Because it gratified his lust to watch her die, to feel her blood moistening his hands as she took her last breath.

This JG who raped my son's wife.

And his mother who thinks her sex and her money will make their evil go away. They *chose* us, these Binders, chose us for death and shame. Now only death can make their evil disappear.

And it was happening, their lives were slipping away. He could *feel* it, his heart beating as fast as a baby bird's. It is the *inevitability* of it all that pleased him so. They run and run to where they had no choice but to be anyway.

"We need but wait."

Meena would see to it. Like all of us, she too has no choice. She hadn't wanted to call Robert Binder last night, but she said what he wanted her to say. *Because it was right. Because I told her.* And after, with Raj at work, Chaudhary had brought her to his bed, which she left an hour later, crying, as always. *Because I told her,* Meena will do what is necessary. She will bring them to me.

405

JG's car wasn't in front of Chaudhary's when Ann drove up. Only a banged-up Honda Civic in the driveway. She parked at the curb and turned off the engine. No bands of unruly rioters around here that she could see. Still, she could hear the sirens, the crowd noises, the intermittent explosions, and she could smell the thick sulfur stench of South-Central on fire.

No lights were on in Chaudhary's. Almost none of the houses had lights on.

Feeling her heart thudding against her rib cage, Ann hurried from the car and slammed the door shut. She was beyond trying to be stealthy. *I'm getting my son, damn you.* She walked up to the front door and knocked loudly. When there was no answer she knocked again, pressed her finger on the buzzer and held it for thirty seconds. "Damn you, open the door."

Furious, she seized the handle and shook it, but it was locked. She kicked at the door, not even feeling the pain that shot through her foot. *Damn them! Damn them! Damn them!* Walking quickly, she went around to the rear of the house. Her heart sank when she saw the door hanging from its hinges.

"Meena? John? Are you here?"

There weren't any lights on back here either. Suddenly she didn't want to go inside.

A police helicopter dipped overhead as if it had been shot from the sky, its spotlight plunging onto Chaudhary's backyard, lighting it up and making her heart leap. Then it shot past, racing along 22nd Street.

She froze as the sound of a moan and a scraping, like a chair dragged along a bare floor, came from the house. Someone was in there. A single drop of icy sweat slid along her spine as she pushed on the door, watched it swing loosely. Taking a breath, she stepped inside. "It's Ann Binder. Who's here? I'm looking for my son."

Nothing.

"John? Are you here?"

Unable to find a light switch, she had to put her hand on the wall to guide her toward the living room, where she had talked to Chaudhary the day before. Where he'd promised to leave California. Promised, damn him! Her fingers slipped across two inches of molding and into nothingness. An open doorway. She stepped quickly past, her heart speeding up. Who had made that sound? It was Chaudhary, had to be. Who else would be hiding?

"JG?" She stopped, listened, then continued, her hand again on the rough plaster wall.

"Meena? John? It's Mom. Who's here?" Her mouth had gone so dry she could scarcely form the words.

Her heart skipped a beat as her fingers found the void of another open doorway.

"Mr. Chaudhary? I'm looking for my son."

She heard a movement again, this time behind her. *Get out of here now!* she thought. But then she was falling, falling as she lost consciousness.

42

THERE were four LAPD and two sheriff's cars in front of the home of Franklyn Mosk, Los Angeles District Attorney. *Why all the excitement?* Robert wondered. Mosk lived in West L.A., a neighborhood of large and expensive homes a continent removed from the raucous trouble over in South-Central. Robert had been listening to the radio and knew the demonstrators had gotten out of hand, but it couldn't be nearly as serious as the news made it out to be. Just another chance to make the central city look bad. People there were pissed off about the movie; they had a right to be. And they had a right to gather in the streets and make a little noise. But riot? That was putting a deliberately negative face on it. Anyway, it wasn't his concern. Meena Chaudhary and her uncle very much were.

He parked next door because of the patrol cars and walked quickly up to the house. But he was intercepted by a patrolman before he could get to the door. "Sorry, sir, you can't go in there. We have an emergency."

"Franklyn knows me." A half-truth at best. "I have to talk to him. It's important."

"About?"

"A problem with my son and his girlfriend. It's serious, believe me."

The cop stared at him as if he were mad. "Your son's girlfriend—"

"The girl's father is homicidal. He's going to kill her if he's not stopped. I'm not exaggerating. We've got to do something tonight. It won't wait until tomorrow."

"Don't you know what's going on in the city right now?"

Robert was taken aback. "You mean the demonstration? Of course I know. I live over there. Obviously it's something that has to be monitored. But it doesn't put an end to everything else happening in Los Angeles."

"Did you know a dozen people, including three police officers, have been sent to the hospital because of injuries? Mobs are rampaging down the streets, stores are being looted—"

"Look, I understand that, but this is more important than stores being looted. It involves people's lives. I have to see Franklyn."

The cop shook his head. "I don't think you grasp the seriousness of what's happening. He's not going to see you. Or anyone else with a personal problem. We've got an insurrection to deal with. Your kid's problems are going to have to wait."

Robert's patience evaporated. "I'm not talking about some teenage tiff. This involves a very

409

disturbed man who's threatened to kill several people. Do you want that on your conscience? Or in your personnel file?"

"Lieutenant?" Fed up trying to explain, the cop yelled toward the house. "You want to come down and listen to this guy?"

A grim-looking middle-aged woman bounded down the steps. "What's up?"

Robert went through his story again, more calmly and rationally this time. But even to himself it was starting to sound trivial. Teenagers and angry parents: it happens all the time.

The woman listened patiently, then said, "I appreciate what you must be going through, but I don't know what can be done tonight. We're on tactical alert. All police in the county, even reserves, are responding to the riot area. The reason Mr. Mosk is working from his home is he can't get to his office. So there's no way we can be taking time to *investigate*. We're trying to keep the city from going up in flames."

"Look, I just want to talk to Franklyn. He knows me. It won't take a minute. Can't you at least ask?"

The woman stared at him a moment, then spun around and went up the steps and into the house. The patrolman looked at Robert as if he were wasting his time. They waited for five minutes, two more patrol cars arriving and leaving in that time. Finally the policewoman hurried down the steps. "Give him a call when the city returns to normal. That's all he can do for you now." She turned to the patrolman. "Get inside. We've got an emergency."

43

"HEY, you, get the fuck over here!" Two cops holding automatic rifles burst from a group of a dozen or so and rushed toward JG as he ran awkwardly down the street, his left knee feeling broken and almost unable to hold him upright.

"I'm just trying to get home," he yelled above the confusion, but one of the cops shouted, "I didn't ask you a question. Get your ass over here."

The other man—or boy, he didn't look older than JG—raised his M-16 with wavering arms. "We told you to halt, goddamn it!"

JG thought, *They won't shoot, I'm not doing anything wrong*, and sped up. But an armored truck cut him off. When he tried to dart around it, a cop flew out the passenger door and tackled him, wrestling him to the street.

Hands tightened on his shoulders and waist and jerked him roughly to his feet. "Fuck you think you're doin'? We told you to stop."

"And I told you I'm going home." Panic made him bold. "Let me go. I wasn't doing anything.

Christ, people are starting fires out here and you're stopping me because I'm *running*?"

"Don't get smart with me, kid. Show me some ID."

"I don't have any. I left it home."
"Why am I not surprised?"

"There's a curfew," a woman cop said as if JG were an idiot or a thief. "To stop looting. Don't tell me you didn't know that."

"What are you looking for?" another voice asked. "TVs? Laptops? Maybe a nice recliner?"

"*Jesus Christ,*" JG shrieked, squeezing his fists together. "I have to get somewhere. It's important. I haven't got time for this."

"Hasn't got *time,*" the first cop yelled, just as a burst of rifle fire came from somewhere nearby. He turned nervously back to the others. "Cuff him and put him in the bus with the other knuckleheads that were out shopping. See how much time he has then."

At that moment they all turned toward the street as they heard a weird musical glass-like sound: *tinkle tinkle tinkle*. Soft and sublime, charming, almost, in its incongruity A quart-sized vodka bottle full of gasoline rolled toward them on the asphalt, a burning rag stuffed in its opening. In two seconds it would land under the truck. "Jesus, hit the fuckin' deck," someone yelled. JG turned and disappeared as an explosion blew out car windows along the street.

And *now*, Sandeep Chaudhary told himself, the next-to-last step. He gathered the cans of gasoline and hurried them to his car, his thoughts reverting as always to the boy and his father. He had no idea where the boy was but knew he'd be no trouble; Meena would see to that. It was her job. This JG and his mother—oh, so brave—they would want to *rescue* the father. They would have no choice. All of life was determined for us. We merely followed the script. And now everything was in motion.

Come to me. I wait for you.

He shoved the cans in the back seat, oblivious to the smoke and sirens and the sobs of his twin boys on the floor of the car. *Less than an hour*, he thought, and felt a sudden calm. He straightened and stared at the helicopter overhead, then closed his eyes and slowed his heart. One hour and everything would be over.

Nothing can stop it now.

Come to me.

Darting behind parked cars and hiding in bushes, trying to stay away from the police, including twenty officers in black cowboy hats riding armor-protected horses, it took JG thirty minutes to cover the mile-and-a-half to Chaudhary's house. When he saw his mother's Nissan out front he felt sick. What was she doing here? He glanced quickly inside the car, then hurried to the front of the house and tried to see in a window, but the blinds were still down. Suddenly headlights swung around the corner and began moving in his direction. Cops or Chaudhary? He hit the ground, scrambled behind bushes at the front of the house. Chin pressed into the dirt, he watched the cop car ease into view. The officers used their spotlight to scrutinize houses and yards. The beam of light moved over his head as the car crawled past, then turned at the intersection and disappeared. JG sprang up and ran to the back of the house just as the air rocked with a massive explosion from blocks away.

Standing at the shattered rear door he heard nothing but the awful beating of his heart. He couldn't see a thing but had to go in—*Hurry, Christ! Go!* He stepped over the threshold, stopped, felt the hot wind prickling his back, took another step... moved along the darkened hallway past... *what?* bedrooms? ...to the living room... his fingers frantically moving along the wall, searching for a switch. He finally felt it, flicked on the light, and screamed.

Meena lay on the floor, tied and gagged.

Falling to his knees he yanked off the gag and fumbled desperately with the twine on her wrists and ankles, not thinking to wonder why it was so loosely tied. "He's going to kill us, all of us," Meena said over and over as he pulled her to her feet. She looked like a child, her hair tangled in knots and her shirt limp with sweat. Sick with fear, she sank back to the floor, but JG lifted her, set her gently on a chair, like something fragile and priceless. She bent at the waist and started to retch but nothing came up.

"Where is he?" JG asked.

It took her a minute to get her breath, then she motioned weakly toward the bedroom. When JG started to run in that direction she jumped to her feet and shrieked, "No! My uncle? Is that who you mean?"

JG nodded his head—of course that's who he meant. She leaned on the back of the chair. "I don't know... Your house, I think. He has the twins. He's looking for your father. He's crazy, he said I'm going to help him kill you. He *believes* that!" Her eyes were dizzy with incomprehension. "He took the gasoline. He told me everyone has to die! He told me that, JG. Because of your father."

"Then who's in the bedroom? Who did you mean?"

But now Meena was sobbing so hard she couldn't talk. He settled her in the chair again and tried to soothe her. When she was breathing more normally, JG hurried to the bedroom and flicked on the light. The room was in shambles—dresser knocked over, lamp in pieces, the bedding in a tangle on the floor. Raj sprawled across the bed, half a dozen bullet holes in his chest. Blood was everywhere, pooled on his torso, dripping onto the mattress, the rug, and the floor.

When JG returned to the living room Meena sobbed, "My uncle did it... when Raj said he wouldn't let him hurt me. He tried to save me, JG, he was going to take me away."

"That's his son!" JG yelled, overwhelmed by it all. How could anyone do that to his own child? Then he remembered the Nissan. "Did my mother come here? Why's her car out front."

Meena hopped up, ran to a closet and flung the door open. Ann was doubled over on the floor, tied up and gagged with duct tape. Kneeling, JG quickly removed the tape. Ann gasped, "Thank God, I heard gunshots, I thought— Meena..."

As JG freed her wrists he asked, "What are you doing here?"

"Looking for you. I didn't know where you went. I guess he knocked me out and then I woke up in there when I heard the shots. What ..."

"I'll tell you later," JG said as another explosion rocked the house.

Ann's voice quivered. "Where's your father? Is he OK?"

"I don't know."

"My uncle's looking for him," Meena cried. "You have to find him. Hurry, please—"

"Could he still be at the DA's?"

"I don't know. I don't think so. Try his cell phone," Ann said.

JG's own phone had disappeared when his car was destroyed. He tried the phone in the kitchen, heard a busy signal, called home and got another busy signal. "I think phone service is down because of the riot." He tried 9-1-1 with the same result. "Now what?"

Ann was frantic. "We have to find him. No one's going to help us."

"Your house," Meena said, and wondered again what Chaudhary meant when he knelt next to her, his lips brushing her ear, whispering that she was going help him kill JG, that it was settled, all the strands of the evening coming together.

44

T HE Vermont Avenue exit from the Santa Monica Freeway was blocked off so Robert had to take the Harbor Freeway and get off at Adams. Two blocks away the LAPD had a heavily-manned cordon set up: nervous cops with riot gear, armored cars, SWAT vans, orange cones and barricades from sidewalk to sidewalk. He argued with a policeman—no, he wasn't a rioter, for Christ's sake. He was going home to 26th Street; he needed to be there to protect his house and family.

But it was no good. Now what? Unable to slow the beating of his heart enough to think rationally, he hurried back to his car, and was backing away from the barricades when a heavy-set middle-aged patrolman came up to his window. He spoke quickly, before anyone saw him. "Go south on Fig to that old Spanish church. Pull into the lot around back and park. There's no one watching there. Just slip through and head west. And stay the fuck away from crowds. Middle-aged guy like you, you got 'victim' written all over you."

Robert thanked him and sped away. His was the only car on Figueroa and it gave him an eerie feeling. Street lights and building lights were blazing like any other night, overhead lights from the elevated freeway to the east, but no cars for the half mile or so he had to travel. *Like a sci-fi movie*, he thought, *some apocalyptic end-of-the-world epic where the hero found himself the last human on Earth.*

At the church he pulled around to the back of the empty parking lot and killed the engine. Stepping onto the asphalt, he stood a moment, looking around. Fires had turned the sky a dull orange punctuated by pillars of black smoke that rose and trembled in the night air like huge exclamation marks. The weird light reflected back gave an artificial luminosity to everything, a Halloween-like shimmer and shake.

The exit from the lot was taped off and the street beyond blocked with saw-horses, but no one was monitoring it. Above him police helicopters thumped the air and sent powerful spotlights shooting across the ground. He could hear automatic gunfire and explosions, but they were mostly south of here, the rioters moving like locusts from field to field. There were no cars on the street, no people. His house was a mile and a half from here. He began to run.

Dodging police cars, it took half an hour to get to 26th Street. People were milling about in small groups in front of their houses, talking anxiously and spinning around when they heard someone running down the middle of the street. They raised baseball bats and tire irons and rifles, then backed off when they saw who it was. A car at the end of the block was burning, and he could hear an elderly woman crying as she looked at the broken windows on the ground floor of her home. Gasping for breath he raced up to the house and stopped twenty feet from the door. Ann's car wasn't in the driveway. Neither was JG's.

But there were lights on in the kitchen.

Chaudhary?

He started up the steps, then thought: *Don't ... wait.* He backed off and moved quickly around to the side of the house, peering in the windows. No one inside. *Did we leave the lights on when we left?* No, someone was inside —he saw a shadow cross in front of a light. Chaudhary or looters?

Moving carefully now he crossed to the rear and was about to try the door when the entire neighborhood went dark. He could hear neighbors shouting, "What happened..." "Where's the goddamn power?"

Two police helicopters suddenly appeared overhead, then another from the fire department. *Damn it, get inside; it's probably JG waiting for you.*

Still, he turned the handle gently. It was unlocked. He took a step inside, and another. Then Chaudhary hit him over the head with the back of a shovel and he stumbled to the floor, unconscious.

When he came to he was face down on the kitchen floor, his hands tied behind him; a candle normally kept under the sink was now flickering in front of him, providing the only light in the house. Moaning, he rolled onto his back and looked up into the hate-filled eyes of Sandeep Chaudhary just inches above his face. The small man was shirtless, his bandages gone and the ugly wounds on his chest oozing blood and pus. He shoved a revolver hard against Robert's forehead. "Where is the boy, Mr. Binder? He should have been here by now."

"I thought—" He tried to sit up but as he did, Chaudhary struck him in the face with the barrel of the gun, breaking his nose and two teeth.

"*Tell me!*" Chaudhary screamed. Sweat flew from his unshaven face. "Where is this boy who ruins my family? This rapist!"

"What are you talking about?" Robert managed. "He didn't rape anyone. Your son—"

As an ambulance roared by outside, brief flashes of red shot around the room. Chaudhary straightened and kicked him under the chin. "Don't tell me about my son. Your JG *killed* him! Your JG rapes his wife."

Robert's eyes rolled and his head fell forward as he vomited on his shirt. He shook his head, trying to clear his thoughts. "You're not well, Sandeep..." He could barely speak through the pain. "JG's just a friend of Meena's..." Blood clogged his throat, gagging him, but he couldn't work up enough saliva to expel it. "He didn't hurt her... he hardly saw her, the way you had her locked in your house."

"Do not lie to me," Chaudhary shouted. "Your family destroyed everything I love. Do you hear? *Everything!*" He dropped to his knees, the light from the candle flickering on his forehead, and seized Robert by the shirt front, yanking his bloodied head to within an inch of his face. "You killed my Nazia, your boy raped our lovely Meena and killed Raj."

"Killed Raj? What are you talking about?"

But Chaudhary's thoughts were already spinning off in a different direction. "It does not matter," he muttered to himself. "Meena will bring him here. He will come." Soothed, he turned his attention again to Robert. "We will all be together, Mr. Binder. And together we will die. Your family, my family. Do you understand?" He shoved Robert back so hard his head bounced off the table leg to the floor.

Chaudhary abruptly straightened and began to prowl around the kitchen as another explosion sounded outside. Again he began pacing, banging his revolver sharply against the cabinet doors. "In India a slum boy started to follow my sister Shumi as she walked to school. Dirty fellow, no schooling. Hoodlum. I told her, make the boy go away, but she would not do it. Even our father couldn't stop her. So he and his brothers beat the boy up, but still he would not stop."

He halted his pacing. "So I made Shumi help me. Do you understand, Mr. Binder? She *helped* me. I told her, 'Shumi, it's all right if you want to meet this boy. I won't tell anyone. Go to the field by Saidapet Road, no one will see you.'" His hand came down out of the darkness. "I cut his throat, Mr. Binder. And her throat, too."

Robert was twisting his arms back and forth, trying to slip out of the cords. Finally he managed to get one free, but Chaudhary was too far away to attempt anything, striding back and forth in the kitchen. "They will be here soon, Mr. Binder. We will wait."

When he again passed in front of him, Robert pushed off the floor and flew at the smaller man, knocking both of them to their knees. The gun clattered from Chaudhary's hand, sliding noisily across the tile to a small rug in front of the sink. Chaudhary lunged for it, but Robert struggled to his feet. His legs felt leaden as he forced himself to race out of the kitchen and down the short hall to the rear door. Chaudhary screamed furiously, ran after him, catching him as he pushed against the screen door, yanking on his shoulder. Robert lost his balance and tumbled onto his back. Chaudhary put the muzzle of the gun to Robert's knee and pulled the trigger. Robert screamed once and tried to pull his leg up but it wouldn't obey. Blood flowed onto the floor.

Chaudhary bent with an angry grunt and pulled Robert back into the kitchen. As Robert held his hand against his knee to staunch the bleeding, Chaudhary picked up one of the cans of gasoline he had brought with him. Beginning with the kitchen, he poured a thin trail of gasoline through the house, ending in the living room, where he put the half-empty can down and placed the other can next to it. A spark anywhere would cause the whole house to explode.

Back in the kitchen Chaudhary lifted the candle and shoved it within inches of Robert's face. "You killed my wife, Mr. Binder! It is because of you we all die tonight."

Fighting to stay conscious, Robert couldn't focus his thoughts. Everything spun together: Meena, John, the dead woman. He forced his mouth open, sought to form the words. "I've been trying to help you, Sandeep. I tried. Why are you doing this?"

"*You killed Nazia,*" the man shouted—an undeniable fact, though Robert was having difficulty remembering anything about it. Still grasping his knee, Robert tried sitting but tumbled on his side, his head hitting the floor. As he lay prostrate, he opened his eyes and saw Chaudhary's twins cowering in the hallway just beyond the kitchen. Urine dripped down one of the boy's legs. They were petrified, sobbing quietly. Robert twisted onto his back and looked up at Chaudhary's face spinning above him.

Slowly his mind resolved into something re-sembling clarity, that night coming back in fits of blurred vision like the images in a child's flipbook.

"Your Nazia—" Robert was having trouble pulling out the truth of that night from weeks of delusion and guilt. He wanted to tell Chaud-hary something important about Nazia, but what was it? Was it that he paid her a hun-dred and fifty dollars, that she had been hiding money from Chaudhary so she could leave him? That she lived daily in fear of the man and was going to flee Los Angeles? But he didn't know how much of that actually happened, how much he invented, how much DeFazio had insisted on. Everything ran together in his brain now. He couldn't think, couldn't remem-ber... *Nazia had demanded more money, hadn't she?* She needed it to leave. *...He's crazy, that man! He will kill me!* Yes. He remembered now. She said she'd go to Ann if he didn't give her more money, he thought, or DeFazio thought, more of the man's wild fantasies. It was hard to keep anything clear in his mind now. *My mu-seum of illusions,* DeFazio insisted... *My ability to deceive even myself...*

The front door banged open and Ann screamed, "Robert? Are you here?"

"Dad?" *His son's voice.*

Chaudhary smiled. "You see," he said calmly. "All together now." And his body went slack.

Panic came on Robert at once. He tried to speak, to yell a warning, but couldn't—*Please JG, don't come in here. Please. Please.*

He pushed his hands on the floor, tried to rise, but collapsed onto his stomach. Tried again, and collapsed again, rolling onto his back. His lips worked, his tongue moved, but no words came out. With a tremendous effort he forced a sound, a loud keening moan. But Chaudhary leaned close, smiled, and shoved the barrel of the pistol between Robert's eyes. Robert's entire field of vision was taken up by the man's sweaty unshaven face and the black mass of the gun.

"Watch me, Mr. Binder. Watch my face, listen, and think about death. Because of you, everything bad has happened to my family. Do you understand? Because of you. *Tell me you understand.*"

Robert's head nodded once, then again, *Yes, yes, I know what I've done.* But as Chaudhary leaned closer Robert grabbed the gun from his hand. Weak with the loss of blood, he still was able to point the gun in Chaudhary's direction and pull the trigger. But the shot went wild and Chaudhary lunged forward, his body falling on Robert.

"No, Mr. Binder, not yet," he said and twisted Robert's hand until he dropped the gun. Chaudhary grabbed it just as Ann raced into the kitchen, followed by JG and Meena. Chaudhary straightened and pointed the gun at them, nodding with pleasure and acceptance. It had come together the way it was supposed to, had to. "You see?" he said to no one, or was it Raj? "You see? Meena brings us together."

Ann shrieked and ran to Robert, falling on her knees, her hands going to the wound in his knee. *My God! What have you done—?*"

Chaudhary kicked her in the ribs, and she flattened on the floor. "Lay down, all of you."

With a terrible howl JG lunged at Chaudhary. The man shot him in the torso, his entire being utterly calm now, thinking, *Yes, yes, everything as it had to be.* JG sagged to the floor, still conscious. "You're fucking crazy –"

Meena was on her knees, sobbing, praying aloud.

"Stop," Chaudhary yelled at her. "Come here, now!"

When she didn't move he grabbed her by the elbow and drew her up. "Now, Meena! It is up to you."

She was crying uncontrollably, had no idea what Chaudhary meant. "Please—" she managed. "Please!"

But as Chaudhary dragged her in front of Robert, her foot hit the candle, which fell on top of the small rug, which began to smolder. "For you, Meena. This man who ruined our family." He seized her hand and his voice was calm, mesmerizing. "You must do this." He placed the gun in her hand. "You, Meena. You *will.*"

Her whole body was shaking so badly she could hardly stay upright. "No," she sobbed. "No, no."

Chaudhary forced her arm straight out in front of Robert's body. "Now! You must."

She twisted out of his grip, screamed, "No!" as the rug at her feet began to erupt in flames.

Chaudhary forced her back, aimed the gun at Robert. There was no emotion in his voice as he spoke: "You are whore, Meena. You are nothing. Nothing. Do as I say. Do as I say." He placed her finger on the trigger. "Now, now—"

When she jerked her hand away he instantly squeezed the trigger, striking Robert in the face, and repeated again and again.

Feeling not the joy of success but only its inevitability, its sublime *goodness*, as the world righted itself, Chaudhary turned to the twins and yelled at them to get in the kitchen. When they didn't respond he began to stomp furiously toward the hallway, ignoring the rug burning at his feet. But he stopped when he heard a voice from the doorway behind.

"*Forget it*," Beth Sylvester shouted, and aimed her shotgun at him. "Figured you for bangers, all the dang noise—"

Chaudhary pivoted suddenly around, smiling almost joyfully, raising his hand, the pistol pointed at her face.

Beth pulled the trigger, the sound in the small room deafening as she blew away half of Chaudhary's head. She looked at the bodies and blood everywhere. "My God," she muttered. "What's happening to this city?"

SEPTEMBER

REBA McEntire's on the stereo—too loud, as usual—as JG waits impatiently for Meena in the parking lot of Cerritos High School in Orange County. He hums with the music, taps his fingers, tries not to worry. Easier said than done; this is the first day they've been apart since he got out of the hospital.

Finally a bell rings and kids begin to dribble in twos and threes from the building and head toward their cars. But five minutes later there's still no Meena and his pulse heats up as he thinks of the time he waited helplessly for her in front of Manual Arts. Then he sees her smiling and his heart skips a beat. Leaning across the seat to flick open the door, he winces as the scar from the operation—Chaudhary's shot had gone through his lung and grazed two vertebrae—still bothers him. Trying to mask his discomfort, he smiles and gives her a quick kiss.

"You OK?" she asks as he turns stiffly back to the steering wheel.

"It's just the pain of seeing my pro-football dreams tragically ended."

She laughs, and he asks about her first day back in Orange County. "I love it. There's so many Indian kids here. And only two blocks from my mom's house."

"Hey, you're not walking. I'll be here at three o'clock every day. You won't be able to miss me." He's driving the Saab now since his mom didn't want it. *A nice car*, he thinks, *safe, reliable. But yellow! Jeez! Maybe a paint job would help.* Then he thinks, *Nah!*

Meena smiles and touches his shoulder as he turns the key. "Where are we going?"

"There's a Tommy's not far from here. Let's gorge on chiliburgers before dinner."

Meena giggles and settles back in the seat, her books in her lap.

Five minutes later they're sitting in the car with Cokes and burgers. Tentatively JG asks, "Do the kids here know?"

About Chaudhary and Raj and the miscarriage she suffered when JG was shot, about her "marriage," and Child Protective Services' weekly checks on her mother's home. If everything goes OK for a year, her mom's going to be given custody of the twins. But CPS is keeping her on a short leash.

Meena looks away a moment. "About some things, I guess. My uncle. Not the baby. But no one says anything. They won't bother me." She looks at him seriously a moment, then smiles with contentment as she takes a bite of her chiliburger. "What did you do all day?"

"Watched TV. Practiced a little. Worked on some songs I'm writing with Mr. Wilkerson."

JG's taking a semester off, then going back in the Spring. By taking two summer classes he can graduate next August and enroll in Eastman in the fall. Meena, too, is on an accelerated schedule, graduating a year after JG.

"Country and western! What do you know about it? You don't even own a pickup."

"Yeah, but I bought a cowboy hat," he says, grabbing it from the back seat. "It's a start." He plops it on his head and takes a long pull on his Coke to give himself a moment to consider again the appropriateness of what he's going to ask. Finally he says, "They're having the Medal of Valor ceremony at City Hall Saturday. Will you go with me?"

"Of course."

During the summer the police department concluded the investigation of the death of Nazia Chaudhary (her real name remained a mystery), with the determination that the shooting occurred as a result of Robert trying to rescue her from kidnappers. Jill Oakley is going to make the actual medal presentation. But Robert deserved it for what he'd done for JG, too. His dad didn't have to come back to the riot zone that night. He did it to protect his son.

"My mom's going to accept the medal. Along with all four grandparents. It'll be the first time we've all been together. Oh, I almost forgot. I've got something for you." He reaches into the glove compartment, pulls out an envelope and hands it to her. "Take a look."

Meena rips it open and takes out a copy of a letter of recommendation Beth Sylvester will send on Meena's behalf to the University of Rochester, where the Eastman School of Music is located. The university has an excellent pre-med program, just what Meena has been looking for. With her grades and recommendations from Ann Binder, Luis Teague and Beth, there's little doubt of her acceptance. Ann wouldn't be very far away either, starting at Princeton the same month JG enters Eastman.

When Meena smiles, JG thinks of his dad, how he wishes he was here, and how much he misses him. But his dad had been wrong when he said nothing important happens until you're out of college. What was happening to JG this very instant was important. And beautiful. The most beautiful thing he could imagine. He wonders sometimes, because of something his mother said at his dad's funeral, what his life will be like twenty or fifty years from now. She sounded as if she didn't believe in progress or the ability of human beings to act rationally. Beth had agreed with her. No matter. His and Meena's love will protect them. The future is limitless, and all theirs.

Meena impulsively leans over and kisses him. JG puts his arms around her. He feels like he's flying a million miles up in the sky. His feet will never touch the ground again, he knows.

He soars.

Go here to be the first to know about new thrillers, crime stories, and mysteries coming from Water Street Crime.

mailchi.mp/waterstreetpressbooks.com/ waterstreetcrimemailinglist

Get the Water Street Crime Starter Library
FOR FREE

Get four, full-length ebooks—**BLOODY PARADISE**, **FROM ICE TO ASHES**, **TROPICAL ICE**, and **SING FOR THE DEAD**—plus two introductory short stories by the author of **STAINED FORTUNE** and lots more exclusive content, all for free!

Building a relationship with our readers is the very best thing about publishing.
We occasionally send newsletters with details on new releases, special offers and other bits of news relating to Water Street Press.

And if you sign up to the mailing list we'll send you all this free stuff:

1. A free ebook edition of the exotic thriller **BLOODY PARADISE**—"...a spicy thriller..."

2. A free ebook edition of the crime thriller **FROM ICE TO ASHES**—"designed to shoot the ice down your spine..."

3. A free ebook edition of the eco-thriller **TROPICAL ICE**—"...well-spun, tautly written..."

4. A free ebook edition of the delightfully noir-ish mystery **SING FOR THE DEAD**—Foreword Reviews' Gold Medal winner

5. A free copy of two introductory short stores from the author of **STAINED FORTUNE**—stories from the childhoods of two his most intriguing characters, Alvaro and Pablo.

6. Advance notice about the release of new Water Street Crime novels.

You can get all this and more,
for free, just by signing up at

**mailchi.mp/waterstreetpressbooks.com/
waterstreetcrimemailinglist**

Did you enjoy this book? You can make a big difference for our amazing Water Street Crime authors.

Reviews are the most powerful tools in our arsenal when it comes getting attention for our books. Much as we'd like to, we don't have the financial muscle of a New York publisher. We can't take out full-page ads in the newspaper or put posters on the subway.

(Not yet, anyway).

But we do have something much more powerful and effective than that, and it's something that those publishers would kill to get their hands on.

A committed and loyal bunch of readers.

Honest reviews of our books help bring them to the attention of other readers.

If you've enjoyed this book we would be very grateful if could spend just five minutes on Amazon or the online vendor of your choice leaving a review (it can be as short as you like).

Thank you very much.

About the Author

BEST-SELLING novelist Zachary Alan Fox's previous books, including *All Fall Down* and *A Perfect Death For Hollywood*, have been praised at "breathtaking" (*Publisher's Weekly*), "The suspense thriller of the year" (*Midwest Book Review*), "absorbing" (*Kirkus*), and "A suspense lover's dream" (*Romantic Times*).

Before turning to writing full time he taught Organizational Behavior at the University of Southern California and Cal State Dominguez Hills under his real name, Richard Nehrbass. *City of Darkness* draws upon his close knowledge of the dynamics of urban America, and is his sixth novel. He lives with his wife in Huntington Beach, California.

ALSO FROM WATER STREET PRESS

Ready for more thrills?

We suggest **Stained Fortune**, by Joe Calderwood, the first in his Clint Kennedy Crime Series.

Have you read all the books in the Water Street Crime collection? Check out Water Street Press at this link and see all the amazing books we have to offer:

www.waterstreetpressbooks.com

Stained Fortune

ENJOY THIS EXCERPT FROM STAINED FORTUNE, THE FIRST BOOK IN THE CLINT KENNEDY CRIME SERIES BY JOE CALDERWOOD.

Chapter 1

I had not planned on ending up back in jail. But when the rewards are great, the risks are often greater.

I remembered how it felt the first time I'd entered jail, the edge of fear that seemed to jab at my nerve endings like the tip of a knife—a sensation I did not find completely unpleasant. Ambition had landed me here, certainly, but I couldn't discount that the nearly carnal satisfaction of an adrenaline rush didn't have something to do with how high I was willing to aim, or how far I'd go to meet my goals.

The other inmates—six in the cell of the Mexican jail I was led to—were hard-pressed to contain their desire to pounce on me as I took my seat among them on the cold, damp concrete floor. Child molesters, rapists, robbers, murderers, assorted minor scam artists—my new compatriots, their hair gelled to porcupine points at the top of their heads, dusty feet in battered flip-flops, dark and shining eyes assessing me.

The prison housed hundreds in cramped cells like this, dungeons with a toilet as the feature at the center of the room, a dank, brown liquid coagulated at its base and a metal seat for seven or more prisoners to use—no privacy and no toilet paper. Weeds sprouted from the cracks in the concrete floor, and the small, damp room smelled of body odor and spent bodily fluids. It was clear the toilet didn't get a lot of use; the inmates pissed wherever they stood.

Pedro, Luis, Gustavo, Manuel, Jose, Carlos —I was the only one with white skin among the mix of Spanish, Mayan, and Mexican prisoners. Most spoke Spanish, or Mayan, with only a spattering of English among them, but I spoke enough Spanish to make myself understood, and to understand that their conversation was about me, and irreverent.

Fortunately for me, Mexico—unlike America in these early years of the new century —was still an aspirational country. My new prison friends appreciated American men like me: they didn't resent my fresh, new, costly clothes or my expensive haircut; they enjoyed the appearance of money, and their proximity to someone who looked like he had a lot of it.

Chapter 2

The intent to make my fortune was what had landed me in jail the first time, but make my fortune I had, in spite of the temporary obstacle of incarceration. At just thirty-four, and with a fat bank account, I'd moved to Mérida, in the Yucatan, "The White City" named for the common color of its old buildings, and for its cleanliness. I'd bought and restored an eight-bedroom colonial mansion for my home. I spent my days drinking beer by my pool, reading a book or watching an old movie on TV, and feasting on the local dishes my houseboy, Pedro, prepared for me—*Poc Chuc* and *Papadzules*. My nights were spent drinking Scotch and making the rounds of restaurants, art galleries and the symphony that made up the vibrant cultural life of the city. The Mérida population includes the largest percentile of indigenous persons in Mexico—Mayans, most of whom were still struggling to reach even the lowest rung of the ladder their Mexican neighbors sat upon —and so I took it into my head that I would help them in their rise, though perhaps in an even more practical way than I'd been helped in mine: I'd bought three additional old colonials, each smaller than my residence, though just a few streets away, and was in the process of combining them into one building and restoring it as a school for Mayan kids. It was a deeply and not surprisingly satisfying way to spend my time, and my money.

Taavi, for one, wouldn't have been surprised. Maybe he was the one who put the idea in my head in the first place—roused himself from eternal sleep and whispered it to me in my dreams. That would have been something he would have done, if at all possible, and who was to say it wasn't?

In any case, my life was paradise, and it wasn't enough.

Who's to say what's "enough"? What is plenty for one man is paltry to another. I had wads of dollars in my pocket and stacks in my safe and rows and rows of numbers on my balance sheets, but when it came to thrills, I was poverty-stricken.

About three months after my move to Mexico, in the early spring of 2008, I volunteered as a worker for the Yucatan elections—the one hundred and six "municipal presidents", or mayors as we call them in the U.S., that were to be elected that May. Those few weeks of volunteer work consisted mostly of answering phones in various campaign headquarters, posting yard signs where they were permitted —and sometimes where they were not permitted, approaching area business people with a fundraising pitch on behalf of the resident power brokers and decision makers. You could call me a "people person". From the time I was a kid, I could always pick out the ones who would be most beneficial to know. I worked my ass off for the local pols and, by the time the elections were over, I had a whole new group of friends. Politics is an inherently dirty business and the pollution among the Mexican political class is deservedly legendary; I figured someone in that crowd could get me into a little bit of much-needed trouble.

Chapter 3

My trouble came with a name: Alvaro.

I met Alvaro—met him *formally*—at the victory party for the candidate in Mérida's Third District. He—Alvaro, not the candidate; the candidate was a forgettable little puke who would later be indicted for removing his opponent's advertising materials and exchanging cash for voting cards—was a solid six feet tall, with a body of lean muscle and a head of wavy, thick black hair. Even at first glance he seemed too lithe and graceful—too *physical*—to be a politician. Periodically he'd throw an arm around the smaller but exceptionally beautiful man at his side; the way he looked down at his companion, the smile he gave him, made me wonder if they were a couple. Both of them were surrounded by the circle of spectators who'd gathered around Alvaro, a crowd of men and women who looked up at Alvaro less as just

449

another guest at the victory party but as if they were his fans. There were a few people among that crowd who looked too alert and wary to be simply guests; they looked like Secret Service guys if Secret Service guys routinely dressed in Irish linen guayaberas.

"Do you know who that is?"

"What?" I turned to the Mayan who'd been on the candidate's PR team. I didn't catch his name, but he looked enough like Taavi to draw me to him when I'd first arrived at the party and he'd taken it upon herself to give me the lay of the land—point out the important people I might like to know.

He gestured now toward Alvaro with the hand that held his frothy cocktail. "You think you recognize him, don't you? He's Alvaro Moreno, the bullfighter—not as well-known as his brother, Oscar, but Alvaro's the one who stabbed and killed the Intimidator."

I nodded. "I've never been to a bullfight in my life."

Chapter 4

"Politicians and bullfighters, there is no difference between them," Alvaro told the crowd. "If you are a bullfighter, the bull is your opponent. He is the one you are trying to beat in the race, the one you do not want to lose the election to, hmmm?" he continued, and the people around him chuckled. "And everything a bullfighter does, every move he makes, is to do one of three things—distract his opponent, so the opponent is confused and can't fight back as well; anger his opponent, so the opponent makes a stupid mistake; cause injury to his opponent, so the spectators will see the bullfighter is strong and his opponent, this massive animal, is weak." By the time he finished, the people around him were laughing in earnest. He didn't need to twist to one side as if to dodge attack, his hands holding an imaginary cape, to keep his audience captive; that flourish at the end was all showmanship.

But when he'd twisted he'd ended up directly in front of me.

I stretched my hand out to him. "I'm Clint Kennedy. New to the area—"

Alvaro put up a hand and let his black eyes wander over my white skin, blonde hair, blue eyes. "New to the area? Who would have guessed such a thing?" he asked, sending the people who were still gathered around him into another gale of laughter.

I might have been put off—distracted—by his greeting, but that was just what he wanted.

"I've never been to a bullfight. I'd love to see you in the ring."

"You would?" he laughed, and he grabbed the beautiful man who'd been standing near to him and kissed him on the neck. "Then what do you say, Javier? I fight again in, what is it? Two weeks? Should we invite this Mister Clint Kennedy to be our guest?"

Javier shrugged, but he smiled as well. "I think Mister Clint Kennedy would like that, Alvaro."

"Then that's what we will do!" Alvaro boomed. He reached out at last to take the hand I had offered him. "Pleased to meet you, Clint. Call me Alvaro—and this is Javier, my brother-in-law."

Brother-in-law, I thought as I began to loosen my hand from Alvaro's grip in order to shake hands with Javier. *This relationship might be more complicated than I assumed...*

But I didn't get to either finish the thought or offer Javier my hand. Alvaro kept his fist tight over mine and yanked me toward him to whisper in my ear, "I know who you are, Mister Clint Kennedy."

www.ingramcontent.com/pod-product-compliance
Lightning Source LLC
Chambersburg PA
CBHW051508250626
47156CB00001B/10